Madman's Monster

Book 2: The Hidden Amongst Us

by
Michael Louis Weinberger

Published by Purple Mountain Publishing

International Standard Book Number: 978-0-9837683-2-6

Edited by Dan Hankison

Cover Art and Formatting: Bill Kutcher: www.pbase.com/ibill

Printed in the United States of America

First Edition

Dedications

To Marc Glassman because everyone should have a crazy uncle to love, cherish, count on and be inspired by.

To Kathy Glassman because everyone should ALSO have a crazy aunt to love, cherish, and remind them that the only rules in life are the ones that you make for yourself.

And, of course and always, to Rebecca, Mikayla, and Natasha who continue to put up with me and allow me to bring these stories to print.

Acknowledgments

There are a team of people that had a huge impact on the outcome of this novel. First I should mention the main editor of this novel, Dan Hankison, who took what could be construed as the digital version of chicken scratches that I typed and them made something legible.

Next are my "quality control experts" who found themselves subjected to being used as everything from editors, proofreaders, soundboards, psychiatrists and proverbial shoulders to cry on. Fortunately, they are all family and were lovingly exploited as such. So to Mom, Dad, Rebecca, and Matthew, a big "thank you" for all you have done.

Lastly, I feel it would be remiss not to mention the "Are you done yet?" squad that has stationed themselves ever vigilantly at the door of the Starbucks where I do the lion's share of my writing. To the whole gang I say, while giving a little extra recognition to Nan and Katie who were nice enough to each do a proofread of the book, "Yes! The book is done!"

Introduction

Excerpt from the journal of Steve Jacobs, 2012:

Sitting by candlelight is something I haven't done in years and the luminous glow momentarily made me nostalgic for a home that I lost decades ago. I smiled as I watched the flicker of the candle's flame create shadows on the walls with the only sound in the room being the gentle breaths of the woman, named Lei, as she slept a few feet away from me. I thought about how much I love her and how beautiful she appeared in sleep as the old, familiar and unsettling pang of worry made itself known in my gut. I rolled the pen between my thumb and index finger for a bit as I considered the blank page facing up at me from the desktop. I closed my eyes and took in a deep breath while searching for the nerve to begin, then I let the air out in a sigh and committed myself to write the words you are now reading.

Truth be told, I have felt the compulsion to write down the history of my kind for decades, but what specific stimulation it was that woke me from my sleep tonight and motivated me to finally put pen to paper, I can't say. If it had been a nightmare that woke me, then I have no memory of it, but I did wake to an overwhelming sense of dread that seemed to be coming from every part of my being. So, should the worst happen, I want there to be some record of who my kind truly are, as opposed to the stories that have chilled mankind and made them afraid of the dark. It is my deepest desire that someday mankind will understand that my family and I are brethren to humanity and not the predators or demons we have been made out to be.

How did this misconception of who and what we are grow to such grandiose proportions? Fear, specifically of the unknown, is the most likely answer; however, let these words I write now reveal only the truthful and factual accounts, without embellishment.

First, my name is Steve Jacobs and, by definition, I am a vampire.

Perhaps you who are reading this are understandably skeptical of that revelation. I can't blame you. After all, you've been told all your life that vampires are merely wonderful antagonists created as works of fiction that satisfy a guilty pleasure. In all honesty, the vampires you have read about or seen in the movies, are exactly that… Fiction.

So let me tell you the three most important facts about myself and what it means to be a "real" vampire… in general terms anyway:

1. As far as I know or can tell we are not demons, fallen angels, aliens or anything else that might be construed as supernatural. What we are, put simply, are human beings born with a particularly rare form of a genetic condition called Porphyria. This condition leaves our bodies incapable of properly making the "heme" portion of the hemoglobin in our red blood cells. As a result, we who suffer the condition have needed to supplement our own blood with "heme" from outside sources. As you may have guessed that means without ingesting the blood of others we begin to deteriorate into excruciating pain, madness and death. In the past we have done terrible things to satiate our needs and preserve our lives… you may note that I omitted the word "monsters" from the opening line of this paragraph. It was an intentional omission as my people have perpetrated horrible atrocities on mankind in the past and, at times, we more than earned that monstrous reputation.

2. Once we learned how to control our condition, my kind flocked together and invented ways to preserve ourselves without having to assault others. One of the more ingenious ways to accomplish this was to partake of an occupation as a barber surgeon. Bloodletting was one of the most popular healing methods from the Middle Ages to less than one hundred years ago. This practice left gallons of blood to be disposed of and allowed

for my kind to easily interact with mankind without worry. As long as the ingestion of the drawn blood was done in secret, no one was any the wiser of who and what we were. Unfortunately, it was a confrontation with the Inquisitors of the Catholic Church in 1528, which led to the discovery of our secret. We have been damned as devils straight out of hell ever since. My people ran for their lives as mankind attacked us with genocide as a goal. We left the cities, towns and villages to live outside the walls of humanity in secret communities crafted in cave systems and old mining tunnels. Many of my kind are still living hidden and away from humanity even now, but more and more of our young have begun to leave the safety of our "off the grid" communities and live among you.

3. The last thing you need to know about us is that all of the other things you have been taught about us are, for the most part, crap. We aren't the undead, can't de-materialize, or change forms with that of a bat, wolf or other creature. We can't fly. We don't have fangs. We don't have superhuman strength or speed. Garlic, holy water, crosses and other mythical items supposedly used to smite or destroy a vampire are pretty useless. If you stab one of us through the heart with a wooden stake, yes, we would die, not because of being stabbed specifically by a wooden stake, but rather because something was stabbed through our heart. On the other hand, our condition did have one very interesting side effect on us. It turns out that after years of needing to survive on the blood of others our bodies evolved as hostile environments to bacteria and viruses. As a result we do not get infections of any kind as the organisms literally die on contact with our blood. Aside from the obvious immediate benefits of this predisposition, the lack of stress on our organs makes my kind enjoy extremely long lives. We look about half the age we truly are and the reality is that we truly are as physically youthful and vital as we seem to be. There are rare exceptions to this rule as some of us just keep going and going, without aging. This is an extremely rare quality and only a handful

of us ever develop this predisposition; however, one such exception would be the founder of my particular community. His name is Alphonso Diemo, but we all call him "Alpha", and he is supposed to be nearly six hundred years old. He insists he isn't immortal and can be killed as easily as any of the rest of us. Although sometimes I have trouble believing it. To give you an understanding of how rare this trait is, Alpha will quickly point out that the only other person in our community known to possess it was a man named William who, along with his wife Abigail, was killed in the confrontation with the Inquisitors back in 1528.

In any case, with those three simple facts revealed it is easy to understand why the world, led by big religion, categorized my kind as demons. What else could we have been in a world without science? Unfortunately, just as science had become advanced enough to vindicate my people and afford a remedy for our ailment, we were betrayed. It was a doctor, named Phineas Whelan from whom we had sought assistance, who discovered both our secret true nature and the unexpected quality our blood possesses. Doctor Whelan betrayed us by reporting his findings to a Pharmaceutical Company, called Pharmanetics, who hunted us down in order to kidnap as many of my people as possible, then hooked them up to machines and harvested the blood right out of their veins in order to make medications for humans. The anti-biotic and anti-viral medicines were expected to perform miracles on the sick and net the corporation billions in profits. In the end it had come down to Alpha, my best friend Chris, and me, supported by those who remained of my kind, to storm the Pharmanetics building and free those of my people the company had abducted. When it was over, we had managed to free everyone, but Dr. Whelan escaped… and not before killing my friend Chris in the process.

It is said that if you find one true friend in your lifetime, then you have done well. Chris was my friend, my true friend, and I have been hunting that bastard Whelan ever since. I swore to my friend as I stood over his grave that when I find Doctor Phineas Whelan I will go "old school" on his scrawny ass and show him why, even though my people are not demons, we did at one time earn a reputation as monsters.

Chapter 1

The Chonburi Jungle near Bangkok, Thailand.

Rain. More rain. It was as if the skies were literally on a spigot that had been turned to its fullest opening, as the rain came down in sheets. The men had been trudging through the jungle for over two hours, which in dry weather would have only taken forty-five minutes. There was nothing to be done about it. The jungle floor had been saturated by the unrelenting rainfall and was now little more than a shallow pool of mud sucking at their boots with every footfall and refusing to let go. Each of the nine men was exhausted from the effort by the time the lights of the camp could be seen. Still, each was a seasoned professional and they broke into their predetermined groups of three before moving into their assigned positions around the camp.

Craig Stanton pressed the button on the wireless transceiver he wore in his ear in order to speak with his team, each of whom had a similar device.

"Position 1, confirm," he whispered as softly as he could.

Within seconds, the barely audible whispers of the other three-man-team leaders acknowledged his transmission, confirming their positions. Craig lifted a third generation night-vision monocular to his eye and scanned the large encampment, which he and his men had surrounded, for any signs of life.

Craig and his men had been hired by the client to work a typical "snatch and grab" mission focusing on the computer systems, as opposed to a human target. The goal had been to infiltrate the "laboratory" inside the camp and secure the main computer, with its hard drive intact, along with any auxiliary data they could lay their hands on. It seemed simple enough of a mission to Craig but, when the client had specified that a heavily armed security force protected researchers in the camp, Craig realized achieving the objective was going to be a bit trickier.

Not that his team couldn't handle it. Craig had assembled his team from men he met while working security in Afghanistan and Iraq. Each man was a former soldier with the necessary experience for what the job required. If the need to "go loud" arose, Craig knew each of his men was morally equipped to do whatever necessary to achieve the mission's goal. After all, professionalism was as much a part of being a mercenary as it was in any other proper occupation.

Craig looked at the images that flowed into his night-vision monocular (with HD television definition and clarity, albeit limited to a black, green and white screen), and his brow furled into a frown at the sight that greeted him.

The camp appeared abandoned.

No guards swept the perimeter with dogs. No silhouettes of men eating their evening meals or mulling about inside the illuminated canvas tents. No signs of guards standing watch from the towers or in front of the building that appeared to be a solid rectangular block of concrete, stretching nearly the entire length of the camp. If that particular concrete building had possessed any windows or skylights it might have looked like a large industrial warehouse, but instead the lack of those structures gave it more of an ominous feel not unlike that of a prison. The rest of the camp was made up of tents in the fashion of those generally utilized for a more consistent, long-term placement, which made the permanence of the concrete building look incredibly out of place.

"What the hell is this place?" the man to Craig's right whispered.

"No idea," Craig replied, "but it looks exactly as it did from the photos we were given."

"Except there had been security in those photos." Craig turned to see the third member of the team staring through his ITT Gen 3 Night Vision scope mounted on his Barrett .50 BMG sniper rifle.

"Surprised you can see anything through that thing with all

this rain coming down."

The man grunted, "I can see enough to be able to locate the targets if they were there, but I don't think I'd risk a shot."

Craig nodded, "then put it away and get your close quarter gear out."

"We going loud?"

Craig considered that option. "Going loud," meant the team wouldn't bother trying to sneak their way in and move covertly to their target. Instead they would open fire on the camp from the safety of the trees and kill everything that moved before storming the concrete building, which their bullets might not penetrate.

Craig frowned, "Not yet. I want to know what's happening in there."

The sniper had already disassembled his rifle and was storing it away when he whispered, "Does it matter?"

Craig turned to his man, a questioning look on his face.

The sniper continued, "I mean, it isn't in the mission objective to keep anyone alive, right? We perforate the entire place, pick off whatever's left, grab what we need, and get out. Easy money."

Craig nodded. It was a simple, straightforward plan and, from all appearances, one that might even work. His only problem was that he didn't know why the client would have gone to the expense and trouble to hire experienced, expensive professionals, when just about any thug would do. Hell, there were enough of the former Khmer Rouge left in this part of Thailand that could have pulled the plan off for a quarter the cost. So why bother with the likes of him and his men?

Craig shook his head, frustrated by the unexpected lack of security forces and considered the possible scenarios. He decided there were only two possibilities; either something had happened within the camp that caused the personnel to alter their routine, or everyone who had been in the camp had, for some reason, needed to abandon it. Actually, there was a third possibility, which was that the client hadn't been completely forthright in telling Craig every detail about the camp and its purpose, but that couldn't be dwelled upon for the moment.

"Boss?" the man to his right spoke softly as Craig considered how best to proceed.

Craig pressed the earpiece and spoke in that same whisper as earlier.

"Target acquisition status report."

"Clear," came the first reply from the leader of the second team followed soon after by another voice in his earpiece from the third.

"Clear."

"What the hell?" Craig hissed as he felt his heart begin to pound harder in his chest, "team three, do you have a visual on the lab?"

"Confirmed."

"Do a perimeter sweep along the fence line, then cut through and check the compound around the exterior of the lab."

"Copy that."

Craig nodded, "Do not enter the lab under any circumstances until the rest of us have a chance to move in for backup. Understood?"

"Copy that, boss."

The radio went silent as Craig used his night vision to sweep the jungle where team three had been taking cover. Craig watched as, exactly as they had been trained, the trio of men in Team 3 broke from the tree line in low sprints before coming to rest evenly spaced out along a portion of the fence.

Craig could hear the voice of the man he had just been talking to in his earpiece, "The fence appears to be set up for electricity, but there is no juice at the moment."

Craig's frown deepened. The lights were on in the camp and the sound of generators could be heard humming over the usual night sounds of the jungle. So why would an electrified fence not be in operation?

"Copy that," Craig whispered back, "proceed."

The trio removed multi-tools from their belts and began to cut their way through the links until a large enough hole was created for them to slip through. No warning sirens sounded or voices were raised in alarm as each man passed through the fence, carefully moving deeper into the camp while covering one another on their way to the lab.

"Team 3 in position. Negative contact."

Craig listened, watching for any signs of life as the seconds ticked by like minutes. When he couldn't see any reason to hold back he once again pressed down on his earpiece, "Teams 1 and 2 move into position, Team 3, silent breech."

The response that came from the Team 3 men were only confirming taps on their earpieces, which made an audible click through the speakers of the other earpieces worn by all the team members. The men from Team 3 raised their weapons and prepared to enter the building checking the door to see if it was locked.

To their surprise, it wasn't.

Trent, the leader of Team 3, looked back at the other men in his trio as he rested his hand on the door knob of the lab building. The men each gave him a slight nod as they watched the door through the red dot sighting systems on the tactical shotguns they carried. The SRM Model 1212 semi-automatic shotguns all had pistol grips and were equipped with extremely short 12" barrels, making the weapon highly maneuverable in close quarters. Each had magazines containing twelve of the 3" double ought shot shells which were capable of cutting an enemy in half in the confined space they were entering.

Trent sucked in a deep breath, then let it out with a grunt, pulling sharply on the door as his partners rushed into the building past him. Quickly, they checked the room, the corners and any blind spots, until each man whispered "clear." They took up a position inside the entryway and covered Trent as he made his way into the room. Despite the ease of initial entry, and the fact that there were no alarms or any indication that the camp was anything but abandoned, something was clearly wrong. Trent knew it and, from the signs of apprehension in the body language of his two partners, he knew that they could sense it as well.

The space they had entered seemed to be a small, maybe only two hundred square feet, greeting area with a couple of chairs lined up, backs flush against the concrete wall. Opposite sat a modest desk that looked as though it was reserved for some kind of receptionist. The desk was sparse with only a computer screen, keyboard and mouse evident on top. A flat screen television hung on a wall behind the desk and several framed photographs of the surrounding jungle hung, evenly spaced, on the walls to serve as art for whomever might be asked to wait in the room. Directly beneath the television was a single door that evidently was the only entryway to the interior of the building.

Trent knelt by the door and listened, hopeful that he might hear something that would shed some light on whatever was happening. Hearing nothing, Trent pressed down on his earpiece, "Entryway clear, there is only a single door for further access. Should we proceed?"

Craig's voice echoed in his ear a moment later, "Copy. I am moving the other two teams to your location and we will work our way to you."

"Copy that." Trent spoke in a barely audible whisper as he flashed his teammates hand signals to get them into position for repeating their procedure to enter the building. Once again Trent rested his hand on the doorknob and tested it. Once again it was unlocked and the ready signals were given.

Trent pulled the door and his men rushed in... only to drop

immediately to the ground and call for Trent to stay behind cover.

Chapter 2

Trent had only a quick glance at what lay beyond the door and he thought his eyes had played a trick on him. It had appeared as though the interior of the lab was little more than a skeleton of large pipes twisting around themselves creating an almost organic appearance. The area was wet with humidity, even more so than the rain-sodden jungle outside, and steam was escaping from what appeared to be a series of pressure valves. The entwining cylindrical system could only be a kind of boiler system. But what purpose could it possibly serve here, in the lone building of an otherwise semi-permanent tent camp? It was impossible to understand.

Trent peered around the door and noticed that the piping was stacked upon itself in such a way that it created barriers stretching from the floor all the way to the ceiling. This in turn created narrow walkways that extended from the dimly lit doorway into the darkness of the room beyond.

"What the hell is this?" one of the men whispered.

The trio scanned their limited line of sight for a target, even though they could only see a few yards into the darkness.

"Goddamn Freddy Kruger's boiler room," the other man responded.

Trent's voice was still a whisper, but the command behind it was easily heard, "Shut it! Stay on task and switch to starlight."

Both men went quiet and tapped their earpieces in confirmation. Each man maintained their sight on the darkness within the manufactured hallway they faced as they pulled the monocular of their night vision optics down to cover their eyes. Instantly the world went from color to green and white as the night vision illuminated the area to high definition clarity. It was at that moment they saw the enormous figure standing motionless at the far side of the room facing them through the darkness.

"Target acquired! Going loud!" one of the men said, his voice no longer a whisper, and he aimed his weapon until the red laser dot rested at center mass of the figure at the end of the hallway.

"Wait!" Craig's voice called out over the earpieces but was drowned out by the explosion made by the shotgun as the trigger was pulled. Incredibly, the target seemed to anticipate the shot and ran to one side as the buckshot hit tearing a wide gash in a six-inch metal pipe. Steam exploded in a white conical plume hissing as it escaped from the newly formed ragged hole, obscuring the room on the other side of the stream of scalding vapor.

"Hold Fire!" Trent screamed over the cacophony of noise. He had no reason to be silent now as anyone inside the entire camp would be aware of their presence at this point. The two other members of his team raised themselves upright and started to move down the hallway until the steam that was escaping the damaged pipe forced them to crawl on their hands and knees in order to pass beneath the vapor plume without getting burned. Trent slung his own shotgun over one shoulder in favor of his sidearm. He knew full well that his Glock didn't have anywhere near the stopping power of the shotguns, but in tight spaces it was far more maneuverable. The Glock was also immune to wet conditions and was renown for being functional even under water. There didn't appear to be any risk of submerging the weapon at the moment, but with all the natural and unnatural humidity in the building, condensation might have soon become a factor for any other firearm.

"Trent! Status!" Craig's voice was a straining to remain a whisper as it demanded to be answered, but Trent was too focused to answer as he made his way under the stream of steam.

Once he was clear of the steam he stood, drew his weapon, searching for any sounds that might give away or dictate the enemy's position. It was possible that the ambient noise of the room could muffle whispered voices, much less any footsteps or other revealing sounds, but that didn't mean the enemy couldn't make a misstep or mistake and give away their position. Trent signaled his men to stop as he made his way forward, continuing down the hallway, with his men protecting his flank and rear until the trio had reached a terminal end.

Static noise erupted from the earpiece and each man reacted by ducking their heads and grasping at the earpieces they wore. Trent could hear Craig's voice in bits and pieces, but the sound of static covered his words, making any message incomprehensible.

Trent raised a hand up again signaling his men to hold their positions and he pressed the earpiece tighter to his head in an attempt to make out what Craig was trying to say.

"Signal weak, say again." Trent spoke aloud as the other two men briefly looked down to see if Trent was having any luck.

The response was only the empty sound of radio static when, without further warning, one of the men flanking Trent suddenly screamed as he was lifted off his feet to dangle nearly ten feet in the open air. His upper body had disappeared in the darkness above them, and all Trent and his team member could see was their teammate's flailing legs. Desperate wet choking sounds gurgled from the man's throat and his shotgun dropped to the ground.

"Jesus Christ!!!" the other man screamed, aiming his shotgun upward.

Trent pivoted from the kneeling position and aimed the Glock at the ceiling but couldn't see what was keeping his man aloft. There were more wet choking sounds that must have been stifled screams of pain, as the man's dangling body began to bounce as if it were a marionette, being violently jerked upward and then allowed to fall back.

"Take the shot!" Trent called out.

"I can't see anything! What am I shooting at?" the partner replied.

Blood, hot and wet, struck Trent's face as it began to pour in rivulets down the dangling man's pant legs.

"What the hell is happening!" Trent heard himself call out.

Then the body bounced one last time as the sound of something snapping or tearing resounded over the other noises in the chamber and the body of the man fell limply to the floor, followed immediately by his severed head.

"Holy shit!" screamed the second man as he began to fire the shotgun wildly up into the ceiling.

The flashes of each triggered round illuminated the area into daylight, but only for the briefest of moments. Perhaps the momentary clarity it provided was insufficient to fully scrutinize the piping and ceiling for any hostiles but Trent still strained to make out any sign of whoever was above them. After firing his sixth shot, the shotgun made a slight clicking sound to indicate it was empty, and Trent removed the night vision monocular and lifted a small but powerful flashlight from his tool belt.

Trent peered first at his still living companion and he called out, "Stand Down!"

Somehow the man managed to pull his eyes away from the ceiling and nodded as he found a measure of self-control.

Trent nodded back, "Good, now reload. I'll cover us."

Again the man nodded and began to fish fresh rounds from his pocket and push them into the appropriate chamber of the shotgun. Trent knelt down next to the body as blood flowed out of the top of the neck and puddled around where the body lay. The wound was surgically straight, almost as if the head had been severed in one powerful quick blow by an enormous razor. There was a portion of the spinal column that had been removed and it left a small cavity in the rear center of the dead man's neck. Then Trent looked to the severed head and noticed that a couple of the cervical vertebrae were protruding from the base of the neck, which explained the cavity in the body, but there also appeared to be something long and thin that was still attached to the bones.

Cautiously Trent approached the head and found that a small loop of wire had encircled the vertebrae at one end while the other end was wound around a short, thick dowel of wood that appeared to serve as a makeshift handle. It appeared as though the wire had been secured to the man's neck from above and is what was used to lift him off the ground.

The bouncing of the victim had caused the wire's loop to sever the tissue of the man's throat, resulting in the shower of blood that had struck his face, and eventually led to decapitation by the force of the man's own weight.

Trent pointed the flashlight up to the ceiling again and shook his head in confusion. The wire was too short to have been thrown over a pipe for leverage. The only possible explanation is that someone had been entwined within the pipes above them and lowered the loop of wire down and around the neck of the dead man. Whoever had been up there had to lift the man aloft using only his strength and bounced his body until he had completed the decapitation.

But that was impossible, wasn't it?... His man weighed over two hundred pounds. The killer would have no leverage to lift with his body or legs while hiding up in the pipes; and therefore, he would have had to accomplish the lift with only the strength in his arms.

No one was THAT strong!

Trent could hear his remaining partner load the final round into his shotgun and ratchet it into the ready position.

"What's the plan boss?" the man said softly but still loud enough for Trent to hear.

Trent looked up and was about to speak when he saw the figure standing just behind his partner. It was a man, or at least it had the same basic shape and features of a man, that stood motionless just outside of the shadows. It appeared to be little more than a collection of scars and tattered flesh. Bright red eyes, cold and vacant, stared back at Trent who momentarily lost the ability to speak at the sight of the monster that faced him. The man holding the shotgun must have read Trent's body language and spun into a shooter's crouch as he pulled the trigger only to have the shot fly just wide of it's intended target. Fingers thick and long as sausages and as powerful as a vise encircled the man's throat as the creature shot past him. Fingernails dug deeply into the tender flesh of the man's neck and then jerked away as tissue and vessels tore away from the man's throat sending, once again, a hot spray of blood bursting in every direction.

Trent screamed and he raised his weapon to fire as his partner flopped down to his knees from the sudden, massive loss of blood. The figure pivoted and changed direction as it dove to the ground. The result was Trent's first two shots flew harmlessly over the creature's back. Despite the sheer immensity of what barreled toward him, Trent realized he was too close to be able to aim properly, so he jumped back in order to create more space. He pulled the K-bar combat knife from its sheath and met the creature as it closed the distance. Trent continued firing the Glock, hopeful that one or more of the rounds might strike home. He then reversed his stance and shot forward toward the creature.

The thing threw its legs out in front of itself, sliding through the large puddle of blood that had accumulated on the floor, and effectively dodging all of the shots. Trent kept firing while trying to adjust to the thing's forward momentum, but the recoil of each shot had the bullets flying anywhere but the location where he wanted them to strike. Trent felt the telltale stiffness of the trigger indicating he was out of ammunition and immediately he thrust the point of the K-bar at the large form. Just as he anticipated the feeling of the knifepoint contacting and penetrating flesh, a massive hand blurred in front of his eyes, grabbing his wrist and wrenching him to the side like a rag doll. Before Trent could recover the thing was on its feet and was launching him up and over as if weightless before he landed head first on the concrete floor. The impact made his vision swim and his thoughts hazy as he placidly watched his arm being twisted...until the snapping of his forearm bones sobered him.

He was about to scream in agony when something solid struck his chest with such force that it took his breath away.

Trent looked down and saw the handle of his own knife protruding from his chest. He couldn't pull any air into his lungs but did feel a torrent of blood force it's way out of his throat as he looked up to the... thing... that stood over him. Once again the blood-red eyes looked down at him as his chest spasmed. He coughed once more before his head fell to the ground. Voices were calling out in the distance but Trent paid them little mind as his vision started to blur. Then the excruciating pain he was feeling in his chest and arm simply flowed away as the darkness took him.

Chapter 3

"Come in Team 3!" The whisper that Craig spoke in, as he knelt just outside the entrance to the lab building, was as close to a shout as he dared. Still, to those who could hear, the emphasis in his voice couldn't be denied.

He had lost contact with Team 3 mere moments after the initial sound of gunfire coming from the inside of the building. The unexpected surprise of the gunfire had sent the remaining six members of the unit scrambling for cover within the camp wherever they could find it. Then the building had gone silent again and the six mercenaries rose from cover, regrouped and stalked along the perimeter of the building looking for any other ways to gain entry.

The building, having been constructed of prefabricated concrete walls and cinder blocks, allowed for no additional points of entry, so the unit regrouped at the solitary entrance. A quick scan of the structure revealed that the walls were of the "tilt-up" variety, which had to have been assembled off site and individually air lifted to the camp location. There was no way to get those enormous structures onto any kind of ground transport that could pass through the dense jungle en route to the camp. That meant this place had come with a large price tag and signified a VERY well funded operation. Whoever had set up this camp was no bush leaguer, not that Craig nor his team were ever led to believe the camp residents were such; however, it was clear that the target was far more capable than Craig had ever considered.

"Trent!" Craig called aloud and the five other men around him all turned to see if their leader was losing his nerve. Craig looked up into the camouflaged faces of his men and sighed.

"All right guys," he shook his head as he spoke, "we're going loud, but no unnecessary noise until we've acquired the package."

All five men grunted their response and returned their

attention to the doorway. They moved into the reception area and cleared the room with the same professional grace that their compatriots had earlier displayed, before changing targets and altering their courses for the boiler area. No orders were given...None were needed as each man was an experienced field operative and they knew their job on an instinctual level. If one were able to discern the look on each man's face it would be one of sheer determination and filled with a drive to complete the task at hand. The whole attitude of the mission had changed the moment the "Go loud" order had been given. Previously, the men would have taken extra care to avoid conflict; however, now every soul the unit encountered from this point on in the mission was to be considered a threat and dealt with lethal force...no exceptions.

Craig watched as the first of his men crawled underneath the scorching vapor that came from a ruptured steam pipe near the end of the pathway. The mercenary gave the "all clear" call on the wireless once he had arrived on the other side and the rest of the team joined him at the end of the hallway shortly afterward. Their boots began to squeak softly as the men trod on a now wet floor, but it was too dark to discern what kind of fluid covered the ground. Craig didn't need to see what was on the ground to know what the substance was and he grimaced as the familiar coppery smell that filled his nostrils told him that they were all standing in blood. The question was, whose blood? Absently, Craig mused that the puddles looked more black than crimson in the sparse lighting within the building and had saturated the floor.

Craig scanned the area, "Anyone see any sign of our men?"

"No sir," an unspecified whisper came through the earpiece so there was no way to tell who had so quickly answered him. Craig looked ahead and in the dim aura of light saw that the walkway turned and split into two separate paths creating a kind of "fork in the road" situation. One pathway led toward the center of the room and to a stairwell that led downward into darkness, while the other path was a serpentine that led along in a gradual arc back to and along the concrete wall of the building past the stairwell and into the unknown.

"What do you think, sir?" one of his men spoke so softly that again Craig could barely hear it through his earpiece.

"I don't think anything of importance would be located in here. The humidity alone would wipe out any kind of computer systems that might be located on this level." Craig considered how he wanted to proceed before he spoke again. "Bingham, stay in the front and cover the stairwell. The rest of you cover Bing from any surprises that might be waiting for him on this level. Once we make it to the stairwell Team 2 will descend and recon the lower level while Team 1 will split up. Two men will cover the stairwell and guard our exit route, the third man will accompany and support Team 2."

"Three guesses who is going with the others..." one of his men whispered in a sarcastic tone that broached insubordination.

It was the first unprofessional act he had ever encountered from any of these men after all the assignments they had been on together. Clearly the unease that had been felt in their first moments of arriving at the camp had now soured the teams' morale.

"Stow it!" Craig spoke with authoritative inflection but with an air of support, as opposed to any kind of reprimand. "Let's just get the job done and worry about how to spend our money when it's over." Craig knew the fine line that he had to walk with these men. They were mercenaries and one had to be more forgiving of breeches in protocol when dealing with mercenaries. They were their own men, beholden to no one and only loyal to the cash of the highest bidder. Teamwork and sacrifice were only vestigial concepts from long ago service in their respective military units. If these values were still present in any of these men now it was because working together and watching each other's back was the best way to keep themselves alive as opposed to any other, more noble or idealistic reasons.

"You're right, I'll be the one going with Team 2 to do the recon of the lower level. Now let's move!"

The group moved as a unit as if they had practiced it a thousand times before. No wasted motions or overt gestures that would give away any advantage for the enemy to exploit. They filed to and then down the stairwell without incident as the pair from Team 1 remained behind as instructed to guard their escape while the others moved deeper into the darkness. The lower level appeared to have been carved out of the jungle floor with the enormous roots of the trees on the surface protruding from earthen walls in a similar snaking manner that the piping had on the ground level. Ahead a large tunnel had been carved on a slight decline as it extended to places unknown.

"Hold positions," Craig instructed as he stopped halfway down the stairwell.

"What's up, chief?" This time Craig could make out the voice of Bingham, the man who had taken the lead of Team 1.

"Something about the floor..." Craig brushed a hand against the surface of what served as the floor for the level they had just been on and ceiling of the next floor down, where they were headed.

The man closest to Craig looked back to see the dirt falling away from something beneath Craig's hand.

"Damn."

"Chief?"

"The floor isn't dirt," Craig hissed, "it's concrete covered by loose soil to give the impression of a dirt floor."

Silence reigned momentarily before Bingham spoke up again, "What's that mean, chief?"

"Not sure," Craig admitted, "but it's definitely queer."

Bingham spoke up again, "I'm a sitting duck here without

cover, do we abort or continue?" A thought occurred to Craig and he immediately moved the starlight monocular down over his eyes.

"We continue, but switch back to starlight."

The men complied as Craig readied his sidearm. The tunnel was the perfect place for an ambush and Craig knew it, but pushing forward might be the only way to prevent being compromised on both ends in a pincher movement. The choice to move forward stung a little as, if he were right about the ambush, the two men he left at the stairwell would be overwhelmed easily, but their deaths would serve to warn the rest of the team that the enemy was approaching from the rear. Craig felt slightly guilty leaving the men out there as bait for whomever might be coming after them, but it was exactly those kind of hard choices that made military leaders.

The team had only traveled a few yards when the outline of a door appeared before them. The door looked to be made of solid steel and had a wheel in the center that appeared to be the same air/water tight sealing mechanism that could be found on the doors between the bulkheads on a submarine or battleship. The door was located in the center of what appeared to be a concrete wall that would have seemed out of place within the natural subterranean level had Craig not discovered the concrete floor/ceiling as they had descended from the stairs. Craig looked to the ceiling and found that the dirt and roots that had been above his head had disappeared and only a layer of concrete, smooth and relatively clean, was above their heads.

The rest of the team followed Craig's gaze before quickly returning their sight to their cover zones.

"It looks like that all camouflage has been abandoned at this point. This has to be the lab," said a voice coming over the earpiece. Craig agreed but didn't vocalize it. Instead he flashed hand signals at his teammates and, with perfect precision, the four men covered each other as they moved to the door.

Craig checked the wheel and found that it turned easily in his hands.

"On my mark," Craig said softly and each man touched his earpiece in affirmation.

Craig took in a deep breath and held it momentarily before whispering, "on three, two, one..."

The sound of a man screaming exploded into their ears at such a volume that it overwhelmed the earpiece speakers and resulted in a high-pitched feedback that lanced pain even deeper into their auditory canals.

"HOLY CRAP!" another voice screamed and then the sound of gunfire exploded along with more screams that now were undulating in resonance as if the man uttering them were being ripped apart from the inside. Each wrenching spasm of sound seemed to be forced from lungs that served as a cry of pain and a fruitless plea for mercy.

The four men at the door took up shooting positions while placing the steel door and concrete wall to their backs, but even with the help of the starlight monocular they couldn't see anything in the darkness or any indication of what was happening.

Craig hadn't taken his hand off the wheel and now he turned it until it reached its endpoint. The feeling of a latch springing free of its housing vibrated into his palm just as the sounds of screaming that were coming from their earpieces went eerily silent. In the new silence it was the only the heavy and panted breathing that could be heard as the remaining four men fought to control their nerves as they waited for the slightest sign of a target.

"Craig!" A voice half shouted between heavy breaths, "I'm incoming, don't shoot me!"

Craig spoke in a voice far more calm than he felt, "Are you clear?"

"I don't..." the man's voice was cut off by his own startled cry and another series of sidearm shots. Silence followed and the man's voice again came over the earpieces but his voice was now panicked!

"I shot you! I know I hit you! Go down you bastard!"

More rounds were fired from what sounded like a sidearm before the voice spoke again.

"H-How can you?! My God! What are you?!"

The man didn't waste any more time on words and only the sound of panicked breathing and hard falling footsteps were heard.

Craig spoke gently, "get ready guys. Wait for the target and be sure of your shots." From the darkness of the tunnel came the first flickers of movement. "Hold fire until sure..."

Craig didn't have to finish the sentence as the illumination in the starlight scopes clearly revealed the figure of a man, their man, and the look on his face was as though he had just seen the darkest nightmare in all of hell itself.

Craig recognized the man as Diego Martinez, one of the most capable and level headed among them...up until this moment.

Craig shouted, "Martinez! Down!" but Diego Martinez either couldn't or wouldn't listen and at the last second he whirled around and emptied the remaining rounds from his sidearm into the darkness of the tunnel behind him. He kept pulling the trigger even after the slide remained open and the last bullet had left the gun. He screamed in terror one last time and turned to run from whatever he could see that the others could not.

He never even managed to take a step as something huge struck him and Martinez fell forward onto his belly with a grunt. His eyes looked beseechingly to his teammates in the distance, "Help Me! Shoot! Shoot!"

"Dammit I can't see anything."

"Anyone have a visual?"

The chatter covered Craig's command of "Just fire over him" as something cried out in the darkness and Martinez eyes went wide with horror. Then Martinez bucked as his hands clawed at the floor in front of him desperately trying to crawl away from the darkness.

"IT'S GOT ME!!!" Martinez screamed and something wrenched him backward and into the darkness as his fingernails scraped against the ground in a desperate attempt to get away.

"Fire God Damn It! Fire!!!" Craig shouted as he unloaded his sidearm into the space that would be above Martinez' prone form. The other three men fired as well until the tunnel was filled only with the sound of rapidly discharging projectile fire. Magazines were emptied and swiftly replaced before the unspecific shooting was resumed. By the end of their second clips each man once again replaced their empties for full stocks of ammunition and held their fire as the gun smoke wafted around them.

"Did we get it?" one man asked.

"Did we get...what?" another responded.

Craig pulled on the door and it slid open with perfect mechanical precision. He peered around the wide steel door to the room inside and couldn't make out any initial threat.

"Everyone inside! We'll make our stand in the lab."

The first two men ran past him into the lab as the third man covered their movements then raced through the door as well. Craig waited for any signs of pursuit but none came.

Still, he didn't hesitate as he too ran through the door to the next room.

His men were waiting for him and aimed their weapons down the tunnel as Craig closed the door behind him and spun the wheel, sealing the room. No sounds came from the outer area and each man breathed a shallow sigh of relief before turning around to survey their new location.

Chapter 4:

Fluorescent lights flickered to life as some kind of automatic switch was triggered. Whether the switch was linked to the door or motion activated, it didn't matter as each man dropped into a shooters crouch and aimed their weapons in different directions, a coordinated military maneuver that covered every angle and line of sight to their position. The men found themselves fully exposed without any accessible cover and high above the floor on a metal grating platform that extended only a few yards beyond their current position. The sheer size and spectacle of the room they had entered was enough to steal their breath in surprise. The room was stark white and appeared as sterile as an operating room, but to call it a room was a complete understatement as the immensity of the space was more akin to an airplane's hanger for Boeing 747 jet planes.

Craig made a quick mental estimate and guessed that this underground space had to be at least double the perimeter of the tent camp that sat on the surface. He then looked to the stairwell they stood upon and saw that it led down to another two levels, each of which was stacked with computer equipment and various machinery that was all painted as white as the rest of the space. The only aspect of the room that was not painted in such a way as to cause snow blindness was what appeared to be a series of metallic gray vents that could be seen imbedded in the walls. There were dozens of the vents spread on each level of the space and they were lined up with such symmetry that they gave the walls a checkerboard appearance.

Craig scanned the lab and realized the computer equipment below them was the main terminal and the one they were supposed to hack.

"Any sign of hostiles?" Craig whispered.

Each man grunted the word "clear" under their breath and

Craig nodded before giving his next orders.

"Stanz. Wrigley. You two take up position here and cover that door. I don't care who or what comes through it, you are to shoot first and I.D. later."

"Sir!" both men whispered with enthusiasm. "Bing, you still have what you need?"

Bingham lowered his weapon and swung his pack from off his back to the ground in front of him. He removed a tablet style computer from the pack and switched it on.

"I'm good," he confirmed. "I don't suppose you can make the connection from here?"

Bingham used the touch screen technology to locate the wireless components, if such components existed, of the main frame.

"I have a weak signal at this point. I can upload the information from here, but it will take time."

"How long?"

"Looks like ten minutes, but I can reduce that by at least seventy-five percent if I can get the signal to full strength."

Craig sighed, "all right. Stanz maintain that door. Wrigley, I want you to cover us the best you can from here. Bing, you're with me. Understood?"

Each man again grunted his ascent.

"Right," Craig continued, "let's get down there, get what we need and get the hell out of this freak show."

Craig and Bingham started down the stairs as Wrigley pivoted away from the door and took up a shooter's position along the railing of the stairwell. They took the stairs three at a time and made it down to the second level and the mainframe in seconds.

"I have full signal strength, initiating download," Bingham declared as a horizontal blue bar began to creep across the screen of the tablet indicating the amount of information transferred versus the amount remaining, "two minutes and thirty-five seconds to completion."

Craig crouched and scanned the lab for any signs of... whatever that was from the tunnels. As he searched, his eyes landed on the various mechanical devices that had been placed neatly against the walls. Each appeared like sterile versions of medieval torture devices that could also be plausible as surgical machinery. Craig had been in more hospitals than he cared to remember and had either witnessed or undergone treatment from the not-so-tender ministrations of innumerable medical devices, but he had never seen anything like these before.

What the hell was this place? Had that huge thing from the tunnels been something they were working on in the lab? If so, why would they have left it as little more than a simple guard dog protecting its master's house while he was away?

"Two minutes." Bingham began to initiate a countdown every thirty seconds when a clatter of noise came from the level below them.

Craig swung his weapon instinctively toward the sound, then realized his mistake and again scanned the room for any signs of...well...anything.

Wrigley's voice sounded in the earpiece, "No target sighted."

"Can you see what might have made the sound?"

"Negative."

Craig pressed his lips together in frustration. "Anyone knock something over or drop something?" No response came from the other men.

"Crap!" Craig's voice was angry now and he was sick of this cat and mouse game. "There must be another way in."

Craig scanned the lab and noticed a row of paneled glass along one wall.

Under his breath Craig whispered, "Gentlemen, we are not alone. Stanz check that door, make sure it is sealed and then you and Wrigley get down here. We're ending this."

Stanz didn't answer but Craig could hear his grunt as he tried to turn the door's sealing wheel further and couldn't. Then the pair of footsteps on the metal grating echoed in the otherwise soundless chamber as the pair made their way down to the second level to join Craig and Bingham.

"One minute, thirty seconds." Bingham announced.

Wrigley was the first to arrive and knelt in a manner that would create a semi-circle next to Craig. Another sound rang out, but this time it came from above their heads. Stanz had just made it to the bottom of the stairwell when he turned on instinct at the sound. No one saw where the figure had come from but it barreled into Stanz with such force that bone could be heard cracking on impact. Stanz whole body was instantly limp, and flopped around like a lifeless rag doll as the two hundred pound man was lifted and carried off as if no more than a toddler. Wrigley and Bingham spun and lifted their weapons, but Craig had been facing Stanz when he was hit and was able to open fire first. Bullets sprayed and left black holes in the otherwise pristine white walls of the laboratory until they found a bank of medical equipment. Sparks flew and glass shattered as the machinery fell to pieces under the trauma from the projectiles. Smoke began to billow out of one particular piece of equipment and filled the area where the figure had retreated with Stanz body.

Craig let go of the trigger when he realized his weapon was empty and he quickly fumbled another magazine from his belt as the spent clip fell from the rifle. He reloaded in an instant and once again scanned the smoke for a target.

All three men stood ready to fire as Bingham spoke softly, "One minute to download."

A loud thud boomed in front of them as something large slid out from under the smoke obscuring their view and Stanz' body slid toward them until it came to a stop at their feet. The body was so broken and unnaturally bent that it appeared almost as if his skeleton had been removed.

An alarm sounded and a red light flashed as unseen machinery hummed to life. Craig could feel the air around him start to blow by like a soft breeze and watched as the smoke was pulled into the various ventilation grills and expunged from the room. As the smoke retreated the figure that appeared from within the smoke seemed to materialize out of shadow and slowly gained clarity and detail with every passing second. The trio all trained their weapons on the figure until it came fully into view.

It was a man, an incredibly tall and muscular man so pale he almost looked like he had the same blue-gray pallor normally only seen in corpses. His hair was long, dark and matted as it fell down from his scalp and covered the majority of his face. He was dirty and dark patches of what might have been dried blood covered the right side of his torso, but they didn't serve to cover the extensive pattern of scarred flesh. The scars appeared to cover nearly every inch of the man's exposed skin and were comprised of either jagged laceration scars, or the insect-like chitinous scars from poorly sutured surgical procedures.

The man must also have been close to seven feet tall, and yet none of those distinguishing characteristics were what drew Craig's attention. The first thing was the man's eyes. They were red where they should have been white. It was as if his eyes had filled with blood from multiple burst capillaries that never receded. The second thing was the device he held in his left hand. The man held out his hand to Craig as if he wanted him to take a good look at it.

Craig recognized it instantly and immediately shouted, "Hold fire! Hold Fire!!!"

"What?!?" Wrigley growled.

"Do not shoot," Craig said in as calm a voice as he could muster, "he's holding a detonator."

Chapter 5

"How can you tell?" Wrigley asked without lowering his rifle.

"It's one I've used before, but it looks like it's been modified."

"Modified how?"

Craig looked down to the man's thumb to see the trigger had already been depressed within the housing of the detonator.

"Best guess," Craig sighed and lowered his rifle, "it's been altered to a 'dead-man's switch.'"

Bingham looked back to his tablet, "Download complete. We have what we came for boss. Any idea how we get through the wild man and back outside?"

Craig looked to Wrigley and gestured at him as he said, "Lower your weapon."

Wrigley didn't look happy but he did as he was told.

Craig took a hesitant step forward as he locked his eyes on the giant in front of him.

"Okay big guy. You got us at an impasse.

What do we do now?"

The man tilted his head to the side in a manner similar to the way a confused puppy would at the sound of Craig's words.

Craig frowned, "Can you understand me?"

The man's head righted itself and returned Craig's stare. Craig looked into the man's eerie eyes and recognized the look behind them. There was nothing more than a soul-chilling, vacant emptiness behind those red eyes that left only the most primal of consciousness keeping the man functioning. The man, whoever he was, had been mentally broken to such an extent that there was very little of what could pass as human cognition. Craig had seen it before on the vacant expressions of POW's who had been physically tortured beyond the point of sanity. Rape victims also carried such expressions with them, most of whom never fully recovered regardless of the time and the excellence of counseling.

It was as if a person was stripped of all things that made them into who and what they were, until only the animal intelligence remained. Craig realized that trying to reason with this man was futile as he, most likely, couldn't comprehend what was being said to him.

Craig looked around the lab. Someone had to be in control of this man and that someone was probably watching what was happening right now.

"Enough of this!" Craig shouted to the area of paneled glass of the lab as Wrigley and Bingham looked at each other uneasily. "Talk to me!"

A voice, mockingly casual came over a loudspeaker, "Mmmmm...yes?"

Wrigley and Bingham raised their weapons, surprised by the voice, but Craig didn't flinch as he held his ground. "You clearly want something. What?"

"I...want something from you?" the voice spoke with a chuckle. "If I remember correctly you are the one's trespassing on my location."

"The whole assignment was a sham from the beginning. I'm thinking it was you who hired us in the first place and manipulated me and my team here for some reason. I want to know why."

Silence came from the speakers.

When Craig had waited long enough he shouted, "This isn't going to end well for anyone! We won't let you take us prisoner and if you have your," Craig pointed to the man holding the detonator, "thing, let go of that trigger, then it's likely the explosion will rupture the chamber. I figure the room is pressurized, so the breach of the air seals will take out the entire area. He'll destroy your entire lab in the explosion!"

Craig let that bit of obvious logic simmer for a brief moment before he again shouted, "So tell me what you want!"

"I'm impressed, you know. You're very smart for a soldier;

however, there is something of which you are mistaken."

A cold and nervous sweat beaded on Craig's brow at those words.

"And what might that be?"

Whoever was talking through the speaker must have moved in closer to the microphone he had been speaking into as his voice turned into a near hiss that was amplified by the volume of the speakers.

"That the detonator is hooked up to...explosives."

Craig frowned in confusion, and then realization hit him squarely in the face as his legs threatened to buckle under his weight. The vents in the walls, the seals on the doors, the lab buried underground, the fact that entire space was an airtight containment unit meant that there could only be one use for such a structure.

Craig's eyes shot wide as he screamed, "WAIT!!!"

The naked feral man in front of him blinked as if he had been surprised by something he just heard and released the trigger on the detonator. The air vents responded to the signal and automatically closed with the sound of metal scraping on metal while an ear popping sensation burst into Craig's ears as the room sealed. Wrigley and Bingham instinctively ran up the stairs for the door. Craig followed but had known that the moment the immense chamber had been pressurized there was no hope of them opening it.

Then the room went silent and all of the fluorescent lights shut off and red emergency floodlights snapped on as a siren began to blare over unseen loudspeakers. Despite the noise, the sound of a couple of the air vents reopening could just be heard followed by a slight hissing noise as dark wisps, not unlike smoke, flowed out of the vents and into the chamber.

Craig tried to hold his breath but the smell of whatever was flowing into the space permeated the receptors in his nostrils and a cloyingly sweet smell registered within his brain. Craig blew some of the air he had stored in his lungs out through his nose in an attempt to rid himself of the smell but it instead grew stronger. A moment later he felt the room spin and his head lolled to one side giving him a clear view of Wrigley who was convulsively retching out what looked like black slime while Bingham grabbed his head with both hands and was screaming as that same black slime oozed from his eyes, ears nose and mouth.

Craig tried to make sense of what he was seeing when he realized he had let out the breath he had been holding. Panic shot through him and momentarily cleared his fogged mind, but not enough to stop him from taking in a breath. The pain shot into him like a thousand red-hot knives that seared him as they penetrated deeper and deeper into his lungs. He tried to blow out the breath of painful air, but instead gurgled on liquid and, as he tried to push out whatever was in his throat, the black slime that had escaped from his companions exploded from his mouth as well. Craig couldn't hear himself choking but his tongue could still taste the substance as it passed up and out of his throat. It wasn't black slime at all, it had just looked that way under the red floodlights. It was blood.

Craig lost all sense of balance next and fell down the stairs to the floor of the lab. His body was so racked with pain that any additional fractures the fall might cause were lost in his background of pain. As he lay there and his vision started to blur with blood that was filling his eyes, he could see the feral man just standing there, watching the scene with that same confused puppy-dog head-tilt that he had worn earlier.

A puddle began to spread across the floor where he lay as all the pain he felt suddenly disappeared. Craig had the strangest sense that he was literally sinking into the concrete beneath him as his mind went blank.

Chapter 6

The creature crouched down, looking at the body in front of him as its flesh melted away, leaving only bones. There was no cognitive process at work as to what was happening, nor why the invaders suddenly fell to the ground screaming as their bodies literally melted before his eyes.

The wordless language of instinct from deep inside his core told him that he shouldn't touch the remains, but there was still the curious need to investigate what was happening that made him shuffle closer. He was aware that he used to understand a large variety of things, but he couldn't put his thoughts together with enough clarity to make sense of what was happening.

He looked to the floor again. The threat that had been lying there was little more than a puddle of ichor, clothes and bones now. He knelt just outside the perimeter of the pool that used to be the man's body and peered at his reflection on the surface of the puddle of blood. The face that looked back was a stranger to him, but he wasn't frightened, instead he studied the unknown face and the strange eyes that stared back. Desperately he tried to put the pieces of his shattered thoughts back together, but was interrupted as the sound of the air vents again shifting position hummed in his ears. Unseen motors whirred to life and he could feel the air in the room rushing all around him. He stood and a thrumming in his ears distracted him from the fact that he had suddenly found it difficult to draw in a breath. The need to escape surged through him but his limbs grew weak and the urgency in his chest kept him from launching into action. Instead he simply staggered back to the center of the room, to his special spot, and sat down. He fought to catch his breath for a few more moments, but the vents had effectively sucked all the air from the room and, an instant later, he fell to the floor unconscious.

An audible ticking sound came from the speakers as another

gas filtered into the room for a few seconds before a countdown initiated.

"Final decontamination procedure initiating in 5... 4... 3... 2... 1... ignition sequence activated"

There was one last slight clicking sound before the entire room exploded into flame as a tiny spark ignited the natural gas that had filled the room. The fire spread everywhere, covering the equipment, floors, walls, ceiling and every nook and cranny of the chamber. The fire was so brilliant that the blood and body fluids on the floor bubbled, but it was short lived as the lack of oxygen in the room limited the burn and snuffed out the fire almost as quickly as it had ignited. The fire, having consumed the remaining oxygen in the room created a natural vacuum and any tinder that there may have been remaining in the room was extinguished as well.

It was only then that the siren stopped wailing and the red floodlights shut down as the fluorescent lights flickered back on. Men appeared at the glass viewing windows on the other side of the pressurized doors, wearing Level 5 Haz-Mat suits while a third hissing sound initiated from within the chamber.

A mechanical voice reported after an announcing chime sounded, "Trace contaminant level: 0%. Air quality restored. Disengaging auto locking sequences."

The wheels on the vaulted doors began to spin as the men in their Haz-Mat suits worked to disengage the seals on the doors that now slid open with a slight whooshing sound. The men poured into the room carrying mops and large plastic bins, followed by other men who rolled carts holding several individual gallon jugs of liquid chemicals inside the room.

Without a word each man began to mop up, or otherwise decontaminate the lab space with the exception of two who moved to the unconscious man lying at the center of the room. Mysteriously, the huge man appeared to have been spared from the fire, which should not have been possible under the circumstances, although his skin had been slightly scorched in places and smoke rose from his hair. One of the suited individuals knelt down and rolled the giant from his side to his back, then removed a stethoscope and began to listen to various locations on the man's torso. The second individual pulled out a hypodermic needle that was already filled with a clear substance.

The individual with the stethoscope nodded and lifted his head up and said, "He's alive. Let's get him back to his holding cell."

"Is he sedated?" an authoritative voice called over the loudspeakers.

The second man with the hypodermic had just removed the now empty needle from the man's neck.

"Just finished, sir."

"Good," the voice over the loudspeaker replied, "I'd hate to find you and the rest of the medical staff in pieces because you had forgotten."

"No problem sir." The medical tech arose and walked to one of the carts as he disengaged the needle from the chamber of the hypodermic and placed both items in a red plastic biomedical waste container sitting on the cart.

Once the floors were mopped clean and sterilized with bleach, including the stairwells and any other surface that the remains of the assault team might have come in contact with, four more individuals in Haz-Mat suits rolled a gurney into the lab. They peered down at the fallen enormous, and still unconscious form that was lying at their feet, as a number of additional techs abandoned their cleaning tools and surrounded the body. Together the techs knelt and, on the audible count of three, strained to lift the heavy man up and onto the gurney.

The unconscious man's body thudded onto the metal gurney like a slab of meat, his skull clanging loudly on a side bar, before being summarily abandoned by the techs that had lifted him so that the men who had wheeled the gurney into the room could now remove him to another area to further complete the decontamination process on him.

One man near the head of the gurney remained in the lab and looked to an electronic tablet as the giant was wheeled out and away. He tapped the screen a couple of times before setting the device down on a nearby countertop. The tech reached back behind his head and disengaged the hood of the Haz-Mat suit, pulled the polymer fabric off his head and took in a deep breath of the lab's refrigerated air that blew generously into the chamber.

Dr. Phineas Whelan let out the breath and turned to the three others standing around the gurney and frowned.

"As I am not currently melting into a pool of meat soup, I feel it is safe to assume that you can remove your hazardous material suits without apprehension."

The three people still in their Haz-Mat suits looked momentarily at each other, as if they were wondering which of them were going to be the first to trust Dr. Whelan's words. Then, hesitantly, each individual began to slowly disconnect his or her headgear and breathe in the "fresh" air of the lab space.

Dr. Whelan had stepped from the remainder of his Haz-Mat suit as a tech wheeled a cart over and lifted the suit from the floor placing it in a plastic garbage bag for later disposal. The tech waited patiently while the other three people stepped from their suits and Dr. Whelan began talking.

"Gentlemen, and lady, may I assume that the results of the weapon speak for themselves?"

No one replied, but Dr. Whelan hadn't truly been expecting any verbal confirmation before he continued, "What you just witnessed is the end result of the biological weapon research that my team and I were commissioned two years ago to assemble. Unfortunately, the parties who originally commissioned the research and development have apparently decided to renege on their original offer, and that is what brings us together here and now."

One of the people who stepped from his Haz-Mat suits was a well-dressed, middle-aged man with dark features. Speaking in a thick Balkan accent he asked "What exactly was it that killed those men?"

Dr. Whelan, clearly aggravated by the interruption, scowled at the man who did his best to maintain his composure under the glare.

"The gas is a vaporized propellant of genetically altered Filoviridae organisms. These are combined with a compound specifically designed to accelerate the organism's ability to invade and replicate themselves within the host's respiratory and renal tissues, thereby causing near instantaneous liquefaction of those organs and killing the host. As you have seen, the effects also have the added benefit of causing particularly gruesome fatalities that bring a certain...shall we say...psychological component to the table as well."

The man with the Balkan accent rubbed his throat uncomfortably, but the other two people from the Haz-Mat suits stepped forward. One was a middle-aged woman who looked more intrigued than ill at ease over the prospect laid before her.

"I thought that all previous attempts to weaponize those particular viruses was proven to be ineffectual by both the United States and Russia. How is it that you succeeded where the world's superpowers have failed?"

Dr. Whelan smiled at the woman and seemed intrigued by her mild challenge.

"In the simplest terms possible, the Filoviridae do not replicate themselves through cellular division. Instead they invade a host and utilize the amino acid chains of the host's cells to create copies of themselves. The host cell is destroyed in the process and a new viral organism is created. Now, due to the anaerobic nature of the

Filoviridae, their transmission could not be relied upon to be distributed via an aerosol emitter... unless we add an additional amino acid to the chain. This additional amino acid serves no purpose other than to protect the Filoviridae from breakdown within an aerobic environment and thus allows for the aerosol distribution."

"That seems a very simple answer," the woman sounded overly skeptical.

"Actually, it is a very simple solution that was, up to now, impossible to achieve given that the technology required to accomplish said solution did not exist. Now it does and, thus, our achievement."

"But you can't be the only one with this new technology."

"I certainly am not."

"So what is to prevent our enemies from creating their own supply of biological weaponry?"

Dr. Whelan smiled, "so what if they do?"

"What?"

The doctor began pacing in front of the three individuals as if he were a professor instructing a class. "As you are all aware, two years ago I developed an anti-microbial, and specifically an anti-viral, vaccination for a company called Pharmanetics. The rather abrupt downfall of the company, which you may have read about in your local or national newspapers at the time, left me searching for the need to find, shall we say, alternative applications for my creation. Due to the limitation of the raw material necessary for me to make additional product, I decided to refine the remaining supply that I had managed to appropriate from the company, and create a vaccination that would extend my short supply. Unfortunately, the ability to synthesize more of the product will be impossible without the acquiring more of the raw materials."

"So, is there a source for these materials?" Some of the color had returned to the face of the well-dressed man with the thick

Balkan accent.

Dr. Whelan breathed out a heavy breath and his face tightened. "Yes. There is additional material out there in the world, but for the moment let's just assume that, well, it is unattainable." Dr. Whelan considered his words. "Perhaps later we can discuss further acquisition of the raw material, but for now the focus shall be on what we DO have and not what we MAY have in the future."

"And what is it that you currently have?" The woman spoke up this time and was clearly growing more excited.

"What I currently have is enough of my vaccine to inoculate approximately ten thousand of your various military men and women. The effectiveness of the aerosol weapon and of the immunity provided by the vaccination, were the main purposes of the demonstration you just witnessed. As you could clearly see, our test subject was able to withstand the ravages of the genetically altered Ebola and Marburg viruses we just misted into the lab."

The two individuals blanched at the casual mention that the two most deadly and incurable viruses known to man had been what was actually released into the room. The third person stood silently behind the other two and didn't react at all to the news.

The woman now looked pale and managed to stammer, "W-What?!?"

Dr. Whelan held up his hands and spoke reassuringly, "Not to worry my friends. You heard the computer inform us that there were no contaminants left in the facility. I assure you our sterilization procedures are beyond the state-of-the-art."

The Balkan man interjected, "But only two countries in the world could have access to such weaponized virus."

Dr. Whelan smiled, "That is very true. However, I would recommend that you curtail any further investigative questionings into the matter, as Mr. Pollard demands a certain degree of discretion as to his many allegiances."

The two individuals looked behind to where "Mr. Pollard"

stood stoically, his body language unreadable.

Dr. Whelan continued in the deep baritone voice he possessed, "If our friend were to feel his identity compromised he might be so inclined as to take certain degrees of action to ensure his anonymity."

The threat did not go unnoticed by the man and woman and they turned an angry eye to Dr. Whelan, who merely smiled and shrugged his shoulders in return. The pair turned once again to look at Mr. Pollard then seemed to dismiss his presence entirely as they returned their full attention back to the doctor.

"So what you are saying," the woman began, "is that you are willing to sell off both your cache of aerosol bombs and inventory of inoculations to the highest bidder?"

Doctor Whelan nodded, "And that..."individual"...will have the ability to immunize an entire regiment of his or her troops against even the deadliest biological weaponry. Imagine the fear that this would instill in your enemies. Imagine the effect this information would have on the world! The ability to utilize nuclear or biological weapons has always been curtailed by the fact that even the victor who wields the weapon could not survive in the aftermath. What I am giving you is the ability to launch a devastating biological attack on your targets and follow it up with multiple regiments of troops right into the "Hot Zone" of the initial biological attack, without concern of cross contamination and, thereby, ensure victory inside that ground zero. There would even be enough antidote to inoculate the specialized technicians who could work unhindered to carry out the clean-up activities and make your 'now conquered' lands habitable once again, which could not be done in a nuclear aftermath."

The doctor inclined his head toward the Balkan, "Can you imagine the price the Palestinians would pay to drop a massive "dirty" bomb inside the borders of Jerusalem? Everyone within Israel would fall to the two diseases, as the Palestinian soldiers marched in, immune to their own bombs, and then kill off any stragglers that might be clinging to life. They could reclaim their lands, with all of the high priced buildings and land developments intact, saving the victor from the need to redevelop the area as they would normally have to do after any major armed conflict."

The Balkan man seemed to shiver at the thought.

Dr. Whelan turned to the woman, "Or perhaps the Chinese would put a similar tactic to use inside Taiwan. Eliminating the resistance to the island's re-assimilation and, once and for all, bringing their wayward neighbor back into the fold that is mainland China."

The doctor turned to Mr. Pollard, "or perhaps something more surgical and precise in nature could be accomplished? Perhaps a specific government agency could be eliminated? Clearing the way for some much needed progress to occur within our own countries of origin."

The doctor looked away and scanned the trio as he held his hands out to them in a beckoning gesture, "THAT is what I am offering you today and I think you are all aware of the significance of what is being laid on the, metaphorical, table in front of you."

The trio stood in silence for a moment before shifting nervously from one foot to another.

"Good," the doctor said as if he had said all he was going to, "I will leave you to contact your respective clients."

The lights of the lab flickered briefly, distracting the doctor as a man dressed in all black combat fatigues seemed to appear from nowhere and stood next to Dr. Whelan.

"My associate will show you back to your tents. Take all the time you need, but I will warn you that the first person to present me with the amount I requested will be the winner. There will be no second chances, so sleep well." The doctor turned his back on the trio and went over to a computer console and appeared to begin analyzing the information on the screen.

The Balkan tried to take one step in his direction but the black clad mercenary blocked his path in an instant.

Politely he held out one hand and indicated a door that was still open, "This way, if you please."

The man looked like he wanted to protest but he held his tongue because the mercenary had eased the barrel of his AK-47 at the man's abdomen. The trio walked from the chamber and out of the facility as Dr. Whelan hurriedly opened his cell phone and pressed a single button.

The line on the other end connected and a voice said, "Yes?"

"This is Doctor Whelan. Can I deduce from the flickering of the lights that you had to use the tasers? "

The voice on the other end seemed to growl slightly before answering, "He came out of the sedation early. Killed one of my men as we tried to get him back under control."

The doctor sighed, "I hope for your sake that the subject is still alive?"

"Yes..." the voice on the other end spoke with clear disappointment in his voice, "We didn't do any permanent damage to your precious Guinea Pig. He'll be hurting for a while, but he'll recover."

"Good. I have plans for him and it would be a tremendous setback to lose my prized possession due to a lack of restraint on your part."

"Be careful Doctor, my people are worth more to me than to be regarded as expendable."

The doctor smiled, "Fair enough, but you should know that to me, they are little more than meat for my beast." Silence came from the other end as Dr. Whelan let his words sink in before adding, "and if you wish to maintain your position above them, then I suggest you remember your place in our little pecking order."

Once again a growl rumbled through the earpiece on the cell

phone and the doctor's smile grew wider.

"I believe I will take that as your understanding, yes?"

The growl continued for a couple more seconds then the voice, now deeper and raspy, quietly hissed, "Yes."

Chapter 7

Las Vegas in October is one of the only times of the year that the weather is pleasant enough for people to actually want to be outdoors in the daytime. Most people know about the famous heat in the summer, but what they forget is how far above sea level the city sits. Las Vegas is a high desert and if it's not too hot in the summer, then it's too cold in the winter and the city has way too much wind at every other time of the year. We also don't have the added bonus of seasons as the landscape remains unchanged year round. No snow, little rain, no autumn leaves or spring flowers to mark the passage of time; however, there is a small window every April and October that we can practically count on to have absolutely perfect weather.

Today is one of those days. It isn't normal for me to close my eyes, but I did and relished the sunshine combined with the cool breeze that swirled around me, as I stepped out of my pickup truck. I don't usually partake in prolonged exposure to the sun, doesn't agree with me for the most part, but I can take it in and enjoy it in small doses. I stretch my arms out to the sides and deliberately bask a bit longer before I shut the door and take a couple steps until my feet are off the asphalt of the street and firmly on the concrete of the sidewalk in front of my office.

Silver State Investigations and Collections

Every morning I chuckle at my sign. I can't help it. It's just so damn "official" sounding to me, which is the complete opposite of what is actually happening inside. I hear the passenger door of my truck close and, with a smile still stretched across my face, I turn to my right to see Lei exit the vehicle. The woman is absolute goddamn candy for the male’s eyes...some female eyes as well I suppose, and the pleasant chill in the air hadn't dissuaded her from wearing her usual attire, which always seems to be next to nothing. The cut of her miniskirt, the tightness of her sweater's midriff, exposing her flat and wonderfully striated belly and the height of the heels on her knee-length leather boots would be perfect stripper attire if they were in fluorescent colors. Instead the grey tweed miniskirt, the white sweater and the grey suede boots were tasteful, but not modest. It was almost as if the clothes had been respectable once but were corrupted as they draped over Lei's body.

And don't get me started about her body. Just don't. I'll suffice to say that every showgirl, stripper, hooker or any other sex worker would starve if they had to work in her presence. They just wouldn't have a chance.

Not everyone felt she had the face to match, what with her Asian features altered by the cosmetic surgeon to appear more Caucasian through the widening of her eyes and plumping of her lips. Still, no one ever thought her unattractive as much as slightly artificial. To me, she had the most beautiful face a woman could ever possess: she did before the surgery, when we grew up together and she still does now. Hell, I still get the same butterflies in my gut when I catch her just as she gets out of the shower, or when she's simply sitting in front of the computer working in a sweatshirt (usually mine) and wearing those nerdy eyeglasses of hers...or pretty much any other time. Oh, I know she's overly smart and every bit as skilled at the same deadly crap that I am, but I still find myself lost in prolonged ogling her even after all these years.

Don't get any ideas. She's mine. I'm hers. That's it.

"God," Lei sighed as the cool desert breeze blew her straight, jet-black hair that normally extended to the middle of her back, into her face, "I wish it could be like this year round."

"Not too cold are you?" I ask, knowing full well that it would take a significantly greater drop in temperature before Lei would ever deign to alter her clothing selections.

Raising one eyebrow wickedly she looked down to what she

was wearing, before she turned to fully face me with that sly foxy grin she could wear so well. My eyes couldn't help but drop down to see her enhanced cleavage and the dual erect reactions the cool breeze had elicited as it flowed around her midriff.

"You disapprove?" she asked using all the practiced allure that had made her the master seductress that she had become.

I smiled and tried to feign mere amusement at her spectacle, "Not at all, but that attitude you're throwing around is not going to be conducive to my being able to get any work done."

Lei smiled, her genuine smile this time, "So? Maybe we should take the day off and enjoy this perfect weather, while we have it."

I started to tell her "no". I really did. But the sight of her was always more than my will power could handle without some extremely important distraction to pull me away.

"Let's at least check in and see if any of our leads turned up something."

Lei pouted disingenuously, "They never do."

My smile widened, it was a really nice day and just the arbitrary thought that my Lei wanted only to spend the day alone with me was too much to resist...and the damn woman knew it.

"Well then, let's at least check the phone messages and, if we don't have anything new, then maybe we can go to the lake?"

A glimmer in her eyes told me I had guessed her wishes correctly and an excited tremor coursed through me as thoughts of the lake cruiser's yacht-like amenities ran through the back of my mind. I walked across the sidewalk to the office door and pulled the key from my pocket.

My name is Steve Jacobs and Silver State Investigations and Collections is the business that I run with Lei these days. We both have our Private Investigator licenses, which I suggested we apply for about six months after I resigned from the Los Angeles Police Department, two years ago.

Don't be fooled, though. We don't take on any clients for "collections" as the sign on the door might indicate, and we only do enough investigative work to keep our otherwise dubious reputations intact. In reality, our entire facility and occupation is more of a front that allows us to work within the boundaries of respectability and legitimacy as we do our real work. Why do we need the public relations veil? Well, it's because our real work is...complicated. I could go into it at length but I'll sum it up by saying that Lei and I spend the majority of our time attempting to track down one single individual, who after years of our searching, is still no closer to being found.

Oh... and there's also the part about Lei and me being vampires. Yes, really. Vampires.

Anyway, the thought of going to the lake would be a welcome respite from all the fruitless searching we had been doing as of late. Maybe it was time to take a break? Just get in the boat, enjoy being surrounded by nature, and luxuriate in the shade that the custom design of the bulkhead would provide. It would be perfectly peaceful, relaxing, and with Lei in a bikini, rather an intensely exotic and erotic experience for me. I suppose Lei has a similar experience, but I don't consider myself on her level, from a physically attractive point. Then again, who could? I don't want to be too self-depreciative, but I have been told that I am handsome and I do manage to possess the genetic predisposition to have low body fat and above average muscularity but, compared to Lei, I think I look like a mangy rat. They say women aren't as visually centric on their men the way men are on their women...and I thank God for that.

I pushed the key into the lock and all the attention I had been putting into Lei suddenly vanished. I didn't feel the expected resistance from the bolt as the key turned effortlessly in the latch.

Lei must have noticed my mood change, "What?"

"Door's unlocked." I said quietly, "You didn't come back for anything after we left last night did you?"

Lei was already on the move to my side, drawing her Smith & Wesson .357 Magnum snub nosed revolver from the thigh holster she barely managed to conceal under her miniskirt. "No! Any chance you forgot to lock it?"

I looked at her, raised one eyebrow in a smirk and shook my head, NO.

Lei smiled back and rolling her eyes heavenward said, "No, I suppose you wouldn't."

I pulled my key out of the latch and drew my own weapon, chambering a round from the magazine of my 9mm Glock 19 with its Crimson Trace laser sight in addition to the standard accessories.

"How do you want to do this?" Lei asked in a whisper.

I was about to answer her, when the doorknob suddenly turned and the door swung wide open. I never saw the person who opened the door as my entire field of vision was obscured by the business end of the 12-gauge shotgun pointed directly at my face.

Chapter 8

I could smell the solvent that the gunman had used to clean the weapon earlier in the day, but I only vaguely heard the voice that seemed to come from further within my office.

"Mikhail! We are not here to..."

Before the voice could finish the sentence, Lei had moved in and pushed the shotgun away from my face as the gunman pulled the trigger. Buckshot flew harmlessly into the air and headed skyward as Lei wrenched and twisted the shotgun around while pinning the gunman's hand to the weapon. She quickly reversed her momentum and sent the man spinning to the ground as his trapped wrist remained immobile and snapped under the force of her takedown.

My hearing was reduced to only a low whining whistle, but I did my best to ignore it and managed to step forward over the fallen man and headed to my office. I knew the man hadn't been alone and, since Lei needed time to secure the man she had just downed, it fell to me to take the lead and clear the office. I rounded the corner of the waiting room and visually checking the hallway that led into the large studio that Lei and I had converted into our shared office space. Seeing no one, I crept forward as my hearing slowly came back to me. I still couldn't hear well, but the miserable sounds that the man Lei had taken down made had started to cut through the shrill ringing that was fading from my ears. By the time I was at the door to the office my hearing had fully returned and the gunman had stopped screaming. I didn't know if Lei had killed him or he had simply passed out from the pain, but that didn't matter at the moment. The important thing was he was no longer a threat and Lei would be coming to back me up.

I quickly peeked around the door to the office and retreated almost in the same instant. There were three men in the office. Two were standing on either side of a third man, who was seated in one of the leather chairs we used for guests. I remembered that the seated man had something laying across his lap, a briefcase maybe, but the other two men had their Tokarev 9mm pistols aimed at my head when I took my look.

"Please! We are not here for violence!" that same voice called out to me.

I wasn't in the mood for explanations at that point so I simply said, "Have your men drop their weapons and kick them over to the door or I swear to God none of you will leave here alive."

It wasn't a bluff. Lei and I were what our people called "Hunters." In the old days we would be the people who were sent out to "acquire" blood for the group...I'll let your mind wander on how we managed to acquire it. These days the Hunters had become protectors and defenders of our people, but our training still included all the deadly aspects of the old days.

"Cton! Polozhite Gus' vniz!" the words sounded Slavic, probably Russian, but I had no clue what had been said until I heard two loud thumps followed by a grating slide of metal on the concrete floor. I peered around the corner again and saw that the two men who previously had been holding pistols were empty handed, with their arms in the air. Surprised, I ducked my head back around and then quickly moved into the room with my Glock at the ready. Lei appeared from behind me and trained her revolver on the man to the right while I watched the man to my left, along with the guy in the center.

"Now would be a very good time to start talking," I said as I backpedaled, knelt down to pick up their weapons and dropped them into the trash.

"Be sure to include the part about why we shouldn't just shoot you in the first place." Lei was visibly shaken at realizing how close I came to having my head removed by the shotgun blast. It resulted in making her very, very angry.

"I apologize for Mikhail," the old man in the chair spoke in that same accented English and his voice sounded very much like a man who had smoked far too much, "The man is an idiot, but a loyal one. Is he dead?"

I didn't know if he was or not, so instead of answering I moved to the first man on my left and spun him until his back was to me. Then I patted him down but found no other weapons on his person.

I backed up and Lei said, "He's just taking a little nap right now, but he'll need a doctor when he wakes up. Probably never play the piano again, but he'll live," Lei said as she repeated my actions by patting down the other man just as I had, and then came back up to cover my position.

I moved to a spot just out of reach of the man in the chair. He was old, really old, if the number of wrinkles and sagging flesh on his face were any indication, but as he rose to allow me to pat him down it was clear he still had full, if not excellent, control of his physical abilities.

I extended a hand for the briefcase and the old man pushed it out of my reach.

"Please, we are here to discuss business. You must accept the work before you see what is inside the case."

I raised the barrel of the Glock up to the man's face, "That particular nicety went off the table the second your man pointed a gun at me."

If the old man was in any way intimidated by the gun, he didn't show it. Actually, it looked almost as though he was about to start laughing and was having trouble holding it in.

I acquiesced, "All right, you hold the box open. I am only looking for weapons, not papers or pictures, and if I don't see any you can close the box before I have the chance to memorize anything. Agreed?"

The old man sighed, "It is acceptable."

He spun the briefcase around, popped the latches and opened

the case. I was able to see a letter size manila envelope, four passports and three stacks of what I thought were hundred dollar bills. Nothing else.

I nodded and the old man slowly closed and latched the briefcase. I looked the old man in the eyes and said, "Take a seat."

He complied easily enough before turning to his two associates who were still standing and said, "My men?"

Without looking I said, "Lei?"

"Mmm-hmm?" she purred in her way.

"Would you mind bringing chairs in for our two friends?"

I could feel her head swivel to the back of mine, "You sure?"

I was still staring at the old man, and something about him was stirring a memory that wouldn't surface.

"I think level heads have prevailed for now." I inclined my head to the old man, "What do you think?"

"Da, I believe so."

Lei chuffed loud enough for everyone to hear, "Easy to say now that we have them dead to rights."

I kept my gaze on the old man, something about his eyes reminded me of... To Lei I said, "I'm not so sure about that."

The old man smiled at my words. His teeth were stained various shades of brown and yellow, evidence of a lengthy relationship with cigarettes...a VERY long relationship.

Lei had been wearing a confident, perhaps even smug, expression at our apparent victory; and then my words had sunk in and her face transitioned instantly back into battle mode.

"You are very perceptive for one so young," the old man drawled in that Russian accent as his face drew together in a mask of limitless rage and terrifying power, "but if I had come here to do anything but talk, then you and your, 'shlyukha', would already be dead."

I lowered the Glock to my side and walked the three paces toward the old man until we stood practically nose-to-nose.

"You sound like you know me," I said in a murderous whisper, "If that's true, then you should also know better than to threaten me," I grabbed the back of the old man's head and shoved the barrel of the Glock under his chin, "or call my woman a whore."

If I hadn't been looking right at his face I might have missed the momentary flash of fear that darted over the old man's face. Apparently he wasn't used to having his threats met with anything but supplication. I could feel the strength building up inside the man as I kept my grip on the back of his head. He was strong, powerful and capable well beyond what his physical appearance would indicate. Despite my entire focus being directed at the old man I could hear a shuffling of feet and the sound of a large object hitting the floor before Lei called out to me.

"Steve!"

I shoved the old man back and into the chair that he had been sitting in then ducked and spun to my right. The fist of the large bodyguard flew over the area where my head had been as my body twisted away from the blow. I extended my gun arm as I spun and centrifugal force brought the butt end of the Glock back around, slamming into the guard's face, effectively shattering one side of his jaw. The man went down in a heap, while the follow through of the blow left me standing once again with the barrel of the gun pointing directly at the chair where I had shoved the old man.

I was aiming at the backrest of the chair. The old man wasn't there.

I heard Lei gasp and whirled to see the immobile form of the other guard lying on the ground in front of her, but behind her the old man had one of her arms trapped behind her back, while his gnarled, claw-like hand seemed to be caressing her throat.

Score one for my instincts: they told me the old man was more than he appeared... and damn them to hell for not giving me any idea how much more.

I raised my Glock, "Easy there comrade, we wouldn't be in this position to begin with if your men hadn't kept attacking us."

The old man's eyes narrowed, "In Mikhail's case, that would be true, however, you made your particular threat plain when you dared to touch me. What were my..." the old man paused and looked disgustingly down at the pair of guards on the floor,"...men to do?"

I sighed, "All right. Enough." I lowered the Glock and holstered it, "Enough of all this posturing. You say you came here to talk? Let the girl go and we'll talk."

The old man's eyes had dropped to the holster at my belt, apparently shocked that I would semi-disarm myself so easily. Lei started giggling at the old man's apprehension and he took it badly. He tossed Lei aside with enough force to send her airborne into a wall of the office. Picture frames fell off their nails as drywall cracked and crumbled in a basic outline of Lei's flailing body as she hit and fell limply to the floor. I tried not to look but the moment my eyes left the old man to see if Lei was all right he appeared next to me. I never even saw him move.

One hand encircled my throat the same way it had Lei's while the other grabbed my gun hand so I couldn't draw the weapon.

His breath stank, though not from garlic or any other pungent food. It smelled of decay. Death.

"You are right young one, I do know you...and I do need your service or I would kill you here and now for your insolence."

I twisted my head around as he held my neck so I could face him. The effort abraded my skin beneath his nails and it took considerable strength to move at all, but I, too, was much more than I seemed to be, and not nearly as outmatched as the old man thought. Still, we could keep up with the "mine's bigger than yours" contest all day and it wouldn't get us anywhere. The truth was that if we decided to take this to a lethal level it would probably end in a stalemate...meaning we'd kill each other...and that wouldn't do for either of us.

I smiled, "So, you done now? Can I go and check on my girl or did you want to throw me into the wall as well?"

The old man's eyes narrowed, but his grip on my throat loosened and he released my gun arm. I walked around him and checked on Lei who was moaning softly as she regained consciousness. People like Lei and myself are tough, a product of our upbringing and training and we heal extremely fast as a result of our genetics, which makes us very hard to kill. Unfortunately, a broken neck or ruptured artery would do the job just as it would on anyone else, so it was always in our best interest to keep any lethal confrontations to a minimum. I breathed out a quick sigh of relief and turned back to the old man and gestured a hand for him to sit. He glanced at the side of the chair he had originally been sitting in, and retrieved the briefcase from the floor where he had dropped it.

I cleared some of the debris on the floor so Lei didn't accidentally cut herself as she came back to her faculties, walked behind the desk and sat in my own leather chair.

"So," I said, "what are you doing in North America Mr. Lagos?"

There was a glimmer in the old man's eyes and a smile crept across his face. "As I said," barely keeping the laughter out of his voice, "very perceptive."

Chapter 9

Dimitri Lagos, leader of the vampire nation whose territory encompassed most of the countries that comprised the former Soviet Union. And yes, I did say "vampire nation." It turned out that the little collective group I grew up in was not unique in all the world. Apparently Alpha had known of the existence of other groups, but it wasn't until communications went global and the world became a much smaller place, that the rest of us found out that we weren't alone or unique. Turned out that there were hidden groups, similar to ours, secreted away on every continent. Dimitri's group was by far the largest as well as being one of the oldest; however, there were additional groups in Egypt, Uganda, China, Brazil, and France, while some younger collectives existed in Canada, Australia and, of course, the United States.

Dimitri Lagos was the Russian collective's version of our Alphonso Diemo. Unfortunately for the populace at large within his territory, Dimitri and his kind rejected modern assimilation and were still the blood sucking serial killers that Hollywood so elegantly tried to reinvent every few years. In a nutshell, the Russians are scary...very scary...and they comport themselves as if they are truly royals from near the turn of the 19th century. Having the enormous sums of money that they seem to have helped them to maintain this ridiculous image. It also seems to keep the authorities from noticing the countless bodies that disappear all over Russia. Where the money comes from, no one really knows. It is also unknown just how they manage to maintain ownership of vast areas of land, in spite of Communism where all worldly possessions and real estate were absorbed into the "State."

I had to tread carefully. Clearly Dimitri was of the few of us who's life had extended beyond even what we can usually expect, which meant that he was hundreds, if not thousands of years old. It was a rare trait amongst our kind, but not unheard of. Alphonso

Diemo, our founder, is long lived and, supposedly, Lei and myself are also, although neither of us have been alive long enough at this point to have experienced, or witnessed an extended life firsthand. It also meant that there was a great deal of the unknown in play. What happened to those of us who "continue on" in life was never well documented by our historians as most of our kind either went mad from our condition in times when blood was scarce or were killed before they ever managed to reach old age. The elderly in our society were a rather new predicament that our people had to prepare for, but Dimitri's people had their own solutions.

They ate the old.

Making it even more distasteful, if that were possible, was the fact that it didn't even serve a purpose, as the blood from our own kind won't sustain us, so the act had more to do with thinning the ranks and removing the weak. True, it made the Russians strong as a group, but physically they didn't have the dubious luxury of growing up underground. Rock climbing was a means of getting around in my world and my people could move up a sheer vertical rock wall almost as easily as could a spider. The Russians might be scary and capable, but none of them can compare to my people physically.

I stared across the desk at Dimitri and waited as he placed the briefcase on the desktop and then set his gnarled hands on top of it protectively. We just looked at one another for a moment. I don't know if we were sizing each other up or if we were both just taking a respite to center ourselves after the earlier violence.

I really wanted to get the monstrous bastard out of my office as quickly as possible, so I dispensed with the formal pleasantries.

"All right Dimitri, as you well know, North America is Alpha's territory and, as his second, I am bound to enforce his will on any who come here. So I'm going to ask you again, why are you here?"

The old man smiled and nodded, "I am aware of the protocols, but I am here on invitation by Comte Diemo himself." He produced a letter, the design on which I recognized immediately as being Alpha's, and held it out to me.

I took the letter and read the familiar script. It read that I was supposed to extend safe passage to the Russians as well as assist them if I were able. I didn't like it. I knew how Alpha felt about the Russians, which was not friendly to say the least, and couldn't believe he would ever willingly want to help them.

I placed the letter on the desk, "This gets you five minutes of my time. Start talking."

The old man looked down to his hands and shook his head in what might have been disappointment. I thought he might drag out the time deliberately, but he started talking quickly enough.

"It has come to my attention that certain of our financial interests are in jeopardy of being taken from us."

He waited for me to respond. I didn't.

With another sigh he continued, "It would appear as though our claims of ownership to certain mineral rich lands in Siberia have come under scrutiny within the new administration. We are at risk of losing these lands and I would very much like this not to be so."

I chortled, "I always heard you Russians had pockets deep enough to sway any political decisions your way."

Dimitri looked confused, "Deep pockets?" It took less than a minute for him to grasp the meaning, "Ah, yes. I see. That is true; however, if a proper bribe was all that was needed I would not be here now."

It was my turn to nod, "I suppose that makes sense. What doesn't is that I am based here in Nevada, which is in the southwestern United States, not Russia. What do you expect me to do?"

"Directly, nothing. This is our fight for our land and my people will turn the soil crimson to a degree such as never been seen since Stalin's time if anyone dares to try to take what is ours."

The look in Dimitri's eyes went bestial and I hadn't initially realized I was holding my breath until the ache to breathe in my chest overwhelmed the apprehension that flowed through me.

Dimitri was looking past me in a kind of daydream and I watched his eyes as they flicked back and forth wildly in their sockets.

"Okay," I said calmly, hoping it would be infective, "so what do you want of me?" Dimitri suddenly seemed to wake from the daydream and his eyes shot back to mine in a deadly glare full of threat and intent. His breathing was irregular and he clenched his fists, but managed to calm himself enough to continue the conversation.

"You," he said and pointed a crooked finger at my face, "I need you to recover some property of mine."

"Excuse me?"

Dimitri nodded, "I have taken steps to counter what is happening in Siberia. Unfortunately, the man I put in charge of the project has betrayed me and I want what he owes me."

I held up my hands, "Wait a minute, are you telling me that you want me to steal for you?"

"Not stealing. Recovering what is already mine."

I laughed, "As you say."

Dimitri's eyes burned into me, "I am not lying, boy."

I shook my head, "No, I'm sure you kept the receipts, right?"

Dimitri clearly wasn't used to the kind of insolence I was throwing at him, but he managed to continue.

"Doing this for me will also serve your own interests."

"And what "interests" might those be?"

Now it was Dimitri's turn to smirk at me, "We'll get to that. First you need to understand what is at stake."

I didn't like how confident Dimitri suddenly looked, which was as if he had some ace up his sleeve.

"Go on."

Dimitri frowned and spat, which I didn't appreciate as I would probably be the one cleaning up the office later, and said, "Everything that is happening is moving through "official" channels, but my own sources tell me that there is a man making claims to being a descendant of the Romanovs who is truly behind all of this."

"Romanov? You mean like the last Tsar of Russia, Romanov?"

"Da, it was thought that the family line had been completely slaughtered back in 1914, but the new administration has taken a stance of being publicly against the crimes committed by the Communists, and they are trying to assign restitution to the victims including the Romanovs."

I shook my head at the whole convoluted situation, "So the government is just going to give the land back to this man just on his say-so, that he is of Romanov lineage?"

"Oh, certainly not!" Dimitri waved his hand as if swatting away a fly at the question, "They are running DNA tests, apparently the latest technology, and if he is proven legitimate then the government will have to decide the best way to compensate all of the parties involved."

"Compensate how?"

"We believe they will either divide up our lands, or assign a monetary increment to each area, based on a geographical assessment value."

I thought about it and, honestly, the idea didn't really sound all that bad a solution to me. "Sounds like everyone will come out a winner, so what's the problem?"

Dimitri Lagos' eyes burned into me, "Do you have any idea the value of the land we are talking about?"

I answered honestly, "Obviously not, because you haven't told me what location is in jeopardy."

The old man's gaze never wavered, "As I said, Siberia."

"Excuse me?"

The old man nodded, "Yes, Siberia."

"What, you mean like, all of it? The entire territory of Siberia?"

All I knew about Siberia is that it was huge, almost as large as the entire United Sates, and was generally considered to be the geographical armpit of Russia. A freezing cold wasteland good only for prison camps and reindeer farms with little indigenous life and even less value. Why these idiots were going to go to "war" over a virtual icepack that no one ever wanted to begin with was beyond me.

"Seriously?"

The old man cocked his head curiously, "Yes, why?"

Dimitri's surprise by my lack of comprehension made me pause. I tried to rack my brain and, failing that, turned to my computer and typed "Siberia" into the search engine. Wikipedia read as my memories of Siberia had always been: home to most forced labor camps and other forms of Soviet prison systems. There was also some mention of herding reindeer and a small patch where potatoes can be grown; otherwise, it seemed a wasteland. And then I saw the section about mining. Apparently after the fall of the Soviet Union the new technology that began to funnel into Russia made an amazing discovery. The region was abundant, dare I say, overwhelmed with precious metals, diamonds, natural gas and oil all of which were now accessible via modern mining methods. The entire region was, quite literally, a gold mine. If I were to read a into what Dimitri was saying I would have to assume that he and his brood were the past and present beneficiaries of these newfound riches, and they did not wish to lose control of 'their' lands.

Dimitri stared knowingly at me and said, "In times past, we used the land as our sanctuary. People died in the camps all the time. Sometimes it was from malnutrition, sometimes from the abuse of their jailers and sometimes they simply disappeared into the night. If fate had brought you to Siberia then, for all practical purposes, you were already dead to the rest of Russia."

Dimitri stood and began to pace around the office as if stretching his legs. "We enjoyed the isolation for years. It served us well during the transition from the Russian Empire to the Tsarist states and then into Communism and we were left alone because no one wanted anything to do with the people, or the land, called Siberia."

"Did you have ever have claim on the land?"

Dimitri nodded, "Da, it was officially assigned to myself and a few of my people as caretakers of the region. We were actually responsible only to track down any runaway slaves or escaping prisoners, and return them to the camps however we saw fit. In return we were granted the right to live and utilize any aspects of the land that were not currently being harvested by the state."

"How long before you realized you were sitting on a treasure chest?"

"Not long. We found the diamond mine first, then the silver and later the gold. It wasn't until decades later that prospectors began arriving and surveying the area for oil, coal and natural gas." Dimitri's nose wrinkled as if he smelled something foul, "Once they found the oil, there was no stopping them. So I began talks with then President Putin about maintaining our rights to the land. He taxed the mines heavily, but we kept all the rights of ownership until the claim was made by the Romanov."

"You're calling him "the Romanov" now? Are you sure his claim is real?"

Dimitri stopped pacing and a look covered his face that wouldn't be accurate to call fear as much as unease, "Yes, I am sure he will prove to be of the Romanov bloodline."

"How distant a relative are we talking about here? There must be hundreds of people with some kind of distant familial tie to the Tsar's family."

Dimitri shook his head, "No, only a direct tie would be recognized in this case."

"But if they were all supposedly killed around the time of World War One, then who is this guy?"

Dimitri didn't answer, but his eyes were distant and unfocused.

I ran the whole story through my head and realized there was something I was missing. I had been so caught up in the tale that I forgot to ask the big question, "So how do you expect me to help? I'm on the other side of the world, and it isn't as though I speak Russian?"

Dimitri seemed to reanimate himself and moved back to the desk to sit in the leather chair. I heard the tinkling of broken glass falling to the floor from behind us and realized Lei was working to raise herself up off the floor.

Dimitri popped the latches on his briefcase and pulled out a manila envelope, full of several papers and some photographs, which he set on the desk.

"We intercepted this." He passed a photograph to me that appeared to be an aerial shot from either a high altitude airplane or a satellite.

"What is this?"

"We believe that the Romanov is funding this base camp and that they are developing new weapons made specifically to kill our kind."

I froze, "What?!? How do they know about us?"

"We don't know, but it would seem that they do, and they are developing a weapon that would enable a military force to specifically target our kind."

I scanned the photograph and some of the papers that Dimitri had handed me and while I didn't look, I could feel Lei watching us as she cleared the debris from her clothes. She started moving in close to Dimitri, but a quick shake of my head let her know the fight was over and to stand down. Dimitri glanced over her way and gave Lei a long, lingering up and down look that was creepy on a level that would put a chill in your bones. Lei noticed him and, in true Lei form, sensually licked one of her fingers, drawing his attention where she wanted it, and then dragged the finger across her throat in a slashing fashion before walking out of the office.

"She is a spirited one. I like that."

I didn't respond, but every fiber of my being wanted to rip the old monster to shreds, never mind whether I was able or not.

I put the last of the papers down on the desk. "This is all very interesting, and, if what you say is true, then there may be a reason for my people to watch and see how it all turns out. However, I don't see a reason to actively become involved yet. I still say this "Romanov" is your problem."

"Da, but this facility," Dimitri tapped a finger on the photograph where it lay on the desk, "it is your problem and your responsibility."

I frowned but didn't respond. The old bastard was working his way around something, holding some kind of trump card back that he thought would obligate me. I waited for him to play his hand, but really had no idea where he was going.

"This is why you owe me your service and you will do as I ask."

My eyebrows went up. "Oh, really?"

"Da," Dimitri's voice became smug and certain as he reached into a flap inside the lid of the briefcase, removed another trio of photographs and slid them across the desk. The first picture had two individuals standing next to each other. One appeared to be a uniformed soldier, although what uniform he wore was beyond me, while the second man was being led away in chains. The second man was also nearly twice the size of the soldier.

"So what?"

Dimitri pointed at the photograph, "The man in that picture is the key. I need him found and brought back to me alive."

I frowned, "I assume you mean the big guy?"

Dimitri rolled his eyes, "Yes, the big guy."

I shook my head, "So who is he?"

Dimitri immediately answered, "That doesn't concern you!"

I stared at him, a little shocked by his outburst, but Dimitri composed himself quickly.

"The identity of that man is unimportant to you, even though he is crucial to us. He is currently being held as a prisoner and we want him back."

"Is he one of yours?"

This time Dimitri just scowled at me and didn't answer.

I relented, "All right, so how do I go about collecting him?"

"The next photograph is a man who might be of some help to you."

I swapped the top picture to the bottom and saw a picture of a United States Navy Officer, dressed in his formal uniform.

"Can you tell me who this guy is?" I said with a degree of sarcasm in my voice.

Dimitri ignored my attitude and said, "His name is Robert Larson and he served in the same Special Forces team that the man from the first photograph used to be in. We believe them to be close friends and he should be willing to help you."

I shrugged, "I still don't see any reason, or obligation, that would make me want to help you."

Dimitri smiled, "Check the next photograph."

I again swapped the top photo to the bottom, but this time just watched Dimitri as he sat there, grinning like a proverbial cat that ate the canary. When I couldn't take the suspense any longer I casually glanced down at the photograph. Immediately I could see that it was a picture of a trio of men, two of whom were wearing the same soldier's uniform as the one from the first photograph, but the moment my brain registered the image of the third man I couldn't breathe and my hands shook as they held the photograph.

Dimitri chuckled softly and rose from the chair. He placed stacks of money and the bogus passports on my desk along with another manila envelope. "All of the necessary documents, maps and other information you may need are in the envelope. I shall assume that I need not tell you to inform me when you have dealt with your responsibility, as well as resolved your debt to me, by retrieving the man and claimed the list of my property, which is also in the envelope.

I was too stunned to speak, just nodding as Dimitri pointed at the photograph I still held, "That man, wearing the lab coat in the photograph, should be able to guide you to everything I require."

My mind and body were numb at the sight, but somehow I managed, "Pick up your men and go."

Dimitri inclined his head and torso in what might have been a slight bow and kicked each of his "guards" until they stirred and staggered out behind him. I thought I heard them dragging away the man Lei had incapacitated by the front door, but I couldn't be sure. I just stared at the image in the photograph.

Lei walked back in, looking over her shoulder at the Russians departing and froze when she saw me standing there incapacitated.

"What happened?"

I couldn’t answer because my voice didn't seem to work.

She moved to my side and placed her hand on my arm as her eyes searched my face for understanding. Then she modified her gaze and checked out the photograph. I heard her gasp and her fingers dug deeply into my forearm.

"OH MY GOD!!!" she exclaimed and her legs buckled slightly before she regained her balance. "It's him!"

I could only nod. After two years of searching, there he was. Dr. Phineas Whelan, the man who murdered over three thousand of my people. And now we knew where to look.

Chapter 10

He woke to pain, but there was always pain. It was a constant, consistent companion for him as he lay alone in the dark strapped to the upright platform that served as his "bed." His eyes fluttered open and he tried to take in the details of his surroundings, but his eyes, though acclimated to the dark from being closed while asleep, still couldn't penetrate the depths of the shadows that surrounded him.

He wiggled his toes and could feel the smooth steel step his weight rested on beneath the soles of his feet. He tried to flex his ankles but, instantly, a sharp pain shot through and around his calf muscles as he made his attempt. The circular clamps that were bolted to the table and tightened around various parts of his body, although not so much as to cut off his circulation, and not viciously painful, unless he tried to move.

He contracted his thigh muscles just to get a sense of feeling in his lower body and again something in the metal restraints seemed to bite into his flesh, increasing the already considerable amount of pain he was experiencing. He knew he was bound by similar restraints around his waist, chest, wrists, biceps, neck and forehead and even the smallest movement would be enough to set the sharp biting pain shooting through whichever part of his being couldn't remain immobile, but still, he tested each and every muscle, each and every clamp, until his body was beaded with sweat from the strain.

He went through the act every time he awakened in the dark place that was his prison, even though he didn't know why. He closed his eyes and tried to make sense of his own incoherent thoughts as each one came into his head. He had no memory of who he was, nor how he ended up here. He tried to concentrate and quiet the chaos in his head, but he wasn't able to focus his chaotic mind. It was as if his own thoughts were functioning and literally screaming at him to act, although in a language he didn't understand. He tried to make sense of anything, to grab onto one single piece of information with some semblance of clarity that might lead him to a place where he could concentrate, a place that would enable him to understand, to recognize the steps needed to be free of the torment that the pain and restraints brought to him.

He tried again and again until the muscles of his body began to quiver at the mental and physical effort he was putting into the attempt to be free. Finally, he slumped, exhausted against the restraints. He closed his eyes in expectation of the oncoming torrent of pain that would come from all the restraints and would simultaneously sear throughout his body as a result, but he just didn't care anymore.

He was too tired of trying to escape, and he knew he couldn't escape the restraints. Or the pain. Or...worst of all...the...

Lights flickered on and off in rapid succession and his eyes shot open at the unexpected strobe effect. There was a slight smell of something in the air that hadn't been there a moment ago. It was acrid and cloying in his nose, but not unpleasant. Something inside him was cheering and he suddenly realized he was no longer in pain.

Surprised he flexed his calf muscles again, but this time there was no searing, biting pain when he felt the meat of his lower leg press against the slick metal that encircled his ankle. Confusion made him test other restraints and when he clenched his fist, when he gently flexed his wrist he could feel the restraints creak and bend with his effort.

The faint sound of voices in the distant background began growing louder and he went rigid. He couldn't let anyone know of the small newfound freedom he had acquired and he hoped that no one would notice him.

The voices continued to grow in volume until he could distinguish the words clearly, "...capacitor probably blown. The readouts all indicate there was some kind of massive power surge, just more than the array could effectively distribute."

"Whatever man, as long as we don't have to hang out in there too long. The guy gives me the creeps."

It was easy for him to determine that there were two voices, both male and both somewhat apprehensive about whatever it was they were about to do. He couldn't distinguish much more as the men hadn't entered the room, but then there was a series of different beeping sounds, followed by a hiss and grind of metal sliding on metal until a loud click sent everything quiet again. Light burst into the room and he had to shut his eyes tightly to keep it from hurting his eyes.

"Is he out?" one man asked.

"No, just doesn't like the light. C'mon let's just get this done," another man answered who was wearing a white doctor's coat over simple green/blue clothes. The doctor hurried into the room and sat in a chair just to the left side of the upright table.

The other man was more wary and was wearing the typical all-black garb of the guards along with a rifle slung over his shoulder and a strange looking gun in the holster at his side.

"Oh yeah, he's awake." the guard's voice wasn't steady and came out in a semi-stutter, "Sh-should we just tranq him? To be safe?"

Without looking up the white coat quickly said, "No, he's had too much of that shit over the last couple days. We aren't supposed to use it unless we absolutely have to."

The “patient” let his eyes follow the guard as long as they could until he would have needed to turn his head to follow. He felt sure he could overcome the restraints around his head and neck as easily as he had those that were around his wrists, but he didn't want to let these two know he could move...at least not yet.

"Well," the guard continued as he moved out of view, "I say it's necessary." The guard pulled the gun from its holster and raised it up, pointing it at the table.

The white coat must have heard the intent in the guard's voice because he did turn around at that point to face the guard, "Then you explain to Whelan why you risked breaking his pet pony with extra tranquilizers while he was still safely strapped down on the gurney."

"I-I," the guard's voice wavered as he turned and looked at the white coat. He seemed to consider that for a few seconds before his arm dropped and he holstered the gun.

The first man nodded, "Good. Now shut up and let me work." There was the sound of multiple clicks and taps as something electronic whirred to life next to him.

He waited, immobile, afraid to even take in a deep breath as the extra movement might draw their attention.

"C'mon, dammit. Reboot already...There we go!" the white coat practically cheered as a computer illuminated and a chime sounded as it restarted itself. "Okay let's see what we are dealing with here."

He listened as the man in the white coat tapped the buttons again and guessed he was mumbling through some kind of checklist when the guard's face suddenly appeared over him.

"Anyone home in there?" The guard's eyes were cold as they peered down at him and, although he didn't recognize the man's face, he knew he didn't like him. In fact, a rage began to build deep inside his core and, unbeknownst to Mr. White Coat or the guard, he instinctively began to clench and unclench his fists in response to the rage.

He couldn't stop himself from opening his eyes and glaring at the guard, who gasped in response.

"Um, doc?" the guard said, stepping back as he spoke.

"It's not nice to taunt the animals, you know." the white coat chuckled.

"Yeah right, but Doc, what's wrong with his eyes?" the guard sounded as though he was about to scream and run in the opposite direction.

"Hmm? What's that about his eyes? Why do his..."

The white coat suddenly appeared in his vision and froze at the sight.

"My God!" the White Coat gasped and was jolted back to his equipment. He hammered a couple clicks onto the keyboard and began to stammer, "Oh no, his readings are spiking! Why the hell would that...?"

The guard cut the white coat off in mid-sentence, "Okay, that's it. Night-night time."

He saw the guard step forward and raise the gun, pointing it directly at his neck.

"Wait!" the white coat called out.

"What?" the guard sounded angry but he held back from pulling the trigger, and turned his head to face the White Coat.

"There's something else...I can't..." the words caught in White Coat's throat as he began to cower away from the table.

"What?!?" the guard yelled at him, "Tell me what the hell is happening."

"Get away from the table!" the white coat yelled right back.

"What! Why?"

"Get away now!"

The guard looked back down at the enormous immobile man as he lay quietly on the table with only those horrifying eyes showing any sign of life.

"Doc, I don't..."

White Coat interrupted, "The electricity to the table restraints is down! He can get free!"

And then the rage that had been building inside his core exploded. Before he had even realized he had moved, his left arm twisted and tore through the heavy metal restraints as easily as if they were tissue. The guard cried out and tried to adjust his aim on the gun, but the feral man grabbed the guard's forearm, and pushed the guard's hand with the weapon off to the side, so that it pointed harmlessly away.

"He's got me!" the guard screamed and tried to twist free of the fingers encircling his arm. The patient squeezed tighter and, kicking one leg, breaking the restraints free from where they had been secured to the table. The guard's voice was still screaming, almost like background noise, but now he screamed in pain instead of fear, as he tried to use his free hand to pry up the fingers that his trapped arm.

Their experiment wrenched his other arm free, pulled the restraints from his head and neck and turned to see the white-coated man fumbling with a keypad by the only door. He frowned as he watched the man repeatedly slide something through a slot on one side of the keypad. It was a clumsy and panicked performance, which might have been why the red light and buzzer kept sounding, while the door remained locked.

Something told him that he couldn't let the man get out of the room. He had to stop him, but how? He tried to sit up but the final restraints around his chest and waist prevented it. He grabbed the one around his chest, which was by far the largest and heaviest of all the restraints and pulled. This time the metal resisted and groaned as it bent under his power.

As he strained he felt something like two sticks shatter in his other hand and the guard shrieked a high-pitched cry that almost sounded inhuman. He turned to see the guard's hand and upper forearm limply flopping between his thumb and first finger like a deflated garden hose. He frowned at the sight, until he realized the guard was desperately trying to get the rifle off his shoulder with his other arm.

He released the guard's limb and, as the guard's body started to fall, the giant man's big hand recoiled and then shot back out like a serpent, grabbing the guard by the face. His palm shattered the guard's nose as it hit and his fingers held the front of the guard's skull like an NBA star palming a basketball.

The guard tried to scream but both the blood in his mouth and the pressure of the steel hand that held him muffled his pathetic sounds. His attention returned to the chest restraint and he strained again for all he was worth until the heavy metal clamp broke free from the table. It was nearly four feet of heavy steel, weighing nearly thirty pounds, but he held it as if it were made of balsa wood.

A light beep sounded and he saw a small green LED light shining on the keypad in the distance. White Coat desperately pulled at the door as the sound of electronic latches disengaged, but the freed man flung the piece of metal he was holding at the back of the departing man. Although the door was partly open, when the restraint slammed into the back of his head with the clang/thud of impact, the white coated man went sprawling lifelessly forward, halfway through the door and he lay prone only half out of the room.

The big man ripped the waist restraint away with significantly less effort than before and sat fully upright. He could feel a strange vibration in his other hand and turned to see that he had literally crushed the skull of the guard as he held him. His fingers had partially dug into the guard's head in five areas corresponding to his fingers while the man's skull had given way beneath the pressure. All that was left of the guard's head was a deformed pulpy mess, and his body was in a death spasm as nerve endings fired chaotically for a few more moments before the body simply hung limply from the huge, partially clenched, fist.

He let the guard's body fall to the floor and looked at his hands in confusion. Deep inside he knew he shouldn't have been able to do what he just did, but another part of him reveled in the fact that he had. He peered down at the dead guard and a slight smile formed on his face. He was glad the guard was dead. He couldn't remember why he should be happy about it, but he was nonetheless.

He stood up from the table and walked to where the man in the white coat was lying. He was face down in a shallow pool of blood that was slowly expanding outward as the restraint had carved a deep gash through the back of the man's skull just above the hairline. When it hit him he had probably died instantly.

Instinct made him kneel down and check the pockets of the lab coat, removing whatever he found. There were some small examination tools that he couldn't make sense of, but nothing that he felt he should keep. He was about to rise when instinct again told him that he couldn't walk away yet. He hadn't found what he was looking for. He scanned the body, but nothing seemed to be necessary, until he checked the man's hand. There was something around white coat's wrist that he thought he needed. Carefully he unfastened the leather strap and lifted the object off the corpse's arm. He looked at the round shiny object that sat between the two straps and watched as one of the little lines ticked it's way around the circle. There were symbols around the perimeter of the circle that seemed very familiar, but he couldn't understand their meaning. Something told him to hold the object to his ear and when he did he thought the rhythmic ticking sound was soothing to him.

Yes, he thought, he would keep this thing.

He tried to fasten it to his wrist the same way the white coat had been wearing it, but it was far too small and barely wrapped around one side of his wrist. Reflexively he reached to his side, realizing he was trying to store the watch in his clothing and it was only then that he realized he was naked. The constant pain the restraints were pouring into him, combined with the added discomfort of immobilization had so preoccupied his senses that he never realized his state of undress. He wasn't cold or feeling particularly vulnerable, but the idea of clothes meant that he would have a place to put things he wanted to take with him. He looked at the corpse and knew the man was too small for anything he was wearing to fit, so he walked over to where the guard's body lay. This man was bigger, but still far smaller than he. He searched through the man's clothing and found several items located in different pockets all over the man's body. He kept a lighter and a small multi-tool because, although he didn't realize what the objects were, once again, instinct told him they were important. He also found that the man was wearing very stretchy clothing under his uniform. It took longer than he would have liked but he removed the shirt and shorts, which were made of a thin stretchy material, that stretched to his size as he pulled them on. They fit tightly against his body, but still had some room left to expand so he wouldn't rip them when he moved, and then he collected the multi-tool, lighter and watch. He dropped the things into the gun's holster he had taken from the guard and then he pulled the belt out of the belt loops on the guard's pants and cinched it around his own waist. The holster clipped onto the belt tightly and had a flap on it that snapped closed and would prevent the loose items inside from falling out.

He stood and looked around the room for anything else he wanted to take. Seeing nothing worth taking, he made his way to the door and stepped over white coat, being careful not to step in the blood that now spread over three feet beyond the body. Looking down at the blood he saw a small, mostly white rectangle floating on the surface of the pool. He knelt down and lifted it out of the crimson fluid, wiping it clean as best he could. There was a small picture of the white coat on one side, along with several words that made no sense to him, and a wide stripe that ran along the horizontal length of the rectangular object. He remembered that it was this object that the white coat had been sliding back and forth on the keypad when he was trying to leave the room.

Now he could use it to escape.

Chapter 11

The flight to Houston was as routine as any air travel can be, which usually meant the preparation before the flight was far more hectic than the flight itself. Lei and I had thrown the barest necessities into two carry-on bags and made it to the airport in less than an hour. I felt under prepared by leaving in such a hurry, but I knew that we were going to have to buy whatever gear and/or weapons necessary once inside our destination cities, so all we really needed were a few spare clothes, passports, cell phones, money and, most importantly our "medicine." I told myself repeatedly that there would always be time to acquire everything else.

"So what's our first move?" Lei asked as we walked out of the terminal in Houston.

"You hungry?" I wasn't actually asking if she needed food. I wanted to know if she had enough of the serum in her system to keep her through the long drive to the military base.

She shook her head, "I'm good. You?"

"Good. Okay let's grab a cab."

"A cab!" Lei spun on me her face aghast.

We had already talked about this. It had started as a conversation about hiring a car as opposed to renting one. Lei wanted to hire a limousine for the long ride out. When I said no, she did her best to convince me otherwise. Lei doesn't like long car rides, unless she can spread out and relax in such a way that only a limousine can accommodate and she began to preach to me about frugality versus style and, failing that, followed her sermon up with several innuendos about the possibilities that would be available to us with the privacy glass.

"Lei," I said in response, "we're going to a military base. No one goes to a military base in a limousine unless they're the President. If we show up in one of those it might give the wrong impression."

"What?" Lei replied, "that we're important? That we mean business?"

"That we are a bunch of pompous civilians who think more of themselves than the men and women in service to this country," I responded.

"That's ridiculous." Lei had this ability of dismissing anything to which she couldn't muster a decent comeback.

"No it isn't. It is a very valid point and one that might make the difference as we are arriving unannounced and unexpected," I said and crossed my arms in front of me to show her how determined I was on this point. "We are not, I repeat, NOT getting a limousine."

Three hours later I had the limousine drop us off in front of the guard gate of Fort Bragg. What can I say? She was right about the limousine, it really made for a pleasant ride. We walked to the gate and were greeted in an official capacity by the pair of guards that were stationed there. They were friendly enough, but were also quick to inform us that the base was off limits to civilians unless escorted or invited by military personnel. It was at that point the MP noticed Lei. She had changed out of her miniskirt into something more professional, which for Lei meant some kind of fantasy executive secretary. I have to give the MP credit as he really tried to keep his eyes on me, but I thought the poor guy was going to fall over when Lei looked up at him over her rimmed glasses and smiled.

I pressed while the guy was "off balance."

"We're private investigators out of Nevada and were hoping to talk to someone about this man." I showed the MP the photograph that Dimitri had initially shown me from the file. "I believe he is stationed here at the moment, correct?"

The MP's eyes darted off of Lei and to the photograph. His brow furrowed slightly and his eyes focused on the picture. The way he was able to so quickly focus on the photo told me he knew the man.

"I am not at liberty to discuss the people who are or are not stationed at this base."

"No problem," I said in as friendly a manner as I could manage, "just put us in touch with whoever has the authority to talk to us."

The MP's eyes rose to meet mine as he appeared to consider something before he said, "I.D.'s please. Both your driver's licenses and your private investigation credentials." The MP held out his hand as we pulled the requested items from our pockets. He then took them inside, saying something to the other soldier on guard with him.

It took nearly five minutes before the MP returned and handed us our stuff.

"Colonel Hatch is usually the officer who accepts the press and other civilian liaison requests. He isn't available at the moment, but if you'd like I can give you his contact information and you can set an appointment."

I shook my head. "We're kind of on a tight schedule here. We can conduct our investigations in other ways if you and your people aren't going to help us," the MP frowned deeply at that as I continued, "but it would really make everyone's life a lot easier if we could talk to someone. Is there anyone else that we could talk to?"

The MP smiled, "I said, if you'd like to set an appointment with the usual officer who handles such matters I can provide you with that information. I did not say that there was no one else you could talk to."

The sound of the gate opening sprang into my ears and I looked to see a topless jeep driving around a troop transport truck and pull forward to stop just inside the entrance. The driver stepped out of the Jeep and, even though the man was wearing sunglasses I immediately knew who it was because he looked just like his picture.

"Hello," the man spoke calmly, warmly but with a slight wariness in his voice, "I'm Major Robert Larson. Was I right to be informed that you were looking to talk to me?"

I nodded and extended my hand in greeting to the Major. Larson shook hands with me and Lei as I made our introductions and thanked him for taking the time to talk with us.

"Not a problem. My trainees are all out on exercise and the lieutenants can supervise them well enough for now." The Major cut a lean and powerful figure. He wasn't a particularly tall or large man, but his chiseled features and easy confidence gave him the presence of someone who was not to be taken lightly.

"So," the Major continued after the initial greetings had finished, "what's this all about?"

I turned to Lei and she handed me the manila file with pictures and information of the John Doe, which I passed on to Larson. He looked confused as he held his hand out to accept the file, but took it, opened it and began to read before quickly and calmly shutting the file.

He looked up and I thought I saw the slightest crack in the man's demeanor, "I think we might want to talk in my office." Larson gestured to the Jeep. "Would you both come with me?"

I nodded and thanked him again before walking to the Jeep and climbing in. Lei was right behind me and was pouring on her charms. The men in the guard gate were openly staring while Major Larson looked but seemed otherwise unaffected.

Interesting.

Chapter 12

We rode in the Jeep with Larson until we arrived at what looked like little more than a trailer park home. I was surprised at how silent the Major had become as we rode through the base. He hadn't seemed the type to be at a loss for words when we met, so either I had misread the man or he was deep in thought about who we were and how to handle us.

The man's personality seemed to return as we all climbed out of the Jeep and he politely invited us into the trailer. The room inside was a small but comfortable office, complete with a file cabinet along one wall and various framed photographs covering almost every other blank spot on the remaining walls.

"Quite a collection of photographs you have here," I commented admiringly.

"Hmm? Oh, thank you." the Major seemed lost in thought again.

"Are you the photographer?" I was looking at what appeared to be a relatively recent photo of a group of soldiers looking as though they had just returned from a mission. They were all wearing strange black clothing and were dirty, bloody, apparently exhausted and smiling broadly as they posed for the photograph.

Larson looked as though he was about to say one thing, when he caught himself and instead pointed to a man who was kneeling on the right side of the photograph.

"That's me."

I looked at the photo and, as covered with mud and camo paint as every soldier was, there was only a vague resemblance between the man kneeling in the picture and the one standing next to me.

"When was this?" I asked.

Larson shook his head, "Can't say." When I looked confused Larson added, "it was a classified mission. It's since been delisted so I can have the picture hanging like this, but civilians still need authorization for any details."

I nodded as I studied the photograph. The scenery looked as though the group was in a swamp, but the flora appeared familiar to me. As I haven't been to too many jungles or swamps in other countries I was guessing that they were in either Louisiana or Florida as opposed to off in some remote part of the world.

"Training? Maybe preparing for an operation?" I said and watched as Larson smiled.

"I am not at liberty to discuss that," but after a heartbeat he added, "but apparently you're a good detective."

It was my turn to smile, "Thanks, but why would the fact that you were training somewhere be classified?"

Larson shrugged his shoulders, "Hypothetically, only two reasons come to mind." I stayed silent hoping he wouldn't cut off the thought there. "First, it isn't the training per se, but the mission we are training for that is classified. As a result all auxiliary information regarding the mission, including the fact that American soldiers were training for it in the first place would be considered top secret."

Again I nodded, "Makes sense. And two?"

"Second, would be to preserve the anonymity of the men in the photograph who may have gone on to other missions where their identities might become compromised, if they could be traced back to this moment."

"Which is obviously why civilians need authorization to access the information."

"Exactly." "So why were you so forthcoming about revealing your presence in the photograph?"

Larson sighed, "Ah, I'm getting old. I've pretty much been reassigned out of field duty and into more of an instructor capacity. He pointed at his left eye, "Caught a piece of shrapnel on my last outing that damaged my eye, messed up my vision and which pretty much sealed the deal on keeping me off the strike teams."

Lei moved to my side and said, "You sound like someone who has come to terms, but are not happy with the arrangement."

"The Navy has been good to me and they continue to be. They could have cut me loose with a medical discharge, but kept me on instead so I could work out another five and get my pension. That was kind of a rare thing, tight as the politicians have been with the budget these days, so I was grateful."

"But?" Lei asked.

Larson turned to her and shrugged, "I've been a Navy SEAL for fifteen years and on active duty with SEAL Team 6 for ten of those years. I still feel good, strong and capable, but I know how damage to an eye can screw up a person's depth perception. My teammates have been supportive, at least to my face, but I constantly worry about what they would say behind my back if I were to try to pursue active duty again."

Larson sighed, "I wouldn't blame them. If I were in their place I would want me off the team as well. I guess it's hard for an old warrior like me to hear he's riding off into the sunset. Hell, I'm only forty years old. Doesn't feel like I should be retiring just yet."

Forty years old, I thought, that was so long ago for me. Strange that now I look back on that time and think what a child I had been, as compared to now. Major Larson, on the other hand, was at the crossroads of middle age, and at the twilight of the life he had always known. I thought about all of the trials and difficulties my people have to overcome being the way we are, but by the time we reach the same point as Larson in our lives we have lived twice as many years and usually have had the luxury of time to secure the remainder of our life on earth. For the first time I thought that maybe, just maybe, the trials that "normalcy" included, could be every bit as difficult to deal with as were our own problems.

"Anyway," Larson gestured at a trio of chairs near his desk, "you wanted to know about the man in the photograph."

"Yes and any help you could give us would be a huge benefit." Lei said as we all walked over to the chairs and sat down.

"I'll tell you whatever I can, and I'm sure I will be able to fill in some of the blanks, but I don't know how much that will be of help to you."

Lei opened a notebook and readied her pen as Larson began, "The man's name is Zach Stonebreaker, and yes that is his real last name. He was a civilian consultant with a team that was created after the attack on the World Trade Center in 1991 and that team was supposed to be a Special Response Team, or S.R.T., in the case of another attack on American soil. Our main parameter was hostage rescue, but we were also trained to take part in any incursions that arose."

When Larson stopped speaking I asked, "How is it a civilian was able to be a part of a military team? And such an apparently elite one at that. "

"The team was training and Zach was brought in as a consultant for a specialized form of combat tactics. Zach was a very talented martial artist and had developed a system that was extremely effective when stealth was necessary. It was a silent killing system that he had been training agents in the CIA to use with incredible efficiency. When word of our needs arose he was sent to show us the methods he had designed. It was during that time that our medic was injured in training and we were about to be deployed, so we didn't have time to find a replacement. Well, it turned out that Zach was also a nurse...or something like that, and because he had been working alongside us, he knew the basics about the mission."

I looked at Lei, skeptical and Larson must have seen the look.

"Yeah I know, but we were really in a bind and, although the entire team protested, Zach was given the go ahead to join us on a one time only basis."

'So what happened?" I asked.

Larson shook his head as the memories flooded back into his mind.

"I had never seen anything like it. See, the mission went completely FUBAR," he looked at Lei and seemed a little embarrassed by his use of the term. "Sorry ma'am," Lei tried to cover her face as she snorted a laugh and did a fair enough job that the Major look relieved, "well the mission was a complete "no go" and we were in trouble. I was cursing a great deal as I was the one assigned to protect Zach, but he had disappeared while I was laying down cover fire. Then the men shooting at us started screaming, we thought they were charging us, would have gotten us too, if they had been, but they weren't. They were dying. Painfully.

Larson was looking straight ahead but he was only seeing whatever images were playing in his mind.

"When the smoke cleared it turned out that Zach had somehow managed to circle around to the enemy's position and took them all out by hand. I'm man enough to tell you that even after all the things I have seen on the battleground, what we saw when we found Zach disturbed me. Funny, but the brass wasn't disturbed at all, they were impressed."

Larson stopped talking for a moment and seemed to be considering something before he shrugged, "I suppose we all were impressed to some degree. Anyway, when we made it back stateside Zach was a part of the team. We put him through the normal training, including SEAL boot camp, thinking we could weed him out that way, you know? Get him to quit on his own, but the guy thrived on the training, he just ate it up and every time we tried to haze or torture him he managed to turn the tables on us."

Larson looked from whatever he had been staring at to my face, "Have you ever heard of someone who was a natural when it comes to sports? Like a guy who just walks into a gym off the street having never played the game before and then the next day he is an All-star at the professional level? Well that was Zach. He told me he had never shot a rifle before, so I showed him how my sniper rifle worked and let him squeeze off a couple of rounds. The guy was able to make tighter groups with his shots on the first try than I could after practicing for years and I'm one of the best sharpshooters in the country. It was like that with everything. You show him how to do something and he was suddenly an expert, I can't explain it any other way."

"So did you go on several missions together?" Lei asked.

"More training missions than actual operations. Most ops usually were called off at the last minute, but yeah we did go on a few together. Guy even saved my life more than once," Larson chuckled, "which is funny cause I was always the loudest one in the room to say he shouldn't be part of the team. But after he pulled me out of a particularly bad scene, I kept my mouth shut and opened my eyes to see what a valuable asset the guy was. I started learning from him, instead of the other way around, and by the end..."

Lei and I waited as Larson's eyes started to glisten just a bit.

"...by the end, we were brothers. Truly the best friend I ever had," Larson's hand began to shake slightly, " and I curse myself every day for not being with him when he died."

"Died?!?" Lei nearly jumped out of her chair.

Larson nodded, "Yes, he was sent of some kind of long term recon mission that he never came back from. It was a couple years ago if I remember right. See, I had just been put on the disability shelf and was feeling pretty sorry for myself, so when he had asked me to go with him I thought he was just being generous, you know? Trying to give the semi- cripple something to do, so I turned him down. I said to him that he didn't need me or, if he did, I'd be a liability to him. He insisted otherwise of course, but I was still stewing in my boots about my being officially taken off active field duty and either didn't believe him or just didn't want to hear what he was saying."

Lei looked at me, I held up a finger in response wordlessly asking her to give me a moment to think. Damn, did Dimitri get it wrong? Were we looking for the wrong man?

"Major," I asked, "you say he never came back from his last mission?"

"That's right."

"Was his death confirmed?"

"Confirmed?" Larson's face began to screw up into a defensive frown.

"Well," I tried to be gentle, "was it a case of him having gone missing and presumed dead or..."

Larson sighed, "No, he had been missing for about a month, but when an operative goes on a deep cover reconnaissance mission it isn't all that unusual for long stretches of silence so none of his superiors were overly concerned. His body was found by one of the locals, his identity was confirmed during autopsy and he was sent home...where I identified him as well."

Lei responded first, "I'm very sorry," Larson looked at her and nodded a silent thanks. I asked, "Locals found him? Where was he?"

This time Larson shook his head, "I'm sorry but that information is still classified."

"How did he die?"

"I wasn't privy to all the details, but the injuries on his body looked a lot like he was in some kind of explosion."

"How so?"

"The amount of tissue damage that could only have been caused by the compressive forces and shrapnel combined with the large percentage of various burns on one side of his body. He was kind of a mess, and the third world preservation techniques for the deceased were...substandard at best."

I frowned, "and you could still make a positive identification?"

"Not by looking at his face, that's for sure. I looked for scars that he had acquired on missions we had served as well as some simple characteristics of his body that I had known about just by being around him for as long as I was. Things like birthmarks, if they were still intact, or the way his knuckles had discolored and flattened having been used to strike heavy bags, boards or people for the majority of his life. Things like that."

Lei and I were quiet for a brief period and Larson said, "I'm sorry if this impairs whatever you are investigating," then he paused to study our faces, "there's something else, isn't there? You aren't disappointed or frustrated, you think he's alive and that I'm either lying to you or trying to deceive you."

"No, I don't think you're lying," I said.

"Then what is it?" I could tell Larson was starting to get irritated. We were treading on thin ice given how emotional the subject matter was to him.

"It's just, that picture I showed you," I removed the photo from the file once again and slid it across Larson's desk until it came to rest in front of him, "we think it's proof that he's still alive."

Larson picked up the photo again and looked at it, "No, I'm sorry, but he's gone. I saw it with my own eyes."

"When?" Lei interjected.

Larson looked up from the photo, "I'm sorry ma'am, what?"

"When did you see the proof with your own eyes?"

Larson had to think for a second, "It was, I can't give you an exact date right now, but it was right around three months ago."

Lei smiled and looked at me, "Bingo."

I smiled back and nodded. Larson looked at each of us and his frown deepened, "Bingo?"

"Forgive us Major, but that photo was taken less than a week ago."

Larson looked as though he might jump over the desk and strangle me, then his eyes widened and he looked back down to then picture.

"No...it...it's not possible. I...I saw..."

"You saw what they wanted you to see," I volunteered, "what they wanted everyone to believe."

"They?"

"The people behind this are extremely well funded and have hired the expertise of a particularly brilliant doctor, who we have a certain degree of experience with, concerning what he is capable of doing. In our opinion," I pointed at the photograph, "we believe that your friend is still alive and a prisoner of these people."

Larson had been staring at the photograph, but when he raised his head the look on his face had changed. There was an edge to his features that appeared to have sharpened and his frown had morphed from anger into intent, but the greatest change was in his eyes. Damaged or not, they shined clear and focused as he picked up the phone and pressed a button.

"Darlene? Do me a favor and get General Hawthorne on the phone please?" Lei and I waited a moment, unsure of what was happening when someone connected on the other end. "Hello General. Yes sir. Thank you sir. Yes sir I am aware of the time. Thank you for taking my call. Yes sir. I am afraid that I need to take that personal time you always said I could take."

I was about to protest when Larson's hand appeared up from under his desk holding a Browning 9mm automatic handgun and pointed it in my general direction. I froze but Lei stood from her chair and Larson swung the barrel of the automatic at her. I was about to respond when Larson held up one finger from the phone and pressed it to his lips in a quiet request for us to be silent.

"Yes sir, I am aware that it is short notice and I apologize for that, but something's come up that requires my personal attention." Lei and I could both hear the silence on the other end of the line that seemed to drag out for nearly a minute, and then the muffled voice of General Hawthorne came once again over the earpiece.

"Yes sir. It is exactly that kind of situation. I appreciate that, sir. No, I do not require anything else, thank you again, sir."

Larson hung up the phone and set the gun down on the tabletop. Lei was about to pounce when I held up a hand asking her to stop. She noticed and complied as I said, "you didn't need the gun."

"Sorry, but I needed to get you quiet quickly. Couldn't let the general know there was anyone else in the room."

"Fair enough, but fair warning," I leaned over the desk until my eyes were six inches from Larson's, "If you ever pull something like that again I will make you regret it." I put enough heat in my voice to make a tiger back down, but the major didn't even flinch.

"Noted." He wrote something down on a piece of paper and handed it to me, "Meet me at this address tomorrow morning at 0800 and bring your passports."

"Passports?" "Yes, you'll need them to get into Thailand."

Chapter 13

"Thailand?" Lei asked with surprise and, perhaps, just a little bit of excitement.

"Yes," Larson said as a matter of fact, "and Bangkok to be precise. Zach was stationed in Bangkok and kept a studio apartment there. He also had a house in Hawaii, somewhere on Maui but I don't know the exact address. Shouldn't be too hard to find as his civilian life wasn't a state secret. The address of the studio in Bangkok may take a bit of searching but that's part of the reason I'm letting you two come along."

My eyebrows went up on reflex, "You're 'letting' us come along?" I couldn't hide the sarcasm in my voice, not that I wanted to. "I thought, if anything, it would be the other way around. And who says I am willing to let you come along?"

Larson met my gaze and smiled, "If you want to play it that way it's fine with me. Truth is I have all kinds of military contacts who either owe me favors or would do anything I asked out of the sheer loyalty that I developed over the years. I can get us out of the country and into Thailand with weapons and technology that their custom officials would never allow through and, as I am guessing the lovely lady you brought along with you," Larson inclined his head to Lei, "appears to be of Chinese ancestry, she probably doesn't speak Thai, and I even have access to a translator, which we are probably going to need."

Larson waited a moment and met my gaze, "It would probably speed the process for me to have a couple of professional detectives along, but I figure that I can put the pieces together on my own long before you set foot in country."

Larson waited again without altering his gaze and I heard Lei muffle a chuckle at my momentary muteness.

"Having said all that Mr. Jacobs, why is it that I need you to give me permission to tag along?"

Damn, I hated being out witted. It was worse for me than losing a fight...and I haven't lost a fight, except to Alpha, in over fifty years.

"I can only think of one reason Major."

"What might that be?"

"You don't know what you are up against. We do, and I can promise you that if you were to try this on your own you would fail and probably be killed."

Larson smiled, "I think I have more than enough experience to be able to handle myself."

I smiled, but it was Lei who gave voice to the elephant that was in the room, "your friend Zach probably thought the same thing."

Larson spun and glared at her, but quickly softened, "No, he knew better, which is why he asked me to come along."

All of the power and bravado went out of his words and Larson dropped his head as the old pain he had been carrying around lanced through him. I deflated my ego quite a bit as well, and walked over to Larson and put one hand on his shoulder, "It sounds to me as though working together we will have the best chance to find him, don't you think?"

He nodded and when he looked up I could see how grateful he was from the look on his face, but there was still something lingering in his eyes that appeared concerned.

"There's something else, what is it?" I asked calmly.

"It's not that I don't appreciate all this, but can the two of you handle yourselves?" Before I could answer Larson quickly followed with, "I'm sorry to have to ask, but I am going to need to know whether I am going to have to watch out for you two or if we can watch out for each other."

"I understand." I really did and that fact surprised me, "and yes, we can more than handle ourselves."

Larson nodded, "Would you object to letting me see for

myself?"

Lei sighed, "Is that necessary?"

"It always is good to know what your teammates capabilities are, or the lack thereof, before beginning any mission."

Lei looked as though she was going to protest more, probably something about not having the proper attire, when I said, "No, it's not a problem. How would you like to do this?"

Larson picked up his phone and pressed the speed dial button again, "Hey Dar, yeah it's me again. Could you ask Sergeant Wilson, Corporal Nash and Lieutenant Takage to meet me at the pit?"

"The pit?" Lei said as she scowled at me, "Well that just sounds lovely."

"Thanks Dar," Larson hung up the phone, "C'mon, let's get the two of you some fatigues so you don't ruin your clothes."

Ten minutes later Lei and I were both wearing camouflaged fatigue pants and the basic olive drab T- shirt that several of the other soldiers were wearing as they went through their daily training regimen. Larson drove us to one side of the base, stopping the Jeep in front of what initially appeared to be a large hole in the ground. The three of us walked to the rim and looked down to see a spectacular obstacle course and three soldiers at various points in the course."

"Okay," Larson began, "this is pretty simple stuff, but will tell me all the information I need to know. The idea here is to get through the course as fast and efficiently as possible." He pointed to what appeared to be a wood tower with a large knotted rope hanging off one side. At the top was a platform where a soldier was waiting next to what appeared to be a table. "Lieutenant Takage is at the first station on top of the tower, where he has a standard AR-15 loaded with nine rounds. The objective once you climb the rope is to shoot all five targets as quickly as possible with as few shots as you can. Slide down the pole then work your way to the next station, which is on the other side of the wall."

The "wall" Larson had indicated was only about fifteen feet from the sliding pole and was a sheer vertical wall with only a few rock climbing polymer hand/foot holds. "Once there Corporal Nash will present you with a sidearm. Enter the house and take out the targets, but be sure not to shoot the civilians." The final stage will require you to climb through the net, get past Sergeant Wilson, and exit through the door at the far end of the pathway."

Larson handed me a pair of binoculars and pointed to the final station. I could see the net laying six feet off the ground and extending horizontally to a pathway blocked in by two vertical nets. Standing midway between them was Sergeant Wilson who was wearing combat training pads. "The Sergeant is going to physically try to keep you from reaching the door." Larson looked sheepishly at Lei, "He will try to physically restrain you and you will need to engage in order to get past him. Don't worry about the Sergeant, those pads will protect him from injury so don't hold back."

Lei looked at me, "At least there's no goddamn water hazard."

Larson actually laughed at that, "Okay, so who's going to be first?"

I was about to volunteer when Lei pushed me out of the way, "Me!"

Larson was surprised by the enthusiasm, but shrugged and said, "Any questions?"

"Nope!" Lei was downright giddy. Hoo-boy, I thought, this is going to be interesting.

Larson pulled out a stopwatch and yelled out, "runner in starting position!" and each of the three men on the track raised an arm indicating their readiness.

Larson turned to Lei, "If you need to stop just raise one arm like those men just did. Understand?"

Lei tsked, "Let's do this."

"Really ma'am, most recruits don't make it through on the first try, or even the twentieth for that matter, and I don't need you to finish to understand what your abilities are."

"Are you going to say "Go" or do I just jump in when I want?"

Larson shook his head, "On my count. Three, two, one, go!"

Lei let out an excited high-pitched squeak as she ran down the incline to the rope.

To Larson I said, "The course doesn't look all that impossible. Why does it take so long for your people to get through it?"

"It's the combination of physical exertion that the rope, wall and net put on your body immediately followed by the need to be precise and methodical that keeps recruits from passing right away. Usually they are too tired to aim properly with the AR-15, or not calm enough at the second station to avoid shooting the civilians. Assuming they reach the Sergeant at the third station they don't have any fight left in them and they get pinned pretty quickly."

Lei stumbled on the loose earth underfoot and slid the remaining distance to the rope. She grabbed a hold and pulled herself off the ground and began to climb.

There was no way that Larson could have known about the kind of upbringing Lei and I had as we grew up in the tunnels of the silver mines where my people had hidden for so long. Rock climbing was part of how we got around and our bodies developed differently over the decades as we spent our lives in such a strange manner. Climbing was as second nature to us as walking, so when Lei began to effortlessly climb hand over hand up the rope without using her legs I thought Larson's jaw was going to dislocate as it dropped open.

"Whoa," was all I could hear the man say as I shook my head.

"She's just showing off." I offered.

Lei spun her whole body around and dangled from the rope as she peered back at the two of us as we watched her. Then she gripped the rope with one hand above her head and the other at waist level drawing the short section of rope taut between her hands. She pulled her body in close and, with the T-shirt yielding to the rope, sandwiched it with her ample breasts. I winced and rolled my eyes as Lei stuck out her tongue, crossed her eyes and proceeded to do slight pull-ups with the rope sliding erotically between her breasts.

"Um...?" Larson looked confused, and just a bit uncomfortable, "that's a new one on me."

I groaned and managed to mumble, "Definitely showing off."

I could see Lei smiling at how uncomfortable she had made the two of us and ended her little exhibition by swinging herself up to the platform, without taking the hand extended to her by the Lieutenant until after she had both feet solidly. The man handed her the AR-15 and pointed to the firing range. The Lieutenant watched through binoculars as Lei fired a total of seven rounds before he tapped her lightly on the head.

"Nice," Larson said out loud although probably to himself, "only missed twice."

Lei slid down the pole and scaled the wall with the same expertise she had used to conquer the rope, and then flipped over the top gracefully before dropping down with as much ease as when she ascended. She ran to where the corporal was standing, took the sidearm from him and made her way into the maze that simulated the interior of a building. I couldn't really see what was happening but could hear a series of two shot bursts.

Larson was nodding approvingly until there was a single shot and silence. Larson turned to me and smiled, "Oopsie-daisy."

Lei's unmistakable voice rang out in a loud screech of frustration, "FUUUUUUUUUUCK!"

I started laughing as did Larson.

"Guess we can scratch one civilian," he said.

There were two more two shot bursts and then Lei ambled out the other side of the maze. Her face was distorted with anger and she threw the sidearm down instead of putting it on the small table in front of the horizontal net.

"Uh oh," I said, "she's pissed now." I turned to Larson, "Better let the Sergeant know he should cover up."

Larson was still laughing, "Oh, he's got a lot of padding on. He'll be fine."

My face went serious, "No, really. Tell him to watch out."

Larson looked at my face and frowned as all laughter went out of him, "What's up?"

I looked back and saw that Lei had just finished climbing over the net. She appeared to be slightly out of breath, but still had plenty of energy in her stride as she moved to the Sergeant.

"I cupped my hands one each side of my mouth hoping to amplify my words as I shouted, "Lei! Don't hurt him!"

Larson frowned at me then watched as Lei's footsteps came to a halt a few feet away from the Sergeant and she flipped me the bird.

The Sergeant moved forward and reached out for Lei who immediately grabbed his outstretched wrist while stepping back and pulling the sergeant off balance. Then she spun to one side while keeping his wrist tight against her body and the Sergeant had to stagger/run to keep from falling over. Lei quickly reversed her spin and the Sergeant flipped neatly over and hit the ground. Lei let go of his wrist and sauntered lazily to the door, opened it and walked through.

Larson looked dumbfounded, "That man is one of my best hand-to-hand instructors and she just walked over him like he wasn't even there." He turned to me, "Who the hell is she?"

I wasn't ready to give a full confession as to Lei and my origins. Let's face it, even after seeing just how much we "civilians" could do, it was still going to be a huge leap to take from "capable" to "vampire" even if we weren't the mythological kind from the movies.

On the other hand there was some obvious logic to letting Larson know exactly what our abilities were, so I thought another little demonstration might be in order.

"We've had some special training." I let the statement hang in the air as Larson waited politely for me to elaborate. His silence made me edgy and I volunteered, "Do you really need to know our history or is it more important to understand what we can do?"

Larson shrugged, "Knowing your history might help me understand your skill set."

"True," I held out my hands apologetically, "but we all have our classified information." I had hoped that the words I used were something that he could wrap his mind around and were as non-offensive as possible. It was also then I realized how much I wanted this man's help and didn't want to alienate our partnership before it had begun.

We stood there in silence until it once again became awkward and I asked, "Want me to take a run?"

"Am I going to see something that I haven't so far?"

I nodded, knowing what I had planned, "Yes, and tell all three men to wait for me at the end of the course."

Larson peered at me, "All three?"

"Please."

"They aren't in the pads..."

"I promise they'll be fine."

Larson looked at me for a beat and then pulled his cell phone out of his pocket.

"Lieutenant, would you and the Corporal please join the Sergeant at stage 3. Thank you."

We waited until all three men were standing between the vertical nets at "Stage 3" and raised their arms to indicate that they were ready.

"You remember the signal to stop the test?"

"Raising my arm or calling out quit."

"Okay, on my mark. Three, two, one, go!"

Chapter 14

I ran down the incline and grabbed the rope, without slipping on the dirt as Lei had, and scaled to the top just as easily, minus the erotic teasing. I could feel the familiar strain in my muscles as I climbed and it gave me a sense of nostalgia for home, or at least, what I had always called home. I flipped up and onto the platform rolled to the table where the AR-15 sat and quickly fired five rounds. I didn't even look to see where the shots had struck, I didn't have to, I knew I had hit every target, maybe not all in the center ring, but definitely in center mass. I set the rifle down and looked at the pole that I was supposed to slide down. The ground was about twenty-five to thirty feet down and I looked over to where Larson was standing. Okay, I thought, demonstration time. I blew out a breath and stepped off the edge without taking hold of the pole.

Normally the only way a person could manage to land without serious injury from that height was to hit and roll with the landing and thereby redistributing the forces that would be traumatic to the feet, legs, hips and so on. I landed on my feet, without rolling or crouching, with as much ease as if I had jumped off a dinner chair. I looked back to Larson who was slowly lowering the binoculars from his eyes, but I couldn't see the look of astonishment that I was sure covered his face.

I turned to the wall and saw that it looked to have been built with four by four wood planks. The hand and footholds were screwed in by bolts, but I pushed my fingers into the slight cracks and lifted myself up the wall by my fingertips. It was something that all natural rock climbers work toward, but I'm sure it appeared to Larson as if I were scaling the wall like Spiderman. When I reached the top I quickly glanced toward Larson but he wasn't there. It made me hesitate for a second but I let the confusion go, jumped down from the wall and walked to where the sidearm lay waiting for me to enter the maze. I moved easily enough through it and two bursts into every "bad guy" without shooting any of the civilians in the process.

I moved on to the horizontal net that was hanging like an elevated floor two feet off the ground and extended about twenty feet across. I stepped back about ten paces then turned and ran at the net. Leaping off my left foot I dove forward, extending my body in mid leap as I saw the net pass below me, then I tucked my head and twisted in preparation of the roll. I sailed over the end of the net and landed on my shoulder as planned and rolled with the impact coming to my feet at the completion of the roll.

It was a good thing that I ended up in a standing position too as the corporal didn't wait for me to make my way into the last part of the course and instead charged me as soon as I landed. He went for my legs and I barely avoided the tackle as I twisted to one side. The Lieutenant was on me a second later and I had to grab his arm to keep him from striking my face. Then the corporal dove for my legs again and this time he got a grip around one ankle severely limiting my ability to move.

I could hear the Sergeant's footfalls as he approached as quickly as he could, given the oversized pads he was wearing, and I countered the two men holding me by rolling my body and trapping the Lieutenant's arm as I held it with my hands. I used my legs to trap the corporal's arm in a similar fashion and arched my body back tightening the lock on their joints. Both men shrieked and began tapping my body in submission from the pressure I was putting on their extremities and I released them just in time to receive a right hook across my jaw from the Sergeant that sent me sprawling.

I stood and was surprised to taste blood in my mouth. It was my own, but my body reacted as if it were a drug and I was an addict that screamed out for more. I could feel the adrenaline surge through my body and a warm sensation flooded me as the need twisted my guts around.

I turned to the Sergeant as he came at me again. This time I let him hit me and barely registered the jab as it struck my face. He followed it up with a boxer's combination that sent another right cross to my already throbbing jaw, a left hook to my ribs and right uppercut to my solar plexus. I stood there and took every blow without defending myself and I still barely felt any of the blows. Sensing that his strikes didn't have the desired effect the Sergeant clasped his hands behind my head in a Thai clinch and tried to pull my head down to strike with his knees. I didn't bend and instead smiled at the man behind the protective facemask. Blood had stained my teeth pink, but I don't know if the man realized it because I pushed out of his clinch and threw a punch into the padded helmet he was wearing. The sound of the impact was a muffled "thump" but the force still sent him reeling back a couple steps. I closed the distance and struck again, this time the force of the punch lifted his whole body off the ground.

The Sergeant fell in a heap and drunkenly raised one arm to the sky; unfortunately, in the state I was in it's meaning didn't register with me and I pounced on top of the man's chest hammering two more blows to the face mask before I heard the polymer crack. I was about to hit him again when I felt two sets of hands grab me from behind. It was the Lieutenant and Corporal trying to pull me off their man. I backhanded the Corporal, which sent him careening to the ground, but the Lieutenant I grabbed by the throat with one hand and by the belt with the other. I stood and lifted the one hundred and eighty pound man over my head before throwing him aside like a sack of potatoes.

I reached down and pushed my finger through the reinforced bars of the facemask and ripped the entire headpiece off the Sergeant. The man was unconscious, but I didn't see his face as much as my eyes focused completely on the small pulsation at one side of his neck. I was about to kneel down when someone slammed into my chest and took me to the ground. I wrapped my arms around the new assailant and felt the familiar shape of Lei's back right before she pressed her mouth to mine. Lei's kiss was violent and forced itself upon me as she grabbed the hair at the back of my head and held on. I tried to push her away and get back to the unconscious Sergeant in order to satisfy the bloodlust that was overwhelming me, but as I pushed at her waist she used the created space to toss her legs around and trap my body in a scissor lock.

I tried to move but Lei was in total control now, so I relaxed my body until my mind came back to me. In the end Lei was still sitting on top of me looking sorry as she said, "Sorry lover, but you lost it there for a second."

I looked around and couldn't see the soldiers. "Did I hurt anyone?" I asked sheepishly.

"Nope," Lei responded, "but Larson is a bit upset."

I groaned, "Crap, how upset."

"I convinced him to wait outside, but he put on a bunch of his gear...and he's holding a rifle."

"Oh terrific," I sighed as Lei helped me up from off the ground, "Well, I guess I better start apologizing."

"Mmmm, might be a good idea," Lei laughed, "But I think he has something else in mind."

We walked through the door and were greeted by several soldiers in the same workout clothes that we were wearing. Larson was the only one clad head to toe in combat gear, including a helmet and semi-automatic rifle.

He walked over to me, "You got your head back on straight?"

"Yes and," I started to say more but Larson cut me off as he announced, "we have been graced today with the presence of a new martial arts instructor. I want you all to watch his style and keep your training in mind." He turned back to me, "I hope you won't mind demonstrating your skills to the men. Any chance for them to see different styles in action can only benefit them in the field."

I looked around wondering what kind of "demonstration" was about to happen.

To me Larson said, "Don't hold back. It won't help anyone learn if you do."

I nodded and Larson instantly raised the rifle and pointed it at my head. I dodged to the side and slapped the barrel in the opposite direction before kicking Larson in the abdomen. My foot thumped into whatever body armor he was wearing and Larson let out a chuff of breath before backing off a step.

The men let out a "HOOAH" and clapped.

Larson walked behind me and raised the rifle again. Again I spun, disarmed him and incapacitated his arm in what could have been a bone breaking hold. The men cheered and clapped again. The look on their faces was respectful but I could tell something was up.

Larson repeated this from several different positions and I realized he was letting me take him down each time.

I extended a hand and helped him up after the last counter and asked, "I thought you said not to hold back?"

"Exactly right," Larson looked to his men, "all right. You all see what kind of fighter this man is. Now let's see how well we work against a new system."

He walked back up to me, "This is an Airsoft rifle," he indicated the rifle he was holding, "It shoots small plastic pellets that sting, but don't do any real damage."

The gun looked incredibly realistic, but I did notice that the hole in the barrel was much smaller than I would have otherwise expected.

Larson looked at me, "Let's try that again," and lowered the rifle to his side before raising it back up again, pointing it at my head.

I spun and grabbed at the stock, but Larson twisted with me sending me off balance. He shoved me back with his foot and fired a trio of pellets into my chest.

Sting?!? "Sting" was an understatement! All three pellets were going to leave welts.

Larson lowered the rifle and said, "Again please."

He assumed a shooter's stance and approached me with the rifle at the ready. I scrambled to one side and closed the distance between us, this time trying to trap his arm and rifle, but Larson hit me with a quick shoulder block, kicked my feet out from under me and then stepped back and shot me again.

I yelped as the pellets hit me and I could hear the soldiers around me politely trying to hold back their laughter. I didn't wait this time and jumped to me feet and charged in. Larson fired the Airsoft rifle but I dropped and rolled under the barrage of pellets and grabbed him around the waist taking him to the ground. I felt the butt end of the rifle slam into my back and shoulder but I didn't let go. I worked my way up from Larson's waist until I had one hand on the rifle and another on his throat. I squeezed and listened to him gurgle as I cut off his air supply. The men around us went silent and I could sense a couple of them stepping forward, maybe to break us up. Larson surprised me by letting go of the rifle with one hand and grabbed my hand at his throat and shifted his weight beneath me. Next thing I knew he had one of his legs over my head and across my own throat.

I'm strong, VERY strong, in fact I am much stronger than just about anyone who isn't a power lifter or "strongman" competitor, but even so my single arm is no match for another person's legs and core strength combined. Larson used his legs and core to extend his body and ripped me off his throat. I came crashing down to the ground with one hand still on Larson's rifle and the other clutching wildly at the leg that was still wrapped around my throat. When my eyes focused I could see Larson holding his combat knife, a particularly wicked looking, spring loaded Gerber Special Forces issue blade, at my throat. It was a double-edged blade and would have cut through my flesh as easily as hot butter but he had his gloved hand pressed tightly against my flesh instead of the blade, protecting me from any accidental injury.

Neither of us moved and Larson's eyes burned into me. It took a moment to realize he was waiting for me to do something, and then I remembered that this was a training session and what the appropriate thing for me to do would be. I tapped his leg a couple times, surrendering.

Instantly the blade moved from my neck and the pressure of his leg across my throat disappeared. Larson stood and put his knife away then offered me his hand. I took it and he helped me to my feet.

The men began applauding and Larson stood back and applauded to me as well.

"All right guys," Larson turned to the men, "remember that, our goal isn't to win a competition. It isn't even to play fair. We are here to learn how to survive and complete our objective by any means."

Then he threw me a "bone," which I'm sure was just to repair any fractures that may have occurred to my ego.

"In a fair fight, this man could take any of us, myself included, but you have to remember we aren't here for that. When on mission our job is to achieve our objective, not to be sensitive to the feelings of the enemy and you should expect no less from the enemy. They will do whatever they have to in order to survive and there is no referee to cry foul when they kill you."

Larson waited and made sure his words sank in, "Understood?" Every soldier replied in unison, "HOOOAH."

"Questions?" Larson asked, but the group remained silent, "All right then, dismissed."

When the men had dispersed I walked over to Larson, who

had retrieved his Airsoft rifle from where it was lying on the ground, and held out my hand. He looked at my hand and then up to my eyes, before extending his own hand and shaking mine.

"Thank you for the lesson," I said sincerely.

Larson kept shaking my hand and staring at my face until he finally said, "I don't know what kind of weird world you two are from, or what the hell that spectacle you performed, I assume for my benefit, was supposed to prove; however, I will say that we are going to be entering the field and the people we may have to deal with are not going to be the usual civilians you two are apparently used to."

Lei and I kept silent as Larson continued, "Soldiers are well equipped with the tools of war and we only resort to hand to hand combat when there are no other options. Everything we train for is designed to work along with our tools and you can be sure that the people we come across are not going to put their guns down if you are unarmed."

I politely said, "I'll remember," and left it at that. Larson was venting and now wasn't the time to tell him that Lei and I had taken on elite soldiers before, or to mention that he had taken me on fully geared up, while I was unarmed. I was more interested in building bridges then pointing out inconsistencies...for the moment anyway.

He nodded and sighed, "Okay, I suppose I should also say that in all my years of military service I never even heard, much less witnessed, what the two of you were able to do today. Maybe someday you'll tell me how you managed what you showed me on the course, but for the time being I think it's safe to say you have the ability to take care of yourselves as opposed to my needing to play bodyguard the entire time."

I smiled and Lei thanked him. "Tomorrow then?"

"Tomorrow," I said, after all, sometimes partnerships can come from unexpected places. I was suddenly feeling a lot more optimistic about the entire endeavor than I had been a few hours ago.

Chapter 15

Dr. Whelan walked over the dead body that laid half in and half out of the cell where he had kept his prize. The creature that had been strapped down in that room was the success he had been working so hard to achieve for the last two years and now it was gone.

Suffice it to say, he was not happy.

"How many are dead?" he asked as he entered the large cell and approached the body of the dead guard lying next to the metal gurney that had stored the creature.

"Six," a raspy voice said from the darkness of the cell. "It looked as though he was trying to sneak out but ran into four guards stationed on the other side of one of the security doors."

"So alone, unarmed and naked, it managed to kill four of your best men?"

"They were there to keep intruders out," the voice replied, "they weren't jailers tasked to be on watch to keep people in. They were taken by surprise."

The doctor chuckled, "Frankly, I don't really think it would have mattered if they had known it was coming. My experiment, my monster, is far more capable than any of you." A growl rose in response from the shadows, but, if a growl was supposed to have any intimidating effect on the doctor, he responded to it in a way that was the opposite of its intended effect.

With derision he asked, "Do you have any idea what we have lost here today?!" The doctor spun in the direction the voice had come from, "Do you have half a clue?! No, of course you don't, you simple minded idiot."

The growl quieted.

"That man was the only one to ever have survived the process!" The doctor repeated each word separately for emphasis, "The...Only...One! And it is entirely possible that we won't ever find another candidate that can withstand the physical and mental torture that we put this subject through."

Silence followed as the doctor kicked the body of the dead guard lying at his feet.

A form walked from the shadows of the room and into the aura of light that emanated from the one lamp near the broken computer terminals, "Why is he so important?"

"It!" the doctor emphasized the word with a pause before continuing, "It is of crucial importance to me. It was my instrument of surgical precision that would cut the one festering canker from my life."

The figure stepped completely from the shadows. He was a large man but no giant, perhaps an inch or so over six feet and he sported a hard, lean build under his all black security gear. He cut the kind of figure that many soldiers who were part of elite groups had, including the scars of experience, but despite the confidence of his posture and demeanor, his hands were shaking slightly. It might not have been fear exactly, and perhaps the effect was a result of uncertainty for a man who relished being in command of every given situation. Nearly every part of his body was covered with some body-hugging garment with the exception of his face, which had the complexion of someone born in the Scandinavian regions of the world.

"If he's gone," the man shrugged, "he's gone. Who cares? He won't survive out there in the jungle for lon..."

"You know nothing!" The doctor interrupted and pointed to the dead man on the floor, "Your man's failure may well be the end for all of us."

"Why?"

Dr. Whelan turned to the gurney and placed his hands palm down on the metal platform.

Quietly, the doctor said, "I needed him to kill someone."

"But that's something you pay me and my men a large sum of

money to do. Just tell me who..."

"No," the doctor spun and started to walk from the room, "You may be something of a legend in your circles Mr. Timberland, but this...this beautiful beast that I made is an absolute force of nature."

The doctor stopped at the door, "I take it you have already sent men out to recover my wayward experiment?"

The man called Timberland nodded as he spoke, "Yes, and I take it you want him brought back unharmed?"

The doctor seemed to consider that for a moment, and then he said, "No, although that would be preferable. The important thing now is to simply bring him back in any way possible. Dead or alive."

Chapter 16

We lost an entire day traveling to Bangkok and, by the time we reached our hotel, Lei and I were both in a heavy need for the serum. The pain of our condition can be moderately uncomfortable in the early stages, but combined that with a seemingly endless plane flight and it is relative torture. Still, we managed to keep it together as we made our way to the room. Once we reached the room and the well-tipped bellman went away, we immediately rushed the cooler and took the serum before promptly passing out from both relief and exhaustion on the king bed while still in our travel clothes.

It was the phone that woke me up. For my part I felt like I had just closed my eyes, but a quick glance out the window told me that the sun had set and the clock on the wall indicated I had been out for almost six hours.

Groggily, I lifted the receiver, "Hello?"

"You better?" It was Larson's voice on the other end. "The two of you looked pretty wasted from the flight. You know, the jet lag isn't supposed to set in until after you get to your destination, not during the travel."

I rolled off the bed and looked at the mirror that was part of the vanity on one wall of the room. I looked tired, and had a serious case of "bed head," but there were no tell tale signs that I had waited too long to take the serum.

"Yeah, we're okay. What's up?"

"Nothing really. I just thought we might get started checking out Zach's place."

"Tonight?"

"That a problem?"

"Might not look good if we go sneaking around his neighborhood, breaking and entering in the middle of the night."

Larson laughed, "I don't think that will be an issue." He didn't explain and instead said, "If you and the girl are too out of it I can go on my own. Let you know what I find when I get back."

I sighed, "No, we'll come along. Like you said, we're the detectives."

"True enough. See you in the lobby in...?"

I looked to the bathroom, the shower was running and steam was wafting up from under the door.

"Call it twenty minutes."

"In twenty then."

I heard Larson hang up and I did the same as the sound of the shower ceased. I walked to the bathroom door and pushed it open as the cloud of steam that the hot water had generated mixed with the refrigerated air of the room. Lei was standing there toweling herself off in front of the mirror and, as was usual when I saw her like this, my breath caught in my throat.

Lei looked into the mirror and saw me standing there watching her. She smiled a genuine, pleased smile that changed to something more wicked as my eyes tracked down the length of her naked back. My eyes weren't strangers to the curves of her body, but that didn't mean I couldn’t get momentarily dumbstruck by the sight of her.

She turned to face me, the hotel towel strategically placed so that her breasts and center pelvis were covered without hiding a single inch of flesh otherwise.

I needed to say something to keep my head from spinning. "Save any hot water for me?"

Lei didn't speak, she simply nodded once and then lowered the towel bringing her breasts fully into view, and she playfully made an erotic spectacle of herself by drying her inner thighs with the end of the towel.

My body was reacting..., which, of course, had been her intent, still I pretended to ignore my own response, and removed my shirt as I began to undress. Her eyes roved over my chest, widening slightly in silent approval.

I turned the water back on and, in the moment I had taken my eyes off of Lei, she moved from her perch against the sink to directly behind me. I could feel her arms wrap around me and the strength of her hands as they slid over my stomach and chest. She raked her fingernails lightly across my skin and it sent electric impulses from my core to the tips of my fingers and toes.

Her body felt warm and her skin was deliciously soft as she pressed herself against me. I closed my eyes and let my other senses take over as I felt her hands work their way down to my waist and then to the button on my jeans.

"Lei," I said quietly, "we're supposed to be in the lobby in less than twenty minutes." The zipper on the jeans yielded without complaint as Lei manipulated it. I felt her lips press against the back of my neck as one arm came back up to my chest and pulled me back against her while the other hand disappeared under the fabric of my pants. She adjusted me gently until I came free of the now highly restrictive garments and let them fall to the floor, stopping around my ankles. Lei pressed every inch of herself against the back of my body and softly began to rock up and down so I could feel how smooth her skin was as it slid over mine. The water had become hot again and steam once again began to fill the bathroom.

"Lei, we need to meet..." She cut me off.

"We're going to be a little late," she whispered as her hands continued to send irresistible impulses through every part of me.

Something like panic filled me and I started to protest, but as my body tensed Lei pushed me forward into the stream of the shower. I spun to face her and found her mouth on mine, her arms around my neck and her body against me.

"We'll only be a little late," Lei spoke softly into my mouth as my mouth searched for her lips, desperate to reconnect.

I pulled her tighter to me, my strength overtaking her own and she let out a small gasp at the effort. In that moment I said, "No fair using your superpowers against me."

She looked up at me sheepishly as I felt her shift her pelvis in line with my own. The look she wore was such a chaotic mixture of emotions. Innocence, lust, and need were all evident, but I knew there was more, much more beneath the surface and I stared into her eyes as she returned the stare. I cupped one hand underneath her knee and raised her thigh up to my waist as her breath started coming in short heaving bursts. When I lifted her body and pulled her to me the whole world went white-hot and every fiber of my being melded with the woman I loved as everything else around me disappeared.

For her part, Lei closed her eyes and let out a deep moan while wrapping her raised leg tightly around my body holding us together and not allowing for any separation or movement. I closed my eyes and reached out with my other senses to feel her muscles twitching as they spasmed and relaxed in syncopated reaction to my own movements and their accommodation of me. A moment went by that seemed to last and last as we stood there, pressed hard against one another without making any attempts to move or disconnect.

Finally Lei raised her head an opened her eyes.

"I love you," she said and her whole body quivered in some kind of release that was anything but sexual.

I understood. I knew what Lei had been through before Alpha found her. She wasn't born into our community, she was one of the afflicted that Alpha managed to locate in time to prevent the condition from ravaging her. Unfortunately, he hadn't been in time to keep the world around Lei from nearly destroying her. From the time she was a little girl, she had been taught that sex was something that was more a means to an end. Adults around her had used and abused her with such severity that she knew nothing of what intimacy or love truly could be like on any other level. In the end, Lei had survived her childhood physically, but there would always be a part of her that would regard sex as something very base, impersonal and very, very, separate from whatever love might be.

She was better now. A few decades would mend a lot of wounds, but every now and again there was a part of her that came to the surface when she let herself go. That was why the seduction had taken the dramatic turn it had.

I kissed her gently, "And I love you. I always have. I always will."

She looked at me and there was sadness in her eyes, "I lost you for a time."

I nodded. Over a decade ago I had run from my people and all that I had known because of a misunderstanding. I had been a fool, but I was back now and nothing on heaven or earth existed that could drag me from her now.

"Never again. Can't happen."

"Why not?" her voice broke a little as she asked.

"Because everything I am belongs to you. My heart, my mind, my soul and anything and everything else there may be is irrevocably tied to you. There is no longer a me without you."

She breathed out heavily and then she began to gyrate her hips as her hands grabbed the hair on the back of my head. Her eyes shifted from the vulnerable and open expression to one that was more excited and feral.

"You are mine," she hissed possessively and barred her teeth at me as she began moving faster, "every part of you, every fiber of you, mine!"

The intensity of what she was doing threatened to overwhelm me, but I knew what she wanted, what she needed and I turned my head away and exposed my neck to her as I calmly said, "Yes."

Lei's mouth opened and she surged forward and bit down on my flesh hard. My whole body jumped reflexively and I tried to twist away from the pain, but Lei only pulled harder at my head and kept me from breaking free as her body moved even faster, literally slamming herself against me as I continued to hold the majority of her weight aloft. My neck was on fire with the intense pleasure and pain as Lei savaged my flesh, snarling and growling as she went, and it was all I could do to hold on and keep us from falling.

Like the woman had said. We would be a little late.

Chapter 17

Larson was looking at his watch as we came walking around the corner from the elevators. He looked a little miffed at being kept waiting, but when he saw the look on Lei's face he rolled his eyes and shook his head.

"Feeling better are we?" Larson said sarcastically.

"Much better thank you." Lei responded cordially but simultaneously cast Larson a look that was meant to tell him to back off.

I don't know if turning his back and walking toward the street was backing off or not, but it seemed to satisfy Lei and we followed as he hailed a cab.

As we climbed into the cab I asked, "So where's your buddy's apartment?"

"Actually it's a rented house, and one that is being paid for by the American government under a false identity."

"It is? Ah, so that's why you don't think it will be an issue to enter the location, you have a key or the security codes or something like that, right?"

Larson was quiet as he seemed lost in his own thoughts before he said, "Something like that. The truth is another member of the special ops team in that picture you saw on the wall of my office was called in to replace Zach. Pick up the pieces as it were and continue whatever mission he was on. He would just move into the apartment and take over the job."

"Just like that?" Lei asked, "And no trying to find your friend?"

"Washington is convinced that Zach was KIA, killed in action, so there's nothing to search for." Larson saw the look on Lei's face and added, "I know it might sound cold but the evidence was pretty convincing. Hell, I was convinced of it as well, until you two showed up with your pictures."

"If Zach was taken by... um... "the enemy", then wouldn't they know where he lived? Your new operative is practically already busted."

Larson chuckled, "You don't know Patrick. No one would ever suspect him of being some kind of operative."

The drive took over twenty minutes as the cab driver wound his way in and around traffic in such a way that no New York cabbie would ever dream of trying. When we finally arrived Lei and I looked out of the cab's window in surprise. The entire area looked as though the houses were built as separate boxes and loosely stacked on top of one another. The ground around the domiciles was unpaved, and the place looked as though it could fall apart if a strong enough wind blew through.

I grunted, "You'd think the American government could afford to house their people somewhere outside of the local ghetto."

Larson cast me a glance, but said nothing as he walked onto the property grounds and checking each building for a number or name.

Lei elbowed me in the ribs, "This isn't a ghetto."

"What?"

"It's actually a pretty decent neighborhood and the apartments around here are for people who we would consider to be the "middle class" in America."

I looked around and shook my head, "It looks like a dump and it might fall apart at any moment."

Lei nodded, "That's the Western view, but the people who live here see it very differently."

I shook my head in confusion and then I saw the look on Lei's face. She appeared haunted and I kept my mouth shut in case it was my vocal observations that were setting her off.

We caught up with Larson, whom apparently found the specific building he was looking for, and waited behind him as he knocked on the door.

"You okay?" I whispered to Lei.

"Yes," she replied, "Just too many memories all at once."

Oh crap, I had forgotten that Lei had..."spent some time"....in Bangkok before Alpha had found her. It explained a lot about the whole shower spectacle that had gone down before we left the hotel. I felt her fingers locate my hand and then tighten on it as if she needed me to help her keep her balance.

A voice called out from behind the door in Thai, but Larson answered in English, "Rogers, open up. It's me."

"Major?" the astounded voice asked in English.

"Affirmative. Open the door Captain."

"Dude, you alone?"

Larson looked back at me and Lei, "Nope, but all is well."

The sound of the locks unlatching could be heard before the heavy wood door swung open and we were greeted by the business end of a revolver from one side of the door jam.

Larson immediately dropped while Lei and I both darted to the side, but no shots were fired. A portion of a face appeared around the door jam and looked down at Larson.

"Whoa! Sir, it is you!" and then the rest of the face popped around the corner including a head full of dreadlocks, circular spectacles and a gaudy tropical shirt.

Larson was clearly not amused, "Yes, it's me and I GAVE the all clear signal!"

Rogers lowered the gun, "Aw dude, cool the jets, what you gave me was an old signal, although I suppose it's still legit. Now, pardon the negative karma vibe, but what the hell are you doing here?"

Lei and I got back to our feet and ambled our way over to the door as Rogers eyed us suspiciously.

"Can we talk inside?" Larson came as close to pleading as I believe I would ever hear and Rogers inclined his head at me and Lei.

"Dude, you vouch for civis?" Rogers asked.

"Yes."

"Personally or professionally?"

"I can only go with personally here. This ain't anything like an official visit."

"Gnarly, I figured that, but was hoping that I was wrong. All right into the abode, all of you dudes."

Rogers stepped aside and the three of us walked into the studio apartment. It was basically one great big room with a couple of small electrical appliances against a wall in the back alongside the only other door, which I guessed was the bathroom. In the center of the room was a large, open footlocker that contained a pile of clothes in various states of disarray and a smaller footlocker that was closed with an unclipped padlock still swinging from the hasp.

Rogers walked to the smaller footlocker in his bare feet. He was wearing white cut off shorts and the entire area smelled like pot. The guy was obviously playing the part of an expatriated American hippie, or of a surfer with an endless summer attitude. Actually, I just assumed it was an act although it might not have been, but whatever the case I understood why the guy wouldn't be seen as a replacement agent and moving back into the old apartment was the same as hiding in plain sight. Rogers removed the padlock, then put the revolver inside, quickly closed the lid, relocking the padlock.

"How long have you been here Pat?"

"Just under three moons," Rogers looked around the room, "Guess I've never been much for setting down any roots and letting the grass grow beneath my toes."

"Not that they'd let you."

That brought a smile to Rogers face and he dropped the accent completely," True enough." He held out his hand to Larson, "Good to see you again Major, whatever the reason."

"Thanks Pat, but let's cut the titles. This is strictly a civilian op."

"Speaking of the civilians..." Rogers turned to me and was about to introduce himself when he took in the full sight of Lei. Initially his reaction was the usual momentary hesitation that most men suffered, but he just as quickly became uncomfortable.

"Major, I can't have any local talent on location."

Bangkok was infamous for the various pleasure houses or discos that graced several of its "Walking Streets" and, clearly, Rogers thought Lei one of the local prostitutes. It was an honest mistake, but Lei was about to pull out the big guns on the poor slob when Larson spoke up, "She's not local or in the business. This is Steve and Lei Jacobs, private investigators out of Las Vegas. They're helping me find Zach."

Rogers turned back to Larson, "Zach?! That's why you're here?"

"I'm going to find him Pat."

Rogers shook his head, "Nah, we spoke on this. Even if you were on a sanctioned search op, I'm not sure there's anything left to find at this point."

Larson nodded, "Maybe so, but I promised all of you that I'd never let any of you get left behind. Way I see it that promise doesn't become null and void just because I didn't go in country with you."

Rogers looked at Larson dubiously, "So you'd do it for any of the team? Not just Zach?"

Larson smiled, "Mostly."

Rogers laughed, "Right then. So what do you need from me?"

"We need to see any of Zach's belongings that he might have left here before he disappeared. Also we're probably going to need a translator at some point."

"Well, the brass cleared most everything out of this place before I got here. There were a few things but it was mostly clothes and some small photos."

"Do you still have the photos?" I asked.

"In the desk. Middle drawer, right side." Rogers indicated the desk by pointing to a pair of short file cabinets topped with what looked to be an unfinished door. I walked over and sat in the wicker chair that barely held my weight and opened the drawer. I could see the pictures resting on the bottom of the drawer but had to lift the large glass jar of marijuana out in order to be able to get at them. Well, at least that explained the smell.

Rogers saw me handling his stash and jumped forward, "Whoa! Be subtle, man."

Larson shook his head, "You asshole Rogers."

"What? It helps me fit into the character."

"You've been living your cover too long for it not to be genuine at this point."

Rogers looked indignant for a moment and then said, "It's medicinal."

I lifted the pictures out and saw that they were the small two-inch by two-inch photos from one of those old photo booths that kids used at carnivals, or in the mall. There were usually four snapshots in a vertical row, but in this case there were only two. An uneven border at the top of the photos told me that the other pictures were cut away. Interestingly the subject was a girl, maybe eight or nine years old, and of Asian, probably Thai, descent. She was a beautiful little girl and wearing a 'Hello Kitty' T-shirt, with her hair tied back in a pony tail, but her expression was very serious, maybe even confused in the first picture. Her eyes were distant and she seemed to almost stare out at me from the picture; however, in the second her face was frozen in a riotous fit of laughter. There was another person's arm and hand in her stomach area and, from her expression, was tickling her ferociously. The contrast between the two shots couldn't be more distant, but both were so perfectly expressive that I could almost hear her laughter.

"Who is she?" I asked as I held up the picture.

Rogers walked over, "That's the million dollar question. I haven't had any luck trying to I.D. her and Washington gave up on the search for any answers once Zach's body was delivered." Rogers paused and screwed up his face, "that's right, a body was delivered and I even heard that you confirmed the identity." Rogers glanced at all three of us, his face showing a sudden onset of concern and confusion, "So what am I missing here?"

Larson walked over to where I was sitting in front of the computer, "Two days ago these guys gave me a picture of a man I believe to be Zach. The picture is supposed to have been taken somewhere between a week and two weeks ago."

"Would you let me see it?" Rogers asked as Lei walked up beside him and handed him the eight by ten photo. Almost instantly his eyes widened, "Whoa! Yep, that's totally Zach. He's looking quite the mess though. What's wrong with him?"

"He's looking quite a bit better than dead, Pat."

Rogers nodded, "True."

Lei asked, "Do you recognize the background?"

Rogers scrutinized the picture for a moment, "All I can see are a bunch of jungle plants that could be from around here. There's no way to absorb anything further as far as I can see."

I put the small photos back on the desk and pushed the file drawer closed when I noticed that the drawer felt sluggish on the rollers. I opened and closed it a couple of times and, even though it seemed to be working properly, it just didn't feel right.

"Excuse me Mr.?" I started to ask.

"No "misters" here, call me Pat."

"Okay Pat, so the few appliances and things, are they yours?"

"I suppose they are now."

"But you didn't bring them in with you?"

"No they were here when Zach lived here, but like I said the brass searched through them pretty thoroughly."

Lei knew something was up and hurried over to the desk as

Larson looked over my shoulder. "What's up?" Larson asked.

"Maybe nothing, but I have a hunch."

I pulled the drawer all the way out and then worked it off its rollers, separating it from the rest of the filing cabinet. I carefully set the contents on the desk, and then turned the drawer down and set it on the desk, too. The bottom of the drawer was the same metallic material that the rest of the cabinet was made of, but felt decidedly thicker when I rested my hand on it. My efforts must have been intriguing as I noticed Lei, Larson and Rogers all watching the drawer intensely as I fiddled with it. Then, as I tried to slide the metal in it's grooves something clicked and the bottom lifted away easily.

It was a false bottom.

Underneath was a manila folder that had been sandwiched between the false and real bottom of the drawer. I lifted the folder up and looked at the surprised eyes of the three people standing around me.

Lei was smiling. Larson chuckled as Rogers shook his head and said, "How could the boys have missed that?"

I shrugged my shoulders and flipped the folder open. Rogers reached over and closed the folder before trying to take it from my grasp. The second his hand struck the folder I pulled back and kept him from taking it while Lei pushed him forward and pinned his body to the desk.

"Whoa! Stop! There might be classified information in there!"

I frowned, "Maybe there is, but its not as though you would have found it without me."

"That doesn't matter in the least." He turned his head to Larson, "Tell them Major, you know the protocols."

"I do," Larson replied, "and I'm sure that if you had explained that little fact to my friends previously it wouldn't be an issue now."

Larson looked up to me expectantly. Crap, Larson wasn't

really asking as much as being polite. Still, I hesitated. We were going to need a translator and maybe even a guide while we were here. Rogers was probably the best choice for that, and I really didn't know if there would be anything in the folder worth burning that potential alliance. I sighed and was about to hand the folder over to Rogers when Larson held out his hand.

Rogers was still pinned to the table as Lei held one hand twisted behind his back, but his eyes widened when he saw Larson's outstretched hand.

"Major?"

"I might not be a field agent, but my security clearance is still active and, if I remember correctly, I have a higher clearance level than you, Captain. That means the appropriate person to see the information inside and make the judgment call on its level of security would be me."

"But you aren't here in an official capacity, that means..."

"Relax Pat, no one's going to know that you didn't clear it first. I'll keep the top secret stuff safe."

Rogers clearly didn't like it, but his body relaxed, "Could someone tell the waihine to let me up?"

Lei dropped down so her body pressed against the back of his, "Why Mr. Rogers, most men would pay a great deal of money to be in your position."

Pat started to resist but hesitated, "Uh."

Lei kissed his neck and I had sudden panic that she was going to feed on him. Lei has never been one who had a tremendous amount of self-control once she gets lost in the moment. My worries were quickly assuaged as she slowly lifted herself off of Rogers and gently righted the position of his arm. Rogers lay there for a second or two as if suddenly awakening from a daydream and not being too sure what was happening.

Superpowers. Definitely superpowers.

Larson was already finished perusing the first few pages by

the time Rogers walked over, "These are all written in...what is that Pat...Thai?"

"Yep, its a legal document that...uh oh."

"Uh oh?" Lei asked.

"Yeah, I think I've seen this sort of thing before. Is there another document under this one that is in English, or maybe German?"

Larson looked up confused and then back down to the folder, quickly flipping pages until he found what Rogers had described.

"Got it, and there's a picture of the little girl stapled to the top corner."

Rogers face dropped, "Oh boy."

"What's going on?" I asked.

Larson responded, "I'm no lawyer, but this looks like a legal document that would make Zach the legal guardian of the girl."

"That's exactly what it is," Rogers said disapprovingly.

Larson scanned the rest of the folder, "That's all that's in here." He looked up to Rogers, "What's this all about Pat?"

Rogers sighed, "It's not good. You might not be too open to hearing it."

"If it sheds some light or gives us a lead, then..."

Larson put the folder down on the table and Lei walked over and put her hand on it, "May I?"

Rogers looked to Larson who said, "I don't see anything else in there Pat. I can't read the Thai, but..."

"No, no. It's all right. The folder isn't a matter for national security," he paused, "but discretion may be warranted."

"Discretion? Why?"

Rogers tried to start speaking a couple of times but the words didn't seem to want to come out. When he finally did speak he said, "I think...I think that Zach may have...um...bought the girl as a...you know...a sex slave."

Chapter 18

Larson and I just stood there dumbfounded, but Lei, who had more than a little personal experience in such matters, started looked like she might kill Rogers for having said those words.

"What! What the fuck did you just say? You goddamn, hippie stoner, motherfucker!"

Lei's tirade immediately brought me out of stunned immobility and I tried to calm her. She shot me down before I could take my first step in her direction.

"No! No Steven! No way! I don't even want to hear it! There's absolutely nothing you can say that is going to make me go along with this!"

I held my hands up in supplication, "We need to find him, but..."

"No we DON'T need to find him!" Lei insisted.

"Lei.."

"NO!!!" Lei turned on her heels and walked briskly from the room, shutting the door loudly behind her as she past the threshold.

Larson looked at me, "Do you need to go after her?"

I looked at the closed door and sighed, "That might be a dangerous thing to do at the moment, even for me. I think I'll give her a minute to cool her head."

Rogers gave me an apologetic look, "Um, sorry?"

I shook my head, "She'll be okay," I turned back to Rogers, "Let's get back on subject. Rogers, it's pretty big leap to go from this guy Zach having an application for guardianship of the girl to becoming a slaver and pedophile."

Larson cut in, "Not to mention that this is Zach we're talking about here."

Rogers nodded, " I know, it's pretty damn unbelievable to me as well, but before I was reassigned here I had been working on an anti-smuggling task force in the Middle East and sometimes the goods that were smuggled were people. This kind of thing is more common than you might think, and these guys manage their businesses by exploiting legal loopholes. One of these loopholes is becoming the legal guardian of an underage boy or girl, but not going so far as to adopting them."

"Explain," Larson said sharply.

Rogers sighed, "Try to remember where you are. This isn't the United States. This is Thailand. Sex is a commodity here, and it really isn't unheard of for a family to sell a daughter into service with a brothel. They tend to hang on to the boys as they grow strong and can work the fields, but the girls are often viewed as just another mouth to feed that can't pull their weight."

"So they just sell their children off as prostitutes?"

Rogers shrugged, "It's something that is perceived differently here. Here it isn't viewed as much more than a dowry would have been in Europe from the bride's family to the groom's, only here it's sort of in reverse."

"You think that's what happened here?" Larson asked.

"Yes, but if it is, then it's only part of the story."

"How so?"

"Okay follow this logic. The girl is sold by her family to a brothel, the idea here being that once she reaches a certain age she will have worked off her debt to the brothel and would be free to follow whatever path she wanted. You follow?"

"So far," I responded.

"Okay, so she's being prepped for her first job, or maybe she's been working a while, whatever, and enter some wealthy foreigner who has a taste for young girls and has an eye on this one in particular. Money isn't a problem and the "madam" or "house mom" would know what remained on her debt. She would calculate what her potential profit earning would be if she remained the entire length of her...ah...apprenticeship and the amount is negotiated until a deal is struck and the foreigner now ‘owns’ the girl. The thing is, the foreigner has a problem. How does he take his property home? If the girl is underage, then becoming her "legal guardian" gives her the ability to travel with him and even potential citizenship in his home country. It's kind of like marrying a woman to get her a "green card" back home in America, only this way none of his assets can be inherited by the girl if something were to happen to him. Legally, everything is above board, unless he does something stupid and gets caught with his hand, or other body parts, in the proverbial cookie jar."

"There's a flaw in that line of thinking," I volunteered.

Larson and Rogers turned to me, "What happens when the girl becomes of legal age? The whole guardian thing gets thrown out the window and any benefits the legal arrangement allowed, like the ability to remain in the country, disappear."

Rogers nodded, "Exactly."

"So what happens to these girls?" Larson asked.

"The lucky ones get abandoned in whatever country they were taken to and become functioning illegals unless INS. catches them. Most immigration offices know about the arrangements, but can't do anything about it so they simply give the girls a one-way ticket back to Thailand. More often than not, the madam that sold them to the foreigner will be waiting at the airport with an offer to work her club again, although this time as a regular working girl with less than half the earning potential as the other girls. Most take the offer, as they have nowhere else to go."

"And the unlucky ones?" I asked.

Rogers sighed, "It's never a pretty story. Some are abused, either physically beaten or hooked on drugs to keep them in line while they continue their lives as sex slaves. Others are sold to the local skin merchants or, even worse, to the organ grinders."

I winced, but Larson looked confused.

"What's that?" he asked.

Rogers shrugged, "An organ grinder? They are an especially

nasty group of people who are in the business of buying and selling other people with the intention of harvesting their internal organs for black market sale."

For the first time Larson looked like he might be ill. He looked down to the picture of the child and seemed momentarily mesmerized by her face. When he seemed to have regained his composure, Larson asked, "How can you think, even for a millisecond, that Zach might be part of this?"

"I didn't say he was. I said that I thought Zach was trying to buy the girl."

"The implication seems obvious," I said and honestly, I was having my own difficulty keeping the bile in my throat from coming all the way up, so my words came out a little checked, "but is there another possibility we might be missing?"

Rogers looked back to the papers and read for a bit before flipping the page. He scanned the next two pages and his eyes widened when he found whatever he was looking for.

Then his eyes dropped and his face seemed to droop.

"It says right here that Zach bought the girl from Chonpak Boonliang for fifteen thousand dollars, American. She was released from her obligations to the Pink Pussy Nightclub." Rogers made a chuffing sound, "Gotta love the names they gives these places. The whole transaction was overseen by the local constabulary with none other than General Praphasirirat signing as witness."

Rogers looked up from the papers, "I'm sorry, but there's no doubt in my mind, he bought her."

"This makes no sense," Larson was still wrapping his head around the scenario.

I had to go check on Lei. The story that had just been relayed to us was very similar to Lei's own personal history and I knew it was going to hit her hard. I opened the door and was surprised to find her sitting just outside on the doorstep.

She was crying. She had heard every word.

"He's right, you know." Lei spoke with the sobs still present in her voice, "I know we have to find this guy Zach in order to track down Whelan," she wiped the tears from her eyes and stood, "so we find him, get the information we need and then I am going to look the sonovabitch in the eyes as I cut his throat."

I was about to agree with Lei when I noticed a white Land Rover parked on the road less than a quarter mile back from where we stood. Nothing overly unusual about seeing a parked vehicle, even one with the kind of price tag that a Range Rover commanded. The general population that lived in this neighborhood couldn't afford such a vehicle; still, there were enough well to do people in Thailand so the odd one or two would pop up on any given occasion. What troubled me was the fact that this one had one of those sparkly white pearlescent paint jobs that glittered in the light...or at least would have if the majority of the vehicle weren't caked in mud. The only off road driving that the people who purchased that color paint job, would be to drive up onto the sidewalk in order to squeeze around another car.

Lei saw my hesitation, but she thought it was in response to what she had said, "Do not try to talk me out of..."

"Lei," the sound of my words made Lei realize something else was up.

"What is it?"

"I think we have company."

Chapter 19

He didn't know how long he had been moving through the jungle, but he hadn't stopped since he had left the compound. When he came to the river instinct told him to follow it as it flowed and something deep inside him knew that whatever he needed could be found at the river's end. Of course he didn't know what that would be exactly, but felt, more than he knew, there would be answers at the end of his journey.

He had been traveling along the riverbank with all its twists, turns and waterfalls for nearly four hours and his feet were beginning to blister from the dampness of the earth beneath them when the smell of cooking meat filled his nostrils. His stomach growled at the allure of the aroma, but instinct told him to stick to the riverbank. Compromise was achieved when he realized that the direction from which the smell had originated was coming from downstream.

He followed the comforting smell of burning wood and the nearly euphoric perfume of roasting meat for another hour until the breeze shifted and directed his nose away from the riverbank. It was close. Maybe only a couple hundred yards away and his empty stomach negotiated with his reluctant brain to seek out the sustenance.

Hunger won and he made his way through the foliage until the area opened up into a man made clearing and a large collection of huts sitting in a seemingly haphazard pattern throughout the area. The smell was coming from a particularly large fire in the center of the village where two boars were roasting on spits as four women patiently tended to basting the rotating beasts. As the meat turned slowly over the fire the crisping flesh dripped fat from small incisions that caused the viscous liquid to collect, and running over the outside of the boar's skin where it eventually fell away into the fire with a crackle and pop.

Men were arriving with large palm fronds to serve as platters for collecting the roasted meat, and set them next to the women who served as the fire pit masters. Friendly words were exchanged that left the group laughing as they worked and a child ran out of one of the huts to see what the commotion was about.

It was a small girl, maybe five years old and she slammed into one of the men who had delivered the fronds. The man playfully pretended to rebound from the impact and teetered from one side to another before pratt-falling, in a display so over acted it sent the child and women into laughter again.

He could feel something twist inside himself at the sight and the pain was almost more than he could bear. He grabbed at his guts and tried to hold in the pain, but it still shot through him until he was unable to stand or even breathe.

He tried to be quiet but the pain made small sobs pass his lips anyway. He hoped the people wouldn't hear him or, if they did, then they would simply think it was a sound on the wind.

Maybe it was the sound of his muffled groans, or it just could have been the fact that the food was ready, that had brought the old woman out of her hut. She was old, very old, but she still carried herself with an ancient grace and power that belied her years. She had been walking toward the fire pit with a wide smile beaming at the innocent commotion when she stopped in her tracks, her face suddenly growing concerned as she turned to face the tree line where he was hiding.

The sight of the old woman caused the pain inside his core to subside and he pushed himself out of the fetal position he had been laying in to kneel behind enough natural cover to hide himself fully. The old woman tilted her head and closed her eyes as she seemed to "sniff" the air, then her eyes shot open and she glared right at him as easily as if he were sitting in an open field. She said something in the same tongue that the others had been speaking and all of their heads spun to look in his direction, multiple eyes were now searching the tree line.

Then everything was in motion, the men hurried to recover weapons and the women scurried into the various huts and sent out more men wielding gardening implements as armaments. Hoes, sickles and machetes were all brandished as the men gathered in a group then headed toward the tree line.

Suddenly his mind was filled with a jumble of thoughts, all of which came upon him so quickly that he couldn't make sense of any single one. All he could do was follow his instincts and, for some reason, his instincts told him not to run. Instead he stood up and revealed himself to the approaching mob of villagers.

Calmly he walked from the tree line and into the clearing. The villagers started shouting and beaconing at him with their weapons, but he kept walking. When the men could see his face they grew quiet. They weren't stupid, and each man could tell something was "off" about the giant that approached them. It was when they saw his eyes that a raw, primitive fear crept into each of them at a different level, but despite the wide-eyed stares and shaking hands, none of them backed down.

He stopped walking about ten yards from the group, opened his palms to the men and closed his eyes. He tried to remain as still as possible as he stood there and waited. He thought about what the edge of a machete might feel like as it slammed into him and sliced through his flesh and bone. He could imagine the pain, but he didn't care.

His brain wasn't capable enough to realize that he wanted to die, or that he wanted, needed his death to come at the hands of these people. All he understood about the moment was that he needed to behave the exact way that he was. So he waited, eyes closed and anticipating the bite of whatever edged weapon was going to take his remaining life.

There was no sound, but something touched his face and it wasn't the edge of a machete or some other implement, but instead the smooth, soft touch of fingertips on his cheek.

"Open your eyes," a quiet voice spoke to him in heavily accented English that he couldn't decipher, but somehow the meaning behind the words sunk in and he opened his eyes. Tears ran out like water from a dam that had just burst and he found himself staring into the concerned face of the old woman while the men looked on in confusion.

His legs gave out from underneath him and he fell to his knees as the old woman cupped his face with her hands.

"I know you," she said as she fearlessly looked into his eyes. She inclined her head to the men behind her and shouted something that made all of their eyes wide with surprise. They began dropping their weapons and hurried over to his side to support him.

He didn't understand what was happening...he had expected to die, cut to pieces by the people who's home he had invaded, but instead the rough hands of the men were gently carrying him toward the hut from which the old woman had emerged, and his vision blurred as his eyelids became too heavy to stay open.

Chapter 20

Lei and I walked back into the apartment and found Larson still arguing with Rogers, presumably about whether or not his theory concerning Zach was true or not. They went silent as we approached and looked at us with questioning eyes.

"We have visitors," I said with enough inflection to convey the message that our guests were most likely unfriendly.

"Where?" Rogers asked as he moved to the footlocker and unlocked the padlock.

"Pearl white, mud encrusted Range Rover less than a quarter mile down the road from here."

"Passengers?" Larson asked.

"None in the vehicle, so either they have business elsewhere or..."

"Or they're doing a recon on the property and looking for the best way to take us as we come out." Larson finished my sentence for me.

"Or the best way to get in," Lei said as she moved to one side of a window and peered out.

Rogers reacted to her, "You might want to keep away from the windows."

Lei turned to look at Rogers and a small piece of the window burst inward as a bullet whizzed past her, just nicking the flesh of her cheek and was immediately followed by the rest of the window glass, which shattered inward and rained all over her head.

Lei cursed, spinning away from the jagged shards in a vain attempt to protect her face. She fell to the floor, as the rest of us dove in all different directions. Larson rolled twice and then crawled to a different window, but stayed behind the cover of the concrete walls. Rogers had dropped behind his footlocker, swinging the top back and was reaching inside. He pulled out a futuristic looking machine gun and lobbed it over to Larson.

Larson caught the gun, flipped it around and chambered the first round to make the weapon ready to fire in one fluid motion.

I dove toward Lei, but before I stopped sliding I could tell she was all right. She had a multitude of small cuts from the glass shards on her face and neck while her cheek oozed blood from the bullet that had grazed her face. Still, she rolled as she fell and came up in a crouch with the most intense look of sheer ferocity that any human being could wear.

My fear for her well being turned into relief as I saw that she was not severely wounded, and noticed the two 9mm Browning semi-automatic handguns that Rogers had slid across the floor, which had come to a stop by her feet. Lei looked up to see Rogers digging into his footlocker again and produce an enormous .50 caliber Desert Eagle automatic handgun with a customized ammunition clip that extended four inches past the base of the grip. He slid the hand cannon across the floor to me.

Lei and I looked down to the guns, then to each other...and smiled ridiculously as we picked up our new arsenal and worked the slides in order to make the pistols ready to fire.

Rogers pulled his own AK47 out of the footlocker with an interesting looking scope perched on top indicating that the weapon had been customized for short-range sniper work.

He was about to take up his own position when the whole world seemed to explode. Outside multiple gunmen opened fire with weapons on full automatic. High velocity rounds blew through the walls like they were made of paper sending the deadly projectiles into the apartment and on through the opposite walls. Concrete dust billowed and swirled as more bullets tumbled through the residue clouds left from the previous volley of shots and impact driven shrapnel exploded in every direction.

The four of us hugged the floor as the various projectiles flew at supersonic speeds over us as the sound of the gunfire and explosions from the impact of their arsenal deafened us.

Desperately we shifted our bodies to cover the windows and doors from our prone positions hoping that the gunmen didn't have the manpower for this barrage to simply be cover fire for an entry team that would be bursting in at any moment.

Then the gunfire stopped. I couldn't actually hear that it had ceased because, at that moment all I could hear was a high pitched whining as my ears fought to recover from the voluminous thundering. However I could see that no new plumes of concrete dust were bursting from the walls, and nothing more was being shot to pieces within the room.

Larson was already in action and flashing hand signals as he strained his head in order to peer out the window. I looked back and saw Rogers already perched on an exposed stairwell and sighting through the same window as Larson with his riflescope.

My God, I thought. When had he moved? Not to mention how had he moved without being perforated into a human Swiss cheese?

Larson sat and flashed three signals to Rogers who never looked up from his riflescope. Good snipers and sharpshooters keep both eyes open when they shoot their weapons as they are expert in absorbing different information simultaneously through each eye. In other words, Rogers was watching Larson's signals at the same time as he was concentrating on whatever he saw through his scope. It's a neat trick, that isn't really a trick. It is a learned skill that can take years to master, and apparently Rogers had mastered it.

He shifted his rifle slightly to the right and immediately fired three rounds. My hearing had returned enough to hear someone scream in shock and pain from outside the walls of the apartment. Larson rose to one knee and fired out the window. More screams could be heard as he ducked back down, but this time the sounds were men hollering instructions to one another in a language I didn't understand.

"They're going to use gas," Rogers called out, "try to force us out of the house!"

"Do you have a target?" Larson yelled back. "I've got one down, but I made two others who dug themselves in. No shots available yet."

"Crap!" Larson spat, "do you have any masks?"

"Just one and it's in the locked..." Rogers went quiet as a low-pitched BOOM sound came from outside. Rogers immediately fired again as something flew through the open window, struck the far wall and clattered to the floor while blowing smoke out each end.

The hissing of the container muffled the cry from Rogers' second target, the same one who had, only an instant before, fired the container of tear gas into the apartment. I gagged as the gas burned my eyes and throat and staggered toward the door. I felt a body drop on top of me and press me to the ground. I could have easily pushed myself off the floor with one arm and lifted whoever was lying on me with the other, but Larson's voice hissed into my ear, telling me to stay down, telling me that the last gunman was waiting for me to go outside. I heard the words, but the gas was getting to me even more and I couldn't think, couldn't see, and couldn’t breathe. I knew that I'd be dead before I took my first step outside the safety of the apartment, but my body crawled for the door anyway. A part of my brain that was still working wondered how Larson could be so rational while the gas swirled cloyingly around us. I tried to see through the burning, stinging tears that ran freely in torrents down my cheeks. Ever feel the sting of onions as you slice them? Well multiply that by about... oh... a million? and you'd only begin to understand what that gas was like.

I squinted and saw Rogers holding a box of some sort. He looked unhappy but otherwise undeterred by the gas that was leaking out the seams of the box, as the saturation of the gas within the air inside the apartment dropped from close to one hundred percent down to an almost passable level. Larson got off of me and moved to the window. His eyes and face were stained with as many tears as mine were, but he barely seemed to notice the pain.

Rogers went to the opposite wall and threw the box through the glass window. It burst through the glass with a crash, taking the box and its noxious contents outside. Lei moved to that window, she had recovered faster than I had, and took in a couple of breaths of the clean air that now was vented into the apartment.

Rogers had barely noticed the gas much in the same way Larson hadn't, or maybe they just had learned to ignore the pain in their training days, and had moved back to the stairwell in order to look through his rifle's scope for the last target. He fired, but must have missed because whoever was outside began pelting the apartment again with another shower of bullets. Larson took cover again and I pressed myself to the floor and turned to where Lei had been sitting.

She was gone. Larson noticed it too, "where's the girl?!?"

I looked around the room, my eyes still screaming as they burned from the residual effects of the gas, I couldn't see any sign of Lei.

"She's outside!" I called back.

"What?!? What do you...?"

I ignored Larson, "Rogers! Pin that guy down!!"

Rogers responded immediately, "No shot!"

"I don't care if you have a shot or not! Open fire on him, make him take cover until Lei can get around the apartment."

"But..."

"Just do it Pat!" Larson screamed.

Rogers didn't hesitate another second and he fired the contents of the AK-47 in the general direction of the last gunman. His rifle was empty in a matter of seconds and Rogers expertly ditched the spent clip and was in the process of slamming a full magazine into the rifle when the sound of Lei's twin Browning automatic handguns began firing in rapid, yet evenly spaced shots burst came through the broken windows.

We had given Lei the time she needed to circle around and get close enough to the last gunman in order to pin him behind whatever cover he had found. I knew Lei's abilities, and how very deadly she was, so I also knew what was about to happen after her wild charge.

The gunman was already as good as dead... and she was angry... and this was going to get messy because Lei had little restraint at holding back her blood lust when she was in a killing frenzy.

I tried to distract Larson and Rogers, "Lei's got him," I yelled to the pair, "see if you can tell if there are any other hostiles."

Maybe it was because Larson had already seen us in action or perhaps it was because he simply thought it was a good idea, but whatever the case he did as I asked and began to scan the area away from where Lei was charging in, but Rogers, on the other hand, kept his eyes on target through the scope, with the now fully loaded clip inserted into his AK-47.

"I'll give her cover," he said, continuing to sight through the scope.

"Rogers!" I tried yelling to jolt him out of his concentration, but the man was an elite professional and stayed on target without even wincing in surprise at my voice.

I could see it all in my head as events unfolded outside. Lei would keep firing until she was within ten yards of the gunman and then, while still running at a full sprint, she would toss the empty guns aside and leap forward. The gunman would peek his head out at the last minute to see her literally flying toward him. Her fingers would be out, extended like claws and her teeth, barred like some feline predator. It would happen in slow motion for both of them. The gunman would try to raise his weapon, or maybe he'd simply raise his arms to protect his face, and Lei would land on him before he could accurately fire a shot. Her fingernails, extra tough from decades of rock climbing, as well as being reinforced by fiberglass and acrylics that literally made them into claws, would penetrate the flesh with little resistance. She would bury her fingers up to the second joint in the space under one of the gunman's armpits while restraining the man's gun hand with the other. He would scream in horror and pain and, as Lei's bodyweight pushed them to the ground, her teeth would sink into the man's throat, biting through mere inches of flesh that she would tear away with a twist of her neck.

The blood spray would be enormous and instantaneous, like the sudden violent eruption of a volcano, and the man would be dead in seconds from the arterial blood loss. In that moment, with a fresh kill and her adrenaline at maximum, Lei would drink. She would press her mouth against the torrent of outpouring blood and swallow mouthful after mouthful of the crimson fluid, trying to get in all in her stomach. Of course, she wouldn't be able to consume it all, and it would pour from the sides of her mouth and cover her face, clothes and body. When the gunman finally died she would stand over him and in every way resemble the demons that mankind has always feared my people to be.

I looked at Rogers as I heard Lei's battle cry when her guns stopped firing, and his eyes squinted. Clearly he thought he was going to have to save the day with a well placed bullet. Then his eyes shot wide and he jolted up from the scope. His face was a veil of confusion and fear. He looked at me, but didn't say a word, before quickly returning his eye to the scope.

There was a scream of pain from outside that was cut off to be replaced by a desperate, wet, choking sound. Animalistic noises, like grunts and snarls, filled the air and Larson called out, "What's happening out there?"

Rogers' mouth moved but no sound came out as he continued to look through the sniper scope.

"Rogers!" Larson yelled when he saw that Rogers was still peering through his scope, "Can you see them?"

Rogers was shaking, in all of his years (perhaps even decades), of training were no match for what he was witnessing through the lens of his scope.

"Rogers!" Larson tried again without response, "Captain!!!"

Rogers head twitched at the sound of his rank and said, "She...she jumped on the last man, and there's blood. A lot of blood, but they fell behind the wall and I can't see them now."

He was lying. I could tell. Larson probably could as well, but if the man wanted to deal with the situation by using personal denial, then I would be okay with it...for now.

From the sounds that I could hear I guessed that Lei hadn't finished with her kill yet and I tried to distract the two soldiers before the final surreal image of Lei covered in the blood of her victim could be burned into their minds for the rest of their lives.

"Larson, any other sign of hostiles?"

Larson was staring at Rogers and seemed a bit spooked at the man's reaction, but he answered me quickly, "No, we're clear. I don't think they expected any significant resistance."

I walked over to Larson and whispered, "You might want to go to Rogers and reassure him that we're all on the same side here."

Larson faced me and his eyes shifted to the window, "What did he see out there?"

"You'll see the aftermath of the body soon enough, but you might want to..."

"I've known Pat for ten years, he has seen some of the worst combat casualties a soldier can see and he's always held it together. What could he have seen that..."

"Robert," I said with extra calm and sensitivity in my voice, "it's not because she killed the gunman, it's the fact that how she did it is...well, it's the kind of thing that your parents told you as a child wasn't real."

Larson looked back at me as I said, "Rogers just learned that some childhood nightmares are real."

Larson turned to Rogers and took a step toward him before he hesitated and turned back to me, "What ARE you?"

I just looked at him with an apologetic look on my face. Despite all he knew, and all Rogers had just seen, he still wouldn't believe the truth...at least not right now.

"What Lei and I "are" is, we're on your side, fighting alongside you, and subsequently, willing to die alongside you if necessary."

Larson simply shook his head and walked over to Rogers. I walked to the front door and went outside to check on Lei with more than a little concern about the heavily armed allies I had just left behind, inside the cover of the apartment.

Chapter 21

Lei was on her feet and stretching her arms out to the sides like a gymnast after a perfect dismount, before bringing her hands back in and gently caressing her body where the blood had saturated her clothes, wetting her to the skin.

Even I had to shake my head at the sight, "You couldn't have just killed him?"

Lei turned and smiled at me, "I've never been known for having a high level of self control. She took a step toward me and unfastened a button on her skirt. I didn't fall to my knees and swoon at her display, even though she was in full seduction mode, only because I knew it was coming. Blood, the real thing and not our serum, has that effect on us. The most obvious feeling is the overwhelming sense of well-being that follows the consumption, and the subsequent, temporary satiation of our condition's underlying symptoms. All of us react differently; I tend to laugh maniacally at the sensation. It's a strange, out of place and menacing sight to see me like that, but Lei goes into full sex kitten mode.

I went to her and held her close to me, more to prevent her from removing all her clothes, than because I was going to acquiesce to her sexual display. She tried to kiss me and I turned my head to the side and whispered in her ear.

"You've given the men inside quite a show already. Let's leave a little something to the imagination, shall we?"

My words were positive and I gripped her tightly to show that I wasn't rejecting her advances because I wanted to, but because I needed to.

Lei breathed her words back to me into my ear and her voice was deep and dripping with lustful need.

"Let them watch! Let them wish that they could ever have what we have. I can give them something to aspire to, the poor normal humans."

With her body pressed against me, I couldn't help but feel the outline of her breasts against my chest, and as she pushed her pelvis against mine I quickly realized my body was winning the self control battle it was having with my head, and my jeans began to grow extremely restrictive and uncomfortable.

"I brought my hands up to her face and made her look me in the eyes, "I think the image would be too much for these men who are most likely currently involved in watching us through their high powered rifle's mounted aiming devices."

Lei hesitated and some rationality seemed to flow into her, followed quickly by remorse and concern.

"Can we still trust them then?" she asked.

I shrugged, "they haven't shot us yet." I said cheerfully, "What say we don't give them any additional reason to consider the possibility?"

Lei looked into my eyes. Honestly, at that moment I was at my limit, if she pressed me any more I would have taken her right then and there in the bloodied earth around her kill. Thankfully, the mischievous twinkle left her eyes and her body relaxed against mine.

"They're still gonna get a show," she smiled as she disengaged her body from mine.

"Oh?" I asked.

"Yep. I'm completely covered in blood. I'd better change out of my wet T-shirt."

There was no passion in her voice as she said it and, despite her ability to get back in business mode, I still balked.

"Um...you didn't bring any..."

Lei looked pointedly at me, "What do you think will have the worst effect on them? The sight of me in my underwear, or in these blood-soaked, see through clothes I'm wearing."

I looked at her skeptically, "you don't wear underwear."

"Semantics."

Crap, I thought, and then helped Lei out of the ruined clothes.

It used to unnerve me how comfortable Lei was in her skin. She wears naked as if it were a suit of armor, and carries herself with even more confidence in that particular state then she does when clad from head to toe. I have always been and am still marveled by her ability even now, and the effect is no less profound than when we first met. Lei had stripped out of her clothes until all she was wearing was the black sports bra, which was also wet with blood and her boots. I tried to take her by the hand but she strode powerfully in front of me as if both hoping and daring everyone to look at her.

When we walked through the front door I had expected bugged eyes and frayed nerves from the soldiers, but I didn't get it. They looked up, held their gazes for a brief moment and then went back to collecting and packing gear. Rogers didn't look up from his efforts when he said softly, "There are some clean clothes in the armoire upstairs. See if some will work for you."

Lei looked at me and then walked right past the two men and climbed the stairs to the loft that served as a bedroom. Once she was upstairs both soldiers looked at me and waited. I wasn't sure what they wanted me to do or say under their respective gazes, so I just opened the door for the elephant in the room.

"What?" I asked simply, letting each man decide what it was they wanted to ask.

They were silent for a time, and then Larson said, "Rogers knows how to find the Madame at the Pink Pussy Club. She's particularly bad news and treats her girls like property, more than like human beings. The girls only work for her because they are under contract. A contract that is enforced by the police as if it were legal. They'd be working the clubs in any case but she gives them only enough money to survive on until their time with her is up, which usually is the majority of their youth. It's rumored that if the girls get too out of line, or are caught stealing then they'll be sold to the organ grinders."

I swallowed, such indifference to life was a foreign thing for me to stomach.

Rogers saw how uncomfortable that made me and chuffed sarcastically. Larson scowled at him then said," At least that's the threat they live under, I don't know if it's true."

I nodded, "So we're going to pay her a visit?"

The soldiers looked worried, but Larson said, "Rogers and I will be paying her a visit. You and the girl should stay out of it."

My attitude turned icy, "Are you trying to cut us off?"

Larson didn't move, hold up a hand or attempt to make any gesture in supplication, instead he just looked up from what he was doing and said calmly, "I'm going to say this one time and after which, I'll expect you to remember who the experts are in this operation. When your investigative skills are needed I will give you the lead, until then you follow my orders or we go our separate ways now. Understood?"

I didn't nod as much as I inclined my head in a gesture that said I understood his words, even if I didn't completely agree with them. He continued, "The girl clearly has an issue with the particular scenario we will be walking into and I believe it best to keep her out of any situation that might be compromised by an emotional response."

Well crap, I thought, that did make a whole lot of sense especially after Lei had reacted the way she initially had regarding the girl's contract.

Larson continued, "You have your agenda Jacobs, and I have mine, which is to find Zach."

I nodded. It was true we needed to find Larson's man in order to locate Whelan...or at least that was what we were hoping. However, the odds were good that Zach and Whelan were going to be in the same location, and as capable as Larson and his friends might be as soldiers, he wasn't an investigator. He was going to need my help at some point to help put the pieces together and he knew it. He wasn't sure how, why or when that was going to happen, and neither did I exactly, but we both knew that it would happen in time.

I turned to walk to the stairs to check on Lei when Larson called out after me, "That is the last time I am going to explain myself to you. Clear?"

I stopped as the amount of pride I could internalize reached it's maximum. I tried, I really did try, to just nod my head and make my way up the stairs. My body and mouth had other ideas.

"I hear you loud and clear. Now let me make something clear to you. Lei and I are professional investigators who have been finding people, some of whom were exceptionally skilled in not being found, for more years than you would care to know or believe. We have, as you have now seen firsthand, more than enough skills to take care of ourselves and plenty of money to hire the best of any particular skill set we don't possess. You may be experts in the art of soldiering, but this is a very different type of battlefield and, when you really break it down, Lei and I are the people who matter here, not you. So, if we were to part ways now, then I'd imagine you and your buddy over there would make the trip to the Pink Pussy bar and ask some questions. Who knows, maybe you'd even get some answers, but in the end the two of you would be wandering around the streets of Bangkok not knowing which way to turn."

I let all of that sink in as Larson's face turned slightly red as he quietly fumed.

I didn't let up, "Your little speech back home was valid as far as getting us out of the country quickly, and without having to go through customs when we arrived, but we are here now, so let's not pretend who needs who more."

Larson stood up and I thought he might come at me, but I still didn't back down.

"Now, for the record I agree with your line of thinking regarding the bar and Lei, but if in the future I ask you to explain yourself, then you will do it, and you will do it happily, because there may be something in those details that will give me some insight in how to better find your friend and our target."

Larson quickly walked up to me and stood with his face less than six inches from mine. He wasn't used to having his authority questioned or countered, but I wasn't a soldier...or at least, I wasn't one of his men.

We stared at each other for a second before I said, "Now, are we clear?"

His eyes squinted slightly, but beyond the rage that appeared to be boiling on the surface, I thought just for an instant I saw the corners of his mouth stretch upward as if resisting a smile.

Larson's face and body relaxed, "Crystal," was all he said before turning his back on me and heading over to Rogers. Rogers face was a mask of unrestrained surprise and he urgently whispered his disapproval to Larson, or so it seemed to me.

Larson answered him quietly, but not so quiet that I couldn't hear, "He's right Pat. We need them, and despite everything else, they are clearly capable."

Rogers' emotions were getting the better of him, "I told you what the girl did out there! I mean, what the hell man?!"

Larson's tone grew impatient, "What exactly is the problem Captain? Did she take out the well dug-in gunman in a way you found objectionable? You'd have felt it was more respectable to have blown his head clean off his shoulders with your AK?"

Rogers face dropped, but he still wasn't done, "It isn't the killing that's bothering me. I think you know that."

Larson took in a deep breath and let it out before putting a hand on Rogers' shoulder, "I do know it Pat." Larson barely turned his head to see if I were listening in on the conversation. I was, of course, and I think Larson knew it too, yet despite that he said, "If it becomes something we have to deal with, then let's do it after we find Zach."

I think Larson was trying to covertly pass along a message to me. In short, he'd make sure we were all on the same team until we found Zach and in that we could count on his full support and cooperation. After that, his loyalty to us was over and if we hadn't earned his trust by then, well, we might just find ourselves on opposite sides.

I started up the stairs as three words filled my head with regards to our Navy SEAL companions...

“Bring it, Frogmen.”

Chapter 22

"Sir, we found him."

The guard was dressed the same as all the others in camp. Black combat gear that looked to be made of the latest breathable athletic wear, with a Kevlar flak jacket worn like a vest covering his torso, and black fatigue pants that fed into his black boots. He was sporting an MP-5 semi-automatic rifle that was equipped with a night vision scope. His face was painted in greasy black streaks of camouflage face paint, and he wore a black recon cap on his head.

The man called Timberland, who was also the security commander, sat at his makeshift desk and looked up from the maps he had been studying.

"Where?"

"He's at the village."

Timberland turned and looked at the clock on the wall and then back at his team member.

"That village is nearly five miles from the camp."

"Yes sir."

"Are you telling me that he made it through THAT jungle and to the village in less than five hours without a map, a compass, or any kind of directional gauge?"

The mercenary soldier looked uneasy, "Sir, I know it seems incredible, but we witnessed the target being taken inside one of the sheds. The natives appear to be caring for him."

"And you didn't think to take him?"

The mercenary didn't hesitate, "There were only two of us, and the village appeared to be protecting him. We'd have needed to open fire on the people of the village, and I didn't want to risk that without at least checking in first."

Timberland was, as a rule impatient, but he knew the soldier had made the right decision.

"Well consider yourself checked in and take however many men you need and get him back, before the doctor decides to take out his frustration on the rest of us."

The phone rang on the folding table that served as a desk, cutting off Timberland's rant. He answered it, "Yes?"

Timberland's face turned from angry to grave.

"How long ago?" Timberland's face grew concerned, "How many did they take out?" His face lost some of its color, "All of them? How could they...?"

There was a long pause and, not wanting to appear out of control in front of one of his subordinates, Timberland waved the guard away. The guard nodded and walked from the room as Timberland listened to what was being said on the other end of the line. Then things seemed to turn crazy, "What was that? What?!?...Did they have a combat dog or...?" Timberland rubbed his eyes, "Okay, keep that part to yourself and get your job done."

Timberland hung up the phone as his eyes stared into the distance before pulling a cellular phone out of his pocket. He tapped the screen a couple of times to enable the encryption code to scramble the call he was about to make and, when the phone indicated the secure channel had been established, he dialed the number.

"It's Timberland. Have there been any reports of any of our kind currently active in the area?" Timberland waited as the voice on the other end of the line responded. "I see. I only ask because a small group in our employ engaged the agent that was sent to replace Dr. Whelan's subject...They were killed...No sir, I meant our agents were killed...Yes sir, and the report is that one member was done "old world" style...No, I haven't seen the body myself but the police we've been paying say..." the voice on the other end suddenly erupted causing Timberland to cringe in much the same way that his subordinate had moments ago. "Yes sir. I understand. I'll see to the body immediately...I've already alerted the pack and we will be going to the location as fast as possible, but I feel there's very little chance of the target or targets still being there...Yes sir, of course we'll do as you say."

The line disconnected with Timberland still holding the phone to his ear. He gently placed it on the folding table as a knock came from his door.

"Come," Timberland called out and the door opened as the man who had just left the room returned with ten others, all of whom were clad in similar black outfits and carrying MP-5 assault rifles. They were comprised of eight men and two women.

Timberland smiled as he looked over the group, "Change of plans. We may have a new threat in the area. We will need to recover a body from the morgue and check the wounds. After that we will be checking up on the local constabulary that we have been so graciously paying all this time. If they are incapable of doing the tasks we have asked of them we are to end our relationship with them."

The group began milling about the room as Timberland spoke. This was not the restless professionalism of trained mercenaries, instead it seemed that the mood in the room was devolving into something primitive and feral. Slight guttural sounds were humming from unspecified throats and Timberland began to feel the tell tale shiver of adrenaline run through his body as he fed off the energy in the room.

Timberland raised his assault rifle over his head from its shoulder slung position, and set it gently on the table in front of him. Everyone in the room froze and watched with far more interest than the maneuver would have appeared to warrant. Then he put his hand on his K-bar tactical knife and pulled it from it's sheath. He flipped the blackened seven-inch blade over in his hand and then slammed it down on the table top while keeping his hand on the grip. The sound of the wood splintering as it stabbed into the wood was like the report of a gun, and when the room went silent again all of the mercenary soldiers were breathing hard.

Slowly, cautiously the first mercenary approached the table and set his weapon gingerly next to Timberland's before pulling his own knife from it's sheath and slammed it home into the tabletop as well. After that it was a near frenzy as assault rifles were set aside and edged weapons of all makes and models were plunged into the plywood until every merc member of the team was holding on to the handle of their own impaled blade.

"Tonight," Timberland spoke to the group with his own breath coming in ragged succession, "we find out who, or what, we are dealing with and then, once we have their scent, we hunt."

On that last word the group let out a collective, anticipatory sound that was more than a simple acknowledgement of their agreement. It was a call to a time that was millennia ago. A time of hunters, prey, the chase… and tonight they would follow the call in their blood.

Tonight they would be the pack that they needed to be, and they were going to find their harmony together.

Tonight the wolves would hunt.

Chapter 23

Larson looked more than a little uncomfortable as he watched the collections of bikini clad girls dancing on the makeshift floor of the outdoor bar in front of the Pink Pussy Nightclub. As I watched him I couldn't help but wonder how it was that a soldier who had seen the kind of "blood and guts" that a SEAL team veteran must have witnessed could still be caught off guard by the enticement of the fairer sex... Or maybe he was just putting on an act for the benefit of any eyes that might have been watching the bar. After all, his demeanor hadn't changed when he had first seen Lei and she could run circles around these girls in the seduction category.

Lei and I were watching our hastily cobbled plan unfold from across the street. Lei was wearing a pair of baggy velour sweat pants with the waist rolled down to a ridiculous level that allowed the top of her G-string to show. The matching, sheer, lacy bra was all she wore for a semblance of a covering for her breasts, and the pose she struck gave the impression that she was just another working girl, putting the moves on a "John." I was, of course, playing at being the tourist wearing a typical island style shirt, and just to make me stand out even more, my jeans and boots.

We hadn't counted on the local talent hassling us when the working girls of Soy 6 seemed to be more populous than the tourists, but we drew their attention in any case. One bribe led to another and to another, until I was starting to feel like an ATM machine. Finally I decided enough was enough and refused to pay a particularly vocal little...pimp? I guess he was a pimp, but the second I stood up to him it was as if the entire area now realized they had pushed me too far. We weren't bothered again, and we had secured our little corner on the street.

Larson seemed to set his sights on a particular girl, but made a scene of being embarrassed or shy about approaching her. The idea was that as soon as he "worked up" the confidence to talk to her, Rogers would bully his way in and try to take her away. The two would argue and then the issue of who would be able to pay the "long time" fee to the bar would require the Madame to negotiate the deal and determine the winner. This would hopefully require a discussion inside a private office where they could corner the Madame away from the majority of her security force. At that point I hoped all that would be required would be a further bribe. I wasn't short on cash, and was willing to use it all to get answers about the little girl and her sale to the man I had come to know as Zach.

It wasn't long before Rogers walked up to the entrance of the bar and passed Larson without acknowledging him. Larson was good and he went about his business outside the club as the girls luridly beckoned him to come in. Overt gestures such as bending over provocatively while pointing at him and then to the small patches of fabric between their legs was comical, but apparently effective. Several other men who had been watching immediately succumbed and walked up to the entrance to be escorted by one girl or another. Larson continued to make a scene of watching the one particular girl for a little longer as she called out every Asian prostitute cliché' from the movie "Full Metal Jacket."

"What the hell is he waiting for?" Lei hissed, "it's not like he hasn't been invited enough."

"He's making himself out to be a selective client."

Lei glared at me, "I know that. I just think he already established that fact ten minutes ago."

"Maybe he's stalling until Rogers can get a good recon of the interior?"

Lei was going to say something back, but then hesitated before saying, "that would make sense wouldn't it?"

"Some," I admitted, "but my concern is for the men that are busy talking amongst themselves on either side of the entrance."

Lei perked up, "Where?"

"The three men smoking, but evidently not interested in what the club is selling to the left of the entrance and the two men sitting at the bar in front of the dancing girls but not really watching them."

There was a crowd in front of the nightclub with pedestrians and potential customers constantly moving back and forth in front of the entrance so it took Lei a second to make out the men I had mentioned.

Once she had seen them she said, "Good eye babe. Who do you think they are?"

"Probably local law acting as covert security for the nightclub." "Do you think Larson made them as well?"

"The man's a pro, so my guess would be 'yes,' but even professionals can slip." I thought about what Larson had said to me back at the apartment, and how he had given me instructions to watch the building from the street "Just in case."

"What should we do?" Lei asked and the anticipation in her voice was unnerving to me.

She had taken in the raw blood less than six hours ago and it was undoubtedly still affecting her. She was going to be all adrenaline and no reserve for a while longer, so I thought it best to give her something to do.

"I'll take the three to the left, draw them into an alley or something, while you distract the two at the bar."

Lei pouted, "Why do you get the..."

I cut her off, "the two at the bar are in plain view. You can't just knock them on the head and make a meal of them."

"I wasn't going to..." as she protested I gave her a look that said, just who do you think you're trying to fool? "...well, okay, the thought had occurred to me, but only if I could reasonably cover my tracks."

"Lei," I said calmly, "what happened this afternoon was a by product of necessity. Tonight is not. We don't take blood, even of our enemy, unless we absolutely have to."

She was going to argue when I said, "Or we'd be no better than Dimitri, or the rest of those Russian scumbags."

Lei's mouth shut and her eyes searched my face until she gave me a slight nod.

"Damn," she sighed, "Its been so long since I had the real thing that I forgot what it was like."

"I know, and you are going to feel the effects for a while longer, so..."

I let her finish the thought, "so, I'll put on a show for the guys at the bar while you get to go and play with the other three."

At that exact moment she drew her hand back and slapped me hard across the cheek. The sharp sound of the smack was loud enough to be heard over the music thumping all around us, and every head seemed to turn in our direction. Lei started yelling at me in Cantonese and stormed away to an empty seat next to the two men of interest at the bar. Larson watched her as she sat down, but didn't break character, and instead took the moment to approach the girl he had been focusing on. It only took a moment before the dancer entwined her arm in his and led him inside, while pressing herself against him and looking relieved that her "John" hadn't noticed Lei and lost interest.

I rubbed my cheek and pretended to be embarrassed by the laughs that were garnered by Lei's little scene and then made a show of sulking away until I had moved nearly a block down the road. When I thought I had covered enough distance I stepped into the sparse shadows that the tacky neon signs allowed and made my way back to the spot where my three targets were still standing. It wasn't easy to be stealthy, given all the animated neon that illuminated the majority of the street into a semblance of daylight, still I found myself in striking distance without having drawn the attention of the trio.

From my position I couldn't see Lei, but she didn't need me to protect her; in fact, it was quite the opposite, because if Lei needed me it would be to stop her from doing too much damage as opposed to someone hurting her.

I staggered out of the shadows, feigning maximum inebriation and flopped around until I basically fell into the first of my targets. The man who was closest to me jumped as I grabbed his arm in apparent support, and dragged his body down with mine as his two partners exchanged looks of both concern and anger at my spectacle. To them I was just another stupid "Farang," or foreigner, who was both the bane and lifeblood of the city. The Thai people have a strange perception of foreigners, and consider then to be unsophisticated, uncouth, spoiled, stupid, naive, and Godless. Of course, the Farang are also wealthy and, therefore, necessary to the inflow of money for their country. I suppose they all remember what life on the farm was like and don't want to return to that life at any cost, or they probably would have kicked all the Farang out long ago.

As a result of this double standard they treat tourists pretty well in general, but if one were to get out of line, or get too inebriated to behave properly, it gives their deep seated resentment an opportunity to come to the surface, and a major beat down isn't that unusual. More than one tourist has found themselves waking up in a hellhole of a Thai prison, broken and bloodied, with no sign of the local party that may or may not have been responsible for their situation.

Unfortunately these guys were keeping their composure, not wanting to give away their "undercover" stake out. I pulled the arm of the man I held and pushed the lit end of his cigarette into the bare arm of his pal, who yelped in pain and slammed his fist down on my back. I barely felt the blow, but I knew I was gaining their attention and intent. I reeled from the blow and stepped on the sandaled toes of a third man before bringing my head up quickly and bashing the back of my skull into the nose of number two who was bent over me, looking for the best angle to punch me again.

Good, now all three of them were pissed at me and their fists rained down on my back in rapid succession. One guy tried to reach under and pop me in the face but I tucked my chin into my chest and protected myself from his attempts as I tried to stagger away. They followed still uselessly pummeling my back with their fists, I almost laughed at their pathetic attempts to hurt me.

It wasn't that my back was so strong or anything...its just that, for the most part, the Thai people are small. I could feel the blows falling on me, but either they were too angry to concentrate on where they should be hitting me in order to hurt me or they just didn't have the mass behind them to inflict any kind of incapacitating effect.

I kept staggering until I found an alleyway and "slipped" into the mouth of it as one of the men threw a kick into my leg. That stung a bit and my apparent response seemed to inspire the trio into launching more kicks that sent me reeling into the back of the alley. I pretended to fall and launched myself to the ground several feet away when we reached the end of the alley. The men surrounded me, trying to stomp on my head or kick my face and I saw no reason to keep the pretense up any longer.

I grabbed the first outstretched leg I could get a hold of and pulled the man to the ground. I pivoted my weight on top of him and slammed my elbow into his forehead that would have made him see stars if the back of his head hadn't whiplashed into the pavement and knocked him unconscious.

The other two went into professional mode as their buddy hit the ground and they jumped on me in an attempt to pin me beneath them, but they still weren't treating me like anything more than a drunk who got in a lucky blow. The look on their faces turned to shock as I pushed free of their grasps and wrapped my arms around the neck of the man who had been lying across my chest. I tightened the chokehold as the man croaked out what might have been a scream while the last man desperately pulled on my arm in a vain attempt to free his comrade. When he realized he couldn't make me let go he stood and reached behind his back for something I couldn't see. I felt the man in my arms go limp and I threw his unconscious body off of me and kicked my booted foot out at the knee of the last man. I felt the crack through the sole as the joint hyper extended and the man's body came crashing to the ground.

A quick flip of my foot brought a heel down on the man's jaw and sent him mercifully to sleep. I got up and felt a queasy feeling in my gut as I saw that the man had a whistle in his hand and not a gun. It was what the police used out here to alert others that they needed backup; therefore, even though I had needed to end the skirmish immediately, I couldn't help but feel badly about the permanent damage I had done to the guy's knee. I tried to justify my guilt by telling myself that if they hadn't been so keen on beating up a drunk foreigner it never would have happened, but that wasn't completely fair. I had goaded them into it after all. I bent down and checked the knee, it wasn't broken, only dislocated, and with a quick pull I reset the joint while the man remained unconscious. It was the least I could do to spare him the pain of resetting the joint when he went to the hospital later.

I walked away from the alley feeling a little dirty both inside and out, as I made my way back to the entrance of the nightclub.

Chapter 24

Larson walked slowly, as the girl who was escorting him inside fawned over him, guiding him toward the bar. There he would pay her bar fee and take her into one of the "short time" rooms located on the upstairs floor of the nightclub. The small male bartender was alone in his efforts, and completely overwhelmed by the multitude of customers that were screaming out drink orders. The girl's voice joined the cacophony of raised voices, vying to be heard over the blaring stereo system, but failed to get his attention.

Good, Larson thought as he craned his neck around to take in every detail he could manage to remember. There were doors that seemed to be haphazardly placed about the perimeter of the club. Larson guessed that they were probably quick getaway passages in case of police raids...or they might serve as entryways for any number of the club's security personnel who could then come out of the proverbial woodwork at a moment's notice. Either way, he knew he'd need to keep his eyes on the doors when...

A fist caught him across the jaw. It wasn't unexpected, actually it had been part of the plan, but Larson hadn't seen it coming and his world spun and he felt his knees buckle underneath his own weight, as Rogers wrestled him to the ground. He heard some of the club girls' scream, as the crowd that had been literally pressing against him suddenly parted in order to give the brawlers plenty of room. Rogers was in full character and pressed his attack by twisting his body and shifting his weight in order to bring another fist raining down. Larson saw the balled fist coming for his face mere moments before it would have struck, but instinctively he raised a hand and palmed the fist as it fell and then reached up to grab a hold of Rogers' left ear. Rogers yelped in pain as Larson pulled him down against his own body. Rogers responded by cursing loudly in both English and Thai.

"Take it easy!" Rogers whispered as his eyes squinted in pain at the force Larson was exerting on his ear before he started cursing loudly again.

"Damn near knocked my head off asshole!" Larson snarled under his breath back at Rogers before he twisted harder on the man's ear. Rogers yelped again and was about to drive a knee into Larson's gut when something heavy fell on top of them. It was the bartender and the little man already had an arm around Rogers throat in the makings of a chokehold. Rogers let go of Larson and quickly grabbed on to the arm at his throat. Now

it was Larson's turn to shift his position. He maneuvered his feet under Rogers' chest and, with a grunt, pushed both men off his chest, sending them sailing backward into a set of tables, most of which were fully occupied.

Rogers and the bartender crashed through a table, which shattered under their weight and velocity, sending the occupants scurrying. Larson sat up in time to see working girls and patrons surrounding them in an attempt to watch the action while staying far enough back to not become part of it. He also saw groups of men step over the prone bodies of Rogers and the bartender, who they must have thought to be unconscious, materialize from the crowd, rudely pushing their way forward and carrying short heavy clubs in their hands.

Damn, he thought, the entire spectacle had grown out of control so quickly that sticking to the plan was going to be difficult. Larson stood alone and held his ground while the oncoming men staggered to a stop in front of him. Apparently they weren't used to anyone facing them down as they ran in. He let his face grow stern, conveying a message that needed no translation: he was no simple civilian, to mess with him was to be in over your head and the result would be deadly. One of the security men seemed to break under the intense glare and took a step back from Larson, while the nearly dozen or so others looked confused and uncertain as how to proceed...that was...until the body of the bartender came flying over the top of their heads and crashed into Larson. In that moment of vulnerability, the security crew found their courage and swarmed in on him raining blows down on his back and legs with the heavy wooden clubs they held.

***

When I finally arrived back at the nightclub's entrance I could see that Lei had the two "undercover" officers, who had displayed so little interest in the club girls, completely mesmerized by her "dance." There was a gathering crowd who had also taken an interest in her, as she gyrated around the makeshift strippers pole that the outdoor bar top sported. By the vacant stares of the pair of men she held in complete control, I could tell that more was going on with them beyond simple gawking. Lei had put them in thrall, a technique some of our kind, Hunters for example, are trained to do involving years of practice. Like hypnosis, it involves a lot of psychologically centered movement, involving the power of suggestion, although it is significantly less formal than clinical hypnosis, in that the goal is just to create passivity, rather than some defined post-session disorder. In the case of what my kind call a thrall, the subject is guided into focusing on a specific object, like a point on the body, followed by that object undergoing a repetitive movement, creating a stimulus causing the brain to slow its own cognitive processes. Eventually the subject is completely drawn in to the moment, and at that point, the subject is simply cognitively "lost" as if in a prolonged daydream or coma, from which they have no interest in waking.

In the more sordid times of my people's history, the Hunters used this technique to trap potential victims, making them momentarily defenseless against the forthcoming attack. Initially, it was only somewhat of an effective method with one major flaw because, just like in the case of hypnosis, the subject had to be a willing participant or it wouldn't work. This is what eventually led the technique being tightly wrapped around seduction, because after all, what else could hold a person's attention more than sex?

To say Lei was one of the best was an understatement. She was a master of the highest order when it came to enthralling a subject. It was her upbringing and her life prior to being brought in by Alpha, and despite how hellish it may have been, that kind of background made her a natural at the technique.

I smiled as one of the men had actually begun to drool slightly as he stared, open mouthed, at Lei while she danced. When the screams began to cut through the music that was blaring over the nightclub's sound system, the entire crowd that had gathered jumped in surprise. My head spun to the entrance and, without thinking I bolted for the opening. The two men Lei had been focusing on shook their heads and came to their senses, but not quickly enough to avoid the heel of Lei's boot as she spun a kick that cracked the first man's jaw before slamming into the second's. Both men fell limply to the ground and the crowd broke as everyone ran in different directions.

I pushed my way past a number of patrons who were going for the exit, and it was as if I was a salmon, swimming upstream. I could "feel" that Lei was right behind me and using my body to make a path for her as we broke through the crowd and into the open expanse of the nightclub. We both froze as a smallish man went sailing airborne past our eyes and crashed into someone, maybe Larson, taking both of them to the floor. A dozen men holding small clubs appeared momentarily befuddled by the surreal flight of the little man, but when he collided with Larson, they quickly regained their senses and pounced on the pair, smacking them repeatedly on the back with the clubs.

I was about to jump in when Lei put a hand on my shoulder as a whistle blew behind me.

The police were already here... and too quickly to be a coincidence. They weren't worried about breaking up the fight either as the first one through the door raised a gun and aimed it at the pile of men. The club's security men looked up in shock and tried to scramble away, too late, as the shot rang out and the bullet struck one of the security members. Blood flew and people started screaming as panic broke out inside the enclosed space.

Rogers hit the policeman in a tackle that wrenched the policeman's body hard enough to break bones, and the gun flew from the man's hand. Larson had fought his way to his feet and was calling out a warning that I couldn't make out over the crowd. Another shot rang out and I spun in time to see Rogers body contort as the bullet struck him. These policemen weren't here to control the situation or restore the peace, they were here to kill. Odds were that they had been paid off to take us out; however, as they had no idea what we looked like, they were probably going to shoot any foreigners that started trouble. Lei and I leapt into the fray, forcibly throwing bodies out of the way as we pushed through the remaining crowd. I grabbed the first policeman I reached by his wrist, and tearing the gun from his hand lifted him over my head and slammed him to the ground hard enough to incapacitate him. The next policeman had just registered me as a threat when my knee drove into his abdomen. As his body bent over from that blow, I brought my knee back up into his face and he fell limply to the floor. A third policeman raised his weapon at me and I was about to dive to the side, but Lei landed on his back with a snarl that would have been the envy of any large predator. Lei opened her mouth but instead of ripping out the man's throat as I was afraid she might do, she instead let out a martial art cry and used the momentum her initial hit had given her to drive the policeman down to the floor. I could hear the man's forehead smack the linoleum despite the intense noise of the club and crowd.

Another policeman fired in Larson's direction and the bullet struck the bar sending shards of wood into the air like shrapnel. Larson moved quickly and confidently in a crouch through the crowd and "appeared" behind the shooter in time to do some kind of abrupt maneuver that flipped the man over and drove him head first into the floor.

I couldn't help but chuckle at the idea that the floor of the club was turning into one of our best assets in this situation, but I stifled the frivolity as I ran for Rogers and nearly collided with two more police officers who emerged from the panicking crowd. They both went wide-eyed as they saw me coming, but quickly recovered and pointed their weapons at my chest. I dropped to my knees and slid across the floor while bending backward until the back of my head nearly touched the ground. One man fired and the bullet sailed harmlessly over me, the other tried to compensate for my slide and fired to one side of my body as I reached the spot where they were standing. I twisted and kicked one man's legs out from under him with enough force to spin him in the air and, right before his head would have hit the ground, I kicked my other foot out and into his face. The second officer jumped back and adjusted his aim just as a set of manicured fingers grabbed onto fistfuls of his hair. Lei leapt back and dropped her body to the floor taking the back of the policeman's head with her. There was a sickening crack as his head struck the floor and another of Bangkok's finest was unconscious on the ground.

What was that now? Floor: 5, Policemen: 0?

I rolled to my feet at the same moment as Lei only to notice the bar had emptied and gone quiet. Larson was hovering over Rogers and was pressing a rag into his side.

"We need to get him to a hospital!"

I ran over and, to Larson's surprise, lifted the nearly two hundred pound man as if he weighed nothing.

"Can we take him to the local hospital with the police after us?"

Larson frowned, "You think they were after us?"

"I think it's too much of a damn coincidence to be anything else. Probably a good idea to play it safe in any case."

Larson blew out a breath and nodded, "So what do we do?"

Rogers was conscious and clearly in a significant amount of pain, but managed through gritted teeth, "I know a doctor, just get me in a cab."

"A cab?!?" Larson clearly objected, and, frankly, it did sound a bit ridiculous.

Rogers countered, "Easier to find, and it will get me there just as fast as an ambulance."

Lei was kneeling behind me and I could feel her bolt upright as something caught her attention. Without a word she leapt onto the stage and took off at a run for the other side of the bar. I watched her go for a door on the far side of the club and she slammed full force into it. The door didn't shatter, but the force of her hit took the hinges right out of the wall and the heavy wooden door fell on top of two men who were apparently guarding the exit. Lei ignored them and sprinted past where their bodies lay beneath the door, while I headed for the front of the club carrying Rogers in my arms with Larson leading the way.

We made our way through the "Walking Street" and approached the area where cars were once again allowed. I quickly realized that Rogers had been right about the cabs as the commotion had resulted in pedestrians leaving the area en mass and a number of cabs had converged on the street to gather up the fares they could gouge for extra money in order to take them away from the action. Larson ran for a cab who's driver immediately wanted to haggle over the cost without even knowing our destination. When Larson pulled out an American hundred dollar bill the man's eyes widened and a smile creased his faces he plucked the bill from Larson's fingers...and then he saw me coming with Rogers and the blood that now covered both of us. Fear and panic can apparently overwhelm avarice as the cabbie desperately tried to hand Larson back the money, but instead of taking the bill Larson brandished one of the police revolvers he had apparently taken from the club.

"Get in and drive. Now!" Larson growled.

The driver quickly and repeatedly "wai'd" him as he cowered into the driver's seat. Larson climbed into the passenger seat next to him as I set Rogers into the back.

Larson looked at me after I closed the door. I cut him off before he could say anything, "We'll put the pieces together here. Take care of your man and get back as soon as you are able. We'll wait for you at the hotel."

Larson didn't reply, instead he turned to the driver and ordered him to go.

Chapter 25

I watched the cab disappear among all the other vehicles on the road as its taillights blended with a mass of multiple flashing lights and multi-colored neon that Bangkok offered to the night crowds. Eventually I turned and made my way back up the Walking Street to the club. Things had begun to calm down and the crowds were emerging from wherever they had sequestered themselves as things began to return to normal. Several electric police vehicles had parked in front of the Pink Pussy Club and I could see some of the newly arrived officers were helping their previously incapacitated brethren out of the club still on shaky legs. One was even being carried on a stretcher while, on the street, a pair of EMT's worked on the security guy who had been shot. Amazingly, that unfortunate fellow was the only one who had been shot, despite the multiple rounds I had heard being discharged inside the club.

I scanned the crowd for Lei, but didn't get too close to the club in case any of the officers fully regained their wits and might recognize me. From what I remembered about the layout inside the club, Lei had run through what I was pretty sure it hadn't been a back door exit, but more likely an entrance to an "employees only" area or maybe a stairway to the "short time" rooms above the club.

Careful to be as unnoticeable as possible, I made my way down the alley next to the club in the hopes of finding a rear door that was unlocked, or better yet, unobserved.

Unfortunately, once I arrived at the potential entrance it was surrounded by club employees, all of whom were speaking rapidly to a pair of policemen who were clearly overwhelmed by the barrage of voices. Part of me wondered if this was a standard ploy on the part of the employees in order to confuse the authorities whenever an incident took place in their questionably legal business. At the moment they weren't being raided and had no reason to stonewall any investigation, as far as I knew.

I was about to turn and walk away when a new voice called out from inside the door. Everyone quieted immediately and began looking around for something, until one small man saw me. Instantly he pointed and called out something in Thai that caused every head to swing in my direction. The urge to turn and run was overwhelming, but I managed to stifle it long enough to realize that no one was running toward me or threatening me in any way.

One of the policemen called out to me in Thai, a complete effort in futility there, but then seeing my blank face, quickly changed into broken English.

"You Steve?" he asked in a choppy manner that made it seem as though he was self- conscious about how bad his English was.

I nodded.

"You want inside."

It wasn't a question, even though the words sounded as though they should have formed one. I was too confused to move, so I said, "uh, yes?"

The policeman rolled his eyes, "No! You want go inside." I frowned and shrugged my shoulders, still not really understanding what was happening.

"You want go inside now!" the policeman pointed to me and then to the door. I looked at the door and took a hesitant step forward. There must have been a dozen employees. Cooks, bus boys, dancing girls and a couple battered security men all watching me in calculated silence that made me fairly disconcerted. I started walking toward the door, but never took my eyes off the policemen. Their fellow officers may have just attacked the club in the hopes of taking Lei, Larson, Rogers and myself out of the picture and who was to say that these new arrivals didn't have the same goal in mind.

I climbed the three steps that led to the doorway, and walked inside without being shot or accosted by the police or anyone else, and found myself in what looked to be a storage space, lined with boxes and various crates of wine, beer and hard alcohol bottles. I kept walking until I passed around a room separator and found myself in the girl's changing area.

I must have appeared a bit stunned as a couple of the girls began giggling at my expression and obvious unease, before returning to their dressing, undressing and makeup application. It seemed none of the girls were fully clothed, and any sort of modesty had apparently run its course with everyone present but me, and not a single one girl bothered to cover herself because of my presence. Strangely, although people might think that it was a fantasy come true, the girls attitude was so 'business as usual' that despite the vast amounts of attractive skin, skimpy costumes and high heel shoes, I felt no stir of desire. Of course, if Lei had been present, I would have received an elbow to the ribs, in any case, and responded with a weak "I only have eyes for you darling." comment, but the truth was that there was a total lack of sexual energy being generated in that room. It actually made me a little sad, as I made my way through their "locker room," and entered the interior of the main club, walking through the tables to the main dance floor. I could only wonder how many of these girls had been sold into the club's service just like the little girl with whom "Zach" had become involved.

A little man wearing what appeared to be a tuxedo ensemble, minus the jacket, walked up to me while holding a bloody dishrag to the top of his head.

"You Steve?" "Yes."

"Boss want to see you. She in her office," he pointed to the far end of the club, "I take you."

I held my hand toward the direction he had indicated and inclined my head, "after you."

The man started to "wai" me but the motion seemed to make the area on his head worse and he grimaced with apparent pain.

"That looks like a nasty bump you've got there. Are you the manager?"

The little man shook his head slowly, "Bartender," he said, and began walking toward the club's offices.

It was then that I remembered a man, apparently flying across the club and crashing into Larson. It had been a nasty fall, but not something that would have cracked his head open like that. I wondered if he had been grazed by one of the bullets that had been fired into another of the club's employees by one of those strange police officers, and if so, how lucky this guy was to still be alive.

We made our way through the dance floor and past various walk up bar tops, until we arrived at another set of doors. He knocked quietly and a voice called out what must have been "Come in." in Thai. The bartender held the door open for me. I watched him, and then realizing that he had no intention of joining me into the office, I "wai'd" him, and walked through the door.

The office seemed initially to be sparse, filled with what appeared to be plastic lawn furniture. There was only man in the room and he was sitting with his back to me and a bag of ice pressed to his temple.

"You wanted Steve?" I felt ridiculous referring to myself in the third person like that, but I didn't know how much English this guy had command of, just hoping it was significantly more than my command of Thai. The man in the chair turned around and peered angrily at me, but something in his eyes changed the second he took in my face and he immediately softened as he stood up and "wai'd" me.

I returned the gesture and watched as the man moved to a wall and felt behind a plastic table. I heard a click and watched as a section of the wall popped open a couple of inches. The man put his bag of ice on the table, opened the hidden door and gestured for me to enter yet another room.

I "wai'd" the man again, and walked through the door, finding myself in a room that could only be described as the most extreme example of over-the-top ultra consumption that had ever been created. It actually felt like I needed to wear sunglasses, as I tried to take it all in, because every piece of metal was bejeweled gold. Exotic woods were used in the construction of all the furniture and a pattern of marble tile were set into the floor. Rare animal pelts from bear and lion to what appeared to be monkey were draped over chairs or strewn about the floor as throw or area rugs, and the ceiling was painted with a blue-sky mural, complete with wispy clouds and a rainbow. Everything, and I mean everything, clashed with everything else in the room. It was the most expensive God-awful mess I had ever seen.

Off to one side was an older woman sitting behind a desk composed of gold and glass. She sat blankly, even defiantly, in an oversized luminous Asian red/orange leather chair decoratively riveted down the front of the arms with what looked like solid gold studs. In front of the desk were a couple of black leather chairs that were somewhat smaller but of a matching design to the large red one, complete with matching gold studs.

I walked over to the woman and stood in front of the desk. Her vacant, yet somehow defiant expression never changed, as I waited for her to say something.

"Hey babe, take a seat."

I blinked in surprise as the woman's mouth hadn't moved when the words came out. Of course it only took me another second to recognize that the voice had not been from the old lady's mouth at all.

"Lei?"

Lei peeked a portion of her head out from behind the chair and smiled mischievously at me as she stood up and walked from behind the throne. I was about to ask what was going on, when she brandished the Desert Eagle, keeping it pointed squarely at the woman's face.

Now it was my turn to smile, although it was mostly because I had been worried about her since she bolted away earlier in the evening. "I see you made a friend?"

Lei ignored me at first and leaned in to kiss me lightly, without allowing the red dot of the gun's laser system to leave the center of the woman's forehead.

Then she said, "Let me introduce you to Chonpak Boonliang, Madame and manager of this hell hole."

"So that's what...who...you went after earlier?"

"Yep, I saw Madame 'Pak making a break for it when the shooting started. I caught her about to climb up to the roof and convinced her not to leave."

I squinted my eyes at her and said, "Convinced her how?"

Lei smiled, "That guy outside is her main bodyguard, and he had been with her when I caught up with them. Once I took him down, well she seemed to want to quietly submit to whatever I told her to do. I think that she believes me to be a former employee, come back for vengeance or something."

I nodded, "Has she said anything?"

"No, but to be fair, I haven't asked her anything, yet."

"You've just let her sit and stew the entire time?"

"After I had her bribe the police to leave us alone, yes."

I stifled a smile, "You've been cruel."

Lei didn't smile back, "No, I haven't even started to be cruel yet."

The chill in her voice sobered me quickly, "Does she speak English?"

"Very well, thank you," Madame Chonpak snorted abruptly.

"Good," I turned to her and looking directly into her eyes, said "that will make everything easier, that is, if you want things to go, easy."

She met my glare, "Easy, how?"

"You see this amazingly beautiful woman with the gun?" I

inclined my head at Lei who sneered a smile back at the woman, "She really, really wants to hurt you. She has issues, most of which came from someone exactly like you and it would be..." I paused searching for the right word, "therapeutic, for her to exact more than a little punishment on you."

The Madame only grunted as if bored by the idea that we might torture her. I turned and saw Lei's eyes darken at the expression and knew I had to get this done quickly.

"You tell me what I need to know and we leave what remains of your club intact." I moved in closer and commanded her full attention, "If you don't tell me what I need to know, then I will burn this club to the ground with you still inside it."

The faintest trace of a facial tick quirked on one side of her face, which told me she wasn't nearly as fearless as she'd like us to believe, but she wasn't exactly singing out her cooperation either.

I pulled one of the photographs of the girl out of my pocket and slid it across the desk so that it faced the Madame. She didn't even look at it. Instead she slowly lowered her hands to her cleavage and removed a small, shiny, silver rectangle. I could instantly tell it wasn't a weapon, as it was very thin and square in shape, still I reached over the desk and grabbed her by the throat until she gagged. The object fell onto the desk and popped open revealing itself to be a cigarette case. Lei picked it up and inspected it for a minute before setting it back down on the desk.

"It's cool," she said calmly, "But feel free to strangle the bitch if you'd like."

I released my grip, but growled, "I really don't have time for this shit!" The Madame's eyes were wide, she was used to dealing with the police, who had rules to follow in how they treated their suspects. It looked as though she suddenly realized that we were something else entirely as her hands shakily plucked a cigarette from the case and placed it between her lips. When she closed the case an internal lighter ignited and she lit the cigarette, puffing the smoke away from me instead of in my face as I had almost expected.

When she was done taking a pair of deep drags she looked to the picture and said only, "Who she?"

Lei reared back to pistol-whip the woman, but I caught her arm. She struggled against me for a moment until we both heard the Madame chuckling at us.

When Lei had regained control of herself the Madame said, "You Americans always think we're a bunch of piss ant people who are small and weak compared to you. You come here, you order us around like we're all you're butlers and maids, here to serve your every wish. But we're a proud people. Ancient people. We strive toward enlightenment, while you soil yourselves everyday with the lives you lead."

Suddenly she spat the cigarette at me, and I was so shocked at the revelation that her attitude had been an act she was playing, that I didn't even flinch as the burning ember touched my cheek. It wasn't until the pain of my skin burning awakened me to what had just happened, and I swatted at the still glowing potion of the cigarette that was stuck to me searing my skin.

Then I let go of Lei and turned slightly, to distance myself from the Madame and regain my composure, before I did something I might regret. Lei, to her credit, held her emotions in check as she kept the laser trained on the Madame's forehead. I walked to the door and leaned against it as I took in a couple of breaths in an attempt to control the pain.

Burns suck. If you don't already know that, ask anyone who has experienced it and you'll find they agree with me. And yet, despite the pain and aggravation, I was still more concerned with how I was going to get the woman to talk before either I, or Lei, killed her. That was when I heard the bodyguard on the other side of the door. I looked to the door handle and saw it slowly turning as if someone was trying to be very quiet before bursting into the room. I stepped to the side and positioned myself so, if the door were to suddenly open, I would be hidden in the space behind the open door.

I turned to the Madame, "Hey," I said nonchalantly enough, but Lei reacted to something in my voice and looked concerned, "I want you to pay close attention for a moment."

The Madame crossed her arms and sneered at me with a "Give me your best shot, Asshole." look. At that moment the bodyguard burst into the room with two more of his security people. All three of them had guns pointed at Lei.

They never saw me as I stepped around the door. I grabbed the two new arrivals by their heads and slammed them together with a resounding crunch and they fell limply down as I shifted my weight and grabbed the main bodyguard from behind by his gun hand, wrapping my free arm around his throat. The man yelped in surprise and pain as I twisted his wrist until the small bones snapped and his gun fell free from the now useless hand.

With another quick motion I wheeled him around and repositioned my grip, using both hands to push the man to the floor. Lei realized what was about to happen and called out to me, although I'm not sure if it was in concern, anger or envy.

I wrenched his head back and exposed his throat before driving forward with a snarl and sinking my teeth into his neck.

I couldn't see the Madame, but I heard her shoot up from her chair in shock at the sight of me twisting my head back and forth as my teeth ripped through flesh, gristle and tendons until I felt an explosion of wet warmth flowing into my mouth. The blood was coppery, salty and familiar. I swallowed as rapidly as I could, not wanting to waste any of the blood, while beneath me the bodyguard went into a full body, spasmodic seizure, just as some of our victims are prone to do when attacked as suddenly and ferociously as this, but I held him fast in a death grip as I finished, just as I had been trained to do over sixty years ago.

It wasn't until he had stopped flopping around and grown weak that I released my grip and let his body slump to the ground. I purposely kept from wiping my mouth clean, holding a small mouthful of his blood, and as I turned to face the Madame I let just a little bit ooze out of the corner of the smile I gave her. She was in full panic mode now and had completely forgotten about the gun that Lei held to her head. I stood and walked toward her while motioning for Lei to attend the bodyguard. I really wasn't sure if Lei was going to save the man, or finish what I had started, but I had to play this out the rest of the way. I felt the euphoria building inside me, and I couldn't stop smiling as I slowly made my way to the Madame, who was now backing away from me as the chair slid out of her way.

I said nothing, just pointed to the photo of the girl still lying on her desk.

The Madame's eyes shot to where my finger pointed, and she raised her hands in supplication.

"Stop! Stop! I'll tell you whatever you want to know."

Chapter 26

He woke to the smell of something both cloying and floral in the air. His body ached terribly, but the pain he felt was a far cry from all those times he awoke strapped down to the metal frame at the camp. Just being able to stretch his legs and move his joints was a near euphoric experience that made a joyful cry escape from his throat. When he sat up he realized he was wearing different clothes. A simple shirt and pair of pants that were loose and worn, but added a basic layer of warmth and protection that was both comforting and familiar.

It was barely a moment later when he realized he wasn't alone. An old, very old, woman was kneeling next to a small brazier in the center of the room and was stirring the coals. Smoke rose vertically up and out through a hole in the domed roof, while a teakettle burbled as the liquid inside boiled.

The old woman lifted the teakettle by wrapping a towel around the metal handle and placed it gingerly on a bamboo tray. She then lifted a small ceramic cup and dumped the contents inside the kettle, making it hiss as the powder contacted the hot water.

"The tea will be ready shortly," she spoke softly without turning to look at him, "in the meantime, why don't you join me?"

He squinted his eyes at the woman, something was strange about her, and some of his instincts told him to get up and run. But somehow, a question wormed its way to his consciousness and he asked himself, “Run where?” He rose to his full height, and barely missed striking the top of his head on the ceiling, as he slowly walked to the brazier and sat across from the woman.

She looked up from her work and smiled at him, it was a nice smile too, and there was something familiar about it that drew him to her.

The woman reached out with one hand and gently patted his thigh, "Now, what has brought you back to me?"

He cocked his head at her in confusion. Her words registered in his ears yet after she spoke them he still couldn't ascertain their meaning, but her mannerisms and tone of her voice told him enough to get the idea.

He relaxed and looked around the room. The room was the inside of a small hut from the village he had happened upon, that much he instinctively knew, but why he had been clothed, cared for, and then invited to sit for tea? It would have puzzled him, if he could have cognitively formed the question.

He looked back at the woman and inexplicably, the sight of her smiling face filled him with sorrow. He could feel something twist inside his core and he shuffled around to sit closer to the woman who, in turn, tilted her head and listened to him move closer, smiling even wider.

Her hand searched for his and, when her gnarled fingers gently grasped his, she lifted his hand until the tips of his large fingers brushed against the corners of her eyes.

Tears filled his eyes, although the sadness that overwhelmed him gave no enlightenment or order to his chaotic mind for any rational reason behind those tears.

"You don't remember me, do you?" the old woman spoke softly as his fingers caressed the skin above her eyes.

When he didn't answer the old woman sighed, "Poor child. What did they do to you?" Still he remained silent and she took his hand from her face, "Well, we all have been wronged and we all have scars, don't we?"

Something in her words made him look down to his body and the clothes that covered him. Carefully he pulled the shirt up and over his head so that, in the ambient and plentiful light of the fire, he could see the labyrinth of angry scars covering the entire surface of his skin. The scars weren't random, but seemed to follow a meticulous pattern, as if his skin had been used as a canvas with the artist wielding a scalpel, as opposed to a paintbrush. Still, the damage wasn't of an artistic design. There was a purpose behind whatever had been done to him, although what that purpose might be, he couldn't understand.

He put the shirt back on and stared into the old woman's face.

"Is Pha still with you?" she asked.

The question sent a shock through his entire being and his whole body clenched as if preparing to fend off an attack. The old woman arched an eyebrow in surprise at his reaction.

"Ah, I see. She is not."

He started to shift his legs underneath him in order to stand when she placed a hand on his arm.

"Wait, you should sit a while and we'll see about clearing the fog in your head."

He didn't understand her and was no longer in any mood to try because all he wanted now was to get away, to hide in some dark place and never come out. His body felt as if snakes were writhing inside of him as something was desperately trying to come to the surface of his thoughts, and yet he knew that remembering could be too painful to bear.

He gently broke her hold on him and stood. He had to get some air, get outside the hut, run… It didn't matter where as long as he could run from the pain, from the old woman, from the village, and Pha... Pha…?

He began screaming the moment the name formulated itself with such perfect clarity in his head. It was a bloodcurdling scream of total and utter anguish and it quieted the wild background sounds of the village, and even the jungle, for as far as his scream could be heard. Only the soft crackling of the fire remained as he drove his hands into his stomach and the serpentine contractions he felt began biting him inside as if attempting to tear their way out of him. His legs gave out and he fell to his side crying and moaning without restraint, as some of the village men poked their heads through the doorway of the hut, to check on the woman inside.

"Shoo!" She flapped the back of her hand repeatedly at the trio of men who had peered in. They had all seen the giant foreigner who was curled up in a fetal position on the ground and bawling like an infant. Finally the old woman's protests registered on them and they respectfully backed out of the doorway.

The woman lifted the teakettle from the bamboo tray and poured its contents into a small wooden cup. He was worn out had stopped wailing at this point, but was still breathing harshly, taking abrupt ragged breaths. The woman creakily stood up and shuffled over to where he lay on the floor.

She set the cup on the ground next to him, "Drink this," she said, "It will help your mind come back to you...although I fear there will be more pain as it helps you heal."

She left him lying there and returned to the brazier where she replaced the kettle on top of the coals. Eventually, his abrupt breathing subsided and the memory of what had happened to him vanished to the point that he now wondered just why he was lying on the floor. He sat up, noticed the cup next to him and took it in his hand. His mouth was very dry and he could see there was liquid inside the cup, but it smelled like something other than water. He looked to the old woman who had heard him sit up and was gesturing with one hand for him to drink the cups contents.

Something instinctively told him not to drink, but thirst won out over his apprehension as he downed the entire contents in one great swallow. The tea was barely warm by now and it had a distinct, yet not unpleasant, slightly, earthy quality that left his mouth tasting as though it was full of flower petals. He set the small cup down and tried to stand, but the room began spinning with vertigo making his eye lids heavy and impossible to keep open. He slumped to the floor as the woman stood, now with a bundle of small sticks that were smoking from one end and giving a sweet, but medicinal smell.

She walked over to him as the smoke billowed around his

head in wispy plumes of white, which he then inhaled through his nose, and out through his mouth. The dizziness increased a bit as warmth began to spread from his head down through his neck and body until it reached his feet and even into his toes. A sense of ease spread through him and the dizzy sensation evaporated as the woman guided him into a supine position leaving him staring at the hut's thatched ceiling.

"So, Pha is gone?" she asked his immobile form, "Strange, that her ghost has not visited me."

Chapter 27

After we were through with the Madame, Lei had helped me strip the bloodied clothes off my body and found suitable, yet probably temporary replacements from one of the larger and still unconscious security personnel. The clothes were ridiculously small on me and tight enough to make me look like some kind of dandy, but they were more than adequate until we could get back to the hotel.

We had found a taxi and were headed to the hotel when Larson had called on his cell phone and gave us his location, which happened to be an enormous and well-known restaurant.

"Larson, how is Rogers doing?"

"He'd lost too much blood, but they've hooked him up to an I.V. and are replenishing his fluids. One of the waiters was sent out to find a couple of pints of blood that matched his type, so he should be okay once that gets in his system."

I had moved the phone from my ear to look at it as if it weren't sending his words properly, "Did you say you sent a waiter? To get blood?"

Larson's voice came back after a sigh, "Yeah, we're in a goddamn company meat locker."

I had switched the phone to speaker so Lei could hear as well, and we just looked at each other in total confusion.

Lei said to me, "You think that's a code for something?"

Larson had heard her, "Sort of, yes. Take me off speaker phone."

I did as he asked and said, "So where are you?"

"We're at the Emperor's Garden Restaurant, less than a block from the hotel and it's famous enough that the driver will know exactly where it is."

"You took a wounded man to a restaurant?"

Larson laughed, "That was my reaction initially as well, but it turns out that my good friend Pat has friends in low places."

I frowned, "So he's what, a sous chef now?"

"Nope, turns out he's got a connection to some 'under the radar' types."

I turned to Lei who raised her eyebrows at me wondering what I had just heard.

"I've seen enough movies to guess you're talking C.I.A.?"

"You got it." I quickly put a couple of the pieces together, "Does that mean...?"

Larson finished the thought for me, "that Zach was also working for the C.I.A.? I can't say I have any evidence of that, but it certainly would make logical sense."

I thought for a minute, as any further enlightenment wasn't forthcoming, and then I asked him, "So how does the fact that Rogers working for the C.I.A. result in the two of you looking for medical treatment in a restaurant?"

"Bangkok is a strange place, but this restaurant has an enormous walk-in refrigerator that they don't need. Deals were made, and now the space is a secret, emergency triage unit for the Agency's field agents."

I really wanted to change clothes, but Larson wanted to get an eye-to-eye update and learn if we were able to find any new information. We asked the driver to make an adjustment in his route, and we made our way to the Emperor's Garden.

When the taxi arrived at the restaurant we made another phone call to get Larson to come out and meet us. He led us through the restaurant into the space where Rogers was lying on a cot with an IV fastened to his arm. His wound was neatly bandaged and appeared to have been well cared for, but his face and skin looked pale and clammy and he made groaning sounds despite being totally sedated.

"Is he going to be all right?" Lei asked.

Larson nodded, "They've already pumped the blood into him,

so he should be. The only danger now is infection, but the IV bag contains a powerful antibiotic so no complications are expected." Larson turned away from his friend to look at us, "Although he's out of the fight, and I don't know what he's going to tell his C.O."

"Truth won't work?" I asked.

Larson looked at me, "Which part about tonight...?" his eyes suddenly comprehended the ridiculousness of my apparel, "Hey, what happened to you?"

I tried to speak, but my own culpability, over what I had done to the Madame's security chief, left me momentarily speechless. Fortunately, Lei came up with the best possible response and answered with, "It's complicated."

"Oh?" Larson crossed his arms in front of himself, as if waiting for an explanation.

I found my voice, "The important thing is that the woman spilled her guts about the girl."

"Really?" Larson uncrossed his arms and looked encouraged.

Lei chuffed, "Literally."

Larson looked at Lei in confusion and then turned to me for clarification. I simply shrugged my shoulders and asked again about Rogers.

Larson couldn't let it drop, "She's dead?"

I hadn't intended to kill anyone. Hell, I had even left the bodyguard sort of alive, yet in desperate in need of a transfusion, but still alive, nonetheless. Sure the Madame may have technically been human, but she was still a monster of the worst kind, preying on little girls and using their bodies to make her, and probably many others, very rich.

Lei just had several other ideas about her fate after the questioning was over.

Maybe it was my years as an officer with the LAPD had mellowed me, from being one of my people's iciest Hunters, and formed me into something else, something that is more...tame?

Well, whatever the case for me, Lei hadn't had that time, and my love for her makes me forget that, in the human world, she is still very much a wild thing that acts as judge, jury and executioner, and doesn't wait for months to pronounce sentence or hold back from what her instincts are telling her to do. Combine that with her sordid childhood at the hands of people very much like the Madame, and the fact that she was psychologically stimulated from having fed so recently, it should have been no surprise that her actions were terminal. Once we had gotten every drop of information out of that evil bitch, Lei was on her, and I was laughing on the surface, due to my blood-drunk state, but inside I was screaming for Lei not to do it, watching as she tore into the woman with her claw-like nails eviscerating her even before latching on to the Madame's neck and drinking whatever blood remained. This wasn't just a feed for her, it was vengeance having roots extending back to Lei's earliest memories as a child.

She looked at Larson without saying a word, but slowly licked her lips, while uttering a satisfied sigh and a slightly coquettish smile .

Larson blanched, turning away from us and back to where Rogers was laying on the cot, "What did you find out?" he asked, staring at the wall of the walk-in refrigerator.

I watched him fighting to regain control, and said, "The girl's name is Pha Lomsah and her mother worked at the club as a dancer and bar girl."

"She was a whore?"

"The mother?" I asked, "Yes. Apparently she had indebted herself to the club, meaning the Madame, due to her particular taste for "Ya Ba", which I gather is a meth and caffeine combination and a particularly addictive drug of choice here in Thailand. The mother got pregnant by one of her clients and hid the pregnancy until it was too expensive for her to afford an abortion. The child was born an addict and would have been put in an orphanage if not for the mother's family who somehow found out about the pregnancy. The baby went back to the mother's village to be cared for and, apparently, they did a pretty good job of raising her. She grew into a beautiful little girl, and when the Madame found a picture that had been sent to the mother from the family, she saw a way to make more money."

Lei walked around to where Rogers was lying and peered down hungrily at the vulnerable man. Larson saw her look and rested his hand on the butt of his holstered .44 Magnum, as a warning, without trying to complete the draw.

"Lei," I said calmly, to catch her attention, and she looked back at me, and noticing the barely perceptible shake of my head.

She looked back down to Rogers and said to me, "Do you feel it too?"

I hated the truth of it, but as I looked at Rogers lying defenseless with a bloody bandage over his wound I nodded my reply. The "IT" Lei's question was about involved the 'temptation' that Roger's blood, and his weakened state, was presenting to our most primal urges. It was like looking at your all-time favorite dessert, and having trouble resisting the urge to have just a taste, even though you aren't really hungry.

Lei backed off but Larson saw what I had done, "What are you people?"

I'm not sure why I answered so abruptly, and maybe it was the guilt, I just don't know, but I blew out an exasperated breath, "I think you know fully well what we are by now. You're just having trouble accepting it."

Larson looked from me, to Lei and back to me before he shook his head and muttered, "Fucking bullshit."

I thought he needed a moment but he quickly followed with, "I assume you found out more?"

I nodded and continued, "The Madame was the one supplying the girls at the club with the Ya Ba and she withheld it from the mother until she agreed to sell the girl in exchange for an ongoing, lifetime supply of the drug. A week later armed men arrived at the village, showed the "contract" to the family, and took the girl away."

"Just like that?" Larson asked.

"Seems like," I answered, "I guess Rogers was right about this country, and it not being an uncommon thing here."

Larson began desperately searching for a place to sit down and finally opted for the floor when he couldn't find anything more suitable.

"So what's the connection to Zach?"

I hesitated. I was hoping to figure out a way to soften the blow that I was about to deliver, but nothing had come to me, so I just laid it all out, "Well, we'd be skipping ahead a bit, but it seems that Zach bought her from the club for his own private use."

Larson shot to his feet, "NO!"

I jumped back as the man was gesturing at me with his hands, without realizing that he had drawn his pistol and didn't understand that he was holding a gun.

"I'm sorry man," I quickly said, while holding my hands up in surrender, "but that was the deal the Madame had made. Local law enforcement even signed off their approval of the sale and provided all of the necessary documentation, just so he could take the child back to America as her legal guardian."

Larson frowned at my reaction, and finally noticed the gun in his hand. He considered the weapon briefly before re-holstering it.

"There has to be more to it than that."

Lei was indignant, "Why?"

Larson looked up and the hostility was gone from his eyes. He shrugged his shoulders and said simply, "Because it's Zach."

Silence filled the room until Larson finally asked quietly, "Did you find out where the mother is?"

I frowned, "Yes?"

"And?"

"She overdosed about a month after selling her daughter. They found her body in one of the hotels, next to a similarly dead foreigner."

Larson cursed and kicked at the ground before asking, "Anything on the "John"?"

"Nope. Guy was clean for anything other than being a drug addict and whore monger."

The room remained silent for a bit as Larson clenched his fists in apparent frustration.

Finally he said, "Okay, so where do we go from here?"

Lei spoke up before I could answer, "I'm going to find the ladies room. Let me know what you guys decide."

Larson watched her walk out of the room and seemed to be in total confusion then turned to me, "Decide?"

I nodded, "Seems we have two leads we can follow. One is going to be tricky and very dangerous, but should pay off if we make it out alive. The other may be a wild goose chase, but the risk seems pretty low."

"Tell me about the risky one."

I took a deep breath and, metaphorically, jumped…

"The men who attacked us at Rogers' place..."

Larson cut in, "The dead ones?"

I rolled my eyes just a little bit, "Yes, the dead ones. They would have been collected by now and taken to the morgue. If we can get into the morgue there will be files, containers with personal effects and..."

Larson's face dropped, "You haven't heard?"

I didn't register what he had said right away, and kept on telling him my plan, "...maybe some distinguishing marks on their...what?"

"You haven't seen the news?"

"Um...no?"

Larson pulled his cellular phone out of his pocket, tapped the screen a few times and then handed it to me. On the screen was a video with a female voice speaking in Thai talking about the building burning in the background. There were scenes of firefighters spraying water from their hoses and emergency crews carrying people to be taken away in waiting ambulances.

"If there were subtitles you'd read that somebody set off a fire bomb in the hospital, and the police think ground zero was in, or near, the morgue.

I snorted derisively, "Someone's covering their tracks."

"Yep." I thought for a second before asking, "Didn't Rogers' say something about the Khmer Rouge? Could they be responsible?"

Larson shook his head, "They are pretty quiet these days, although they do hire out for mercenary work, and are behind the occasional kidnapping for ransom. Their organization is more or less dead, otherwise."

I sighed, "Well that rules out plan "A". On to plan B."

Larson squinted his eyes as a thought seemed to occur to him.

"The family."

I inclined my head, "What about them?"

"Did you find out where they are?"

"Yes."

"We should go there." I smiled as Larson had pretty much described plan "B."

"Yes..." I agreed, "Yes we should do that."

Chapter 28

There was no paved road to the village, and what passed for the dirt trail that we were taking was more like a snow ski mogul run, if you replaced the snow with mud. Between getting occasionally stuck in the deep mud, and bouncing hard enough to be concerned that the borrowed Jeep's suspension wouldn't stand up to the stress, we were all relieved when the jungle decided that the vehicle would go no further. I never thought that I'd actually look forward to walking through such a wild and foreign landscape, but I was on the verge of motion sickness by the time we left the vehicle, and moving on my own two feet immediately started to clear my head.

Before we left Lei had taken the opportunity to go shopping, and somehow managed to put together some appropriate clothing for us to wear on our trek through the jungle. They weren't military fatigues as much as tourist camo for camping, but they had the appropriate earth tones of khaki and olive green that would blend in to the surroundings if our situation called for it.

Larson provided the munitions as well as the Jeep, which he said belonged to Rogers', and he took the lead as we headed into the dense dark jungle. After about fifteen minutes Larson stopped and pulled out a handheld device that looked like a large cell phone.

"GPS says we are about a mile and a half from the coordinates on the map. Normally I'd say it'd take us the better part of half an hour to make it there, but in this terrain, we'll be lucky to cover it in two hours."

"No sense waiting around then," Lei chimed in with mock cheeriness, "Lead on!"

It turned out that it wasn't simply a case of a two-hour hike through the woods. Each of us ended up knee deep in the mud at one point or another, and it threatened to suck the boots right off our feet as we pulled ourselves out time after time. We also had to cross over several fast moving yet thankfully shallow creeks, and even climb down one short waterfall before we found some partially open terrain.

Larson stopped us as we reached the level ground and checked the GPS again, "Looks as though it will be just beyond the next tree line."

"How is it there could be a clearing like this in the middle of the jungle?" Lei asked while removing a boot to let out some of the accumulated river water."

"Don't!" Larson called out to her, but it was too late and Lei froze as she turned to look at him while holding her boot upside down.

"What?"

Larson grumbled something about amateurs, before he said with a certain degree of restraint in his voice, "You should have waited, now your feet will begin to swell and you may not get that boot back on comfortably."

Lei hurriedly tried to slip the book back on, but it was clear that Larson was right. She managed, but had to loosen the laces significantly before she appeared only partially satisfied with the way the boot fit.

"Should we eat now or wait until we get to the village?" I asked Larson, while Lei was struggling with her boot.

He thought for a second, "Well, we don't really know what kind of reception we are going to get in the village. I think we should eat some of the trail mix you guys brought, and maybe even try for a catnap. Better to be as fresh as possible when we get there."

"You expecting trouble?" Lei asked as she stomped down hard on the boot heel.

Larson ignored her animated display, "No, but we are arriving unannounced. These people could leave at any time and join the modern world in Bangkok, or some other city, but they choose to live out here in the sticks. To me that means they don't want any part of the modern life, and they may feel as though we are intruding. People never react well to having their domain intruded upon, so respectful caution is probably warranted."

It was just then that we heard a gunshot "boom" in the distance.

All three of us spun to look in the direction where the shot had sounded. It seemed to all of us as though the shot had been fired at the distant tree line, and it was also in the same general direction as the village. We were facing that direction as we looked stupidly at each other, and then all three of us broke into a run toward the source of the shot.

Chapter 29

Timberland had barely gotten the taste of smoke out of his mouth, since igniting the firebomb in the police morgue, before it was time for him to go back to work. The whole snatch and grab at the morgue ended up being simple enough. He and his team had simply bribed the usual policemen into letting them enter through the rear doors, that were normally reserved for the ambulances arriving with patients, or in this case corpses. The dead were normally taken into the morgue for autopsy, storage, and eventually were picked up by the doctor who served as the city's coroner. Of course, no one had realized it had been their intent to set the station ablaze, but sharing that information hadn't been in Timberland's plans. The fire was supposed to be a lesson to the police, letting them know that they needed to start holding up their end of the arrangement. In any case, the fire would char the corpses beyond any reliable identification and whatever information may have been gleaned from any completed autopsies would be destroyed when the fire reached the computer terminals in the adjoining office, so the mission was accomplished.

Now it was time to see to Whelan's missing guinea pig. Timberland planned to raze the village in order to see if Whelan's wayward pet was still holed up inside. They hadn't far to go as the village was only about five miles from their camp, so the team ran the entire distance. Truth be told, this was exactly what his people really needed, something more primitive and able to take them back to their roots, as opposed to a scrupulously planned and detailed raid. They were simply going to the village to seek their prey, and kill everyone who happened to be at the wrong place at the wrong time.

There were eleven of them in all and they encircled the village as they silently arrived. Eyes darting back and forth, targeting every soul that moved within their kill zone as the excitement of the blood sport that was about to come threatened to overwhelm their ability to remain civilized. Timberland could feel it too and knew that he couldn't hold his people back for long. They lived for the hunt. They lived for the kill. They were predators, and predators need prey.

Timberland watched as a middle-aged woman swept dust and debris out of what passed for her home. He would be the first to go in, the first to kill. It was his responsibility, as much as his right, and he focused on the woman who would fall beneath him, as the one to die at his hands before all others.

A quick whisper into his mouthpiece, and Timberland confirmed that the rest of his team were in place and ready.

"On my mark, breech the village."

Timberland readied himself to burst from the jungle and onto the woman before she could let out any sound of alarm. He had expected her to stay in her doorway, but she turned as if to go back inside. Then she bent over, with the sheer fabric of her dress clinging to her body, outlining the curves of her legs and waist.

Timberland smiled at the sight and thought, maybe there was more he could do beyond simply killing the woman. He ran from the tree line in a crouch and was closing the distance to the woman, when a child screamed from the other side of the village. The woman stood up quickly and turned to look at what was causing the commotion, but her eyes opened unnaturally wide when she saw Timberland coming at her, now at a full run with a K-bar in his hand.

He pushed for more speed, but instinctively ducked and rolled at the sound of a gunshot being fired. A bullet struck the woman in the chest and cut off her scream in an instant, and she was dead before her body hit the ground.

Timberland cursed and pulled his own Glock 23 from its holster. He had hoped to keep this entire exercise a quiet endeavor. Opting for the use of knives as opposed to guns was a kind of personal preference that he and the rest of his team shared. It was so much more satisfying to be able to look into the prey's eyes and really, truly feel the blade as it parted flesh and took life. Hearing the screams and moans undulate in a cacophony of sound as the blade is pulled free, and thrust back in over and over again drove directly into the core of what it meant to him to be a hunter and predator. Now that the scenario had lost the element of silence there was no reason to be quiet anymore and Timberland turned to see the rest of his people working their way inward from the perimeter they had created and it looked like all of them had abandoned their knives for their pistols.

Some of the villagers ran into their huts, while others had stuck their heads out just to see what was happening. A pair of older women began to corral the children and drive them into their various living quarters, while men ran toward the fallen woman carrying an assortment of sharp farming implements and machetes.

Timberland couldn't believe how quickly the scene had deteriorated into chaos, but it really didn't matter. They were here to kill everyone in the village, yet he hoped his people would remember they needed a couple of the villagers to question regarding Whelan's pet, just in case they didn't locate him in the village. Timberland fired a single round into each of two men who were running at him. One was holding a machete and instantly crumpled in a lifeless heap while the other continued to charge with what appeared to be a gardening hoe and took the round to his thigh. Other gunshots resounded and more people screamed as they feel into the dirt crying out in pain at the wounds the 40 caliber handguns were inflicting, when a sound echoed in Timberland's earpiece that he hadn't expected. One of his team screamed first in terror and then in pain before going silent leaving only static in the earpiece.

"Who was that?" one of the team called out.

"What just happened?" another one responded.

Timberland immediately took control, "Keep it together people. We know who and what we are up against. Looks like our target is still here. Pair up and complete your sweeps. All other targets are now expendable."

Timberland felt more than he heard the heavy footfalls behind him and he tried to spin into a shooter's crouch way too late, as an enormous blur slammed into him, lifting him off the ground and carrying him through the wall and into the nearest hut. The breath was driven from his chest, and the taste of blood filled his mouth as he crashed down through a bamboo table and into the ground.

The gun flew from his hand and he made no attempt to retrieve it as he felt for the knife at his side. He could still hear the sounds of his team members in his earpiece running to his aide as he pulled the blade from the sheath and drove the point into whatever was wrapped around his waist. The knife tip found it's mark and penetrated deeply into flesh causing the tightness around his core to release the pressure.

Whatever had him let go and Timberland rolled away to gain some distance between himself and his foe. It was, of course, Whelan's pet project, nearly seven feet tall and well over three hundred chiseled pounds of primal force. Timberland wasn't afraid, but instead felt the rush of adrenaline burst through him as he faced his enormous foe. He had his K-bar and years of training in hand to hand combat, while Whelan’s "Pet" had nothing beyond his size and hardened skin. Timberland also knew he had reinforcements who would be beside him in seconds, while this medical monstrosity he hated stood alone.

Timberland let out a battle cry that was more of a roar than an actual word, and lunged with the knife, but to his surprise, the enormous figure just lazily slapped it aside, and with enough force to potentially break bone. Timberland backed away and readied himself for an attack when the first of his team arrived at the ruined wall of the hut. The "Pet" spun away from Timberland and grabbed the new arrival by his gun arm, wrenching downward and dislocated the man's shoulder. Timberland could hear his teammates joint pop as the gun dropped harmlessly to the floor. His teammate screamed in pain, but only for the briefest of moments as the giant encircled the man's neck with his left arm, twisted and squeezed. The sound of the man's neck breaking was more like the sound of bubble wrap being popped than a crunch or repetitive crackling. Timberland didn't wait to watch the aftermath but dove for the fallen gun, grabbed it and aimed to fire when a foot from the giant caught him in the chest to send him soaring backward through the rear thatched and broken wall of the hut.

This time when Timberland sat up he spat a mouthful of blood onto the pieces of the hut that surrounded him and watched as the "Pet" turned to confront the rest of his team as they charged in.

***

Lei and I ran as fast as we could but, due to our inexperience of traveling over such wild terrain, we couldn't pick out the easiest path in order to keep up with Larson. He was nearly thirty yards ahead of us when he reached the tree line and disappeared into its foliage. As Lei and I reached the edge of the tree line we heard the report of a pair of gunshots that sent us to cover and stopped us in our tracks. Quickly we looked at one another to make sure neither of us had been struck by a bullet, and cautiously proceeded into the tangle of jungle trees, resuming our trek toward where we believed the village to be.

It only took a minute to see the outline of the village beyond the trees and Lei and I crouched behind a large, gnarled, and exposed root to watch as people darted back and forth between their thatch huts or scurried to get away, leaving at least one man lay twitching on the ground.

Something from the corner of the village was crawling out of the ruins of what must have been a former hut, and then limped back and into the cover of the trees that surrounded the village. Less than five feet in front of us came another gunshot from where Larson had taken up position to fire. I had to blink in surprise as, despite how close he was to where Lei and I crouched, I never would have known he was there. The man was very, very good at his job, regardless of his injuries.

I pointed out the man escaping into the trees to Lei, "I'm going after that one, let's see if we can take one alive. You help Larson with the crowd control."

Lei didn't even bother to nod her understanding, as she immediately moved forward toward Larson until the Special Forces commander held up a fist for her to stop. Once I realized that Larson was aware of Lei, I made my way around the jungle trees in the hope of cutting off the escaping...whomever he was.

***

Timberland worked his way painfully to the edge of the village and turned to see how his men were faring against the freak when, suddenly, one of the team jerked wildly to the side and fell as a gunshot exploded from the other side of the village. All heads turned to look where the shot had originated, but no one from the village could be seen. The shot had apparently come from the far side of the village near or past the tree line but it wasn't until the second shot rang out and another one of his people fell dead to the ground that Timberland realized he wasn't dealing with an armed villager. The shots were too well placed for any farmer.

Then an unfamiliar Caucasian man wearing military camouflage while aiming an AR-15 moved out of the tree line and knelt to fire another round. Timberland watched as a third member of his team crumpled when his head burst as the round blew the side of it away. The remaining six members of his personal security team opened fire, forcing the new arrival to take cover back in the trees, as a barrage of bullets headed his way.

Timberland tapped his earpiece and found it to be miraculously still functional despite his many trips through the walls of the hut.

"Unknown hostiles have engaged! Retreat to the compound and regroup!" Timberland yelled the order and watched as each of his team immediately changed direction, heading for the tree line that they had originally come out of. One of his team, a woman who was a particularly wonderful marksman, slipped on some loose dirt and was grabbed by the giant freak before she could regain her footing. Without effort or consideration the freak tossed her bodily back toward the center of the village with such force that she bounced several times before coming to a stop almost thirty yards back and away.

He considered moving to help, but suddenly was mesmerized by another stranger who ran from the forest and charged at the fallen woman. The stranger was also woman, looking more like she belonged in a red California lifeguard's swimsuit, as opposed to the hiking gear she was wearing, but when she reached his teammate the sight turned so surreal that Timberland couldn't turn away. The woman literally leapt onto his fallen teammate and began clawing at her with her fingers like she was some kind of a bear. It looked comical until larger and larger streaks of blood began flying with every slash. It was just too much to take in, so Timberland followed his own orders, retreating into the jungle. He had barely made it into the trees when his path was cut off by another man, also dressed in what looked like urban hiking gear.

"And where do you think you're going?" the man said almost laughingly as he blocked Timberland's path.

It didn't take a genius' intellect for Timberland to realize he was going to have to go through this man, as opposed to around him. He reached first for his sidearm, which wasn't in its holster, and then for the K-bar that he had managed to slip back into its sheath, before he was kicked in the chest.

Timberland crouched down and spread his arms wide in preparation for his attack, while the man in hiking gear shifted his feet and circled to the right. Timberland knew that each of them were looking for the opening that would give them an advantage. Timberland saw the opportunity he was looking for as the man in the hiking gear stumbled ever so slightly on an exposed tree root, and he leapt forward with a snarl while slashing with the knife. Unable to dodge or shuffle out of the way, the man was forced to block the oncoming knife with his arm. Timberland tried to twist the edge of the knife around to slash the man's arm as he pulled the blade back in, but the man had regained his footing and spun back and out of range. Timberland didn't let the man rest, as he darted forward, feigning a strike at the face, but shifting mid-strike to drive the point of his knife in low for an incapacitating wound at the opponent's legs.

The man seemed to take the bait as he lifted his arms to block the strike at his face, but moments before Timberland would have driven the blade of his knife to the hilt into the man's thigh, the man lifted his leg and leaned back allowing the knife to pass harmlessly through empty air.

Panic filled Timberland as he realized he had overextended his thrust and was caught off balance as the man pivoted and brought the heel of his boot back down and around in a powerful kick. Timberland did the only thing his momentum would allow and he rolled forward past the oncoming booted foot and into the man. The man's leg did strike his head, but the blow came more from the thigh are as opposed to the heel or shin, which reduced the power behind the impact. Unfortunately Timberland was also too close to properly slash or stab with his knife, so he pushed off with his legs, driving his shoulder into the man's abdomen and sending him to the jungle floor.

Timberland immediately fell on top of the man driving his knife straight for the man's throat. The man saw the attack coming and twisted so the knife drove deep into the soft earth beneath the spot where his body had been. Then the man's hand whipped out and grabbed at Timberland's wrist just as the knife was pulled free of the ground and Timberland shifted to point it at the man's face. He pressed down on the knife with the point mere inches from the man's eye, but the man beneath him was so strong that the blade made no further downward progress. Timberland tried to shift his weight as he lay on top of the man and he put his other hand behind the blade to add the extra force of both arms and even more of his body weight behind the stab. Yet incredibly, despite the added leverage, the man beneath him compensated for the difference and started to push his way out from under the point of the blade. The knife rose slowly away from the man's eye and Timberland growled as he desperately tried to push the blade back down again.

***

It was all I could do to keep the knife away from my face as I held onto the guy's wrist and kept him from stabbing me in the face. Then he started thrashing around like a wild animal, which lessened the direct downward pressure but made it even more difficult to hold on to him.

What was going on? I should have been able to take this guy apart, but he was moving faster than a regular human and also seemed stronger than his physical appearance would have otherwise suggested. I could hear Lei calling out to me from the distance, and I supposed that the rest of the people who were strangers to the village had retreated, but that didn't help me in my current predicament.

I brought my leg up and wrapped it around the man's waist

while shifting my weight and rolled both of us over. It was a neat little trick I had learned from one of the martial art instructors at the police academy, and it left me sitting ontop of my opponent in a dominant position. The quick shift in leverage had also enabled me to pin his wrist to the ground and I raised my fist for the punch that would have sent him to sleep when his head darted to the hand which I was enforcing the pin, and he sank his teeth into my forearm.

I cried out with more shock than pain, and couldn't help but to see a beast pinned beneath me, instead of a man. He took advantage of my moment of confusion and managed to kick me off of his body sending me rolling down the path and away from him. I deliberately rolled with the force of my fall, and sprang to my knees in preparation for the attack I was sure was coming, but the man was gone.

I stood and ran forward a few steps, but quickly stopped to listen for the sounds of the guy running through the dense foliage and giving away his position, but all I could hear was the background sounds of Lei and Larson, as they called out to me from the village.

I looked down to my arm and saw a perfect semi-circle of teeth marks where the guy had bitten me. The bite was deep and it bled a little, but I ignored it as my particular physiology left me insusceptible to infection, which is what normally would be the only concern. I tore apiece of my shirt away and wrapped the bite to staunch the bleeding in any case.

Lei called out again and I answered with a quick, "I'm okay!"

I was going to turn and walk back to the village but couldn't keep myself from taking one last look into the trees. That guy had been too strong, too quick and too...what? My head searched for the right word, but all I could come up with was, “wild.”

He clearly had been well trained, but I still should have been more than a match for him, yet he had held his own against me without much difficulty.

What the hell was going on?

Chapter 30

I wandered back into the village, as many of its inhabitants began emerging from wherever they had been hiding. I watched as mothers hugged their children and men gathered in small groups over the bodies of the men Larson had shot. They were whispering to each other, and then looking at us, before turning to what might have been the largest man I had ever seen, both in height and stature, who was moving gracefully throughout the village. Once my eyes had settled upon the man I couldn't look away. Even Lei, who was perched like a bird of prey over the woman she had subdued, couldn't maintain my attention. The guy was even bigger than Alpha, who was one of the most imposing figures that anyone could ever hope to gaze upon.

It wasn't just the man's size. I had seen athletes, basketball players mostly, who grew to such proportions, but there was an air about him that simply couldn't be ignored. He also seemed strangely familiar to me, but I quickly brushed that thought aside as I saw Larson slowly approaching the giant.

Larson kept his weapon trained on the man, but his eyes weren't focused on aiming as he made his way forward. The giant saw him coming and froze, hands clenched in fists, and his whole body tense as if ready to spring.

Finally, when he was less than ten feet from the man, Larson lowered the rifle and his voice cracking as he said, "Zach?"

The giant looked surprised at the name and his head tilted in a fashion similar to the way dogs will tilt their heads when confused.

"Zach, it's Rob," Larson engaged the safety on his rifle and let it hang loosely in his hand as he spoke to the giant. I watched nervously as Larson came within striking distance of the massive arms the giant possessed.

Larson had apparently found his friend, but the reality that the man who stood in front of him may no longer be the same friend he had known previously didn't seem to register with Larson.

I looked to Lei, who looked back, as if asking if this was the man we had come to find, I shrugged my shoulders and took a step in her direction. As soon as I moved the giant swung his head in my direction, and I got a clear look at the man's eyes.

I gasped at the sight, because those eyes didn't look human. They were blood red where the whites should have been, and the circle of each eye, that should have been his iris and pupils, were totally black. I felt a fear erupt from somewhere inside of me unlike anything I had ever felt before, and in that moment, I was more terrified than I had ever been in my life. I wanted to run away, or fall to my knees and curl up in a ball to hide. But instead I just stepped back and looked over to Lei who had been watching me. The color had drained from her face when she saw my reaction, and she immediately turned to see what had affected me so. When she realized what I had seen her reaction was even more severe than mine, and as I watched she encircled her arms around her middle and begin to shiver.

It was an old woman who broke the spell for all of us. I remembered having heard her voice in the background, calling out to her people who had begun to follow the commands and requests she had been giving to them. Then she walked right up to the giant and took his hand with Larson watching her curiously, as she pulled the big man the couple of steps closer to stand in front of him.

"Drop rifle on dirt," she recommended quietly and with authority to Larson.

Larson didn't have the rifle raised and he looked confused, but the woman spoke again in the same severely broken English, "He is focus on rifle. Can't see you, only it."

Larson looked from the old woman to the man he called Zach and shrugged his shoulders while dropping the rifle where it landed softly on the ground. Instantly the giant reacted and looked to the rifle and then back up to Larson's face. A smile broke out over the big man's face and his mouth began to move as if trying to speak, without being able to form the words. Larson began smiling as well as he walked forward and extended his hand to the giant. The man, Zach, looked at the hand and extended his own. Larson's hand disappeared completely inside the giant's who was smiling fiercely as he pulled Larson in and embraced him in a manly hug, complete with slaps on the back, and a sound that I took to be a laugh.

Larson accepted the hug , but was letting out grunts of pain with every back slap he received. When Zach finally let him go Larson seemed to finally notice the man's eyes. He had a much less visible reaction than Lei or I had, but it was clear from how his smile faded and his expression turned to concern that it did have an effect on him.

"Oh Zach, what did they do to you man?"

"Come," the old woman said, "we talk."

Chapter 31

The five of us sat around a small fire inside one of the huts as the woman, who we were guessing was possibly the village elder or something akin to that, made us tea. Every time one of us tried to speak she would shush us and tell us to wait until the tea was ready.

Larson was staring at the man he knew as Zach, who happened to have nearly every inch of his skin marred by scar tissue that looked only recently healed. His face was spared to a degree, but there was still evidence of trauma that made it clear his visage wasn't completely unscathed.

When the kettle started to whistle, the steam erupting from its spout made a little cloud, the old woman removed the tea and expertly shifted the kettle to each of us and poured the precise amount into a small bamboo cup. Larson, Lei and I all stared with fascination at her casual catering to our needs, before she ended her formalities by sitting down next to Zach and patting his knee.

"So," she began in heavily accented English, "we thank you for help against demons, but you not here for them, yes?"

Demons? I thought, what did she mean by that?

Larson spoke before I could ask, "Yes, we came to find Zach," and he pointed to the big man who began to sway as he knelt before the fire. The old woman kept her hand on his knee and inclined her head in Larson's direction.

"Why you want find my son?"

That statement left everyone speechless.

"Ho! I ask question," the old woman had sounded protective of Zach when she had called him "Son." Now she sounded as if she was getting angry at us.

Larson found his tongue first, "Sorry, but...your son?" He looked at Zach who began to slump his body forward as if fighting off falling asleep, "I'm sorry ma'am, but I don't understand."

"Shah, shah, shah..." the woman waved her hand in apparent disgust, as she rose and shuffled her feet to a small set of drawers that appeared to have been carved from the trees that surrounded the village. There were only two drawers in the piece and she opened the top drawer and felt around inside. We could hear pieces of metal or glass clinking softly together as she manipulated her hand inside the drawer, before she closed the top drawer and opened the bottom one. Her hand dipped inside and immediately pulled out a manila envelope, holding it to her chest with one hand as she closed the drawer with the other.

She shuffled back over to the fire and tossed the envelope to Larson.

"This tell you," she said cryptically and I guessed that she wanted to let the envelope's contents explain because she lacked the ability to express herself properly in English.

Larson looked at the envelope, but set it aside and asked, "Can you tell us what happened to him?"

Lei leaned over and took the envelope from where Larson had set it down. Larson shot Lei a glance as she took it, but she calmed him quickly enough by saying, "Ask your questions while I look through this. I won't take anything."

Larson's face softened, and he turned back to the woman as Lei opened the envelope and removed the contents.

The old woman had been watching Lei carefully throughout the exchange and, when the moment had ended she smiled warmly at Lei as if understanding some kind of silent joke.

"Ma'am," Larson's attention had returned to the woman and he pointed to his friend, "Do you know what happened to Zach?"

"Yes, I know," she said quickly and confidently, "but he tell you himself...in moment," Zach flopped forward and then fell over sideways from the kneeling position he had been in. The woman didn't catch him as he fell on her as much as she guided him to the ground.

Larson jumped forward and immediately checked his friend for a pulse, "What happened? Is he wounded?" I moved to the opposite side of the giant and looked him over.

"No sign of any injury beyond the single knife wound at his shoulder," I called out.

"Then what the..."

The old woman was waving her hands and speaking in Thai, which although we couldn't understand her language, she was clearly saying and indicating that we should all calm down.

"I give him much tea," she pointed at the kettle, "He should be ready to tell what happened to him and Pha."

"Pha?" I asked out loud without really meaning to, "Who's Pha?"

A heart-wrenching groan came from behind me and I turned to see Lei as she dropped the papers she had removed from the envelope and clutched her midsection.

Fearing the worst I moved from my position next to Zach, and was holding onto Lei in less than the span of a heartbeat.

"What is it?" I momentarily thought the old woman had poisoned us, but Lei looked up at me and her eyes were filled with tears that just began to fall. Her whole body was shaking with the effort she was expending to keep from crying and I suddenly realized that no poison could have had that effect on her.

She tried to speak, but couldn't without breaking down and instead pointed to the papers on the floor. Larson and I looked to each other before he went back to caring for his friend while I gently lifted the stapled papers off the floor.

The first few documents were in Thai and appeared very similar to the ones that we had seen earlier regarding his "purchase" of the child.

When I flipped past the last page that was written in Thai and saw the words written in English that were centered on the top of the page in bold typeface all the breath left my lungs in a manner similar to Lei.

"What is it?!" Larson called out in frustration.

I turned sadly to him and looked down at the big man who now lay unconscious on the floor.

My voice was barely a whisper as I said softly, "It's a legal document applying for a permanent naturalization certificate.

Larson frowned, "He applied for a green card? For who?"

"For the girl in the snapshot...Pha."

"But if he had already legally established her as his ward, why would he..."

I held up the papers so Larson could see the words on the top of the page and his eyes went wide as he read the header, "Application for Adoption."

"He wasn't taking her back to the states as a ward or some kind of sex slave," I said gravely, "He adopted her and was taking her back as his daughter."

"My grand-daughter," the old woman said with a sorrowful pride in her voice, "He now Pha's papa, that make him my son."

I felt Lei lean into me and, although she didn't make a sound, I knew she was crying. Lei had told me several times how she had prayed every night as a child that any one of the "clients" she "entertained" would take a special interest in her, and buy her out of the life she was in. Even the more sadistic ones would have been preferable to the life with the Triad. She tried to make her clients fall in love with her by doing more than they asked of her, no matter what that might have been, but it never worked. They always left and tipped her manager/pimp handsomely for her efforts. It made her a favorite, but didn't improve her life, and instead of appreciating her they just made her work more and beat her if she said she was too tired or sore.

Then one night a man arrived at the brothel clad all in black leather, with skin and hair as white as a ghost. She had never seen anyone like that before and was initially afraid of him until he unexpectedly requested to pay off her debt so she would be allowed to leave with him immediately. Confused by the man's interest, since he had never been a client, she nonetheless found a glimmer of hope that her long ago prayers had been answered. When the triad refused to accept money for her debt, she had started to cry softly and decided to finally follow through with a plan to end her life. She had been contemplating it for months, and now, with her last hope seemingly gone, she decided to go through with it.

It was the sound of raised voices that drew her attention back to the white haired man as the manager tried to force Alpha to leave. The raised voice of the manager had alerted several of the triad men, who began filling into the room, brandishing long knives. Alpha had only smiled, before he slaughtered every single triad in the building.

It had all happened so quickly that Lei only remembered how red the blood had looked as it streaked across Alpha's porcelain white hand when he gently extended it to her. She took it, her hand small and shaky as it came to rest in his, and they walked out of the brothel together, forever leaving her old life behind. Lei could remember in realistic detail how mangled the bodies of the triad were, as she and Alpha stepped over them, but the horror she might have felt by the bloody scene never came. Only the elation of finally being free made her legs feel weak. She had collapsed then, and Alpha lifted her into his arms, carrying her away to her new life with the people she and Steven now knew as their family. Lei had been in the life since infancy and was forever grateful to Alpha for having saved her, but the life had scarred her in ways that would never fully heal.

I knew that this man Zach, in Lei's eyes, had suddenly become a hero of epic proportion. He was the answer to the prayers that Lei had as a child, except that he had answered the prayers of another little girl, and he had done it before the child was forced to endure the years of rape, torture and humiliation that Lei had endured.

I gently ran my fingers through the length of her long black hair and caressed her head as she wept into my chest.

"I would have killed him," Lei whispered in between sobs, "I wanted to kill him. I was only waiting until the right time, when he was away from Larson and the old woman."

I put my arms back around her and held her tight, "I know. It's all right."

Lei shook her head against me, "No, it's not. Can you even begin to understand what I would have done? What would have happened if I had gone through with it and then learned all of this after it was done?"

A little chill went through me because I know how Lei can get. She takes her kills personally, and even though I had seen it first-hand several times, I've never gotten used to it.

I took a deep breath and hoped that it might subconsciously influence Lei to do the same.

I whispered, "You're under the blood influence, and feeling everything more than you normally would."

Lei tried to argue but I cut her off, "You haven't hurt him, so there's no need to feel guilt over what you would have done." I felt Lei's body stop shaking as I spoke, and her breathing began to return from ragged sobs to a more normal cadence.

I put my fingertips under her chin and gently lifted her face up to look into mine, "We have a chance to help him, and get revenge on this man, for what he did to him...and to us."

Lei's eyes narrowed and there was a kind of twinkle in them, perhaps at the thought of what she was going to do to Whelan when we found him. Involuntarily I winced at her expression, and Lei smiled wickedly at me, knowing what I had realized.

I have never wanted someone dead as badly as I wanted Dr. Phineas Whelan dead, but knowing Lei the way I do, I couldn't help but think, God help the poor bastard when she gets a hold of him.

Larson was still tending to Zach, unsure of what to do.

"How are we going to get him out of here?"

"He not ready to go yet," the old woman informed us.

Larson wasn't listening, "So do we take him to a hospital or to Rogers' doc?

Lei and I turned to Larson not sure how to answer. So where was this Pha? And how were we going to get answers we needed if the guy couldn't speak?

Chapter 32

"Ask me what you need know, I tell you," the old woman said as she moved away from the fire and made her way over to where the giant of a man had flopped onto his side.

The three of us sat quietly for a moment, looking to one another for enlightenment, and thoroughly confused by what was apparently transpiring.

"What do we ask first?" Lei volunteered.

"Ask where Whelan is," I said immediately.

Larson tried to say something when the old lady closed her eyes and placed her hands on each side of Zach's head. Initially she looked to be supporting him, but when she didn't let go, and made a grimace with her face that appeared to be an effort of concentration, we could tell there was more going on than what we could see with just our eyes.

The old woman answered us in her normal heavily accented English, "He say there several people who look like doctors in prison camp. No names, but one in charge usually in underground. Spend most of time there."

The woman stopped talking for a moment and opened her eyes to look down with sorrow at the face of the man whose head she cradled. Her voice sounded slightly choked when she started talking again, "The one in charge is who kill Pha."

Lei, Larson and I all suddenly sat up straight in total shock. We hadn't expected the girl to be dead, in fact, we hadn't even known she was involved beyond anything more than being a means to find Zach. Now it appeared that she was more than a side note in whatever was happening.

Lei looked as though someone had let all the air out of her and she wrapped her arms around herself and turned away from the rest of us. I placed a hand on her shoulder, just to let her know I was aware of her pain, but I was also giving her the space she needed.

Larson looked crestfallen as well, although he tried to maintain a professional demeanor when he asked, "What happened?"

The old woman sighed, "They torture him," she began, "Never ask questions or want anything, just hurt and hurt, more and more, but he never break. Until..."

She went silent as she caressed Zach's face and stroked her fingers through his hair.

"Until what, ma'am?" I tried to ask gently, as the answer was clearly going to be something significant, and very, very bad.

"Until they begin use electric," the old woman whispered and tears began falling from her eyes, "So much pain. Couldn't fight now, but they still not ask questions. The one in charge, he get upset. He get angry that something not working, so then they bring Pha."

"What?!...How did they ever...?" I began to say, but the answer was obvious. They probably found her at Zach's apartment. After all, they knew the address and had undoubtedly gone looking for something to use against him. The girl might have been a surprise, but they guessed right when they took her with them back to the camp.

"They bring her to lab and one in charge threaten to kill her," the tears were falling freely now as the old woman seemed to relive the event as it happened, "He beg them ask what they want. He tell anything. He do anything, but no hurt girl. The one in charge just laugh and then...cut..." the woman stopped and lifted her hand away from his head and covered her own face as she began to sob.

Lei had turned around and moved across the room to the woman's side and embraced her as together they cried. Larson and I just looked at the three of them, not wanting to say anything, because there were no words that could possibly be appropriate in this particular moment.

"He broke then," the woman continued as Lei held her, "for first time since there, he scream...and then, something inside him just shut down, and he die."

I had been looking at the floor of the hut, but my eyes came up at that last part.

"Die? What do you mean he died?" I asked.

The old woman opened her eyes and turned to face me, "Die...like dead."

Larson and I looked at each other, confused.

"Ma'am," Larson started, "I'm sorry, but I don't understand. Zach isn't dead."

"Not now," the woman shook her head as she spoke, "They bring him back with electric, but now he not same. He come back and not person anymore. Chains not hold him and he start to kill. Try to kill one in charge, but stopped. Guards shoot him, kill him again and then, once again, doctor bring him back. Then they change him, put things under skin make stronger. Put things in blood too, but not fix mind."

I leaned over and whispered to Larson, "Do you have any idea what she's talking about?"

He shook his head, "It sounds a little like a brainwashing technique."

I raised my eyebrows, "That stuff is for real? I thought it was all just fiction."

"I thought vampires were just fiction."

I screwed up my face and said, ironically, "Touché."

"Sorry," Larson continued, "Not the right time or place, I know. Anyway, the whole practice of brainwashing for military application was deemed unreliable, so most of the work in that particular field was abandoned, but it still did exist. It really isn't all that dissimilar to hypnosis, but operates on a much deeper psychic level. Although I have never heard of anyone going to such lengths to pull it off."

"Why?"

"Because the subject is at too great a risk of dying." Larson turned and looked at Zach, "I guess that wasn't much of a deterrent in this case."

"So what you're saying is, that in order to achieve the kind of results that might be reliable, a normally unacceptable risk had to be taken?"

"Basically, yes. According to the little information I know, all the research was stifled by the fact that to make further progress, within the science, there would be a need to put the subject into mortal peril. There was some thought about using inmates and prisoners, but the scandal proved too horrendous for anyone to personally accept the responsibility."

"So if someone could work without concern for the wellbeing of the subject, then...?"

Larson nodded, "Then he might be able to achieve results that are comparable only to what has been written about in fiction."

I shook my head, "Goddamn Whelan...the bastard is turning into a twenty first century's Doctor Mengele."

Larson nodded, "The question is, why? What were they programming him to do or become?"

"Not to mention," I added, "why my client is so interested in him."

Chapter 33

Silence reigned in the hut, but the somber moment seemed to be fading as the women parted, their crying over, and Zach began to shift around on the floor as if waking up.

Lei moved across the floor, sat down next to me and asked, "So what do we do now?"

"We got what we came for," Larson answered with a sigh, "Mission complete."

Lei and I turned, eyeing him as he casually picked up his rifle, checked to see if it was loaded, ratcheted a round in the chamber and it was ready to fire. The threat was anything but subtle, yet Larson didn't raise the rifle, but instead held it loosely in his hand, ready to use in case it turned out to be necessary.

I never took threats well and stood to face Larson, "You got what you came for, but we aren't done."

"My part of this was finding Zach, that's it."

"And those men who came to the village?" Lei was standing now as well, and was slowly circling around Larson as she spoke, making it difficult for him to target both of us simultaneously, in case it turned out to be necessary.

"You know," Lei continued her thought, "the ones who were responsible for Zach's kidnapping, torture and murder of his child."

Larson didn't answer, but he didn't back down either.

"We are here for the man responsible for what was done to Zach," I pointed at Larson's friend and hoped that whatever the ancient woman had done for him had cleared his mind enough so that Zack could understand me. "And we don't want to get him because of what was done to Zach, although I admit it does add fuel to that particular fire, but because of what he did to us and to our people."

"You said that your client wants Zach brought to him, like a piece of lost property."

I laughed, "My client is every bit the sadistic animal that Whelan is and I'm not doing anything here for his benefit."

"But you still plan on delivering Zach to him?"

I shrugged, "That's up to Zach. I agreed to find him and extricate him from Dr. Whelan's compound. What he does from this point on was never up to me."

Larson frowned, and I couldn't tell if that was because he was surprised by my statement, or for some other reason known only to him and his people, but he asked. "Why does he want Zach?"

"I never asked. I didn't care then, and I don't care now. This is about stopping Whelan."

"Really?" Larson cocked and eyebrow at me, "Stop him from doing what?"

I opened my mouth to answer, but realized that I didn't have one.

"I don't know," and I turned to Zach, "I don't suppose you could shed a little light here?"

Zach had sat up and was looking around the room with those strange red eyes. He faced me, but he didn't answer.

"Back to the silent treatment?" Lei joked.

The old woman joined the conversation, "He cannot say. His mind not ready, but it fix itself slowly. He talk soon."

"How soon?" I asked and the woman only shrugged her shoulders in response.

Larson looked at each of us and began to walk to the door, "Let's get started, it's going to take us a while to get back to the Jeep."

I stepped in front of him, "I don't think we have resolved our little...difference in opinion."

Larson bounced the rifle a little bit as it rested in his hands, "No we haven't, but do you think it would it be possible to hash all this out back in the city? You know the place, where there is indoor plumbing and real mattresses?"

"And what if those men come back?" Lei asked, "We can't just leave the village undefended."

I agreed with Lei, "She's right, they'll be back and this time they be loaded for bear."

Larson's stance wavered a little, "I know, and we were successful against them this time because they were taken by surprise. Next time they'll be ready for us and, with what we currently possess as far as weapons are concerned, we'll get slaughtered if we take them on like this."

"We?" I said reflexively, and my mood was suddenly lifted. Apparently, Larson wasn't as ready to abandon us as completely as I had thought.

Lei had heard the slip as well, "So what you're saying is..."

Larson scowled and looked disappointed, but he said, "We can dip into Rogers' stash and, maybe, he'll have access to something that might even the odds."

I smiled, "Doesn't the United States Government frown on the distribution of armaments to non-military personnel?"

"Officially or unofficially?" Larson said with heavy sarcasm in his voice. I laughed at the innuendo.

"So again I ask, what's the plan?" Lei asked.

Larson turned to Lei and said, "We'll get back to the city and I'll head to Rogers' place to gather the crates while you three take Zach to the medics at the restaurant, and see if he needs his shoulder patched up."

A snapping sound came from where Zach had been sitting, and we all turned to look at him. He was gone.

Larson looked at the spot where he had been lying, "What the hell?"

The old woman spoke up, "My son stay and protect village. He get people to safety."

Larson had started to walk to where Zach had been, but stopped and looked at the old woman. He appeared as though he was about to say something, but then dropped his head and said, "Always the goddamn protector. Yeah, that sounds like Zach."

"You sure you want to leave him?" Lei asked when Larson changed direction and headed for the door.

"I know my friend and, even though he can't tell me so, he wouldn't want to leave these people completely vulnerable. C'mon, let's go already," Larson still seemed a little cranky, but I felt confident that we were still on the same team...for now anyway.

***

The trek back to the Jeep didn't take as long on the return trip, or at least it didn't seem as long. It can be hard to tell when you know where you're going, as opposed to looking for your destination. In any case, it was just before noon when Larson pulled the Jeep up to the front of our hotel.

Larson watched as Lei and I climbed out of the Jeep and said to us, "I'm going to get whatever gear I can from Rogers' place and come back as quickly as I can."

"We'll be here," I said as I gave the Jeep's windshield a quick rap and Larson drove back into the humid afternoon streets of Bangkok.

We took the elevator up to our room and, as I slid the key card into the slot and looking forward to a hot shower, with as much sleep as I could manage to squeeze in before Larson came back with more guns and whatever. The instant I walked into the room I sensed something out of place, something was wrong. I froze putting out my arm to prevent Lei from walking past me. She initially had a confused look on her face, but caught on immediately, and pulled out the Glock that had traveled back from the village with her.

I went in first, and could hear the speakers of the TV were producing the unmistakable voice of Jack Nicholson, who was in the middle of some long-winded dialog meant to enthrall his audience, but that was of no interest to me as I moved further into through the door. The room was laid out in typical motel fashion, and as you enter, the closet and bathrooms are on either side of a small hallway leading into the bedroom. I carefully walked past the closet area in order to get a better view of the room and saw someone sitting on the bed. I hadn't been particularly quiet as I unlocked and opened the door so it would have been a surprise if he hadn't heard me. I just assumed he had, and then the size of the man registered, as did the long white hair flowing past his shoulders and draping over the back of his dark overcoat.

What the hell? I thought.

"Alpha?!" I nearly spat the name out in surprise. As Lei heard me, she immediately pushed past and, with a huge smile on her face while giggling like a little girl, ran in and jumped into his outstretched arms. Alpha's eyes sparkled initially, but were concerned when he saw the gun she was holding. She had flung her full weight at him, and it was all he could do to catch her and not be knocked backwards off the far side of the bed.

"And hello to you too, beautiful one," Alpha still talked with an accent, but it was very difficult to determine the exact origin of it, "Now do you plan to shoot me or smother me?"

Lei, reminded of the gun she was still holding, said in a voice that sounded around ten years old, "Oopsie."

I walked fully into the room and extended a hand to Alpha, who shook it firmly continuing to smile that peculiar smile of his. It almost made you miss the fact he wasn't wearing his contacts.

Alpha's real name is, Count Alphonso Diemo and yes, he's a real count, or "Comte" as his title is actually pronounced, and bestowed upon him by King Richard of France and Navarre. He is the founder and leader of our little family and stands nearly six and a half feet tall and wears long sleeves year round to protect his alabaster skin, yet he still looks more like an elf out of Lord of the

Rings, than a powerful vampire Lord.

Except of course, for his eyes, which are completely black, and I don't just mean his irises and pupils either. It looks as though the entire contents of his eye sockets were replaced by Hematite spheres. That strange metallic black stone is the closest thing I know of to match the appearance of Alpha's eyes now. It sounds unnerving I know, but on Alpha it has more the appearance of the eyes of a stag, as opposed to a shark or an alien. I remembered Alpha as having beautiful, amber-colored eyes for as long as I knew him, but that was prior to the change. Why they changed no one knew, but Alpha suspected that it was due to his advancing age. He was one of the oldest of our kind, and that meant there were a great many unknowns when it came to his future, and what would happen to him, or us, over time.

"I may not be a real policeman anymore, but I'm pretty sure you are breaking and entering, Alpha."

"Nonsense," Alpha said as he straightened his clothes, which had become disarrayed from Lei's uninhibited pounce, "I didn't break anything."

"What about entering?"

Alpha laughed, "Didn't you know, a vampire can't cross a threshold without being invited? And, since I am already in your room, it stands to reason you already invited me in."

I laughed, "That would makes sense if the whole threshold thing wasn't complete bullshit."

Alpha nodded and laughed as well, "True enough. I still love the concept."

The three of us had finished exchanging pleasantries, and Alpha asked, "So, where is the person that Russian Devil, Dimitri, is so interested in?"

I sat in a chair and kicked off my shoes, "We left him at the village where we found him."

Alpha looked confused, "I thought you needed him to direct

you to Whelan's exact location?"

I nodded, "We do, but he's..." I thought about how best to explain things without dragging it out forever by creating confusion, "not himself at the moment."

"Oh?"

Lei readily agreed with me, "He's definitely different."

Alpha was still smiling, "Any idea why Dimitri is so interested in him?"

"They did something to him back at that place where they held him," I shook my head, "but what was done, or why, we have no clue."

Alpha shrugged, "So tell me about him."

I started to describe him, and Alpha listened happily at first, but as I continued to describe not only Zach's physical appearance, but the way he made you feel when he was around you, Alpha began to take on a more serious expression. I used the cliché', "gives you a chill, like someone walking over your grave." and Alpha went from being interested, to looking uncomfortable and somewhat drawn. I was describing what little I had seen in the way Zach had fought the mercenaries at the camp and Alpha reacted as though he might fall over.

Lei moved to his side and steadied him, "What is it?"

"Are you all right?" I had moved to catch him as well when he looked like he might topple over. It was alarming to see. Alpha may have white hair, but he is not frail. His strength and dexterity are near superhuman, which he would say was another of the benefits of being so long lived, and he was not prone to dizzy spells or otherwise.

"I...I'm fine," Alpha was breathing fast and Lei looked pleadingly at me to do something. I had no idea what to do, but Alpha seemed to read my mind and said, "It's fine children. You just reminded me of someone I knew long, long ago."

"An enemy?" Lei asked.

Alpha shook his head, "Far from it. My closest friend."

Lei and I instantly knew to whom Alpha was referring.

Alpha's first and best friend William, who shared the condition affecting all of our kind. The two had met while both were suffering the madness and together they had run rampant all over Europe, killing indiscriminately and were every bit the monsters that legend would have you believe. That continued until Alpha, for reasons that elude us to this day, began to come out of the madness. He was the first of our kind ever to do so, at least as far as we knew, and somehow he managed to bring William back from the brink as well. After that the pair devoted their lives to the search for our kind in order to rescue them from themselves, and hopefully before they hurt anyone else.

Happy to change the subject Lei asked, "So what are you doing here Papa?"

Alpha wasn't really Lei's father, but they had taken on the whole father/daughter thing after he had saved her so many years ago. Truth be told I pretty much considered Alpha my father as well, which made my relationship with Lei especially kinky in some ways, but as none of us were actually blood relatives, there was no harm. Lei and I never considered each other to be siblings and the whole relationship started out with Lei trying to manipulate me with her sex appeal. She was successful, just not in the way she had intended. We became instant friends, later best friends, and later still, lovers. It wasn't until a gross misunderstanding had come between us that we spent any time apart. OK, mostly a misunderstanding on my end, to be truthful. But we reconnected and have been together for the last several years as if we had never been apart since that first day when we met.

"I come bearing gifts." Alpha stood and sauntered dramatically about the room as he spoke in the way. It was just something he did. I don't know if that was an old school thing, or just his sense of humor, but it was always fun to watch.

I looked around the room and, seeing no boxes or anything else out of the ordinary, I asked, "Gifts? What kind of gifts?"

"You two are my best Hunters, I fully expected you to be successful in finding your quarry, and thought it might be a good idea to bring a little backup."

"Backup?" I asked incredulously, "You?"

Alpha smiled, "No, not me."

Suddenly Lei looked worried, "Um...shouldn't we tell..."

Alpha raised his hand, "I'm telling him now. It's time Lei. He's ready."

Lei stared at Alpha and nodded before sitting in one of the two chairs that the hotel had provided. I looked from Lei to Alpha, and back again, just feeling that uncomfortable feeling you get when everyone is in on the joke but you.

"I'm ready for what?" as I spoke the hotel phone began to ring.

Alpha cleared his throat, "Not you...well, I suppose you are ready too..."

The phone continued to ring and Lei said, "I'll get it, maybe it's the Major."

I nodded and turned back to Alpha, "You were saying?"

I always found it surreal when someone as old and experienced as Alpha could look uneasy. Honestly, I couldn't imagine what he had to say that would make him so nervous.

Alpha looked as though he was about to start again when there was a knock at the door.

I turned and looked at the door, "Oh you have to be kidding me!"

Alpha looked suddenly concerned and, when I saw the look on Alpha's face, I asked, "So, you're expecting someone? Is this our backup?"

A voice behind the door called out, "Room service."

Alpha let out a breath and mumbled, "That idiot. He actually ordered room service."

I frowned as Lei hung up the phone, "Larson says he has the stuff we need, but we should meet him at the restaurant where Rogers was recovering."

Lei walked to the door and was about to peer through the peephole when Alpha seemed to notice something out of place and faster than my eyes could follow, he jumped across the room and pulled Lei away from the door just before it exploded inward.

Chapter 34

Men clad in black poured into the hotel room and each carried a sidearm with longish barrels that could only be silencers. I was in motion a second after the debris from the door had slapped into me, and tackled the first man through the door before he could get a round off. The others behind him hesitated as our bodies rolled into their legs and threatening to make them lose their balance and fall into a huge pile. For a moment I thought they might shoot into the mess I had created, but the threat was cut off as Alpha leapt from the floor and grabbing both men by their shirts, flung them back to the far corner of the room.

Lei was in motion a second later and jumped to the bed and leapt for the door. I don't know how she realized another man was coming through, but just as he cleared the doorframe she landed on him driving his body to the ground.

The man I tackled had lost his weapon and was futilely struggling against the chokehold I held him in as I watched Lei raise an arm and bring her fist down hard on her opponent. There was a loud thud/crack as her fist dropped, and I immediately knew there was one less enemy to worry about for now. My guy was weakening but wasn't out of the fight just yet.

Lei turned to me, "You okay babe?"

"Yep, thanks hon," I answered as casually as if we were shopping for fruit while I squeezed tighter on the man's throat and he made some choking sounds. "Maybe check on Alpha?"

Lei looked up, but the expression on her face shifted and her body relaxed, "Nope, he's good."

When the man I held finally went limp, I pushed his body away to see Alpha standing over the two men he had thrown into the wall. They were lying very still, one on top of the other, and had apparently been neutralized. I turned away to check the man I had choked out and found a pulse at his neck easily enough.

"Lei," I called to her, "keep an eye on this guy in case he wakes up. I'm going to check the hall."

Lei nodded and moved to kneel beside the man lying next to me as I got up from the floor. Quickly I moved to the doorway, and risked a peek by pushing my head around the corner. I saw the next man immediately, and the surprised look on his face told me he hadn't been expecting anyone besides his own people to exit the room.

I saw his gun come up, and ducked back into the room as the silenced rounds burst into the wooden doorframe. I kicked the door shut and announced to the room, "We have one more party guest outside."

Splintered wood began spitting from the door leaving small holes as the bullets fully penetrated the door. I scrambled back and away, as Lei and Alpha moved to pull me back into the room.

I asked, "I don't suppose either of you picked up a gun from one of those guys?" When I received only silence as a reply I guessed the answer. As a group we all ducked behind the bed hoping the mattress would stop any bullets fired at us by the man who we expected to burst into our room.

We heard multiple muffled sounds as the silenced bullets plowed into the mattress and box springs. One bullet struck the floor next to my leg, bouncing twice, before coming to rest on the carpeting, and I could see the shoes of the man standing just inside the doorway. He had just started to move around the bed to improve his firing position.

Then a voice, shouting in a surprised tone, and in English, came from what had been the doorway, "WHAT IN THE BLUE HELL?!"

I could see the attacker's shoes stop and turn back to face the door when suddenly there was a resounding "CLANG!" followed by complete silence before another loud "CLANG!" was heard. I could see the last gunman's feet pirouette drunkenly as something cut through the air, and I saw the gunman's silenced sidearm fall to the floor as another pair of shoes appeared into view.

I risked a look, and my jaw literally dropped open as I saw the last of our attackers shake his head as if clearing his vision and pull a knife from his belt to face the man entering .

Standing in the doorway of my hotel room, and holding a heavy room-service silver serving tray...was Dracula.

Chapter 35

Yes, Dracula.

Now I don't mean it was Vlad the Impaler, nor the fictional character that Bram Stoker had written about. This was a cheap theatrical costume reminiscent of Bella Lugosi from the famous black and white film of the 1920's. The shock of the flamboyant spectacle had rendered me momentarily speechless, as I took in the full regalia of slicked back hair, black jacket, pants and vest. His tuxedo's frilly white shirt, complete with cuffs and red ribbon with pendant, all were consistent with that ancient movie, but it wasn't until I took a closer look at the powdered face and a brandished set of cheap plastic vampire teeth in the mouth of the actor, did I notice who was standing there.

Chris Barnes.

My best friend, former LAPD medical examiner and dead man these past two years.

At first I didn't recognize him. I was too shocked by the absurdity of the costume he was wearing, but when he raised the aluminum room-service tray over his head and shouted, "HAVE AT YOU!" at the remaining enemy, his identity clicked. Truly, I had never known anyone else THAT crazy. Chris ran into the room and I just watched in stunned fascination as he brought the room-service tray down once again on the man's head. Then a final resounding "CLANG" deformed the tray around the man's skull in a manner that suggested a professional wrestling scene; however, this tray was no prop and had the density to deliver a force strong enough to incapacitate the recipient of the blow.

My legs were weak, because I had held my dear friend as he died helping to save my people. I had watched over his body afterward, carried it to the coroner and attended his funeral. In the days that followed, Alpha had cryptically mentioned Chris once, but when it never came up again, I just assumed he was helping me cope with the loss. Now Chris stood in front of me...well, he was actually on the ground kneeling over the man he had just clobbered, dressed as Dracula, fully animated and alive.

I stood and tried to get my bearings as Chris repeatedly hit the man on the head with the tray, screaming at the top of his lungs with every blow as he hit him again and again...

"I got him!"

CLANG!

"I got him!"

CLANG!

"I got you now!"

CLANG!

"You're mine!"

CLANG!

"Show a knife to me!?!"

CLANG!

"I'll teach you!"

CLANG!

Of course the man was completely unconscious at this point, but Chris was just...being Chris.

"Chris?" the word barely escaped my throat, as my voice was gone, amidst the shock at seeing my dead friend so fully animated.

"This is for me!"

CLANG!

"This is for being too damn tall!"

CLANG!

"This is for the Titanic!"

CLANG!

"This is for Ole Purdue!"

CLANG!

"Chris!" I had to shout to get my voice to work, but all the noise and chaos he was creating was more than I could register and, frankly, I would have probably shouted anyway.

Chris froze in mid-strike, still perched on top of the man as he looked at me,

"Into the breech, Steve! Into the..."

Chris' words were cut off as Chris seemed to suddenly realize the man beneath him was totally out for the count.

"Oh right," Chris climbed off the man and stood smiling in front of me. He was about to say something when a moan escaped from the man on the ground.

CLANG!

"Chris!" I shouted and ran to my friend.

Chapter 36

"He the last one, or do you need to clear the halls? Go ahead, I've got this one covered!" Chris was holding the room service tray over his head ready to slam it down again.

The insanity of the scene had me mumbling, "He's got him covered...with a room service tin?"

Chris apparently heard me, "Never argue with results."

"Chris..."

"The LAPD should make these things standard issue."

"Chris!"

"WHAT?!"

"How is it you're still alive?"

Chris looked confused and then turned to Alpha, "You were supposed to tell him."

Alpha dismissed Chris' statement with a wave of his hand, "I was in the process, before our friends so rudely interrupted us."

Chris set the tray down and walked over to me. My long dead best friend just walked over, with his ridiculous cape waving behind him, and he just stood in front of me and held out his arms, "C'mon bro, man-hug time."

I let out a sound that was a half laugh and half cry as I embraced my friend. He was really here. Alive, well, and as eccentric as ever.

Chris laughed along with me, and when we held the hug a bit longer than two men, comfortable with their heterosexuality could properly excuse, we began giving each other manly slaps on the back as we let go.

I managed to stammer out, "How?"

Chris nodded and turned to Alpha as he said with heavy sarcasm, "Good a time as any for explanations."

Alpha merely shrugged, and stepping over the bodies to check on Lei.

We began moving the bodies into the room, were checking them for heartbeats, as Chris started talking.

"I was gut shot remember? Those ass-faces literally blew my guts out in the Pharmanetics lobby and left me for dead while they hunted you and Alpha down. I lost a lot of blood, not to mention that the junk in my intestines was going to poison me. I figured I was done and the last thing I remembered was telling Alpha to go and help you before, I guess, I passed out. Well, next thing I knew I woke up and was hooked to some machine with a couple of IV bags pumping life back into me. Turns out your boy Alpha pushed some of his own blood into me back at Pharmanetics, which kept me from dying from the systemic infection that gut shots are known for, and was pumping even more of his blood into me through a direct transfusion."

"Alpha gave his...a direct..." it was the process where a healthy person had their blood pumped directly into the body of someone who needed it via a clean tube. We had done it with many of our kind who were in the throes of madness, but Alpha never used his blood for the process. He had said that over the centuries his blood wasn't really compatible with human blood anymore and it would have strange side effects on whomever received it.

"Yeah," Chris continued, "I've heard that it isn't a regular thing?"

"No," I said, still stunned. "It's not."

Chris shrugged, "Oh well, guess there has to be a first time for everything. Anyway, I recovered pretty slowly, and it took me nearly six months to be able to eat solid food again, and another six before I could walk normally. I guess I was pretty messed up. In the meantime Alpha and his people treated me like royalty, and when I could finally move around on my own again I found out there were some new...shall we say "rules" I had to follow to keep myself alive."

I looked at Chris' face and guessed what was making him so

cheery, "You're one of us now, aren't you?"

Chris bowed formally and adopted an Hungarian accent, akin to the Bella Lugosi Dracula costume he was wearing, "I am a fully-fledged, card carrying Vam-Pire," Chris pumped his fist, "Yeah baby!"

Lei turned away from Alpha and muttered in mock disgust, "There goes the neighborhood."

"Hey!" Chris responded with equal mock indignation.

Lei flashed him a look and Chris pointed two fingers at his eyes and then pointed them at Lei in a threatening manner.

I shook my head, "Why didn't anyone tell me."

Chris saw my face and toned down the frivolity, "Man I am so sorry about that. I thought you knew. Alpha said that he was going to tell you when the time was right, but I never thought it would have been this long."

Lei moved to my side and I asked her, "Did you know?"

She looked a little uncomfortable, but she didn't lie to me, "Yes."

I let out a breath I had been holding and shook my head as I pinched the spot between my eyes where a headache was creeping in.

"Why all the secrets?"

Lei shrugged, "He needed to recover without distractions. You felt so guilty you would have wasted your life at his bedside and distracted him from properly recovering. That wouldn't have done you or Chris any good."

I wanted to be angry about that, but knew she was right. Chris had gotten shot helping me with a fight that wasn't his in the first place. He was helping me because he was my friend, so the responsibility fell on me when he died. I would have babied the hell out of him if I had known he was still alive.

"That doesn't explain why I wasn't told after he recovered."

Alpha decided to join the conversation and said, "Your friend had to learn what it meant to be one of us. That took time," Alpha paused to look at Chris and snorted, "a lot more time than most."

Chris rolled his eyes.

"But, what did you mean when you said that I was, ready"?" I asked.

"I meant that Chris was finally ready," Alpha looked back at Chris, "Could you take the ridiculous costume off now?"

Chris sighed, "Spoiled my big entrance, dammit."

"I take it Chris is our back up?" I asked as if already knowing the answer.

"That was my intention. I had thought that this might be the perfect time to..." Alpha seemed to search for the proper words.

Lei sighed, "Test him?"

"Test?" I repeated the word in confusion before the realization struck, "You want him to be a Hunter?!"

Lei covered her face with her hand, but if she was shocked or stifling a laugh I couldn't tell.

"What better time to test him than with my two best Hunters, just to make sure he isn't overwhelmed?"

Lei had recovered from...whatever... and pointed out, "We don't usually test new candidates in the middle of active operations."

Alpha nodded, "True, but my point remains."

"You want him to be a Hunter?" I asked again, although this time it was more of a statement to myself, than a question to Alpha.

Alpha looked at me and raised an eyebrow, "Yes."

"A Hunter?" I asked again.

Alpha looked even more confused, "Yes?"

I pointed to Chris, "Him?"

"Hey!" Chris said indignantly, but was half laughing when he did.

Alpha seemed to suddenly understand, "A lot has happened in

two years. Perhaps you will learn something as well?"

I hadn't completely come to terms with the fact that my best friend was still alive and now I was supposed to accept that he had been trained as a Hunter. And in less than two years?

"Alpha you have got to be…"

Lei interrupted me by saying, "Can we work this out on the way to the restaurant? Larson is waiting there for us."

"…kidding me!" as I finished my thought. I don't like being cut off.

Chris turned away from me and looked at Lei, "Restaurant?"

"It's a medical clinic, too." Lei volunteered

Chris' eyebrows went up, "Huh?"

Lei nodded "Don't worry, we'll explain."

Chris' drew the cape around his body and half of his face, and scowled at me, Dracula style, and with a terrible Transylvanian accent he said, "Vell den, allow me to put on something, less formal," and he sauntered out of the room never dropping the cape from his face.

Chapter 37

Chris changed out of his Halloween costume in favor of a pair of jeans, hiking boots and a T-shirt that read "Team Edward" as he headed for the lobby with Lei. I wanted to stay behind and talk to Alpha, but with all the bodies lying around I figured we needed to clear out pretty quickly. Alpha and I strode out of the hotel and found a walk-up bar less than two blocks from the hotel. My intentions were to talk, they really were, but I wasn't sure I was going to be able to resist the urge I had to beat the crap out of the man. I had always considered Alpha like a father to me, which made it even harder for me to accept the fact that he and Lei had kept the secret of Chris' being alive away from me for so long.

I barely waited for the waitress to walk away with our drink order before I started in on him.

"How could you?!" I demanded.

Alpha just peered inscrutably at me, those bottomless black eyes of his now hidden behind mirrored sunglasses.

"No - No! None of that Lord and Master vampire attitude crap!" I was pointing an index finger in his face before I had realized I had moved, to which he simply sat on the edge of his seat and rested his elbows on the bar as he watched me.

I continued, not trying to regulate the volume of my voice, "This is Chris we're talking about here! MY friend, my respons..."

"There!" Alpha slapped my finger away and pointed with his own, cutting me off before I could finish, "There is the answer to your 'why' for what I did."

I started to protest, but Alpha cut me off again, "You want me to take away the "inscrutable" attitude? Well then, don't take an indignant one with me."

I shut my mouth and let Alpha continue, "What have you been doing this past year and a half?" Alpha asked.

I was a bit shocked by the question, but Alpha answered for

me when I didn't speak up right away, "You and Lei have found over a dozen lost and abducted children, found nearly two dozen of our people and saved them by bringing them into the fold, not to mention the way the relationship between you and Lei has grown."

Alpha seemed to consider that last statement before saying, "I really don't understand why you haven't married the girl yet. Anyhow, look at how much you have accomplished, and then think about how much you would have done if you had sat at his bedside the entire time, holding your friend's hand throughout his recovery because you felt it was your fault."

My voice caught in my throat, "I..."

Alpha waved a hand, "No, you may not like it, in fact I'm sure you don't like what I did, but that doesn't mean it wasn't the right thing for me to do."

My face tightened and I probably should have just dropped it, and moved on, but sometimes my anger can override the filter between my brain and mouth, "It doesn't matter if I had wasted my life, Chris' life, Lei's life, or anyone else's. The real point here is that you took the choice away from me. If I had decided to waste my life and support my friend above all else, then that should have been my choice. It might be a selfish choice, given the way you just presented it, but the choice of how MY life was spent would have been mine, not yours."

Alpha blinked at me and a half smile crossed his lips before he bent his head forward and ran his pale fingers through his snow-white hair. Then, with a sigh he said, "You're right."

I was so ready for a rebuke that I actually stuttered, "A-A-and...uh...what?"

Alpha rested his face in his hands and nodded before raising his head up to look me in the eyes, "You are right."

"Um...yes, yes I am," was all I could say.

Alpha sighed, "I've spent the last five hundred years being a leader and making decisions for our family that, I will admit, at times were extremely painful. I have had to do things that, if given a choice, I would have rather died than do and I justified my actions at every turn because I HAD to know what was best for the entire collective."

As I watched him, Alpha, who always had been the pillar of a strength that was superhuman in proportion even for us, began to look tired and maybe even a little frail as he spoke. It was as if the front he put up had crumbled, and for the first time ever I could see the toll centuries of life had taken on him.

"I'm sorry Steven," he spoke the words quietly, but there was no doubting the sincerity in the words, "I played the father figure for far too long. I suppose it would be accurate to assume that I don't always know when to leave it behind."

With all of the steam having gone out of my sails, I simply turned back to face the bar top and we both just sat there in silence for about a minute before the waitress brought over our drinks. She set two bottles of some kind of Thai beer that I had never heard of in front of us before placing two small menus next to the bottles.

"No trouble here," she said quickly as she gave us a stern look of warning. She might have wanted to say something more, but the expressions on our faces were enough to tell her to give us a little space, and she walked off to serve other customers. I picked up my beer and tilted the bottle toward Alpha. His head turned slightly as he processed my actions, then he picked up his own bottle and clinked it against mine. We both drank half the contents before setting the bottles back down on the bar top, and I looped an arm around his oversized shoulders. Alpha didn't flinch away, and I pulled on him a couple times, "You are a very good father, you know."

Alpha snorted a laugh, "So good that a misunderstanding sent you away from me for over a decade? So good that I apparently made the wrong decision about your friend?"

I laughed, "I didn't say you were perfect, but at least I can understand why you did it."

Alpha turned his head and regarded me for a time. And then he smiled and patted me on the back a couple times before saying, "We all right then?"

"We're good, as long as we learned our lessons."

Alpha chuckled, "Nearly six hundred years, and I wonder if I have really learned anything." He took another drink and asked, "So what now?"

I thought for a moment before I said, "I guess it's time for dinner."

Chapter 38

Dr. Phineas Whelan was pacing the floor of his lab waiting for Timberland to report concerning what had happened at the village. The man had returned several hours ago and was extremely upset about something, not that Whelan cared about whatever concerns Timberland and his band of maniacs might have. What he wanted to know, needed to know, was the status and whereabouts of his patient. He was relying heavily on that individual's success to protect him against both his enemies as well as his dubious, though necessary, allies.

The sale of the biochemical weaponry had gone off without a hitch, as did the sale of the accompanying "vaccine" for the special forces brigades of the buyer, but Whelan knew that without his personal monster he would be vulnerable if...no, not if, when the buyer turned on him, after the sale was fully over.

He had barely escaped two years ago when he had run from Pharmanetics and was forced to abandon all of his technological breakthroughs, but he hadn't lost the knowledge that he had gained while he had worked there, including the prize of his achievements, the "Flash Box." The device emitted a little strobe of light that resembled the red eye-reduction effect of a camera's flash but, in fact, sent an energy impulse into a subject's Optic Nerve, thereby traveling to and influencing the brain. Now he had reached the pinnacle of his work in mind control by creating his personal monster and protector that would stand between him and the vampires if they were to ever come for him again. True, he hadn't figured out the unique variant allowing this particular subject to survive the process when all of the other test subjects had died, but Whelan didn't care. He had his weapon against the vampires now and, most delicious of all, it was his genius that had created the giant.

Unable to control his patience any longer, Whelan walked to

the phone in the lab and pressed a button that should link him directly to Timberland's tent. When Timberland didn't answer, Whelan threw the phone against the concrete floor, smashing it to pieces. He stormed out of the lab and walked through the corridors until he found and ascended the stairs, reaching the boiler room, which had to be shut down for the time being, and then made his way outside the building. The night was cloyingly humid, and Whelan felt perspiration condensing on his brow the instant he left the refrigerated air of the lab. He walked toward the huge tent that Timberland's mercenaries shared.

There was no way for Timberland to have known that Whelan was headed his way, but just before the doctor, arrived Timberland stepped from the door of the tent to face him. Whelan had stopped short at the sight of the man who stood wearing only the bandages covering a minimum of his physical body. Timberland's hair was matted with what was probably perspiration and his skin was filthy, giving his body look of dark and light patches on what Whelan knew to be his otherwise totally pale skin. He stood hunched over slightly, but whether that was due to injury or some current battle induced ferocity infecting the man's state of mind, couldn't be ascertained.

"You shouldn't be here right now," Timberland was growling more than talking and began shifting restlessly as he peered into Whelan's face.

"You were supposed to check in with me as soon as you returned," Whelan put as much authority into his voice as he could, which normally wasn't an issue for him, but for the first time since signing on with Timberland he felt perhaps, now wasn't the time to push the issue.

"We weren't able to retrieve your pet."

"I assumed as much as you're back and the holding chamber is empty," Whelan conceded, "But what happened out there? Did you at least manage to find him?"

Another low growl rumbled inside Timberland's throat, "We did."

Something moved in the shadows behind the door to the tent. It appeared to be one of Timberland's crew, whose skin reflected momentarily in the moonlight as he, or she, passed through the minimal illumination let in by the open door.

Timberland noticed as Whelan looked inside, and wordlessly growled into the open door. Whelan thought that whatever the man had uttered, sounded very much like the deep basso bark of a big dog.

A growl came out of the tent and Timberland's eyes went up in surprise and anger. He immediately turned his back on Whelan and faced the open doorway, apparently daring anyone inside to step forward. Whelan resisted the urge to run because every instinct his mind and body had told him that he did not want to see what would happen if Timberland had to clash with whoever was lurking just out of sight.

The low growling sound from inside the tent began to decrease in volume, as whoever was making it seemed to move away from the door and back into the interior of the tent.

"What are you people doing in there?" Whelan heard himself say although he really hadn't intended to say it out loud.

Timberland slowly turned back to Whelan keeping his eyes on the door until the last possible moment.

"Call it...family squabbling." Timberland said cryptically.

Whelan looked from Timberland to the tent and back. Was it possible that all of the people in Timberland's crew were related to him? Whelan shook that thought away. It really didn't matter. What mattered was whatever information he could get out of Timberland, while he had his attention.

"So, what did you learn?" Whelan asked again, this time in a quieter voice.

"Your little pet project had the support of the village and some unknown outside reinforcements as well. Three of my people are dead as a result."

Whelan scratched his head, "What outside reinforcement?"

"Can't say, but at least one of them was a professional, probably military or ex-military."

Whelan shook his head as the words registered, "I thought those Khmer Rouge thugs, whose bodies you retrieved earlier, took care of the new CIA Spook."

"They did, but that doesn't mean he didn't have back up."

"Would that be normal for a spy?" Whelan asked.

Timberland shook his head, "Not normal, but given what happened to their last operative, they might have been issued partners, or a team of emergency personnel just in case of another loss of communication."

"Do you think that's what happened?"

Timberland was pacing again and was clearly getting more and more agitated the longer he stayed outside the tent, "No. I think these were the people who were with the spook when the Rouge hit the house, but I don't think they were at the house in any official capacity."

"Why?"

"The way they killed that one Rouge. It was primal, angry and not professional. I fought one of them as we retreated, and he wasn't military."

"Is he dead?"

"No."

Whelan shook his head in amazement, "And how is that possible? You and your team were supposed to be the best."

Timberland didn't seem as though he wanted to answer, or maybe it was more that he didn't want the rest of his crew to hear what he was about to say, because he moved closer to Whelan and whispered, "Something...was different about the man."

Whelan frowned, "How so?"

Timberland shook his head, "He was strong...way too strong for his size."

"Like you and your...team?" Whelan volunteered.

"No, it was...it was more than that. He had training. Extensive training from the skills I saw. But they weren't military, or like any martial art I've ever seen."

Whelan was growing impatient. He wanted to know about his subject and not about how this fool let his opponent get the better of him.

"Ever seen anything like it before?"

Timberland had been staring at the ground and his head propped up at the question, "Yes, in fact I have. Your experimental freak fought in a very similar manner."

Whelan watched Timberland's face as he spoke, and a chill of apprehension found its way into the hair on the back of his neck.

Timberland either didn't notice or didn't care and he continued, "Your monster was bigger and stronger, of course, but there's no question that they fought in a very similar fashion. That mean anything to you?"

Dr. Whelan's eyes darted back and forth across the ground as he played possible scenarios out in his head.

"Did you see anyone else who wasn't part of the village? Anyone who may have looked very out of place?"

"Sure."

"Was he also a tall man? White hair, white skin, maybe dressed all in black?"

"No, he looked like a regular grunt, although probably special forces if I had to guess."

Whelan let out a breath he had been holding, "Any others?"

Timberland thought back to the village, "Maybe. After that freak of yours tossed one of my people to the ground, a woman jumped her."

Whelan froze, "A woman?"

"Initially, I had thought she was one of the villagers, because she had Asian features, but after realizing what she was wearing, along with the positive way she jumped into the fight, I'm pretty sure she was part of the group that hit us."

A mental image of the makeshift operating theater back in Los Angeles, and the naked body of a woman who had been tied to the gurney began to play through Whelan's mind. He remembered using his scalpel to slice into the woman's abdomen as she lay beneath him. Remembered how she didn't even flinch as he cut her and, later, how he had watched in a rear view mirror as she had killed the man who was his head of security, by ripping his throat out with her teeth.

Timberland frowned, "I see you do know her?"

All the blood had drained out of Whelan's face, "We've run out of time. We need to get the subject back now!" Whelan started to walk backward toward the lab, "Forget the village! Get back to town and check the hotels, the tourist shops, whatever. Do whatever it takes to find out where they are and get my subject back!"

Timberland frowned, "What are you expecting?"

"Not what," the doctor turned to run, "Who!"

Chapter 39

Alpha didn't go to the restaurant with me after our lengthy discussion. He said he needed some time to be alone, I wasn't sure why, but I suspected that it might have something to do with the way he reacted when I had told him about Zach. I couldn't take the time to figure out what Alpha was thinking because the threat to our people by Dr. Whelan, who was still out there, was of major importance. If the man had any kind of self-preservation or even common sense, then he was certainly beefing up the security around him, along with preparing whatever he was concocting in that lab of his to use against us.

As I walked the street back to the restaurant I resisted the temptation to call Dimitri in search of answers. The man may have been our employer, but I certainly didn't trust the sadistic SOB. I needed to get a straight story about what was going on and what his real interest in Zach was all about? Why was he so important to whatever Dimitri had planned? As far as I knew, or had ever heard, Dimitri Lagos and his followers liked to be the "things that went bump in the night." I suppose that someone like Zach would add to the fear factor in whatever arena that he might be plotting in, but what it was I had no idea.

I tried to piece other parts of the puzzle together from what I already knew. Whelan was here in Thailand and working on some kind of project that Dimitri had perhaps been a part of, but Whelan betrayed him, and now both men wanted Zach because…what? How was Zack a key part to their plans.

My head started to ache, and as I rubbed my eyes, a thought occurred to me. Larson's friend Rogers had said, before the gunfight, that the CIA had placed him in Thailand because of information they had received about a terrorist group that had secured a cache of bacteriological and virulogical agents with the intention of creating dirty bombs. Would it be a coincidence that

Whelan was in the same area? Not a chance, but how did Dimitri and his plans fit into that? Biologically dirty bombs, due to our body's inherent immunity to all things bacterial or viral, would have no effect on Dimitri and his followers, so it posed no threat. Could Whelan be trying to reproduce that effect in normal human beings? Is that why he had done all those things to Zach? Is that why he had gone way beyond the simple act of torturing the poor guy and instead drove him to the point of madness?

I just didn't know and it was more than a bit embarrassing. Some great detective I was proving to be.

I walked up to the restaurant and pushed past the hostess who wai'd me graciously, but as she recognized where I was headed, she made every effort to pretend she had never seen me.

I passed through the dining area and into the kitchen where a collection of young chefs were prepping the evening's ingredients. None of the chefs looked up from their large Chinese style cleavers, probably more as a result of the rapid and precise chops and slices they were executing on a variety of cutting boards, as opposed to being concerned about my privacy. I have to admit the smells coming from the kitchen were wonderful and fragrant with the cilantro, lime and garlic overwhelming anything else trying to share the air.

It really was a perfect cover for the makeshift hospital that had been converted from a massive walk in refrigerator in the far corner of the room. I had asked how the restaurant could afford to lose such a giant appliance and was told that, due to the frequency of power outages in the city the refrigerator became unreliable. Most of the restaurant ran on propane including the lights, which were hooked up to a propane fueled generator. In the end, the removal of the walk in was too costly to be worth doing, and when the owners were approached by some crazy Farang who wanted the space inside the box, they jumped at the outrageous rent he was offering.

Larson had filled in the rest of the details about the Farang, who was a CIA field agent, looking to set up a place where his operatives could get some emergency care, as well as take an occasional 'interested' party to a quiet place for...questioning.

I saw Larson first. The man was all smiles as he was asking a shirtless Rogers questions, while Chris made like a doctor, re-inspecting the work that had been done on Rogers.

Lei was standing on the far side of the box, and brought a finger to her lips telling me to keep quiet.

"...you really look like shit Pat," Larson sounded like he was playfully chiding Rogers."

Pat smiled as he lifted his arms for Chris to check the stitches as they wound around his shoulder from the back. Then Chris noticed me, and looked up from what he was doing.

"Hey," Chris nodded to me and immediately returned to his work.

"Hey," I said back with equal nonchalance. I knew Chris well enough to know that when he was completely enthralled by his work trying to interrupt was fruitless. It was so surreal to see my friend working, much less walking and talking, as I recognized those little personality traits my friend owned, and that I had been convinced I would never see again.

Larson turned to me and his smile never left his face as he excused himself and walked over to where I was standing.

He held out his hand to me and said, "Listen, I never got around to thanking you for helping me find Zach."

I took his hand and shook it but couldn't keep the inquisitive frown off of my face, "No problem. It's been a crazy few days."

Larson's smile faded, "Yeah, it has, hasn't it?"

"How's Rogers doing?"

Larson turned to where Rogers was sitting up on the makeshift cot, submitting to whatever examination Chris was currently performing.

"He seems okay. Lost some blood, but in the end just needed to be stitched back together. Nothing broken or otherwise damaged, lucky bastard."

"How's his head?" I asked in a very serious tone.

Larson looked at me, "His head? He only had a shoulder wound."

"Not what I meant," I said cryptically, but Larson read the meaning behind my words.

"He's not happy on several levels. Being shot is bad enough, but being shot as a result of something that wasn't what you had signed on for in the first place… well, that makes it a bit worse."

I nodded, "I don't suppose you could convince him that it was more about finding Zach as opposed to helping Lei and myself?"

Larson smiled, but there was no humor in it, "I tried. Sure, he's happy as hell we found Zach alive, but..."

"But?"

Larson let out a deep sigh, "Rogers isn't the same man I served with when we were part of a team all those years ago. He's changed, you know? Grown as a person and as a soldier, and he has moved on with his life and career. I'm the one trying to hold on to what I used to have, as opposed to moving on, because probably there just isn't any moving on for me."

I shrugged, "I don't know about all that, but I meant that I get the distinct impression that we aren't real popular with him on any level."

Larson raised his eyebrows, "You think? After what went down first at the house when Lei ripped that Rouge gunman apart and..." Larson was growing angry and he took a second to lower his voice so the others wouldn't be alarmed.

"And now the whole city is talking about the state they found the Madame and her bodyguard? Yeah, I'd say there was good reason."

"They've been found already?" I hadn't expected what Lei and

I had done at the nightclub to be discovered so quickly.

"You mean, what's left of them."

I answered defensively before I could stop myself, "They deserved what they got and more. Is that going to be a big problem for you?"

Larson grew impatient, but kept his voice at a low volume, "I saw what your girl did at Rogers place. To that Khmer Rouge gunman and as far as I'm concerned, dead is dead. I don't care what it looks like, or how it's done, but what happens afterward is another story. Seems to me there was something far darker at work and that worries me, if in no other way, then on a strictly professional level."

"So we're off Rogers' Christmas list...what about you?" I asked.

Larson looked directly at me, "What about me?"

"Are you still on board? If not, then now's the time to say so."

Larson stepped his feet back as if getting ready for me to attack him, "Is that so?"

I crossed my arms in front of me, "Yep. This is where we can part as friends, even if we can't work together anymore. But I do need to know that you're all in. One hundred percent in, or nothing."

Larson eased off on his defensive posture and turned to look at Rogers, who now had a blood pressure cuff cinched around his arm, but for some reason Chris was pressing the receiver of the stethoscope to Rogers' forehead instead of the crook in his elbow beneath the cuff.

He turned back to me, "Your friend Chris, he does know what he's doing right?"

I turned and saw the spectacle that Chris was creating and chuckled, "Yeah, he's legit, but he also goes for the cheap laugh whenever he can get it."

Larson watched as Rogers' eyes and his whole expression

turned from wary and confused into almost jovial, as Chris finally managed to coax a smile from his patient.

"Zach's still out there," Larson volunteered. "That means we're not done here. If Zach wants to finish this, which he apparently does, then I'm with you," giving me a very serious look, "one hundred percent."

I nodded, "Good."

I approved of the lengths that Larson was willing to go to in order to protect and defend his friend. That kind of friendship was rare indeed.

I looked at Chris as he wrote something on a post-it note pad while he told Rogers, "Make sure the doctor reads and follows these instructions." He then peeled the single sheet off of the pad and stuck the adhesive part to Rogers' forehead, before quickly turning and walking away without another word.

I looked back to see Rogers smiling but looking confused by the paper attached to his head and I had to squint my eyes to read what Chris had written before Rogers could peel it off.

The note simply said "I love enemas."

Chris walked up to me, "I'm going to see if this joint actually serves food," then he grumbled under his breath, "although I doubt fajitas are on the menu. Anyway, want to come?"

I turned to look at Lei who hadn't so much as glanced in my direction since I had arrived, "Definitely, but give me a sec?"

Chris followed my gaze to Lei and said, "Sure thing," before he walked out of the converted fridge headed for the dining room.

I moved to stand next to Lei. She seemed a little uneasy as I eased up to her as she crossed her arms, in what might have been an unconscious response.

She didn't look at me and instead made a point of seeming more interested in what Rogers's reaction to the post-it note was going to be as he pulled it off of his forehead.

Finally she asked, "Are you still angry with me?"

She had asked in a rather meek voice that didn't suit her personality. It wasn't an act, or at least I didn't think it was one. It was simply that she was afraid we were on shaky ground, which would be unusual for us."

"Yes and no," I said honestly, "I understand why you did what you did, but I still don't like the idea that you might be keeping secrets from me."

She looked hurt by the words, but I still felt the air needed to be clear, "Makes me wonder what else you might feel is more important than trust between us."

I knew the words were going to cut into her, but I wasn't trying to be deliberately hurtful. Lei looked at me, wanting to protest, but I held up a hand and she bit off whatever words she might have said.

"It's not that you weren't acting in any way, other than what you thought was best for me. You were, and it's not as though you were doing it out of anything but affection, but the fact is that you put the importance of keeping a secret from me ahead of the trust we have in each other."

I could see tears forming in her eyes and I caved just a little, "To be fair, I blame Alpha a lot more than I blame you. He shouldn't have told you what was going on and then asked you to keep quiet about it. He was wrong and he knows that, now. Frankly, I think he knew it when he made the decision, but he's so used to doing the wrong thing for the right reasons he didn't balk at the deception."

I waited to see if she was going to argue. When she didn't I said quietly, "Still, even though I love Alpha like a father, I'm not in love with him. I am in love with you."

Lei's head had dropped as I spoke, but as I said those last words she raised her head and her voice cracked as she spoke, "I love you too. More than anything."

I nodded and kept my expression neutral, but inside I was

falling apart. In all the years we had known each other we had barely ever said "I love you" to each other. I don't know why, maybe we felt like we didn't need to, but it seems that based on the reaction we were both having to those wonderful words, well, we should have been saying them far more often.

"Please Lei," I said weakly, "No more secrets. I don't care how devastating the truth may be, because I know that not trusting you will destroy me faster than anything else ever could."

Lei nodded immediately but didn't say anything until, "There's something you should know."

I sighed, "More secrets?"

"No, no more secrets. That was the only one I ever kept from you, and the only one I ever will. I swear."

I nodded again, "Then what?"

"I told myself that I'd kept the fact that Chris was alive a secret because it was the right thing to do. Alpha even said as much to me when I found out, but it isn't really the reason I didn't tell you."

I waited patiently, as Lei searched for the courage to continue. In my head I didn't think the reason was going to matter, but it obviously had a big significance to Lei, as she seemed to be 'confessing' something.

"I had just gotten you back!" she exclaimed, and then her words came out in a rush, like water through a burst dam, "It had been ten years since we were together, and we were finally back on track and I didn't want anything to get in the way, and I know how loyal you are to your friend, and the guilt you felt over what happened and I didn't want to lose you again or share you with anybody, not even Chris. I wanted you to be mine and mine alone. At least until Chris couldn't be kept a secret anymore."

Lei was crying now, but she didn't sob as the tears flowed down.

"I had been away from you for so long. I was selfish. I'm

sorry."

I was wrong, it mattered a whole lot more than I had ever thought anything could and I could feel the anger rising in me. Lei hadn't just kept it from me, she had made the choice regardless of what Alpha had asked her to do. She'd done it deliberately, and not out of any motivation more altruistic than simple selfishness.

I guess she could see that I was growing angry again and looked away from me. "I don't blame you for hating me right now. I'd probably feel the same if the situation were reversed."

"Hate you?!" I got angrier, "Oh No, you don't get to guilt me into forgiving you by going to extremes."

"I know."

"Do you?" I didn't mean to raise my voice, but in the enclosed space sound reverberated more than normal. "I'm no 'mark' you can manipulate, I know you too well."

"I never could manipulate you, Even when you didn't know me ‘too well’."

I sighed, "No, you couldn't, could you?" I began searching my thoughts, because something was nagging at me, "What were you worried about Lei? Alpha and I had already cleared the air, and I’m not going to leave again."

She was very still and hugging herself tighter she whispered, "You did once."

Those three words hit me harder than any punch I had ever received. I looked at her, as she continued to stare at the floor.

She was right.

When I left I hadn't just left the life, and the family, but I had left Lei behind as well. If our paths hadn't crossed by necessity there was a very good chance that any possibility of Lei and me being together would have been slim at best. In my defense, I had thought Lei to be part of the betrayal that had driven me away, but I should have, at the very least, given her the chance to explain. I had left abruptly because I didn't want my heart to make me do something other than what my head knew, with only the 'facts' it had at the time, was the right thing to do. Did that mean that if the circumstances were "just so" that I could leave again?

A thought occurred to me, something Alpha had said earlier during our own confrontation.

"You know," I said calmly to Lei, "neither of us have any living blood relatives."

Lei looked up to my face confused by the change in subject. Gently I put one hand on her shoulder and turned her to face me. She didn't fight me but didn't lift her head to look at my face. I wiped away some tears that had stopped falling, yet remained on her face, and then lifted her chin to look into her eyes.

"I suppose...I mean, when this is over, you should consider who you'd rather have, to give you away."

Lei frowned, "What? I don't..."

"Technically Alpha isn't really your father any more than mine, but he's the closest thing we've got. Then again, Chris is basically family, so either could be appropriate."

"Are you...? What are you...?!" Lei's confused reaction wasn't what I had expected, and I felt a nervousness I hadn't known since my teenage years swirling within me.

I heard a crash, but my whole world revolved around Lei now as I took her into my arms.

Lei gripped me tightly with one arm and hand, but was pushing away with her free hand.

"Lei, I want you to know that whatever comes from this point on that we'll be together, no matter what."

Lei got it at this point and her face peered disbelieving into mine, "You better not be doing this just..."

I cut her off, "No. We've been together nearly five decades. That's longer than most already married couples, so forgive me if I've grown complacent, or too familiar with you to say how I feel, how I have felt for all that time, or act as I should have done long,

long ago."

Lei put her hands on my face, which made my heart speed up, beating so hard that I thought everyone in the room could hear it, as I said, "At this point, if I have to get on a knee I'll probably makes us fall."

I started to kneel anyway and Lei dropped right down to her knees with me.

"Lei," I looked around at the interior of the refrigerator, saw Larson peering down at us, ignored him, and turned back to Lei, "Despite my taking you to all the fanciest places, and although this is happening in front of the strangest collection of witnesses in the history of all proposals… Will you, Lei, marry me?"

She let out a sound that was half cry and half a laugh and her body started to bounce up and down before she said, "Mine," and kissed me fiercely.

When we finally parted I asked dumbly, "That meant 'Yes' right?"

She kissed me again as I stood us both up.

I took it as a "Yes."

Of course, as ever, Chris had returned to break the mood.

"Oh will you look at that," Chris was looking at the pair of us on our knees holding each other, "Two assholes in love." He pretended to swoon and placed the back of one hand against his forehead, "...So romantic, couldn't ya just plotz."

Larson looked at Chris and frowned, "Plotz?"

Chapter 40

Chris led us out of the walk-in refrigerator and toward the dining area. Our table already had a collection of beautiful looking plates of food and a large bowl of steamed rice that made my stomach growl in response. "Well, here we are," Chris chuckled as he scooped some rice onto his plate.

"Yep," I smiled as I helped myself to some of a noodle dish that had shrimp and green onions spread evenly throughout, "Deep in it as usual."

Chris nodded, "And you two are engaged to boot!" Chris pointed with the rice ladle as he continued, "You know, you two have the absolute worst timing and sense of romance that I have ever seen."

Chris lifted a spring roll from another platter and took a big bite as he turned to Lei, "And just so you know, the bachelor party is going to be on a deep sea fishing boat headed for an eight day trip to Guadeloupe Island."

I nodded, "Right time of year for that."

"Sure is," Chris reclined into the back of the dining chair, "Think the old ball and chain will let you go when this is over?"

I shrugged and looked at Lei, "Um...honey?"

"You aren't going tuna fishing without me, asshole."

Chris rolled his eyes, "Well, that didn't take long."

I smiled, "What didn't?"

Chris didn't answer directly, but made the sound of a whip cracking followed by a uttering a high pitched, "Meow."

"Hey!" I protested.

"Goddamn right," Lei agreed.

"You know the thing about newlyweds and the jelly bean jar, right?" Chris spoke conspiratorially.

I felt my shoulders go slack, "Chris..."

"Okay, so the first year of your marriage you put a jelly bean in the jar every time that you guys fu..."

"Chris!" I interrupted, "I know the story of the jelly bean jar!"

Lei looked sideways at Chris, "You do realize he's marrying me right?"

Chris nodded vigorously, "Yeah and it's really gonna suck to see your ass blow up like the Hindenburg."

"My ass?!" Lei announced in a loud voice to the entire restaurant, as she stood up from her chair and with the few patrons inside the place looking up from their food to see what was happening, Lei turn her backside into Chris' face.

"Does it look as though my ass has expanded? Even one inch in the last fifty years?"

Chris had to sit back as far as he could in his chair to keep Lei's posterior from bashing him. For my part, I was now holding my breath to keep from laughing.

"...Ah..." Chris stammered, "You know your boobs are going to drop to the ground as well."

Lei spun around, "How DARE you!" and unselfconsciously grabbed her chest and tested to see if gravity had already started taking a toll.

"Enough you two," I somehow managed while still laughing.

"Wait, wait, wait!" Chris objected, "She might shove those things into my face too!"

Lei suddenly realizing what she was doing, sat back down, "In your dreams, sweetheart."

"Guys?" I was still smiling like an idiot as I spoke.

"See Steve," Chris was in full 'Eureka' mode, as he pointed at Lei, "She called me sweetheart! She IS in love with me! I knew it!"

"Oh please." She said.

"Guys?" I implored....

But Chris was on a roll, "Oh please nothing!" He turned to me, "I'm sorry Steve, but until Lei and I resolve our unspoken attraction for one another I can't let you marry her."

"Chris...?" I said.

"Unspoken attraction!" Lei sounded aghast.

"Lei...?" I asked

Chris looked sorrowfully at Lei, "We shouldn't try to fight it anymore."

"Fight it?!" she exclaimed.

"Guys?" I was practically begging now and my voice needed to take a sip of water just to clear the laugh from my throat.

Suddenly Chris slapped the table with both hands, "All right! Fine! I'll sleep with you just this once, but that has got to be the end of it!"

At which point I spit the water out, as I couldn't contain the laughter inside me. Chris laughed too, and pointed at me as well. Lei just crossed her arms and tried to look angry, but she was making a poor showing of it, as her face looked as though she might start laughing, too.

After a minute or so the moment of frivolity ended and we ate for a bit without speaking further until I asked, "So what's up Chris? I don't think you brought me out here just to talk about the fishing or having sex with my future wife."

Lei cooed, "Mmmm, future wife. I like that."

"You're right," Chris confirmed, "First, I guess I wanted to apologize."

I was so shocked that I almost lost the food in my mouth as I spoke, "Apologize?! For what?"

Chris pushed himself away from the table, "A bunch of different things, I guess. Letting myself get shot, mostly. It had been my fault for not paying any attention to my surroundings."

I shook my head, "You were busy trying to help me, and Alpha!"

Chris nodded, but said, "True, but after the training Alpha has been putting me through, well it seems obvious to me now that I should have been more careful."

"You're a Medical Examiner, not a Soldier and not a Police Officer."

"S'pose that was the case," Chris was growing more and more somber, as he sat looking down at the tabletop and tracing his fingers along tablecloth, "But as I said, I had quite a bit of training since my recovery. Learned a lot in that time. I know a lot more now than I did before and I just wanted to let you know it won't happen again."

I was confused, "What won't happen again?"

"I won't compromise you or anyone else when we hit the camp."

I just stared at him. I didn't really know what to say, but fortunately, the waiter had returned to remove the empty plates, which gave me a chance to collect my thoughts.

"You weren't going to let me go with you, were you?" Chris said knowingly.

I hadn't even thought it was a possibility in the first place, and there was no way I was going to let him come with us. I didn't give a damn how much training he thought he had.

"Chris..."

"No, don't even try." Chris interrupted, and the lovable jester that had dominated Chris' personality was gone. What replaced it was something more determined, and maybe even a little scary, "This isn't a conversation I'm going to have with you, I'm sorry, but this guy Whelan pretty much killed me, man. You don't know the pain I've endured, how I had to wear a colostomy bag, as my guts knit themselves back together. How I had to learn how to function again, and I don't just mean walking around, I mean learning how to eat solid food, and take a shit without screaming in pain."

I cringed at the visual Chris was painting. The turmoil inside me diminished and I felt a certain degree of my person shift to a different mindset. I didn't like it, but who was I to deny Chris his chance for revenge? Most of my own motivation was vengeful, for what that man had done to me, my people, and most of all, Chris.

"If you do come along, you follow the lead of either Lei, Larson or me."

Chris smiled, "You're the lead Hunter, and as I'm part of the community now, I know my place."

I didn't like the sound of that, "Place? What exactly did Alpha teach you?"

"After I recovered and was able to walk again, I was kind of lost," Chris wasn't even looking at me any more, "I was afraid, afraid of pretty much everything. I had come so close to dying, I was actually dead, and after that I was afraid to do anything, regardless how benign...and I hated being afraid. So when Alpha came to see me, after my body had fully recovered, I asked him, begged him, to train me to be like you, to be a Hunter."

I almost bolted out of my chair, "What?!"

Chris laughed at my reaction, "He figured you would react like that. It's why I didn't make contact with you sooner. I needed to finish my training before I saw you or you might..." Chris paused and thought about his next words before he spoke them, unusual for Chris, "...get in the way."

Incredulous, I repeated those four words, "Get in the way."

Chris looked at me, "Don't take it like that. You know what I mean."

I did. It didn't really help, but I did understand.

Chris looked at me, "I needed it, you know? I needed to not be afraid anymore, and I had seen how you handled yourself, your confidence, your competence, I needed that."

"Who trained you?" I managed, "One of the hunters, or Alpha himself?"

Chris frowned, "Alpha. Why?"

I shrugged, "It's just that he hasn't personally trained anyone for decades."

"Maybe, given our relationship and the fact that I was shot while freeing your people from Pharmanetics, he decided to take a personal interest?"

I nodded,

"There's something else I need to tell you."

I groaned, "What else could there possibly be?"

"I'll get to that in a second. What can you tell me about that guy Zach."

I took a moment and filled Chris in on what I knew and his history with Larson, up to now. Chris took it all in without saying anything, but every now and again he'd nod his head while he just sat there listening until I'd finished.

And I finished with, "I don't know why they held him as a prisoner, or why Dimitri Lagos has an interest in him, but there must be a reason that we are missing." I stopped and thought for a second before asking, "Does what they did to him make any sense to you?"

Chris nodded, "Maybe a little. I'm only guessing here but I think those surgical scars are actually implantation sites."

"Implants?" I remembered the ugly winding scars that covered Zach's arms and torso, "What do you think they would implant?"

"Don't know for sure, but my guess is that if you actually touched the scars you'd find that there is something solid beneath each of them."

"Ok, for argument sake, what would that mean? "

"Well I doubt they would be microchip tracers or anything like that. I mean, if they were as simple as location devices, then why would they need more than one, plus a backup or two? From what you are describing this guy literally has hundreds of these things in his body."

"Hundreds?" I asked in astonishment.

Chris shrugged, "It sounds to me like they were targeting the major muscle groups."

I nodded my understanding, "So the purpose would be?"

"I think they might be delivery systems."

I frowned, "You just lost me."

Chris nodded, "I think they implanted a slow dissolving capsule of concentrated chemicals, not unlike the prescription pills you swallow, but only release their contents when they come in contact with another chemical, probably one made naturally by the body, and probably, I'm guessing here, but adrenaline."

"That's even possible?"

"Sure. A few years back a hormonal implant called Norplant was in the news. It was basically a birth control pill, but instead of a woman needing to swallow it daily, the pill was implanted into a woman's arm or hip, and released hormones slowly over the course of time. It freed the recipient from the burden of having to take pills on a daily basis, and it was proven to be just as effective."

"So why the hundreds in Zach?"

"I am assuming whatever is in the implants isn't systemic. It's local, but they wanted a systemic result, so they just put it everywhere in his body where they wanted to get the effect."

"Why adrenaline?"

"Because it's only released at times of stress. If it were a constant then he'd either run through whatever was in the capsules too quickly, or burn himself out. My thought is, if these guys were trying to build some kind of, I don't know, super soldier out of Zach, then he'd be releasing adrenaline whenever he came under stress, which is also the time he'd need whatever was in the capsules."

I supposed that made some sense, "Anything else it could be?"

Chris nodded and looked a little queasy, "They tortured him?"

I nodded, "We believe so."

Chris paused and shuddered, "They were trying to break him. Break him in every conceivable way."

"Yes, but… Wait, what do you mean?"

Chris raised his beer bottle in the air and showed it to the waiter, who waved that he got the message, and held up two questioning fingers in response. Chris gave him the thumbs up, and then looked back down to the tabletop.

"Okay, just guessing here, but I think the only way to accomplish what you are describing is if they killed him, Steve. Literally tortured him until his heart stopped, and then resuscitated him only to start the whole process over again."

I felt my mouth drop open slightly, "My God."

"It would show on the EKG as if he'd had a heart attack.

"Why would they do that?"

"The brain can last about three minutes without oxygen before it starts to deteriorate. Hypoxia can lead to severe brain damage if the oxygen supply is cut off much longer than that before resuscitation. Now, remember this is all conjecture, but from what you describe I am fairly confident that they were inducing a controlled amount of brain damage."

I thought a second, "You think that's why he's having trouble talking, isn't it?"

"Maybe, a side effect of multiple resuscitations could be why his eyes seem to turn more red when he is excited or stressed and why they ebb when he is more relaxed."

I looked at Chris, "Yeah, what the hell causes that anyway?"

"Just capillary fill. What you're seeing are the capillaries filling with freshly oxygenated blood at a massive rate, which happens whenever his blood pressure rises. It's actually pretty benign, despite how it looks, but the talking problem could be something more sinister."

"What?"

"I have only heard stories or rumors about this, and no actual practice, but it seems to me that they were trying to program him."

I frowned, "Yeah, that's what Larson and I figured as well, but why so much torture and why risk killing him?"

"So they could rebuild him. Just like I had to learn how to move again after being shot, maybe the recovery from the brain injury involved a degree of re-education and the psychological input of ideas or directives? I don't really know...I'm no psychologist."

I thought about it and shook my head, "But brainwash him to do what?"

Chris just shrugged, "Don't know, but didn't you say that guy Dimitri was interested in him?" I nodded as Chris continued, "Well maybe it's something that Dimitri wanted? There has to be some kind of trigger that will set his programming off."

Again I asked, "But, to do what?"

"A guy like that? My guess would be to send him into a place where the human version of a tank is required."

Chapter 41

The four of us went back to the hotel in two separate cabs. Larson rode alone in one cab while Chris, Lei and I rode in the other. We didn't really speak, Lei and I weren't in the mood and Chris was occupied taking in the sights, wowing at the neon and the women sexily dancing outside the bars and trying to entice new customers inside. I was watching him closely. He had over exerted himself, both physically back at the hotel, and mentally, while working on Rogers. I probably shouldn't have been concerned, because after all, Alpha himself said Chris was ready to get back into the real world, and that meant he had a certain degree of self-control to use our medicine whenever he felt the pangs of the thirst start to build inside him. It was one of the first lessons any of our kind had to learn before they were allowed to leave the collective, but the way he was eyeing the working girls made me worry.

Then again, and in all fairness to Chris, it could very well be that he was hungry for something very different. I had always known the guy was a "horn dog", and throwing him into the middle of the largest sex-tourist city in the world was like throwing an over-eater into a Las Vegas buffet.

"Chris?" I asked softly.

He didn't stop looking out the window of the cab as he mumbled, "Mmmm?"

"You okay, man?"

He was silent for a time and then he turned from the window, "I guess," he said sadly, but he also sounded in control.

He began shuffling around in his seat as all eyes turned to him, "I was just checking out the girls. You know, seeing if I could locate any accidental, or deliberate, nakedness. I'm getting pretty riled up too, and have started undressing the girls in my head, you know, just good clean American fun, right?"

"Sure," I said, agreeing with him maybe a little too quickly.

"I was thinking about what I might want to do, you know, after this is all over."

I smiled, "I thought we were going fishing?"

Chris nodded, "Yeah, but before that. Maybe before we head back stateside."

"You thinking about getting some?" I said it with as non-judgmental a tone as I could, but it just sounded stupid coming out of my mouth.

"Well...sure. I mean, it has been almost two years."

Lei immediately chimed in, "What?! Two years!"

I put a hand over my eyes to try to stop the headache I knew was about to come from lancing into my head.

"Two years!" Lei said again, "Oh God, how can you even think of anything else. Want me to have the driver pull over? You can meet us back at the hotel when you're done. Probably only take a minute or two at this point, we could probably wait for you..."

Chris laughed, then realized she was serious and looked at me, "Man you got a good one there, bro."

"I do," I said and winked at Lei, "But you were in the middle of saying...?"

Chris nodded, "I was thinking of how soft skin would feel as I ran my hands over it. How it would taste as I kissed it. I miss the physical contact, you know?"

"Sure," I spoke very quietly, I knew where this was going.

"And then, I was kinda getting aroused as I thought about the more sexy bits and could even see myself, you know, "doing it". All tied up in the arms of someone pretty and stuff when, and I don't even know where the thought came from, but I had a sudden vision of grabbing on with my arms and legs and going for her throat."

I watched Chris' eyes and saw such a confused and frightened look in them that the awkwardness of the confession was lost on me. It would have been lost on any of our kind, because we knew about it. We had all been there at some point and had an entire community of support to help us through it. Chris was on his own, and dead center in the middle of the most sexually tempting place on earth. He shifted around some more in his seat and pulled what looked like a large ballpoint pen out of his back pants pocket. I recognized it as an Epi Pen, normally used as an emergency delivery system for administering Epinephrine, to people allergic to bee stings, in order to stifle the reaction of the poison in the sting, and prevent them from going into anaphylactic shock. He looked at the pen, took a deep breath, and slammed it into his thigh. There was only a slight snapping sound, as the pen's delivery system injected a dose of our special serum into the large muscles of his thigh. He tensed slightly, as it took effect on his body, and then he relaxed as the relief of what he had been feeling washed over him.

"Better?" I asked, more to break the silence inside the vehicle, than for any other reason.

He nodded, saying nothing, as he once again peered out the window. A look of sad longing was on his face as he said, "Any idea how long it should take before I can tell the difference between the early stages of the hunger, versus simply being horny?"

"How do you feel now?" I asked.

"Depressed mostly," Chris admitted.

"Then you do know the difference," I said matter of factly, "You just took the serum, and you don't "want" girls anymore. That means you were more hungry than horny."

"That really sucks, you know?"

"Not really," I continued, "If you ever get confused, just take a shot. Besides, like you said, it's been two years for you, so you're bound to have some conflicting signals, especially in this city.

Chris shrugged. I wanted to say more but Lei put a hand on my arm to keep me quiet. She was right. This was Chris' battle and he needed to figure some of it out for himself. We could help and we would, but first Chris was going to need to come to terms with who, and with what, he had become, and that was the one thing we couldn't help him with.

Our cab arrived at the hotel first. Lei and Chris made their way to the elevator while I waited for Larson to arrive in his. Maybe I should have been worried about leaving Lei alone with Chris, given the delicate state he was in at that moment, but I wasn't. Lei could take care of herself, and even if she couldn't, I figured if Chris had any self-control, he could at least hold it together around my girl out of respect for our friendship.

I paced around the outside of the hotel's entrance, just trying to clear my head and think about our next move. Obviously we were going to have to infiltrate the camp, but it was going to be a daunting task. We were more than a little outnumbered by the mercenaries protecting Whelan, which brought up another issue to mind. Who was funding him? Mercenaries cost a lot of money and they certainly don't risk their lives on the cheap, so where was the money coming from? My first thought was that he sold off the stockpile of medicine he had taken from Pharmanetics two years ago, but it only took a few seconds to discard that idea. Dr. Whelan was the only one who knew how to turn the blood of my people into the medicine that Pharmanetics had been developing. He didn't have the time to have produced enough of it to pay for the tents in the camp, much less the small army at his disposal. That meant someone was financially backing him.

My thoughts pointed toward our "friend" Dimitri. The Russian clan was certainly wealthy enough, no question there, but if Dimitri and Whelan had a falling out, then how was it that Whelan was still able to afford the men at his disposal? It's not as though they worked for free. They'd walk out on him the instant his checks didn't clear, so where was the money coming from?

I shook my head, as if that would clear the fog that had built up inside my brain, just as a cab pulled up to the front of the hotel. I saw Larson as he climbed out of the back of the cab and began walking toward me. I greeted him with, "Hey Larson, Lei and Chris went upstairs about five minutes ago and are gathering what they need from the room."

Larson had simply nodded his head in response, when I heard a soft tinkling sound that seemed out of place in the moment. It was as if the normal noise of the city was intruded upon by pieces of glass hitting the pavement. What peaked my interest about the tinkling noise was the absence any initial crashing sound of glass breaking.

"What?" Larson asked when he read the look on my face.

I shook my head, "I don't know. I thought I heard, something..."

I turned, walking along the sidewalk running parallel to the front of the hotel, with Larson following behind me. I still hadn't seen anything, but something crunched under my shoe, and when I lifted my foot there was a small circle of white powder sparkling in the light. I quickly realized I had stepped on a piece of glass, explaining the sound I had heard, but as I looked around I couldn't see any broken windows or other sources of the glass.

I looked over to Larson and noticed him looking up the side of the hotel. I stepped back and trained my eyes up the side of the building as well. At first I didn't see anything particularly interesting and then something burst out the side of the hotel in a cloud of broken glass. I just stared stupidly upward and watched the black spot fall and grow larger in my vision until my brain again clicked back to the "on" position and I realized that I was standing almost directly below the falling debris.

I shot back, and to the side a few feet, never taking my eyes off the falling material. I don't know when I realized that the black spot was a person. I'd like to say it was instant recognition of the flailing arms and legs that tipped me off, but the truth was that it had been the scream that grew from nothing and increased in volume as the body plummeted. The scream stopped abruptly when the body landed on the concrete, right shoulder first, and the smack of the skull against the pavement was as sickening a sound as I had ever heard. It left a smear of blood at the initial impact site and then actually bounced a few inches up and to the left before coming to rest in an abnormal tangle of limbs.

I turned away at initial impact, more to protect my eyes and face from any additional glass or body parts that might shoot off the ground, as opposed to not wanting to watch the unpleasantness of the man's death as he hit the ground. As soon as the sounds subsided I looked back, but I didn't stare at the brains smeared on the ground, or the grotesquely dark puddle that began slowly spreading away from the body. What caught my attention was what the man was wearing. It was all black combat gear just like the people who we fought back at that village.

"Oh crap!" I cursed as I bolted for the hotel entrance. I had reached the door before someone who had also seen the body hit finally registered what they had seen and screamed. Everyone on the street was turning to look and see what had happened, some people were even rushing from the hotel, while a couple of security people were talking into their radios, probably trying to figure out from which room the body had fallen.

I knew the room, and I just hoped that I could get there before it was too late.

Chapter 42

I arrived at the elevator, saw that there was one car that was standing open at the ready and decided it would be faster than the stairs. I jumped in and started hammering the button for the twenty-ninth floor and tried to will the doors to close faster.

I almost screamed when Larson stuck his arm in between the closing doors and caused them to open again. Somehow I managed to restrain myself from throttling him as he climbed in and the doors closed again. Larson looked relaxed as the car rose while I began pacing in the limited area that the elevator car allowed with the three of us inside.

We were barely halfway up when Larson said, "Let me go first."

"What?" I said, shocked by his voice, which was louder than the wordless, classical rock being pumped through the elevator’s speakers.

"They might be covering the elevators. I'm armed," he showed me his sidearm, "and I'm guessing you're not?"

He was right. I had stashed the guns before we went to the restaurant.

Larson looked at me calmly, "Let me clear the hallway before you go rushing in, okay?"

It was not "okay", not "okay" at all, but I knew he was right.

"...Okay," it was all I could manage as the two most important people in the world to me were under attack and I was stuck in the middle of what seemed to be the world's slowest elevator, listening to a musical rendition of "tie a yellow ribbon ’round the old oak tree."

Hell. I was definitely in hell.

What was even worse, was that when the elevator arrived, I had to wait for the all clear from Larson before I could leave the elevator and get to my people.

Of course, the elevator did finally arrive, and the two of us hugged the sides of the car as the doors slid open. Immediately there was an explosion of sound and the back wall of the car seemed to come apart in tiny pieces of metal and wood, but Larson had made a good call about the bad guys covering the elevators, and I watched as he calmly readied his weapon. The instant the gunfire stopped he pivoted and shifting his body position so only his arm and one eye peered around the edge of the door, his pistol jumped twice as two rhythmic double taps exploded with a sound that might have destroyed my eardrums inside the confined space of the elevator car if I hadn't protected my hearing with my hands.

No further shots riddled the walls of the elevator. I waited for additional shots, but when none came I turned to Larson and watched as his eyes darting around, apparently scanning the area for additional hostiles, but it seemed as though he didn't find any.

I could see but not hear as well as I would like, because even protecting my ears as best as I could, the two earlier bursts Larson had fired pretty much deafened me for the moment. Larson mouthed out a command and ran from the elevator. I wasted no time and bolted down the hall after him and nearly ran into some women who were running the other way, towards the elevator.

I vigorously pointed them toward the stairway, and hoped they caught my meaning, before I continued after Larson. Following closely on his heels, I was in time to see him stepping back from the door to our room, as he dropped his shoulder and broke through the door as if it were paper. Screams that had been muffled by the closed door could be heard now, as well as the shrieking sound of a woman. My heart skipped a beat as I pushed my legs to run faster, but I skidded to a stop as a black-clad figure backed out of the ruin that Larson had made of the doorway.

The man was clad all in black and desperately trying to fire his handgun back into the room. Unfortunately for him, he was out of bullets and as he realized it was empty he threw the gun into the room, turning to run. Larson emerged with his own handgun up and pointing at the man, but couldn't shoot as I was in the line of fire.

The man tried to run past me and went face first into my fist. The punch landed with such force that the man simply crumpled to the ground at my feet. I ignored the still form and walked into the room, which was completely torn apart. Not a single piece of furniture remained intact or upright and blood was covering everything. It was even dripping from the ceiling, and there were bodies lying around haphazardly in grotesque unnatural positions like a painting by Dali. Needless to say, it was a particularly ghastly sight, even for me.

Lei and Chris were so covered in blood that it took a moment for me to realize that each of them was holding a black clad figure in a lethal embrace, as they fed from the arteries in their necks. Larson stared wide-eyed into the room and his gun wavered between aiming at Lei, and then Chris, and back, and I finally put a hand on the barrel, breaking the trance he was in. I pushed the barrel down gently, and initially Larson resisted the push, but dropped his aim under his own power a second later. For just a moment there I thought he had reached his mental limit.

I couldn't have blamed him for a second.

Lei 'finished' first, pulling her mouth away to take in a deep breath, like a person who has been underwater far too long. Blood had poured from her mouth as she opened it, which made her already blood soaked clothes even more crimson, and Chris coughed and hacked like a child who drank too fast and choked on his beverage. He spat some blood against one of the few remaining white spots on the wall of the hotel room, clearing it from his throat. It made an interesting splatter pattern, and a few drops ran vertically downward from the center. He stared at it for a moment, looked down at the lifeless body he was holding, and dropped it with a "thump" that only dead weight can make.

My heart felt like it was going to break seeing the look on Chris' face at that moment. The reality and potential ugliness of his new existence had just come crashing down on him without anything to buffer it. He could have killed them with a gun, knife or his bare hands without thinking twice if he had to, but the feeding was going to take a toll on his thinking.

Larson was running his fingers over his stubbly hair, while I just walked around the room and took in the shambles that had been made. Nothing seemed salvageable and, even if something were, there wasn't time to sift through the ruins. I knew we only had a few minutes before hotel security was going to figure out from where the body had dropped onto the pavement, and if we were caught in the middle of this we were going to have to fight our way out.

My nose had just begun to take in the stench of the dead as it began to overpower the pine cleaner that the maid service had used in their duties, when Lei walked over to me and interrupted my thoughts. She was still lost in her bloodlust and she ran her hands over her body longingly before reaching out and tearing open my shirt. I immediately grabbed her wrists and held them up and away from me, but she shot her head forward, kissed and licked my bare skin, sending a chill through me and leaving a wet red streak that ran diagonally across my chest.

"We need to go!" I whispered to her urgently even though I knew she was going to ignore me, "We can't afford to be detained by the hotel security, or the police. Chris!"

Chris had been looking at his blood smeared face in the bathroom mirror and seemed lost in the gothic horror of what he saw in his reflection. My voice snapped him out of his daydream...or nightmare...and his head spun toward me.

"Get the guns! We need to go now!"

Maybe it was the urgency in my voice that cut through to his addled brain, but he nodded and moved to the hotel safe and opened it. We had stored the handguns in the safe, as well as a couple boxes of ammunition. The rifles, shotguns and Desert Eagle were safely stashed in Larson's room, which was why I spun to Larson and said, "You too Major! Go get the guns from your room and head down the stairs to the second floor. We'll meet you at the bottom of the stairwell."

Larson still looked stunned. Couldn't really blame the guy, could I? Problem was I didn't have time to let him slowly recover his senses. I pushed Lei down to the floor and she moaned with pleasure apparently thinking I was going to mount her. Definitely didn't have time for that either.

Shame.

Larson let out a soft sound that made me turn my head to him and ask, "What?"

"I asked where we were going to go?" he sounded sheepish, which was a complete one hundred eighty degree change of personality for the man.

Not good.

"Major!" I tried to sound like my old police academy drill sergeant, "Let's get a move on!"

Larson responded to the tone of voice I used, and immediately stood up straighter and seemed to pull himself together as he ran from the room. I only hoped he wasn't bolting for the lobby before retrieving the guns from his room.

We were really going to need them. And very soon.

Chapter 44

Larson had been right. I didn't know where we were going to go. We all made our way down to the second floor via the stairwell. My guess had been that this hotel, like many other large hotels, kept most of the internal workings lodged on the second floor. Room and maid service, laundry, hotel maintenance and the like were located on the second floor, which also meant that there was likely going to be access to some service elevators that would lead us outside. It took us less than a minute to steal some clothes and towels from the laundry bins, bottled water from a room service cart, and then find our way out of the hotel.

The four of us stopped in a nearby alley, where Lei and Chris changed clothes as Larson and I dampened towels with the water so they could wipe away as much blood from their skin as possible. Once everyone had changed and cleaned up we headed to the garage where we had stashed the Jeep we had borrowed from Rogers. We had left the keys hidden under a floor mat so Rogers could collect it if he needed it, apparently he hadn't as the vehicle was sitting right where we had left it. Larson had the long guns in an army duffle bag to which we had added the handguns and ammunition and stashed it in the back.

I asked Larson, as we waited for Chris and Lei to climb into the Jeep, "have you checked on Rogers?"

"No, why?"

I had my suspicions, but I wanted to tread as lightly as possible for the time being. Larson had just witnessed something that he had always believed was purely fiction and it was going to take a little time for his mind to wrap itself around what he had seen.

I just shrugged, "He hasn't collected his Jeep. I just want to make sure he's okay."

Larson frowned at me while Lei and Chris settled into the

back of the vehicle, "If you have something to say, just say it."

I looked sympathetically at Larson and tried to sound diplomatic, "I don't have a statement to make, okay? I'm just trying to figure out how they found us at the hotel."

"Rogers wouldn't rat us out," Larson said with a level voice filled with one hundred percent conviction.

I raised an eyebrow at him, "I certainly believe he wouldn't rat you out, but they weren't waiting in your hotel room. They were in mine."

Larson shook his head, "I don't know the reason, but I do know that it wasn't Rogers. You're way off base here."

"If you have any other explanations, now's the time." I knew that I had left the subtlety behind at this point, but the gunmen had shot at Larson as well. He had to know that we needed answers, even if the questions were uncomfortable to ask.

"What about you?" Larson asked as he walked around to the driver side of the Jeep.

"Me?" I was so shocked by the question that I just repeated it back to him, "What about me?"

Larson retrieved the keys from under the floor mat and climbed into the driver seat, "Sure, you."

"You think I told the enemy where we were staying so they'd come and attack me?" I said dripping sarcasm off each word.

"Not exactly," Larson said as he started up the Jeep.

"Then what?"

"Think about it, who else knew you were staying at the hotel?"

I rolled my eyes, "Outside of the people sitting, here I can't think of anyone."

In the periphery of my vision I saw Lei's head turn to look at me, her beautiful eyes wide with shock.

I shook my head, "Okay, Alpha knew, but it isn't as though he was going to..."

"No," Lei said urgently, "He isn't the only one."

I frowned, not getting it, when Larson finished the thought for me, "What about your client?"

Initially I was too dumbfounded to put the pieces into an actual thought, then I think my mouth dropped open a bit as everything came together.

"Oh Goddammit! We even knew he was involved with Whelan before they had their supposed falling out." I shook my head in disgust for not having figured it out sooner, "How didn't I see that?"

"Simple distraction," Larson said matter of factly, "He had you convinced they were adversaries from the beginning. Hell, they may really be adversaries, but you have what he wants now."

I was trying to clear my head as I said, "He said he wanted information, but he also wanted Zach."

"Maybe he was willing to cut his losses and just settle for Zach?" Larson suggested. "Any idea why he wants him in the first place?"

I thought for a bit, but my head was still spinning from the revelation that Dimitri might have set us up.

Larson started up the Jeep and pulled out of the garage, "Any idea where I should go?"

I shook my head, "I'd say back to Rogers' place, but the chances are good they're watching it. Can you call him?"

"Sure, but why?"

"See if we can meet him wherever he's staying. It's probably off the board."

Larson nodded, "Good idea."

It took Larson a couple of tries, but he did manage to connect with Rogers. Surprisingly, I was very wrong about him being "off the board" as he was at the bungalow apartment where we had previously visited him. I wasn't able to distinguish most of the conversation as Rogers apparently did most of the talking, but Larson had pulled the Jeep around and headed toward Roger's apartment before he had hung up the phone.

"We aren't actually going to the bungalow, are we?" I asked fearful that I already knew the answer.

"We sure are," Larson said a bit too jovially.

"Is that such a good idea? You agreed with me a moment ago when I said there was a good chance that the place was being watched."

Larson nodded, "As a matter of fact, it was."

"Was?" I asked.

"Yep," Larson agreed with a big smile, "Apparently, Rogers had some recent visitors who cleared the area before he went home."

"What kind of visitors?"

"The U.S. Marines," Larson said proudly, "They've cleared out the area, actually came across a couple of people who appeared to be watching the house and took them into custody."

"Custody?" I shook my head, "who's custody?"

"Not sure. Looks like whatever Rogers was working on has been turned up significantly. He said something about the fact that because his cover was blown, the military was moving from a subtle role to a more aggressive one. Rogers let me know that he is being transferred and he's currently packing his things, but wanted us to come by and talk before he left. I think he wants to know if we found anything he can report before leaving. If there's something he can add to his report that will help, well, it will make up for the last couple days, and if not, then at least we can return his Jeep."

It didn't take long to reach Rogers' place and as we rounded the corner we could see a pair of black sedans pulling away from in front of Rogers' bungalow. The cars drove past us as we approached, but I couldn't see anything or anyone beyond the sedans' heavily tinted windows.

Larson looked uneasy as the cars past the Jeep, which made

me wonder if he had some idea of who might be inside.

"Friends of yours?" I asked.

Larson shook his head, "I was expecting Navy personnel, given the Marines having been here, but those vehicles weren't military."

I looked around, but couldn't make out any signs that there were soldiers in the area.

"Your boys still out there?"

Larson nodded, "That's what Rogers had said. They're probably dug in around the perimeter. Keeping a watch."

Everyone in the Jeep started looking out the windows as Larson pulled the Jeep onto the dirt road that served as a driveway.

"Okay," I said, "If they weren't military, then who were they?"

Larson just grimaced and shook his head as he took the keys from the ignition and stepped from the Jeep. The rest of us followed his lead and exited the vehicle to walk the short distance to the Bungalow.

When Rogers answered the door Larson's pushed his way in angrily, "You were holding out on us Pat...holding out on me."

Rogers initially smiling face dropped and was replaced by a look of regret.

"Listen..."

Apparently Larson wasn't in the mood to listen, "Just when, exactly, did you start working for the Agency?"

Rogers sighed, "Why don't we all go inside?"

Chapter 45

"Everything I told you was true," Rogers wasn't making excuses as much as explaining himself, "I tried to help you any way that I could, without revealing myself. The problem was that since Zach was considered KIA the mission was already in serious danger of being scrapped before I even got here."

"What mission?" Larson asked.

"You know I can't tell you that," Rogers voice sounded both apologetic and disdainful at the same time, if that were possible, "Besides, the help I was giving you was legitimate."

"Was it?" Lei asked accusingly.

"Huh?" Rogers looked confused, then angry, "Who the fuck are you to ask that of me?"

Lei bolted toward Rogers more quickly than the eye could track, and stopped right in front of his face, "I'm the fucking bitch who's gonna rip your throat out if it turns out you set us up."

Rogers didn't back down, but his expression turned more confused and less angry as he stepped back and asked, "Set you up?" He turned to Larson, "What's this bitch talking about?"

Larson sighed, "We had some unexpected visitors at the hotel. They were waiting for them in their room...and you knew where we were staying." Larson let the question hang in the air unspoken.

Rogers mouth moved a couple of times with no sound coming out, but when he found his voice the indignation sounded out clearly, "That is a hell of a thing to accuse me of."

Larson nodded sadly, "It would have been."

"Would have been?!" Rogers was losing his temper apparently at the defamation of his character.

"Yes," Larson said calmly, "Right up to the point I found out you're working with the so called 'intelligence' agency."

"Oh give me a break with the inter-departmental distrust shit!" Rogers had turned from Lei and faced Larson, "It's 'me' were talking about here."

"Oh, really?" Larson said with equal indignation, "Then tell me what the hell is going on here?"

When Rogers hesitated Larson softened without relenting, "Look, I still hold the rank of Major, and I'm still assigned with Special Forces, so I'm sure I have the necessary military clearance for whatever the classified information might be."

Rogers shook his head, "At this point it's not military. It's Agency. That, and the fact that the freaks you are traveling with are complete unknowns to the system, that's why I don't want to let unnecessary information out."

If this wasn't my cue to speak up, then I couldn't image a better time, "Then use us...freaks."

Rogers and Larson both turned to look at me. Rogers didn't have a happy look on his face, but was too curious to not respond, "What?"

"It seems pretty obvious that this assignment, or whatever, has been taken out of your hands. Maybe they are passing it on or doing whatever you people do, but we aren't part of your collective organizations. Hell, for the most part we don't even officially hold United States citizenship, but I have a strong feeling that our interests are very similar, right? Otherwise, why would you have been so willing to help us?"

Larson looked at Rogers with an interested gaze, while Rogers just looked at the ground.

"Is that right?" Larson asked.

I cut in before Rogers could answer, "I'm sure that there is a strong friendship between the two of you, but the CIA doesn't do anything, unless they see some kind of potential benefit to them."

"Rogers isn't just CIA," Larson countered, “He’s still one of mine.”

Rogers sighed, "No, he's right."

Larson turned back to his former teammate, "He's right? How

so?"

Rogers walked a couple of steps away from Lei as he spoke, "Zach didn't know he was working a CIA angle when he was assigned to the detail here in Bangkok. He was simply given a long-term undercover recon assignment. Obviously, the OP went south when he was discovered, but if you were right about him being abducted as opposed to KIA, then it would be all the excuse we would need to launch a rescue offensive into the territory. Hell, we could have probably even gotten the Thai authorities to assist in the assault and recovery."

"So?"

Rogers shrugged, "So I saw an opportunity to accomplish two things at once. Potentially finding Zach, as well as making a case for the Agency."

Larson didn't seem too upset, but I added, "And if we presented a potential threat to your mission?"

Rogers looked sheepish, "I would have had the Thai police detain you, until I could arrange for your transport back to the States."

Now Larson started to show the first signs of tension in his face, but I wasn't done.

"Transport for all of us?" I asked knowingly.

Rogers initially shot me a look of fury, but it cooled quickly and was replaced by a helpless look, "No, just the Major."

"What?!" Larson didn't bother to hide the betrayal in his voice.

Rogers held his hands up, "What else could I do?" He pointed at me, "He even said it himself, the part about technically, they are not American citizens. How would I have been able to justify that?"

Larson stepped up to Rogers and looked him in the eye, "So what were you prepared to do with them?"

Rogers couldn't meet his eyes, "The Agency would have had them turned over to the Thai authorities on some trumped up charges to keep them incarcerated until the crisis passed."

"And after the crisis had passed they would certainly have taken every step to see us released from whatever pit of a prison that we were stuck in, right?" I added.

Rogers just shrugged, "It's not like that's what happened. Don't punish me for something I didn't do."

"No, but you were prepared to do it," Larson volunteered, "Damn man, what happened to you?"

Rogers grew indignant, "What's that supposed to mean?"

"This isn't like you," Larson spoke softly, but the disappointment in his voice was clear, "Even if they're not official U.S. citizens, we don't throw our assets into a meat grinder when they're no longer convenient."

Rogers was quiet for a couple ticks of the clock, but then said, "The Agency does."

The two men looked at each other and I could see the years of trust and bonds forged under the trauma of battle experience dissolve as the truth was revealed. I have to admit it was a little disheartening to witness.

"In any case," I broke the silence, "Lei and I can be your best assets, if you'll trust us and if you will let us," I was putting extra emphasis in my words to help ease the tension that was now in the room.

Rogers turned and looked at me, "How?"

"We're going back."

"Back where?"

"To the village, and from there to the camp where they held Zach."

Rogers' eyes shot wide and he whispered in surprise, "You found their encampment?"

I shook my head, "Not the exact location, but I'm almost certain that Zach knows how to get back there. And for the record, Zach was adopting the girl as his own daughter. He had nothing to do with the intentions you had described to us."

"Was that scenario even real?" Larson hissed.

Lei chimed in, "Of course it's real."

Larson waved a hand dismissively, "I meant in this case Rogers. I meant with Zach, or were you just trying to put us off the trail?"

"It was legit," Rogers confirmed.

"Doesn't matter now," I said confidently, "What does matter is that we are going back in and we are going to finish this mess."

"You'll never get through the security," Rogers volunteered.

"We will...with your help."

"Me?"

"You?"

"What do you expect me to do?"

"We need equipment and information."

Rogers shook his head, "As you can see, I'm packing everything up for extraction. No way that I can get anything shipped in at this point."

I shook my head, "No need. You have everything we need right now. Or at least you did last time we saw you."

Now Rogers looked interested, "The entire operation has been taken out of my hands. Not my call anymore."

"You didn't have us on the table before. Now you have a team that can be completely disavowed. Now you have us, to do your dirty work and if we are caught, you can wash your hands of us, thereby taking none of the guilt or blame for whatever we do."

Rogers thought about that, and his interest was obvious, but his face screwed up in a look of concern as he asked, "What information do you need?"

"There's a piece of this whole thing I am not seeing. Zach's abduction, the experimentation on him, Dimitri Lagos involvement..."

"Who?" Rogers asked.

"Dimitri Lagos," I said, and when Rogers blank expression didn't change I explained, "He's kind of a...secretive character, who runs a vast portion of Russia."

"What? Like a crime boss?" Rogers asked.

"Sort of. In any case he's involved in this."

"Involved how?"

"I think that he and Whelan were working together on something, but they had some sort of falling out and are now working against each other."

Rogers shook his head, "I can't believe I'm having to play this much catch up, but who's Whelan."

I just looked at him, incredulous that he, and therefore the CIA by default, had absolutely no idea who they were dealing with.

"Dr. Phineas Whelan. He's a medical doctor, specifically a neurologist, and scientist who has taken a particular interest in how to disrupt the normal processes of the brain."

"To any specific end?" Rogers asked.

I decided to remain a little vague at this point, "Lei and I came up against him before and, at the time, he was short-circuiting the transmissions between the skeletal muscles and the brain with one of his inventions he uncreatively called a "Flash Box". Later it was revealed that the device was only the tip of the iceberg. His true intention was to synthesize a vaccine that would make a person completely immune to all viral and bacterial pathogens for a short period of time."

The part I held back was that the vaccine was derived from the blood of my people, due to our natural immunity to bacteria and viruses that we all possess. A culture founded on the consumption of natural blood products would have to develop an immunity over time, or it stands to reason that we would have been wiped out by blood-borne diseases centuries ago.

Rogers nearly exploded toward me, "WHAT?!"

I had to jump back to keep him from grabbing me, "What?

What's wrong?"

Rogers was completely unhinged, "Oh My God! It all makes sense now! I need to call this in and..."

Rogers moved in the direction of a phone, but Lei grabbed him by his tropical shirt, spun him around and flipped him into one of his chairs.

"Don't move," Lei had left her foot on his chest and pressed him into the chair, "Talk."

Rogers pushed Lei's foot off and started to get out of the chair, "Let me up! I need to..."

It was Larson who pushed him back down, "Give."

"Rob?" Rogers looked surprised at Larson, but what he...what we all saw in Larson's face at that moment, told Rogers that he had run out of time to keep information from us.

Rogers face turned from Larson, then to Lei and then me. Eventually his shoulders dropped as he gave in, "All right listen, Zach was assigned to investigate the possibility of someone having delivered some particularly nasty bugs to the area."

"Bugs?"

"Viruses. Controlled pathogens so virulent that they can be potential threats to the world's human populations."

Larson lifted his hand from Rogers's chest, "What pathogens?"

Rogers looked at him, "In this case, Hantavirus. Two strains, specifically Marhburg and Ebola virus."

"Oh Christ!" Larson looked very frightened, "How could they risk moving it? It's a damn death sentence if it gets loose from the containment units."

"Exactly," Rogers agreed. "The Center for Disease Control in the states keeps a very close watch on the presence of any outbreaks that may occur worldwide regarding a wide variety of pathogens. The World Health Organization operates in a similar capacity in Europe and Asia. Anthrax, cholera, small pox, AIDS,

Ebola, Avian flu and more, way too numerous to mention all the ones having a high priority for regulation and control for obvious reasons. Anyway, there are very few stock piles of these diseases within government agencies..."

"Why the hell would anyone deliberately stockpile the diseases?" Lei jumped in, "Why not just destroy them and remove them from existence?"

"Because even without the disease being present at this time, that doesn't mean it won't manifest again in nature at a later date. The stockpiles are kept in case of a new outbreak so vaccines can be synthesized as necessary. One such stockpile is in Atlanta with the CDC, while the other was in Russia, when it was the former Soviet Union. Unfortunately, since the collapse of the USSR, the security of the stockpiles have become increasingly questionable. Rumors of the sales of small pox and anthrax to terrorist organizations are common, even if there is no direct proof, but the potential is real enough. So whenever we get information that someone is dealing in biologics we investigate."

Lei and I never had any fear of diseases, after all, our immunity was something we had been born with, "So assuming Whelan has some of this stuff, what's he going to do with it? Let it loose in a specific area or something?"

"Unless he's figured out how to weaponize it," Rogers suggested.

"Not possible with hantaviruses," Larson cut in, "Our unit had to prepare for chemical and biological contingencies, so I know something about them."

We all turned to Larson, Rogers even looked impressed as his former teammate continued, "I know our best and brightest people have been trying to make those particular bugs viable within a delivery system for years and without any success. Something about the structure of the DNA chains that makes it impossible. I doubt one man, even this mysterious Dr. Whelan, had any success where the top American scientists failed."

"You don't know this guy," Lei stated with irony in her voice, "but why do it?" He'd poison any area he released it in for generations."

"Again, unless you had a vaccine to protect you, and of course others that you selected," I said with a nod. "It would be a more effective deterrent that any wall or army ever could be, because who would ever want to cross your borders and risk certain death by Ebola or Marburg?"

"Exactly," Rogers agreed, "it's the perfect dirty bomb. Better than a nuke because it does no damage to the property or the environment. It just kills off all the people. You could just walk in and take over without firing a shot, if you had immunity."

"And if Dimitri wanted to keep people out of Siberia without damaging the resources he's coveting..." Lei suggested.

Rogers looked at Lei, "Dimitri? Siberia?"

Larson ignored Rogers, "But Dimitri's people wouldn't need the vaccine, so why all the experimenting and interest in Zach?"

"I don't think Zach was part of that plan. My guess is that Dimitri wants him specifically for something else."

"What?" Rogers asked.

"I don't know, and last we saw Zach, he wasn't in any state to tell us, so that will remain a mystery until Zach regains his senses."

"And if he doesn't?"

I frowned, "Then I figure we'll have to ask Dimitri ourselves."

Silence fell after I said the words, and I supposed that I might have put a little too much lethal intent into them.

Lei broke the silence, "There's one thing I don't quite understand. If Whelan and Dimitri had a falling out, then who is he making the dirty bomb for?"

Larson and Rogers simultaneously said, "Terrorists."

They looked at each other and Larson nodded to let Rogers explain. "The Middle East is full of money, and people willing to use such an extreme measure, specifically on Israel. They could easily buy nuclear weapons from the stockpiles in Russia. The dissolution of the Soviet Union left a great deal of weapons of mass destruction lying stagnant and unaccounted for in numerous locations. Problem is they'd be dropping the Bomb on their own holy land and would have no way to celebrate their victory. On the other hand, these dirty bombs would clear out the "infidels" and leave the buildings standing."

"Ah crap!" I cried out as everything just fit into place for me, "That's why Dimitri and Whelan had their falling out."

Lei got excited, "What?! Why?"

"Think about the kind of person we know Whelan to be. He figured out what Dimitri was up to and realized he could double dip by selling the bombs to any well backed terrorists, which according to Rogers would be in unlimited supply, and then sell the vaccine as well for an additional fee. He could double or triple his money by dealing with people who weren't naturally immune, like Dimitri and his followers."

Lei nodded, "That does sound like our guy."

"Exactly," I said, "Dimitri could probably get another type of dirty bomb made, maybe not one as sinister as what Whelan came up with, but deadly enough, but if Whelan turns around and sells the vaccine to Dimitri's enemies, then he'll be hopelessly outnumbered by an army equally immune to whatever biological bug that might be out there. Dimitri and his people will end up losing their edge and have no chance. They'd lose everything."

Lei cut me off, "And that's why Dimitri needs Whelan's head on a platter and the information in his computers. He needs to know if Whelan sold any of the vaccine so he can take whatever steps necessary to be certain that it can't be used against him down the road."

Larson nodded, "But that still doesn't explain Zach."

I agreed, "No, but it does explain an awful lot that we didn't know before."

"So where does that put you?" Rogers asked from the chair Lei had thrown him into, "and can I get up now?"

"As I said, we're going back to the camp to get Whelan." I shot Rogers a look that let him know I would not be deterred. "He doesn't leave the jungle alive."

Rogers looked as though he might put up a fight on that issue, but he kept his mouth shut on the topic, changing the subject.

"Okay, so assuming that I give you the supplies you need, how does that help me?"

I thought for a second, "Now that it's out of your hands, what will the next person in charge want to do?"

Rogers shrugged, "Locate the camp. Then the priority would be to initially send in shock troops and scour the grounds for the pathogens."

"And if that fails?" I asked.

Larson finished for Rogers, "The military is concerned first and foremost with containment. They will want someone to laze the camp for a scorched earth contingency."

I turned to Rogers, "That right?"

He nodded, "Most likely."

I paced a couple of steps in each direction, "Okay, you call your people. Tell them your good friend Major Richard Larson is with you, and he has a team ready to infiltrate the camp. Once they look up his record they will know he is both capable and expendable, no offense?"

Larson was smiling ear to ear, apparently thrilled to be going back into action, "None taken."

"They should also love the fact that the team he has put together is just as capable, but as off the record as it gets, so there will be no risk of it coming back on the United States."

Rogers raised his eyebrows up and I knew I was speaking a language that the CIA couldn't resist.

"They will need to provide you with the laser targeting system so that, if we are compromised, you can provide them with their contingency plan." I waited for Rogers to voice any objections and when he remained silent I asked, "Do you think they'll go for it?"

He looked at me and then at Larson, who just shrugged his shoulders and said. "They're not my people. You'll know how they work better than I do."

Rogers nodded, "Yeah, they'll probably go for it. It will save them days of searching the jungle with their drone spy planes."

Larson volunteered, "Satellites a no-go?"

Rogers shook his head, "The jungle canopy is too overgrown for any direct imaging and the thermals were coming up with too many possibilities. The heat here screws everything up. That, along with the deniability will make your idea a viable scenario for them."

"So you'll call and sell them on it?"

Rogers nodded, "If they go for it I can have the targeting system in a matter of hours. How soon do you want to proceed?"

I turned to Larson and then to Lei. Both of them had wide toothed grins on their faces.

I chuckled and shook my head, "Immediately. We go as soon as you get your laser."

Chapter 46

The ‘designated conference room’ was never truly suited to be any such space. Tucked away next to the computer mainframe was a small area left for additional storage, and it was little more than a walk-in closet modified for that purpose. At least, that was what it represented, now that the folding table and chairs had been set up. Three chairs, one for each person that would be attending the "meeting."

Timberland was the only one who had been sitting in a chair, but now he paced the tightly enclosed space like a caged animal in a zoo. He had been on time: 1400 hours was the time the doctor had said to be here and he had arrived exactly on time. It was fast approaching the half hour mark, and he had been waiting and waiting. He told himself that if he was kept waiting a full thirty minutes, then he'd leave, and the two others would have to come to him. Come to him inside his tent and among his crew...his pack.

He respected both of the men who were going to be present, but respect was a two way street. Earned, not freely given, and if he was going to be disrespected like this, kept waiting like an inconsequential pedestrian, then he'd remind them who he was and the power he controlled.

At exactly 2:29 p.m. the only door of the conference room opened and Dr. Whelan walked in followed by a man Timberland hadn't seen since the "demonstration" that had taken place over a week ago. Mr. Pollard looked as though he hadn't changed his clothes in all that time. Sure the clothes looked fresh and pressed, but exactly the same style and color as last time. He felt a slight trickle of tension gather at the base of his skull as Pollard looked at him through dark shaded sunglasses.

"I was told two o'clock," Timberland pointed out unhappily, "it's two thirty."

Pollard said nothing and the doctor merely shrugged without

looking at him and said, "So?" He spoke casually, as if he held so much authority that he was beyond the courtesy of promptness.

Timberland was too on edge and he tried to let his rage out with each breath, "So I do not like to be kept waiting...especially when I've been asked to attend someone else's meeting."

The doctor looked up from the computer tablet he was fussing with and stared into Timberland's eyes. He seemed surprised that Timberland had found the nerve to speak out against him. Timberland met his gaze, and stifled a slight growl that was growing in intensity within his throat.

The doctor's face cooled and his eyes narrowed to slits. He stood up straight and took two steps to stand next to where Timberland was standing, looking straight into the mercenary's eyes.

In his naturally deep voice Dr. Whelan whispered, "You want me to fit you with a dog collar, Fido?"

The words hit Timberland like a bag of rocks, making him stagger back a step in surprise. Then he let the growl erupt from his throat in a roar and he grabbed at the tall but frail looking scientist. His fists scooped big handfuls of the doctor's clothing and he lifted the man off his feet and raised him over his head before slamming him back down on the plastic table. The knife was out of it's sheath before Timberland had even realized that he had pulled it free and the edge of the blade was pressed against the doctor's throat.

The doctor went wide-eyed with shock and fear as, apparently, he hadn't believed that Timberland would ever follow through on his threats and posturing.

Timberland's mind came back to him as he held the knife at the doctor's throat. Every fiber of his being was screaming at him to slice through the delicate flesh and let the blood spray warm and wet over his face. His mouth started to water at the thought of how the blood would taste in his mouth and the feel of it on his skin as he imagined cutting deeper and deeper into the doctor's body, until his blade found the spinal bones.

If it hadn't been for Pollard pressing the barrel of the .44 magnum revolver against his temple, Timberland might not have been able to resist making the cut. Now, even with the threat of impending death pressed against his head, Timberland still had to struggle to keep his hand from killing the obnoxious bastard.

"You pull that trigger," Timberland's voice was raspy and deeper than it should have been, "and my team will eat your guts before the sun has set."

"Your team?" Pollard spoke softly, "Don't you mean your pack?"

Timberland's eyes widened in surprise. Pollard knew.

He let the shock of the revelation wash over him before he spoke again, "Call it what you like, the results will be the same."

"Surprised? Don't be. It's what we do. What I do." Pollard moved his head in close to Timberland's ear and hissed, "Now get that knife away from his throat and sit your ass down in the fucking chair."

Timberland could feel the words as much as he heard them and the threat within each syllable was enough to dramatically cool his ire. He felt his hand shake slightly as he withdrew the knife from the doctor's throat and made a point of sheathing it slowly before shifting his body and sitting in one of the three chairs.

Pollard moved to another chair and set the gun down on the tabletop in front of him as he sat. This left only the doctor, who was still lying on his back where Timberland had pinned him, who rolled off of the table and onto to his feet, pausing next to the third empty chair. He didn't sit right away, but instead massaged his throat where Timberland had gently pressed the blade. His expression was complete indignation, but both Pollard and Timberland ignored it, so eventually, the doctor sat down in the last chair.

"Now if you two idiots can keep from killing each other a little longer, we have things to discuss." Pollard looked at the doctor, "My sources are telling me that you have the first weapon ready?"

The doctor was staring at Timberland, but he answered the question, "Yes, and not a prototype either. This is exactly what was requested, and is representative of what will be delivered in volume, pending the orders."

"Not a prototype?" Pollard sounded concerned, "You've run a test already?"

The doctor broke his vision away from Timberland, "What? No, but the technology is sound. We didn't have to invent a new delivery system as much as make the pathogens viable and dispersible inside the existing technology. Simple."

Pollard shook his head, "I have seen the pathogens work as intended, and I have also seen the bombs work when delivering and dispersing other materials. Now I want to see them both work, as intended, as a unit, or there will be no payments and no future orders."

The doctor raised his chin slightly, "Not from you, you mean."

For the first time Pollard's face showed expression as a thin pressed smile stretched across his lips, "Don't even think of it. You got into bed with me and my people on this. There's no backing out now."

Now it was Timberland's turn to stare at Pollard, "What?" he turned to the doctor, "You made a deal already?"

The doctor remained silent, but Pollard spoke up easily enough, "Oh yes, the good doctor here has made the decision concerning with whom he wishes to deal." Pollard turned to Timberland and smiled warmly, "It was the right choice, by the way as any other would have forced us to turn this little camp of yours into a parking lot."

Timberland stared blankly at Pollard, reading everything about the man's body language and expression before turning to Whelan, "Who does this guy represent? Who does he speak for?"

Pollard exploded forward in his seat, half standing, with his face a mask of rage and his words hissing through clenched teeth, as he answered for Whelan, "For the biggest fucking fish in the pond, that's who!"

Timberland jumped back in his chair at Pollard's words and just stared openly at the man.

Pollard peered down at Timberland, effectively cowing the mercenary before he shifted and sat back down in his seat.

"Timberland is it?" Pollard straightened his sunglasses and his voice returned to its normal octave as Timberland nodded, "You will find the other two buyers, and their escorts arriving from the south. Make sure to round them all up?"

Timberland felt relief wash over him as he was given something to do. Something...anything... that would get him outside of the tiny room in which he currently sat.

"How do you want them delivered?"

"Alive please. Beyond that, I don't care."

Timberland nodded, "Where?"

Pollard thought about that for a moment, "You say that Whelan's specimen was seen in that village about two kilometers from the camp?"

Timberland and the doctor both nodded.

"Is the first weapon ready for detonation?"

Dr. Whelan frowned at Pollard, "I suppose so. Yes."

"Good," Pollard spoke as if he had just figured out a riddle that had been plaguing him as he turned to Timberland, "Take them to the village. Leave them there."

Timberland nodded, "And the villagers?"

"Don't let them interfere."

Chapter 47

It took less time than I thought it would for Rogers to get the briefcase with the laser targeting system delivered. We were still loading ammunition into multiple magazines when there was a knock at the door. Rogers answered it and spoke with the young man standing outside. There was a quick and terse exchange of words before Rogers called for Larson to join them. Larson handed me the clip he was working on and strode out of the bungalow. I could see the young man snap to attention, salute and Larson returned the salute, then taking the clipboard the young man handed him and he began signing documents. He returned the clipboard and the young man handed him what appeared to be a legal size briefcase, saluting again and turning on his heel to leave.

Rogers and Larson walked back in with Rogers shaking his head in what appeared to be disbelief.

"That what we were waiting for?" I asked.

Larson opened the case and immediately nodded back at me, "I carried one of these so many times in field that holding it now is like coming home again."

"That was fast," I volunteered," wasn't it?"

Rogers nodded, "Thanks to Larson here it was."

Larson looked up, surprised, "Me?"

"Yup," Rogers confirmed, "It turns out, that when they took the assignment from me it no longer remained in the jurisdiction of the Agency. Now it's interdepartmental with the Navy, even though no one is particularly happy about that on either side, but Major Richard Larson's reputation apparently still has enough clout to expedite the process."

Larson looked as surprised as any of us, "Really?"

Again Rogers nodded, "Not that I'm complaining or anything."

The four of us finished our prep and loaded up the Jeep for the drive back to the village. It hadn't rained for two days, and despite the humidity we made much better time now that the ground had the time to dry out. Well, dry to a greater extent than the last time we tried to make our way in. We had saved maybe an hour of travel time when we passed the same checkpoint as before and this time the guards just waved us through so Larson didn't have to break anyone's arm to get it done.

By the three-hour mark we were at the end of the road and had to make the remaining trek on foot. It was nearly six o'clock when we arrived at the edge of the jungle and found ourselves at the grassland we had needed to cross just the same as last time. We decided to skip taking a rest and kept hiking for the village. Our intention was to try to cover the remaining distance before the sun had a chance to completely set.

We were only about fifty yards from the clearing in the jungle when Larson stopped us.

"Something's wrong."

Rogers knelt and surveyed the jungle, "What?"

"Listen," Larson indicated by pointing a finger to his ear, "You hear anything?"

We all listened, there was the usual chirping sounds of crickets, or whatever bugs made those sounds in Thailand, but there was something else. A buzzing sound that seemed out of place.

"Bugs?" Chris asked.

Larson nodded, "Yeah, but it sounds like a whole lot of bugs."

Lei shrugged, "It is a jungle."

Smiling crazily, Chris asked, "You ever see those movies where there's this huge army of ants that swarm over the ground and devour anything it crosses down to the bare bones in seconds?"

Everyone looked uncomfortably at Chris, who shrunk down under the scrutiny.

"It's not ants," Larson sounded confident about that conclusion, but still confused as to what might be the cause.

I was looking in and around a collection of exposed roots when I saw a small patch of yellow and black. I moved to the colors and knelt.

"Guys?" I called out, "Over here."

The four of them walked cautiously over and peered down at the ground where I was indicating. It was a bird. Small, beautifully colored and very dead. There was no sign of what might have killed it except that it had only empty sockets where it's eyes had been.

"Bugs do that to its eyes?" Lei asked.

"Don't think so, the rest of the body looks untouched...and fresh. It hasn't been lying here very long."

"So it's a dead bird?" Chris was getting anxious, "I mean this can't be the first time something died in the jungle, right?"

"Maybe," Larson didn't look convinced that it wasn't a sign of something sinister, but Chris did have a point. "Okay, let's keep moving, but keep alert for anything out of the ordinary."

We all stood and followed Larson as he led the way for another fifty feet before stopping abruptly again. We all waited but he just stood there looking ahead at the path we needed to travel. Rogers slowly began to move to Larson's position.

"Rob, what's..." Rogers went silent as he focused his eyes on where Larson was looking. He froze as well, just staring off into the jungle ahead of us.

Lei and Chris looked at me as if I knew what the appropriate military procedure should be. I just shrugged and began walking to where Larson and Rogers stood with Lei and Chris on my heels. We arrived and stared out at the jungle. Initially everything seemed normal, then I realized the buzzing sound from earlier had grown louder and that there were...objects on the ground in front of us that seemed out of place. Even in the dim light I could make out what the things were.

Dead things. Wildlife of all kinds were just lying there.

Dozens of birds and rodents, along with a couple of larger mammals including some small pigs and a deer. The mammals were in a poor state, as they looked like they had been deflated, like when the air had been let out of them it had left only their skins behind.

"What the hell?" Rogers looked like he was going to take a step forward when Chris caught his arm.

"Wait," he spoke urgently, "You said they were using biological warfare stuff right?"

Rogers's eyes shot wide and his hand reflexively, and uselessly, covered his mouth and nose.

I stepped forward, "Let us go first, but cover us in case we're not alone."

Larson nodded and pulled Rogers back to take up positions with their rifles as Chris, Lei and I walked into the kill zone on the jungle floor. We had only moved about twenty yards when we began to see even more dead things strewn about the ground, all leaking a black ichor that was probably blood, mixed with dissolved internal tissues. Some of the animals, like the birds, appeared relatively intact, but minus their eyes, while the mammals seemed to have fared even worse. There was a small pig on the ground that resembled little more than a deflated skin balloon that was practically floating in a puddle of what had once been its internal organs. The smell was unique as well. Not really the smell of death or decay, more like freshly killed meat stored in a refrigerator. It was still an unnerving, unpleasant and odor, but not nearly as noxious as it appeared.

The three of us walked on until we reached the edge of the jungle, after which, the village stood in a clearing. The village looked abandoned without any signs of life. There were no people moving around, no animals roaming haphazardly between the huts and no smoke coming from the fires within the shacks. We exited the jungle and began to cautiously walk through the village. We began checking huts for any signs of life, but every structure seemed to be empty. It appeared as though everyone had simply disappeared.

I pulled a two-way radio from my pocket and called Larson, "The place looks abandoned. No sign of anyone."

"Any indication that a biologic has been loosed?"

"Not in the village, but the wide and nonspecific species dead in the forest would convince me that something happened along those lines."

I could hear Larson grunt a curse and say something to Rogers before he spoke again into the radio.

"So how can we tell if it's safe for us to enter the village?" he asked.

I looked to Chris who had walked over when he saw me speaking on the radio. He said nothing, but shook his head.

"I think you and Rogers had better back out of there. We'll need to...wait."

Lei had been out of my vision for only a minute, but when she came back into view she was carrying something large in her hands. It was the old woman without her eyes that we had met earlier. She was limp in Lei's arms, the life gone from her body and her face was covered in a stained mask of black blood.

Chris sprinted toward Lei without realizing he was too late to be of any help. Lei put the elderly woman's body down gingerly as Chris arrived and he immediately checked for a pulse, but his hand recoiled at the cold feel of her skin. His head dropped as he could tell she had been dead for some time.

I walked up to them and to Chris I asked, "How long?"

Chris was coping by going into doctor mode, "I doubt two hours, rigor hasn't set in, but the body feels like a water balloon without any structure to it."

I nodded and Lei lifted the body and walked toward her hut.

"Where you going?" Chris asked.

"I'm taking her home," Lei kept walking and entered the woman's hut, where we had been guests only a couple days ago. I could see in my head how Lei walked her to what served as her mattress and gently laid her down on her back and propped her head up on her pillow. I guessed Lei arranged the bed linens in what would have been a comfortable arrangement on top of her before saying a quick prayer over her then moving to rejoin us.

"So what do we do now?" Chris asked, breaking me out of my introspective daze.

"How safe do you think it is in the immediate area?"

Chris shrugged, "No way to tell, but if your theory is correct then the nefarious Dr. Whelan didn't give his bugs a speedy half-life. He wanted them to hang around and take anyone out that hadn't bought his vaccination. I think we were very lucky not to have had those two military guys we brought with us infected."

I nodded, but Chris wasn't finished, "They should probably clear out of here. Put some distance between themselves and this place."

Again I nodded and picked up the two-way radio, "Larson, you and Rogers better head back to the Jeep. We found a body, and it looks as though she died the same way the animals had."

"Are you guys going to be okay in there?"

"Our unique genetics protect us from whatever hit the place, so we should be fine."

"If it WAS a biologic weapon you're safe, but not if it were chemical. Are you sure of what you're dealing with?"

I hadn't thought of that. I turned to Chris who just shrugged unknowingly, "Chances are if it's biological were fine, and if it's anything else, we'd already be dead or dying, so the odds are we're gonna be okay."

I sounded far more confident than I was, "We're going to take a look around and see if we can find anything that might lead us to their encampment."

Larson's voice sounded choppy over the radio, "We're currently moving back, but how are you going to find the camp now? Your whole plan rested on Zach taking you to the camp."

"True, but we only found one body, the rest of the village is empty. It's just a guess but I'm thinking that they had a warning of what was going to happen and evacuated. If we can find the rest of the villagers, then we'll probably find Zach as well."

Silence fell over the radio for a minute before Larson responded, "Okay, it's worth a try. Hell, it's not like we have anything else to go on. Listen, that radio you're holding is also a GPS locator. Keep it on you so we can find you when you need us."

"What's the range?" I asked.

"Just under a mile. We'll keep a watch on the map and if it looks like you are moving out of range we'll drive the Jeep closer to keep you in range."

"What about the hot zone?"

I could hear Larson sigh before he answered, "You take your chances, and we'll take ours. Over."

I smiled, "Copy that."

Chapter 48

Lei rejoined us and wore a sad look on her face.

"You take good care of her?" I asked.

"She seems...at rest," Lei said softly.

"Good," I said and put a satisfied sound in the word, "We owe her that much."

Chris looked from Lei to me and back again before saying, "So what do we do now?"

I turned and surveyed the village, "Best thing we can do now is to check the perimeter and see if there are any tracks leading away from the village."

"Why?" Chris asked.

"There were nearly a hundred people here and we only found one. Chances are they somehow caught wind of what was about to happen and took off. We need to find them."

"There's a flaw with that, you know?"

I turned to Chris, "Oh?"

"Sure," he said sincerely, "If they were warned and everyone took off, then why didn't they take the old woman with them?"

I shook my head. I had wondered that, but Lei spoke up, "She wouldn't leave."

Chris and I both turned and looked at her, but Chris asked, "Why not?"

Lei looked down at the ground as she spoke, "She lived here her whole life and, as wise as she was, it was the only home she knew. What they did here, whatever they loosed upon the area, would make it so she could never come home again. Somehow she knew that. Just as she knew she was too old to start over and call somewhere else home."

"So she stayed behind and let the virus kill her?" Chris asked, shocked.

"It was her choice, but it was also a sacrifice to show whoever discovered her what had happened here...assuming they could survive the virus."

Chris protested, "But if she knew what was happening, and that she could never come home again, then she would have also known that no one would ever be able to find her. Anyone who came into the area would drop dead from the virus."

"Unless she knew we would find her," I said softly.

Chris turned to me, "You told her about us?"

Again I shook my head, "No, but she just seemed to know things. She probably realized what was going to happen and made everyone leave. Stands to reason she would also know about us."

"But how could she know any of that?" Chris' logical scientific mind was in flux.

I turned to Chris and, without a trace of sarcasm or humor in my face I said, "She could talk to the spirits."

Chris rolled his eyes and chuckled, then took in the seriousness on my face, "You're serious?"

I shrugged, "That's what she told us. Who was I to argue?"

Chris shook his head, "Jesus, Steve..."

"Look, it doesn't matter why. What does matter is that the rest of the villagers are unaccounted for and there's a good chance that if they are alive, then so is Zach, and we need him to find the camp, right?"

Chris and Lei both nodded.

"So let's check the perimeter and see if there are any signs or tracks of a group of people leaving the village."

The three of us spread out and began walking along various pathways within the village until we made our way to the outskirts of the huts. Almost immediately Lei called out, "Over here! Tracks, and a whole lot of them!"

Chris and I jogged over to where Lei stood, but on my way over I found something as well.

"I have tracks over here too!" I called out as I stopped to study what I was looking at before heading over to join Lei and Chris.

When I arrived at their location I was surprised to see so many different footprints spreading out over a ten-foot span and heading into the jungle. The prints were definitely a human foot, some of which were barefoot while others were a solid flat shape indicative of the simple sandals and shoes that the villagers wore.

"I'd say you found them," I said as I reached Lei and Chris, "Well their tracks anyway."

"What'd you see?" Chris asked.

I shook my head, "Much fewer tracks. Several people, but they were moving nearly in single file, practically stepping right on top of one another's footprints, and they were wearing modern shoes."

"Modern shoes?" Chris asked.

"Yeah, from the tread and depth of the prints I'm guessing a military style boot, and very recently too. I think we just missed them."

"Think they were the ones who planted the bomb?"

"Doubtful. Anyone who wanted to use such a device would want to deliver it from a missile most likely. My guess is that they were more than likely here to see if the device did its job."

"They were ready to kill everyone in the village, just as a test to see if their damn bomb worked?" Lei's voice was angry, but she already knew the answer.

Chris raised his eyebrows and whistled, "Wow, that's brutal. So now we go after the villagers, see if your "boy" is among them, and hope he can take us to the camp where we can commence laying collective boot to ass?"

I was nodding along with what Chris was saying and had to stifle a laugh as he finished. Damn, I had missed the guy.

Lei immediately replied with an exuberant, "Goddamn right, you crazy mother-fucker!"

I tried to interrupt the oncoming rant, "Okay, wait a minute."

"What? What wait? We can't wait!" Chris was fairly bouncing up and down on his toes.

"Chris..."

"C'mon man, I'm pumped! Your uberbabe is tingling with anticipation, and she said the F-word while referring to me! We gotta go!"

Chris' attitude was infectious and I desperately wanted to join in, which made what I was about to say even more difficult.

"I'm not going with you two."

That sobered them both up real quick.

"Excuse me," Lei said angrily, "But what the hell do you mean you're not coming with us?"

I nodded, "Yeah, I'm going to follow the tracks over there," I pointed back to the spot where I had found the extra set of tracks made by people wearing combat boots. "Who knows, they might lead right back to the camp."

Chris protested, "Right, but that's what we're doing following the villagers tracks, you said yourself, Zach is probably with them and he's going to lead us where we need to go.

"True enough," I agreed, "But I also said 'probably', and we still need another plan in case those tracks end up leading nowhere. The ones over there appear recent enough to follow clearly."

"Then let's all follow them." Lei suggested.

I shook my head, "It'd be better if we have two options, as opposed to only one."

Lei crossed her arms in front of her and scowled at me, "So what you're telling me is that you are going to try to follow those tracks back to the camp solo, while I am supposed to find the people of this village with the walking hard-on over there." Lei inclined her head at Chris.

Chris' head popped up at hearing her description of him, "Hey!"

"It's the best approach," I said patiently, "You know that."

Lei huffed, and her eyes drifted to the ground, "Maybe, but I don't have to like it."

"Like it?" Chris interjected from somewhere in the distance, "C'mon, you know you love it!" then he started gyrating his pelvis at Lei, as if he were a Chippendale dancer.

I had to stifle a laugh, but Lei, who initially went wide-eyed with rage at the sight, ended up covering her mouth with her hand so Chris wouldn't see her smile at the spectacle.

I put my hands on her shoulders, "If nothing else he'll definitely keep your spirits up. Besides, I can't let him go alone.

Lei frowned, "But Alpha said he trained him personally, and he did fine at the hotel."

I nodded, "He has the training, but none of the experience. I need you to make sure he's got the support he may need, just in case."

I pulled her in close and kissed her hard on that pair of soft lips that I cherished to the core of my bones. In that moment my eyes closed and the whole world melted away around me leaving nothing but the sensation on my own lips and the pressure of her body against mine.

When I broke the kiss Lei still had her eyes closed and I could see them dancing behind her eyelids. She breathed out a heavy breath and opened her eyes instantly peering into mine.

"I love you," she said.

"And I love you." I whispered back as I let my arms drop from her body.

Lei turned and mumbled, "Goddamn right you do," as she began walking back to where Chris had finished his dance of love.

I collected the gear that I had set on the ground and began walking the perimeter back to where I had found the tracks. When I reached the edge of the clearing I looked back just in time to see Lei and Chris disappear into their spot in the jungle. I waited and watched the jungle canopy where they went in for a moment, then turned and ran into the jungle following the tracks of the combat boots. Whoever had made them was an hour or two ahead of me, and there was a good chance they were already back at their camp getting ready to report their findings. I only hoped I could find them before they could move on to whatever their next step was going to be.

Chapter 49

Timberland closed the seal on the laboratory door, walked to where the doctor was sitting at his computer terminal, waiting while the doctor's fingers flew over the keyboard.

Doctor Whelan didn't look up when he asked, "Is it done?"

Timberland nodded, "It's done."

"And were we successful?"

Timberland shrugged his shoulders, "Sort of."

Whelan frowned but didn't look up from his computer, "Sort of? What does sort of mean?"

Timberland just shrugged his shoulders again, "It means that the device and the air dispersal system was effective in distributing the plague quickly and efficiently. Everyone in the village was exposed and died as a result. Also, the vaccine you gave to me and my men was efficient in protecting us as well."

"I gathered that last part by the very fact that you are standing in front of me as opposed to having melted into an organic puddle of goo. So what's the 'sort of' in the equation?"

"As I said it killed everyone in the village; however, it turns out there was only one person in the village when the device detonated."

Now the doctor looked up in surprise, "Only one?"

"I can't explain it. We watched that village for months and it was never empty like that."

The doctor rolled his chair away from the desk and cupped one hand under his chin.

"Could they have been warned?"

Timberland pressed his lips together before saying, "By who? I only learned of the test a few minutes before you launched the drone. Did any other people have the prior knowledge, or time to get to the village, warn them and then initiate an evacuation that would take them out of the exposure zone?"

The doctor shook his head, "The launch was spontaneous. I hadn't even anticipated that Pollard would want another test beyond what he saw the other day in the lab, and only Pollard and I knew the plan."

"Could Pollard have warned them?"

"He didn't have enough time, and even if he did, why would he when it was he who requested the test in the first place?"

Timberland shook his head, "Well, explanations or no, it seems obvious that somehow they were warned."

The doctor frowned, and his eyes darted around the room as if searching for the answer written on the white walls.

"Well, that...is unnerving."

Timberland watched him. It was the only time he could remember when the doctor didn't appear to be completely confident and in control. The "helter-skelter" rapid eye movements gave a visual picture to the insanity that Timberland had always thought resided in the man.

Slowly, the doctor regained his composure and he calmed before saying, "It doesn't matter. We are so close to the end of this project that once the money arrives and the products are driven out of here we can finally leave this cesspool and rejoin the civilized world."

Timberland chuckled, "Maybe you can."

The doctor wheeled his chair around to face him, "Ah yes, you and yours will be moving on to the next assignment, correct? And what might that be exactly?"

Timberland shrugged, "It will be wherever we're sent. Doesn't matter to me."

"Doesn't it?" The doctor stood up from the chair and walked toward Timberland, "Aren't you tired of being a simple lackey for your master? He sends you and your...what did you call it? Ah right, your "pack" out here where you are in charge with total autonomy. Why is that exactly?"

Timberland clenched his fists as the doctor peered into his eyes.

"Is it because he has such absolute faith in you that he feels you need no checking or guidance?" The doctor waited for an answer, but when none came he continued, "I didn't think so. It's because you are one of the few who have any remaining sense of self control."

Timberland's eyes shot from where he was looking to the doctor in surprise.

"Oh yes, I know all about the 'condition' that you and yours live with. Frankly, I am surprised how well you all function as a unit, but then again, that's one of the traits that...'things' like you are supposed to be good at. That is, as long as there is a clear-cut leader within your little 'pack.' "

A low growl emanated from deep within Timberland's core and his instincts were screaming for him to strike out at the source of his discomfort.

The doctor could see he was agitating the mercenary and he smiled at the effect his words were having on him, "How does it feel to be a mere foot soldier? To be the one who does all the work and will never reap any of the benefits of your abilities?"

The growl was still in his voice when Timberland answered, "We don't operate like that. What we do, we do for the benefit of our...family."

The doctor smiled but also appeared unconvinced, "Really? And how have you benefited by putting your life on the line for your master?"

Timberland was ready to explode and he hissed, "Not my...master!"

"No? Then what exactly?" The doctor mockingly made a show of trying to think and then having an epiphany, "Oh! I remember now." The doctor's face screwed up in a mask of disgust as if the next words he would speak had a sour taste, "Your 'Alpha,' right?"

Timberland could feel the emotions swirling inside him, forcing adrenaline into his limbs and readying him for the imminent kill.

The doctor walked right up to him and patted him on top of his head a couple times before saying, "I understand your frustration. It would seem we both have a problem with our..."Alphas"."

The inclusion statement caught Timberland so off guard that he actually let out a small yelp as his body reacted to the confusing information. He knew the doctor wasn't like him, didn't suffer from the same needs and drives as he did, but he did seem sincere as he had said those words. Timberland had an instinct that told him when someone was lying and he could tell the doctor wasn't lying now.

"Alpha? You?" he managed to stammer as he fought to regain control of himself.

The doctor had walked off a couple of steps, but turned at the question, "Oh yes, and a very different kind to be sure, but just as problematic in any case. You see, where your conflict stems from a superior...and I use that term as a reference only, in the case of mine, "Alpha" appears to be his title and he is a particularly mortal opponent."

Timberland listened carefully now. his body had relaxed and his emotions were again under his control as he listened with interest to every word the doctor was saying. In the short time he had known the doctor he knew the man always had an agenda for whatever he was doing and Timberland knew that the man was going somewhere with this line of reasoning, but he wasn't sure what he was attempting to suggest.

"So here we are, at the tail end of our particular mission together with no clear cut destination to follow afterward?"

The doctor had phrased the sentence as a question and waited for Timberland to respond.

Hesitantly Timberland said, "Right."

"Of course I am, but I am thinking," the doctor swirled his hand in the air absently, "just wondering aloud if you will allow me the pleasure of doing so, that with you and yours having received the vaccination that keeps you immune to the little cocktail we have concocted here, it would be very easy for your particular 'Alpha' to find himself, and any others that might be ahead of you in the...'pack' exposed to a particularly nasty little virus."

Timberland listened and when the idea was laid out before him his eyes went wide.

The doctor continued, "Did you think your people would be in any way immune to my little creation without the vaccine?" The doctor didn't wait for an answer, "I think not and I think that this could easily clear the way for you to take your rightful place as the leader of your kind."

Timberland's head was already spinning with the possibility when a thought occurred to him, "But all of the product was to be shipped to Pollard. It was part of your deal with him."

"True, but I always keep a little for myself at the end of a deal. I wouldn't have been able to vaccinate you and yours if I hadn't kept some in reserve from my last endeavor."

Timberland nodded, "But if Pollard finds out there'll be hell to pay. I don't want the kind of heat that man can bring to come down on me."

"It won't."

"Sure it will," Timberland said angrily, "If there is an outbreak with bodies found anywhere other than where Pollard decides to use the device, IF he decides to use the device, then he'll know we were involved."

The doctor smiled, "Trust me my friend, I have a little surprise for Pollard and his people. They won't be an issue fifteen minutes after their money clears into my account."

Timberland just stared a the doctor for a time before saying nervously, "You're insane. You know who he represents!"

The doctor just smiled wider, "I do and I am telling you it's nothing to worry about."

Timberland stared at the doctor and again he couldn't perceive any deception in the doctor's words.

"So what is it you want?"

The doctor looked mortified, "Want? Me?"

Timberland screwed up his face in a "Be serious" look."

"Well, I suppose our newfound friendship could benefit from a certain return of the favor."

Timberland nodded, "And what would that be?"

"Isn't it obvious? I said, like you, I have my own "Alpha" that needs handling. I want you to 'handle' him."

"Me?"

"Why not? It isn't as though I am unaware of your abilities. You're pretty competent most of the time and I am guessing that when your life is on the line you'll be even better."

Timberland tensed, "Is that a threat?"

"What?" the doctor was clearly shocked, and then he understood, "Oh, no I'm not threatening you. I meant that by going after my 'Alpha' you will either be successful and kill him or he'll kill you. There really won't be any other possible outcome, so it should serve to properly motivate you."

"One man? You need me to kill one man?"

"Don't be overconfident! He, like you, is far more than he appears to be."

Timberland almost laughed out loud, "If I'm prepared, then no one man is more than I can handle."

The doctor shrugged, "Okay then, we have a deal?"

Timberland thought about it and couldn't really find a downside. All he needed was the courage and conviction to take on the leader of his group...and betray him.

"Tell you what," Timberland walked over to the desk where

Whelan had been sitting and picked up a pen and notepad, "I'll do your little favor for you and, when I get back," Timberland wrote something on the notepad and tore the sheet free, "You will either have one of your little devices ready for me or a briefcase filled with this sum."

Timberland handed the paper to the doctor who then read the number on the paper before saying, "Thinking a little highly of ourselves are we?"

"It's a fair amount, given how much you are going to be taking in on your deal with Pollard. Besides, what is it worth to you to have me solve your little problem?"

"And what about you and YOUR little problem?"

"I need more time to think about what I want to do. After all, my real loyalties have always been to money, because no matter whatever else I may be, first and foremost, I'm a mercenary."

Chapter 50

I wasn't trying to be quiet as I ran, hopped and crawled through the dense foliage as I followed the tracks from where they had started. I lost sight of them a couple times and had to back track in order to reacquire them, but for the most part it didn't seem as though whoever had made them had been concerned about anyone following them. Certainly they had made no attempts to conceal their presence, which made my efforts easier.

I had only been on their trail for about an hour, when I began to hear the rumblings of machinery and engines. The sound wasn't particularly loud, in fact it was barely audible, but due to the noise being so starkly artificial and out of place within the jungle surroundings, it was easier to recognize than it would have been otherwise.

I abandoned the tracks and followed my ears toward the sounds until the smell of campfire and cooking food wafted in on the breeze. I had gotten close, but still couldn't make out any visual sign of the camp, so I slowed my pace to a creeping stalk and kept my footfalls as silent as possible as I pushed forward.

The camp appeared all at once as I pushed a tangle of vines to the side revealing the clearing beyond. Unfortunately, I realized in less than a second, I had completely exposed my presence to anyone who might have been looking in my direction. I let the vines drop back into place and dove to the jungle floor as fast as I could. I waited and listened for any raised voices or sirens that might indicate whether anyone had seen me, but after a minute went by, then two and even three, without any change in the natural sound and rhythm of the camp, I guessed that I hadn't been seen.

I sighed and tried to convince myself that I had gotten lucky, before I slowly raised myself from the jungle floor, carefully peered through the vines and took in as many details of the camp as I could.

The first thing that registered was just how many people were moving around. It was like watching an ant farm with too many insects moving at too quick a pace to be properly counted. I guessed over thirty people, who were clad in black uniforms and well armed, watching over a couple dozen more, as they hauled crates from the only building in the camp that wasn't made of canvas.

That had to be the lab and, by default, Dr. Whelan had to be inside. As the realization hit me I could feel the adrenaline shooting through my system and sending butterflies into my stomach. My breath was growing erratic and my thoughts turned to how I could get into the building without being seen.

I studied the rest of the camp, which looked a lot like that Army M.A.S.H. unit that used to be on television, with the large tents spread apart unevenly throughout the length of the area cleared of jungle foliage.

None of the tents mattered. The only thing that they represented were obstacles to be avoided, in order to get into that one building constructed of, I thought, concrete. I watched and waited, until I thought I saw a flaw that I could exploit. There appeared to be one tent with only three soldiers inside. Each of them moved slowly as if weary and ready to go off duty for a while. It also happened that they were in a tent at the edge of the clearing. I guessed that two of the three soldiers would be close to my size, and a plan hatched in my head.

Admittedly, as plans go, it was a pretty basic one. I would sneak up to the tent using the jungle for cover and hit the three men inside. Afterward, I could dress in their uniforms and make my way to the lab with a little "on the go" camouflage. I'd have to move quickly as the headgear they wore would only partially cover my face, but it might be enough to keep from drawing attention to myself.

I waited another minute or so, just in case some other plan came to light. Nothing came to me, so I stood and began to work my way around to the edge of the camp.

Suddenly I felt something big and heavy cave in the left side of my body. I don't know what it was that hit me, but the impact was tremendous and it took me off my feet and carried me several yards before slamming me back down on the uneven earth. My head was spinning from the impact, but I could tell by the pressure around my chest that something had a hold of me. I tried to push myself away, but it's hold shifted itself to tightening around my waist as instinct took over and I twisted my body against the force. I knew that I could gain enough leverage to throw the thing off of me if I just had the time to worm myself around. Just a couple more seconds was all I needed and I'd be free, but a loud rustling in the trees to one side warned me that another something was approaching fast. I pushed with everything I had and, with a jolt I felt the grip around my body break away.

I tried to stand, but opted instead to roll out of the way and just barely avoided whatever charged me. I came up in a standing position from the roll and turned as the sound of yet another attack came from behind me. This time I saw the body of a man clad in black combat gear as he broke through the jungle foliage and charged at me with incredible speed. I also saw the glint of the blade he was holding and barely maneuvered myself in time to avoid the strike.

More rustling from my back forced me to turn again as another charge came from another direction. I leapt to the side too late as I felt the white hot pain of a knife's edge bite into my leg just below the meat of my calf. I rolled again and slammed my shoulder into an exposed root as I brought my legs underneath me and stood in a crouch. My leg and foot was still working despite the damage, but it was painful as my mind scrambled to figure out how best to counter these attacks.

I anticipated the next attack and spun to face the oncoming charge, only to have that attacker dart back and away once he realized I had changed my stance. Almost instantaneously another attacker charged in at my back from the new angle and again I was forced to dodge to the side without being able to make up any ground on my opponents.

I was getting frustrated and, admittedly, starting to fatigue as every evasive maneuver I made resulted in an attack by another adversary, from whichever direction my back was facing without giving me a moment of rest. If I spun to face the oncoming attack the charge faltered and a new one began from the new direction that my back was facing. It was almost as if I was being attacked by a pack of wolves.

My thoughts went back to the man I had fought in the village. I had thought something seemed unusual about my adversary, but what was I up against? It's not like these men were some kind of werewolves; being all fangs, claw and fur; so were they just using wolf tactics as a strategy against me? It seemed crazy, but if they were, then I had to admit that it was working. I had to turn the tables on them, and quickly before I lost what remained of my strength and stamina.

I rolled again to avoid the latest attack and angled my roll so I would be able to come up to a standing position with my back against the trunk of a wide tree. Now I had an effective barrier between myself and the direct path of attack to my back. I faced out to the foliage as I pressed my back against the wide tree trunk and heard the now familiar sound of the charge coming through the brush. I heard the hesitation and the hard planting of a pivot foot on soft earth and anticipated which side of the tree the attack would come from as I threw my elbow out to the right side of the tree.

The impact was incredible and the sound was a loud sickening snap and crunch as my elbow caught the charge as the attacker had veered around the tree. I had driven the point of my elbow back hard and caught the man in the face just below and to the right of his nose. I felt it as the bones of his face caved in on themselves as his head was stopped abruptly in place by my strike while the rest of his body was carried forward by his momentum and was lifted from the ground like a counterweight arcs from a pendulum. The man had been moving with enough speed and force to carry his body up and over while the top of his head plummeted toward the ground. He landed headfirst and his neck twisted awkwardly as his bodyweight came down in a near vertical landing.

For my part I felt that strange funny bone shock shoot through my arm from my elbow followed by a weird heaviness that I only realized later was my arm going numb. The impact had been so tremendous that I had given myself the equivalent of a nerve strike and my arm was going to be useless for a while...time to initiate plan "B."

I fished my good hand into my pocket and felt for the small two-way radio. I flicked the switch and pushed down on the button that would send my voice to Larson's unit, but never got a word out as I had to spin and shuffle to the side to avoid another attack. Foolishly, I assumed that the oncoming attacker would be trying for another knife strike to my body and I realized too late that the attack had targeted my hand that held the radio. The impact didn't cut my flesh but did send the radio flying off into the jungle. It seemed to float in slow motion as it tumbled through the air as I watched my only form of communication disappear into the tangled web of plant life that the jungle contained.

Turns out that it didn't really matter anymore because I then felt something strike me in the back that kind of reminded me of being stung by a wasp. It hurt, but not enough to be a gunshot. I was going to ignore it until my entire body seized up in a painful spasm. Imagine getting the world's worst cramp in not just one muscle group but in your whole body and you'll only have an idea of how painful the seizure seemed. I toppled to the ground and flailed around uncontrollably for a bit as I tried to scream from the pain, but couldn't even get my body to respond on that most basic level.

When the spasm stopped I was completely spent. I had no strength and couldn't feel any part of my body with certainty, as at least three of the attackers piled on top of me raining punches and kicks anywhere they could. It was only then that I dimly realized I had been hit with a taser, which mercifully explained why I couldn't feel most of the blows as they struck. I only hoped that they weren't breaking bones as I was eventually rolled onto my stomach, my arms placed behind my back and my wrists and ankles were bound and immobilized by heavy duty zip ties.

I forced my head to look up only to see the heel of a boot coming rapidly toward my face. Instinctively I pushed my head down into the earth to protect my eyes, but the impact of the kick still made everything go black.

Chapter 51

Lei and Chris had been walking for nearly three hours by the time the tracks ended and left them spinning in circles, wondering which way they should turn.

"All this time spent and we lost the trail," Chris was shaking his head as he sat to give his legs a rest.

Lei was pushing leaves and scrub brush aside as she studied the ground, "We just have to find the trail again."

Chris chuffed at her, "Oh really? Is that all? Well, can you see any sign of their tracks?"

"No."

Chris rolled his eyes, "Well, that's just great."

Lei lifted her head and smiled at him smugly, "But I do see how they tried to cover their tracks."

Chris grew attentive, "What's that mean?"

Lei looked back down and pointed to a spot on the ground, "Their tracks are gone, but that's only because they tried to conceal them." She knelt down and lifted a couple of leaves away from where she was looking. "See how the dirt here is so even?"

Chris walked over and knelt beside her. He dropped his gaze, but it all just looked like dirt to him.

"No, sorry, but I can’t see anything."

"Okay, take my word for it then. Someone has moved the earth around here to erase the footprints, probably with a branch of," Lei held up a couple of the leaves that she had been brushing aside, "leaves."

"Why do you say that? Beyond the dirt thing I mean?"

"Look at these leaves," Chris did so, still uncomprehending. "They're quite green. They didn't fall off their branches naturally."

Chris looked all around at the jungle floor and noticed that, although other types of leaves were spread haphazardly in different places, there were almost no other leaves like the one Lei was holding except where she was kneeling. When he looked past her he could see the odd collection of leaves leading away and deeper into the jungle.

Chris whistled, "Damn, they were trying to be so careful and they practically left a trail of breadcrumbs to follow."

Lei nodded, "Be careful. The fact that they suddenly started covering their tracks probably means they realized someone was following them. "

Chris' face grew serious as he nodded his understanding. Carefully the pair started to follow the obscure trail of leaves as it wound around the jungle floor. They had only covered about fifty yards when Lei suddenly stopped in her tracks and knelt.

Chris did the best he could to move quietly to her side and whispered, "What's up."

Lei didn't answer, but instead kept her head down, as her eyes darted from one side to the other. Slowly she pivoted and turned her head around to look behind her and then let out a quiet sigh of frustration.

"What?" Chris asked.

Lei took a tighter grip on the rifle she carried, "Don't make any sudden moves, but we're surrounded."

Chris' whole body shook as he physically fought to control himself from bolting upright, "What? How? I didn't hear anything."

"They were waiting for us. The trail must have been bait and, when they heard us coming, they took up positions along the trail and just let us walk right into the snare. I only heard them when they moved to block the path we came in on."

Chris flicked the safety switch off of his rifle, "Who are they?"

"No clue, but we're not dead yet, so they must either be interested or friendly."

Chris scanned the jungle, but couldn't see any sign of a human being, "So how do we keep it that way? Us being "not dead yet" I mean."

Lei seemed to think for a second and then said, "We stop playing games."

Lei slowly stood up with her hands held out to the sides. She made a show of extending the rifle away from her body before dropping it on the ground next to her and then held her hands in the air. Chris blinked a couple times in disbelief and then understood what Lei was doing and mimicked her every move. Almost as soon as he had dropped his own gun on the ground and had his hands in the air the sound of people approaching rapidly became loud and clear.

They broke through the jungle and stopped as soon as they were clear of the foliage, bringing their rifles to bear on the duo. They were all men. Small, wiry, dirty and wearing clothes that looked like homespun. At first there were only a few that emerged from the surrounding bushes and trees, but in a matter of seconds that number quadrupled, and every pair of their hands carried old bolt-action rifles. Each gun seemed to be in greater disarray than the one next to it, and were crafted to be best suited for hunting at over one hundred yards. They would be particularly clumsy at the close ranges they were now being used, not to mention the fact that rifle bullets would probably pass right through them, and then through the people standing on the opposite side, so the danger to themselves was likely to be greater than anything Lei or Chris might do to them.. Still the bullets would more than do the trick to kill or incapacitate both Lei and Chris, if the men decided to fire.

Lei and Chris just stood their ground passively and waited while the men closed in on them. Then something large moved through the jungle toward them and the men parted to let it through. An enormous man standing nearly seven feet tall moved into the open. It was Zach. He had removed his shirt and was standing with every inch of his exposed skin caked in mud that had dried and gave him a monstrous appearance.

Chris craned his neck upward to look into Zach's face, "Lemme guess," he said to Lei without facing her, "This is the guy we're looking for, right?"

"Yep."

Chris sighed, "Do any of you people even know someone besides me who is under six feet tall?"

Lei frowned, "What?"

"I mean, seriously! When this whole little adventure started between me and Steve, the first thing that happened was I ran into Alpha, who happens to be a damn giant in his own right. Now here I am, face to face with the missing link and, from what I can tell, I ain't never going to look him eye to eye."

Zach turned his head to concentrate on Chris who was becoming more and more animated as he spoke.

Lei was gesturing with her hands for Chris to tone it down, but he either didn't notice or he ignored her outright.

"Best I can hope to do with this guy is stare eye to tits with him. I mean, how is anyone going to take me seriously as a bad ass if I'm staring at them eye-to-tits?"

"Chris."

Chris turned casually to Lei as he continued, "Oh sure, I know that works for you..."

"Chris!"

"...two of your biggest assets..."

"Chris!"

Chris stopped talking and looked up from Lei's chest to her face, "...What?"

Lei frowned, "That whole little tirade was just so you could gawk at my boobs, wasn't it?"

Chris' face instantly look indignant and he seemed as though he was going to protest, but then he pressed his lips together, "...Um, well...I mean...maybe."

Lei shook her head, "Chris, if we get through this alive I'll give you a damn lap dance if you'll just shut the hell up right now."

Chris' eyes went wide and he made a gesture of locking his lips closed with an imaginary key and then tossing it away.

Lei stepped forward toward Zach, "Do you remember me?"

Zach didn’t say anything, but he did nod his head.

"Then you know we're not the enemy here, right?"

One of the villagers said something that sounded urgent in whatever Thai dialect they spoke. Lei practically jumped out of her skin when Zach responded fluently in return.

The villager looked from Zach to Lei, his face softening and then he looked at Chris and frowned before spitting on the ground.

"Hey! I get that!" Chris pointed his finger at the man, "that means the same thing in every language!"

"He can speak now?!" Lei said out loud to no one in particular, then she looked at Zach, "You can speak now?!"

Zach removed the sunglasses from his face and his eyes had lost the majority of their red coloration leaving only a slight pink tinged coloration that appeared very similar to someone who had been swimming in a chlorinated pool for too long.

"San!" Zach called out, and a small boy, maybe eleven years old, walked around the adults and hid behind one of Zach's legs. Zach said some words in a very calm tone and the boy appeared to relax, then Zach flicked his head at Lei and the boy stepped forward.

The boy's voice was high, evidence of him not yet having gone through puberty, but he carried himself as well as any professional translator when he said, "Pha's father would like to know if you saw what happened at the village."

"Uh oh," Chris mumbled under his breath, but Zach heard him and swiveled his head in Chris' direction. He studied Chris a moment and then his shoulders dropped as he let out a sigh and turned back to Lei.

Lei nodded, "Yes, it's as bad as you think. I don't believe

anyone can return to that village for now, maybe ever."

The boy started to tremble as Lei spoke and when he translated the words his voice broke and tears began to fall from his eyes. He was tough and didn't break down and cry outright, but the profound effect that the loss of his home had on him was evident. Some of the other men with rifles wiped at their eyes, but otherwise maintained their composure, as Zach softly laid a large hand on the boy's shoulder before asking something else.

The boy nodded and wiped the tears from his face before asking, "Pha's father asks if grandmother escaped?"

Lei bowed her head and then shook it slowly from side to side. Now the boy did start crying and Zach knelt and quickly pulled him to his chest. The boy ignored the mud that had caked on Zach's skin and bawled. Zach held him with arms that nearly encompassed the entirety of the boy's body until one of the adults tapped the big man on his shoulder. Zach looked up and nodded then gently pulled the boy off of him and led him into the arms of another man who quickly picked him up and carried the boy back into the jungle.

Zach stood and watched them go as they disappeared into the jungle, then he turned to Lei and held out his hands and shrugged his shoulders.

"What?" Lei asked, "I don't understand."

Zach repeated the gesture and then pointed to the rifle Lei carried.

"Oh, you're asking what are we going to do now?"

Chris chimed in, "That's the sixty-four dollar question isn't it?"

Lei asked, "Can you lead us back to the camp where they held you?"

Zach clearly didn't understand her words and only frowned in confusion as she spoke. Lei kicked herself for letting them take the child away before she could get all the information she needed.

"Oh this is just perfect!" Chris was stomping around clearly frustrated.

"Chris!" Lei scolded and would have said more but Chris interrupted her.

"No! I have had about enough of this confusion crap! He understands English, he's just psychologically scarred and can't make his mind work properly as a result." Chris moved toward Zach despite several of the villagers raising their rifles and pointing them in his direction. Chris ignored the rifles completely and stomped right up to Zach and stared straight into his chest while pointing an index finger at the giant as he spoke.

"Listen up Sasquatch, I don't like the jungle. I don't like bugs, or the wetness, or the humidity, or the dark, or the smell of anything else that is jungle. But here I am, walking around with an uncomfortable chaffing developing in my crotch and ready to possibly get killed by a bunch of hired guns bent of ruining the world in the name of money. What's more, there's this insane scientist who likes to tinker around with people's brains before he melts them into goo from his own recipe for biological terror."

The villagers all looked confused but Zach stood motionless as Chris continued his rant, "He's responsible for killing my friends," Chris pointed to Lei, "killing her family," then he waved his finger at the men of the village, "killing their family," and then Chris stood on his tip toes and looked up and into Zach's pinkish eyes, "and if I'm not mistaken, your family. So we need some neurons in that gigantic cranium of yours to fire straight and true again so the message gets through to you that it's time for some serious and permanent payback."

Chris lifted his rifle and thrust it sideways into Zach's chest. The big man didn't flinch at all and Chris rocked back slightly as the impact rebounded back up his arm and threw off his balance. Chris shook the rifle and Zach gently cradled it in his hands.

"Okay, right now the guy who is my best friend in the whole world is trying to find that damn camp on his own and I am not going to let him down by not having his back if he needs me. So either get your head in the game Frankenstein," Chris paused and pointed at the rifle and waited. When Zach didn't respond he ripped it back out of Zach's giant hands and cocked the levers readying it to fire, "Or get your useless carcass out of my way."

There was a moment of silence that followed. Lei watched as the men of the village looked at each other as if asking if they could shoot the crazy person amongst them while Chris kept his countenance stern and directed solely at Zach, who's expression was completely unreadable.

Then, ever so slowly, the big man smiled.

Chapter 52

As plans go mine apparently could have been thought through a bit more thoroughly. I remembered the ambush just outside the perimeter of the camp and then getting my ass kicked, but how I had arrived in the room I was now in was a mystery. I suppose I should have simply been grateful that I wasn't dead, but any joy I might have felt along those lines was tempered by the fact that my wrists, ankles, waist and throat were all entwined by what felt like rough leather straps. I tried to pull with my arms but even with my way above average strength I couldn't even feel the leather give, much less tear.

I looked around, and found myself in a room lit only by the ambient light coming from a computer screen and a collection of electronic monitoring equipment that appeared to be of medical design. The cold I felt on my body where it touched whatever I was strapped upon told me that it was made of metal. I rolled my eyes, when I realized that how widespread the cold felt, over the entirety of my body, could only mean that I had been stripped of my clothing. Taking away a prisoners clothing was by no means a new tactic. It left the prisoner with a sense of vulnerability and self-consciousness that weakened their will and resistance, but if they thought it was going to have that effect on me they were in for a surprise.

I lay there in the near dark for what seemed like an hour, before I heard an electronic beeping followed by the sound of someone turning the doorknob. The sound of footfalls on a concrete floor were now easy to make out, as what I guessed to be two people entered the room. They stopped by the computer and the monitors studying whatever readouts they were interested in, before turning to me. I couldn't make out their faces but the white lab coat that one person wore was clearly visible while the other was wearing something dark, but not the mercenary jumpsuit that I had been seeing so much of recently. This, I guessed, was more like a business suit.

Then a face appeared above me an instant before a flashlight burned my vision away.

"So what do we have here?" the voice was a deep, full basso tone that might only have been rivaled by the late Barry White. I didn't answer the question because, after all, I wasn't even sure it was directed at me.

The flashlight was moved away and orange moons remained and clouding my ability to see for another few moments as the voice asked again, "I said, what have we here?"

I coughed, cleared my throat and answered hoarsely, "Where am I?"

I heard a sigh and then a click that sounded very similar to a key on a keyboard being pushed. I was immediately followed by a jolt of pain that caused my whole body to arch up as I felt every muscle in my body spasm uncontrollably and it was as though my own strength might actually cause my back to arch beyond it's abilities and potentially snap my spine...and then it stopped. My body flopped back down onto what I could now tell was a kind of hospital gurney as the man in the lab coat manipulated a lever and caused the bed to tilt until I was positioned in a near upright attitude.

"That was to help you focus," the deep voice said, "Open your eyes please."

I hadn't even realized I had shut my eyes until the voice had told me so. I slowly opened them and could see that the light in the room had been turned up. I could see the two men standing in front of me, one was a stern looking man in a business suit so dark that it could have been black, but was probably a charcoal number of some sort. An all-black suit would be way too cliché, although suitable for the CIA agents. I can't explain how I knew that this man was part of the agency, I suppose it just felt right, but I was more interested in the other man, the one in the lab coat. That man was Dr. Phineas Whelan and was the man I had come here to kill.

My eyes went to slits, but my mouth smiled as I hissed, "Hello doctor Whelan."

The doctor's eyes went slightly wider in surprise, "Have we met?"

I nodded, "I know you."

The doctor stared at my face and then began to walk around the gurney, "Strange then, that I do not know you."

"Our paths didn't cross, but I am well aware of you and your 'work'."

"Really?" the doctor moved back to the front of the gurney to face me, "Any particular work that interested you?"

"I know most of it."

The doctor chuckled, "Oh, do you?" he then fished something out of his pocket, "Then you should know that the single CC of liquid in this vial will is enough to kill you should I drop it on the floor."

I just smiled.

The doctor's eyebrows rose in patronizing scrutiny, "You think I exaggerate?"

"No," I spoke calmly, "I just don't think you would risk you own life by dropping it."

The doctor nodded quickly, "That's true, and normally you would be absolutely right. But you see, Mr. Pollard and I have been vaccinated against the effects of the virus in this test tube. It's a little cocktail of my own creation that you haven't had the luxury of receiving."

I frowned. The doctor not only didn't know who I am, he also didn't know what I am. That left me wondering who he did think I was.

I decided to do a little fishing, "So what do I have to do to keep you from dropping that vial?"

The doctor's face immediately became cheerful, "Ah, so you are quick to grasp the parameters of your situation. That's good as I don't like wasting time."

The doctor gestured to the man he called "Mr. Pollard" who walked forward and peered down at me.

"Recognize him?" the doctor asked when Pollard had moved in close.

"No."

The one word was all he said, but it spoke volumes as I heard the Russian accent color the word.

The doctor frowned and looked back at me, "Is that possible?"

"I don't know everyone in the CIA, but I am familiar with the agents that are assigned in the field for this part of the world. I do not know who this man is, but I can tell you that he is not one of those agents."

I was hardly listening to the words and was instead concentrating on the accent. It was all going down exactly as we had predicted. The man must be part of the Russian government that Dimitri and his people were planning on going to war against. The doctor had betrayed Dimitri and sold the vaccine to Pollard and was not only going to provide the Russian government with a level playing field against Dimitri, but he was going to sell the biological weapon to them as well.

"So who is he?" the doctor sounded a little freaked out that there were things he didn't have answers for.

"Don't know," Pollard said calmly, "Why don't you ask him?"

The doctor looked surprised and then understood, "Oh right, right." He turned to me, "So, who are you?"

"I suppose you could call me the past that's come back to haunt you."

Yeah, that might have been hokey but I wanted to stall for time...Why? I'm not sure, but what else was I going to do?

"I see," then doctor said calmly and he moved his face very

close to mine, "I think you need to focus."

He reached one long spindly arm out and touched a key on the keyboard. There was a static sound and a hum of what sounded like an electric generator before the pain shot through me again. I tried to fight it but I was screaming through clenched teeth mere seconds after the onslaught had begun. When the electricity ceased my body again dropped back to the metal gurney and only supported by the restraints, having been arched again and totally worn out by the full body muscle spasms, and I noticed that there was a slight smell of burned hair in the air as I panted for breath.

"Are you more focused now?" the doctor asked smugly, "I asked who you were."

I was still trying to catch my breath when I garbled my name, "S-Steve Ja..Jacobs."

The doctor smiled, "See how easy that was?" He turned to Pollard, "That name mean anything to you?"

He shook his head "no" but was already typing it in on his smart phone.

The doctor looked down to the small screen and squinted his eyes trying to make out what Pollard was looking up. It appeared as though he wasn't able to see anything because he appeared to give it up and turned back to me.

"So, are you CIA?"

I shook my head "no" as I fought to collect my breath.

"If you're not CIA..." the doctor thought for a moment then an idea struck him, "Did Dimitri Lagos send you?"

Pollard looked up from his Smart phone at the mention of Dimitri's name.

I didn't see any reason to lie and I definitely wanted to extend the time between shock treatments, "He told me where I could find you."

"So you work for Dimitri."

"No."

"No?"

"I took his money," I turned my head and spat something vile tasting from my mouth, "But I'm not one of his people."

The doctor froze, "What do you mean 'one of his people'?"

I thought a little diversion might be well suited here, "Only that I am not one of his employees. He wanted your research and knew that I have been trying to find you."

"Trying to find me?" the doctor ran his fingers through his hair, "Why have you been trying to find me?"

I smiled, "I don't like you."

The doctor frowned and held up a finger, "Ah, ah, ah. You seem to be losing focus again."

I heard the panic in my voice more than I realized or felt it, "W-WAIT!"

The doctor ignored me and pushed the key on the keyboard. Again the pain shot through me, but this time I didn't have the strength to scream. The muscle spasms did force a strange moan from my throat and I felt a tooth crack as my teeth bit down harder and harder.

When the excruciating electrocution finally subsided the first thing I realized was that I was swallowing my own blood. I guessed that at some point I had bitten my tongue and it was all I could do to open my mouth to let the fluids dribble out."

When my hearing returned I could see that Pollard and the doctor were arguing.

"…Won't find out anything if you kill him."

"Don't tell me how to do..."

I opened my eyes and saw the doctor looking at me, wide eyed with all of the color drained from his face. Pollard obviously noticed the change in his colleague as well because he immediately quieted and glanced from the doctor to me and back to the doctor.

"What is it?" Pollard said with a note of impatience in his voice.

"His blood..."

I cursed myself for being a fool at having not swallowed my blood. The blood of my people is not quite the same shade of red as normal people. Due to our dysfunctional hemoglobin our blood appears more a translucent pinkish color as opposed to crimson or red, almost as if our blood had been over saturated with water. I looked down to the floor where my mouthful of blood had splattered and could clearly see the concrete floor through the transparent pink hue. I looked up to see the doctor staring at me as he started to back away from the gurney and computer bank.

"He's one of them," the doctor sounded as though he was on the verge of panicking.

Pollard seemed unimpressed, "So he works for Dimitri, so what? He practically said as much and we knew they'd be coming at some point."

The doctor shook his head vigorously, "No, he's not one of Dimitri's people."

Pollard looked confused, "How can you know that?"

"The blood of Dimitri's people doesn't look any different than ours." The doctor pointed at the blood spot on the floor, "Blood that appears that color is a side effect of having been on a particular type of serum for decades. I spent a significant amount of time working on donors with that particular color blood. I'd know it anywhere."

Pollard looked down to the blood splatter and then at me before asking, "So who is he?"

Doctor Whelan fidgeted with his hands for a moment, then reached in his pocket and pulled out a large syringe.

Pollard immediately reacted, "Wait, we need to know who he is and how many others might be with him."

The doctor checked the level of whatever fluid might have been in the syringe and shook his head, "No, we're done here. Get your men to load as much as they can and then get out as quickly as possible."

"What?" Pollard was clearly not used to being in the dark and not in complete control of the situation.

On the far wall came the sound of a phone ringing. It's electronic tone beeped loud enough to break the doctor's concentration and he turned, unsure of what to do first.

Pollard turned in the direction of the phone, "I heard you ask your people not to disturb us."

The doctor nodded and, begrudgingly, pocketed the syringe and walked into the shadows of the room in the direction of the ringing phone.

He picked up the receiver, "What is it?" and then went quiet as he listened to the voice on the other end.

When the doctor spoke again he was shouting into the phone, "Get some people out there now! And set up some kind of perimeter defense around the outside of the lab, in other words do your damn job!"

There was the sound of the doctor slamming the receiver down on to it's cradle and then his footsteps hurried over, "We're out of time! We need to get what we need and get out as fast as possible."

Pollard was already moving to the door, "What? Why?"

"Motion sensors in the jungle are going crazy. Maybe fifty or more unknowns headed our way."

Pollard didn't argue, but turned back to look at me, "What about him?"

The doctor didn't stop moving toward the door, "No time for the drugs now. Just shoot him."

Chapter 53

The camp had come alive with activity and Timberland's group called out orders to multiple squads dividing their company of mercenaries into two basic teams. An offensive unit was going out to head off the incoming threat, while a second team was given selective fall back and defensive positions, in case the first team couldn't stem the oncoming tide of hostiles.

The mercenaries moved with experienced precision and were about to deploy into the jungle when the first explosions of gunfire caught them much sooner than they had expected. Blood erupted, as men began to contort and fall from the projectile's impacting their flesh and any coordination the mercenaries had dissolved. The location of the gunshots, obscured by the surrounding jungle, subsequently gave the mercenaries little indication of which direction the fire was coming. The men who stopped to look for the attackers were gunned down while those who instantly and desperately scrambled for cover found themselves pinned down.

It was also immediately clear that they weren't under an attack by a modern assault team as there didn't seem to be any of the quick repeated shots that would indicate semi-automatic, or even the automatic machine gunfire. Unfortunately, any initial confidence this might have instilled in the mercenaries never manifested itself, due to the fact that the shots had an extremely high degree of accuracy. Some of the men tried to return fire, but without any definitive targets there was no way to tell if the rounds they haphazardly sprayed into the jungle were meeting with any success.

Panic took over and, as mercenaries are want to do when the chips are down, their ranks broke. They ran for the only solid structure in the camp, which was the concrete walled lab in the center of the development. Some of the mercenaries who tried to make a run for it were literally cut to shreds by sniper bullets that struck them from seemingly every direction. Their bodies twisted and jerked wildly as they were hit by the individual rounds from the left, right and behind, before their bodies fell lifelessly to the ground.

Three figures broke from the jungle and ran after the retreating mercenaries. They fired no weapons, but moved with such speed that they caught the diminishing troops in a matter of seconds. Glints of light flashed, and blood flowed from multiple lethal wounds, as some of the men were rendered apart by unforgiving steel while others were crushed under the fist and heel of the giant who struck with enough force to splinter bone with his every blow.

The only thing the mercenaries could appreciate about their attackers was the merciful swiftness of the death they dealt, and in a matter of minutes only the three figures of Lei, Chris and Zach were still standing in the compound.

"Well that went better than expected." Chris was ambling around and still looking for someone to fight.

Lei was checking the bodies, as was Zach, while Chris watched them curiously, "What are you looking for?"

"These are all grunts," Lei called back.

Chris frowned, "What does that mean?"

Lei cursed, "It means these aren't the men we fought earlier at the village."

A voice called back from the jungle in Thai. Zach shouted back an answer when a knife slammed into his back and sent him sprawling to the ground. Chris and Lei spun to see five men and two women walking out of the jungle where they had apparently taken cover during the firefight.

Chris moved to Zach, "Who the hell are they?"

Lei shook her head, "I don't know exactly, but we caught them in the process of attacking the villagers a couple days ago."

Chris inspected Zach's back, "The knife was stopped by his shoulder blade, don't think it penetrated beyond it. Painful as hell, but he'll be fine.

***

Less than two miles away Larson and Rogers sat in their Jeep. They had arrived and Rogers was shaking his head, as he stared at the screen of a laptop that was showing real time satellite images over a part of the jungle canopy.

"It has to be them," Rogers said as he touched the screen where the thermal imaging pictures were being relayed to their screen. , "Only a fire fight looks like that on thermal."

Larson nodded his head in agreement, "So what do we do?"

"I don't know about you, but I don't want any part of whatever death bugs they were developing out there."

"You mean the biologic?"

"Damn right I do."

"So you just want us to sit here?"

"Nope," Rogers tapped a few keys on the keyboard and hit "Enter". He then closed the laptop and reached for the key in the Jeep ignition.

Larson grabbed his hand, "What the hell are you doing?"

Rogers wrenched his hand away and then slammed the back of his fist into Larson's nose. Blood burst from his nostrils and eyes as the nasal bone shattered under the force of the impact. It took a few seconds for Larson to shake off the pain and disorientation that the blow had delivered, but once his vision had cleared he found himself looking into the barrel of Roger's 9mm Browning sidearm.

"I'm sorry Major, but you saw what we're up against. This isn't about recovery anymore. It's about containment."

"What?" Larson's voice sounded as though he was in the throes of a terrible sinus cold as he tried to speak, "What did you just do?"

Rogers frowned, "I did what needed to be done. Think about

it. Can you actually say you would allow any chance for that biological horror those fools developed to escape? To escape into the hands of God knows who?"

Larson understood the protocol, but couldn't believe that Rogers would so be so willing to sacrifice Zach and the others.

"Pat, you can't just..."

"I can and did. It's out of our hands now."

Larson stopped fumbling at his nose and looked at the man that had been one of his closest teammates back in the day, "What's out of your hands?"

“In fifteen minutes the Navy is going to launch a series of air strikes on the exact location where the thermal revealed the gunfight. They will destroy the jungle canopy and all standing structures that remain. After that we have another fifteen minutes to be at least five miles from that spot."

Larson's brain suddenly clicked in to what was about to happen, "Oh my God. The Navy is going to drop a MOP on a friendly nation?!"

At 20 feet long, a massive 15 tons in weight, and packing over 5,300 pounds of explosives the MOP or Massive Ordinance Penetrator bomb can penetrate up to 200 feet into the earth before detonating its ordinance. This made it not only the largest, non-nuclear, bomb ever created, but the ultimate “bunker-buster” as well.

Rogers laughed, "We already made our deal with the Thai government as a part of a contingency plan." Rogers stepped from the Jeep and started to walk around the front of the vehicle all the while keeping the gun trained on Larson. "If it's any consolation, it's a relatively surgical strike. Everything located underground, including the stored pathogens will be vaporized by the blast and then covered in God only knows how many tons of earth as the ground settles back down afterward."

Larson found himself asking, "What about the collateral

damage?"

"Our experts say it will be minimal, although there will, of course, be some. Oh, and you will probably want to know that the concept of dropping the MOP on foreign soil will be covered by the story of a terrorist cell that blew itself up while trying to transport a stolen nuke through the Thai jungle. Back home the public will cry out for us to increase our vigilance against the terrorist threat, now that they suddenly seem to have access to nukes and such." Rogers smiled ironically, "A win-win for the good guys."

"And I suppose you and your new friends in the CIA are the good guys?"

Rogers rolled his eyes as he stood in front of the passenger door, "Oh knock it off. You know damn well we're the good guys. You just don't like the idea of leaving anyone behind. It's against your nature. I understand and respect that about you, always have, but now we aren't dealing with the typical battlefield scenario you trained for."

Larson's face was starting to contort in anger, "Bullshit."

"No Major, no bullshit. Think about it for a second. If you were sent in to destroy the biologic stockpile and had to sacrifice yourself for the mission to be a success, then would you do it."

Larson didn't answer and simply glared at Rogers.

Rogers nodded, "That's what I thought. Now tell me, would any of us from the old unit?" Rogers waited and when Larson kept quiet he answered for him, "Of course we would. Wouldn't even have a second thought about it either. Well that's what's happening now. Your new friends are making the noblest sacrifice they can to the world, even if they don't know they're doing it."

Rogers opened Larson's door with his free hand, "Move into the driver's seat."

Larson hesitated, but he knew the truth of what Rogers was saying...even if he hated it, and begrudgingly slid into the driver's seat.

Rogers climbed into the passenger seat, keeping the gun trained on Larson as he moved, "Okay, start the engine and get us as far away from here as you can. The clock is ticking you know, and I'd prefer not to get caught in range of the air strike if I can help it."

***

Lei tried the door to the lab, but found it locked.

Chris noticed and said, "Probably a good thing. They undoubtedly have the door covered by anyone and everyone inside."

Lei shot a frown at him in frustration, but knew he was right, "So what do we do?"

Chris turned to look at the quiet standoff that was happening just behind them. On one side were seven expertly trained and unorthodox mercenaries while on the other side was the singular entity that was Zach. Chris looked at the big man's back and could feel the strength flowing from him. The wound to the shoulder blade had barely bled and, as painful as a broken shoulder blade should have been, Zach showed no signs of feeling the pain. He stood tall and confident, as he faced down the group that milled restlessly across the clearing from him.

Chris turned back to Lei, "What do we do?" Chris reached for his rifle and pulled the clip to check his remaining ammunition. Finding it empty he sighed, "Well, there goes the easy way," and dropped the rifle to the ground. Chris stepped forward to stand next to Zach, reached behind his back and pulled his Karambit blade from the special sheath that was tied to his belt.

Lei smiled and her eyes widened at the prospect of what was about to happen. From a special holster attached to her side, which was normally meant for spare clips of ammunition, she removed a small metal box. She opened it and removed a small vial of liquid, carefully unscrewing the cap. The cap was a makeshift paintbrush and Lei dabbed a small amount of the liquid first onto the fingernails of her right hand then switched hands and repeated the procedure.

Chris glanced away from the small group of mercenaries in front of them to see what Lei was doing and laughed, "Yeah, good time to make sure your nails are done up right."

Lei winked at him, "Girl's gotta do what a girl's gotta do."

Chris rolled his eyes, "Sure. You ready?"

Lei's smile spread across her face, "Bet your ass I am, but that still leaves us with the small problem of the locked door...assuming we survive of course."

Chris shrugged his shoulders and watched the group pacing back and forth, brushing up against one another as they moved, all of their hands held pairs of similar combat knives, "One catastrophe at a time, right?"

Chris didn't turn to face Zach but he slapped one hand on the big man's chest, "Ready big guy?"

Zach didn't make a sound or even flinch and the quiet made Chris look up to Zach face. The giant's eyes were so red that there were no signs of his pupils in his sockets. It reminded Chris of the black eyes of a shark, but red and just as terrifying.

The without any warning Zach lunged forward and sprinted toward the mercenaries. A collective shout arose from the group as three charged forward while two-darted left and two more darted right in an attempt to encircle their enemies. Chris watched as Zach closed the distance with the three mercenaries while Lei had darted left to prevent the two others that had bolted in that direction from getting behind Zach. Chris wasted no more time and ran right in a mirror image of what Lei was doing. Zach met the three mercenaries head on as each extended one of their knives toward various vital parts of his anatomy, but the big man hunched down lower as he ran and, at the last possible moment, launched his body forward, leaping in a near horizontal lunge into the trio with tremendous force and speed. His shoulder hit the first mercenary before the man could alter his course and with enough force to shatter the man's spine. The sound of the backbone shearing apart was like a gun going off and seemed to shake the surrounding trees. The mercenary's body folded around Zach's shoulder as if were made of twine instead of flesh and bone and was lifted off his feet and carried along with Zach's leap. The other two men staggered, stopping their forward momentum, and darted out of the way as Zach's body flew past them. Zach rolled with the impact as the mercenary on his shoulder fell away limply, either disabled or dead...didn't matter which as either option meant he was out of the fight.

Lei caught up to the two she had pursued, and blocked their path. Initially they were wary, but when they saw that she was unarmed their courage returned a thousand fold and they split up to attack from the front and rear simultaneously. Lei let out a laugh as the first one charged in with combat knives waving in the air in front of her face. Lei instantly realized it was a mere distraction, albeit a lethal one if she didn't take care to avoid the blades, as the woman that had circled behind her came in low and tried to cut the back of her legs. Lei let her come and dodged a right to left swipe of the combat blade that flew horizontally in front of her eyes and let herself fall backward to the jungle floor as the woman's knife sliced the air cleanly where the back of her thighs had been.

The female mercenary was so surprised by the move and the lack of impact with her knife that she lost her balance and had to roll forward to keep from falling on her face. Her partner realized what she was doing and jumped over her rolling form and lunged forward with the tip of his knife like a fencer. Lei had rolled backward and came up to her feet as the man had jumped over his partner and she reversed her direction and shot forward a split second sooner than the man was able to get his footing. She moved in from a low point and brought her right hand up, her fingers in a claw shape as her fingernails sank a centimeter into the flesh of his neck and then tore through the surface of his skin until they exited the far side of his neck.

Blood flowed in copious amounts as the man spun away from her. Lei made no attempt to pursue him as she turned her concentration on to the woman. The man covered his neck with his hand and glared in surprise at Lei. He lifted his hand away to see it coated in a thin layer of his blood, but realized instantly that there wasn't enough blood to indicate his jugular vein or carotid artery had been damaged by the attack. The woman came out of her roll and spun back to face Lei. Her face turned from a mask of combat rage to one of surprise as she saw Lei's face spattered in small droplets of blood that she was joyfully wiping away with her hand and then licking off her palm like a cat. Seeing no wound on Lei, the woman's head swiveled to her partner who was just looking up from his hand.

"I'm okay," he said, "get h..."

The man's voice caught as his chest suddenly seized and his throat felt like it had collapsed upon itself. His eyes flew open in panic as he realized he couldn't get the breath of air he had just pulled into his lungs back out again. The woman stared as the veins in her partner's neck bulged with the effort of his attempt to push out the air that was trapped inside his chest as he fell to his knees. By this time the man's face had turned bright red and was now darkening to purple as he tried to let out a scream, but only the slightest of hisses made its way out of his mouth.

"What did you do!?" the woman shrieked at Lei with such raw emotion that everyone in the immediate area stopped and turned toward her in surprise.

Chris' eyes squinted in order to see what had happened, and looked from Lei to the man kneeling on the ground with three large gashes in his neck and a fourth beneath it that had only raised a welt.

"Oh," Chris nodded, "That's what you were doing."

The two men Chris faced looked horrified by the sight of their compatriot kneeling purple faced on the ground, now with copious amounts of foam bubbling out of his mouth, as he tried to scream either from the pain or knowledge of his imminent death.

One of the men shook the image off and turned back to face Chris as he leveled the knives he held in readiness, but the other man just let one of his knives fall to the ground.

"Fuck this," the man said as he reached for something behind his back.

Chris rolled his eyes at the man, "You're no fun." Chris nonchalantly tossed the heavy Karambit with what appeared to be minimal effort, almost as if he were throwing the blade away in disgust and surrender, but directly at the mercenary that had dropped the knife. The mercenary found the sidearm that had been holstered behind his back and had raised the gun up just as the Karambit slammed into the center of his throat. The heavy, wickedly curved, double edged blade shattered through the man's hyoid bone as if it were made of paper, and then continued to penetrate through the soft tissues before hitting the back of the cervical spine. The point of a Karambit blade is made to be extra fine so it can do it's intended job at cutting open human throats more efficiently; however, in this case the fine tip wedged it's way between the vertebrae and just barely nicked the man's spinal cord.

When the mercenary simply toppled over and began hacking up blood even Chris looked surprised.

Chris looked at the dying man, "Whoa...um...Yahtzee!"

The second man let out a scream that might have been a battle cry but sounded more like a roar as he charged forward. Chris braced for impact when out of the corner of his eye he saw something large coming toward him from the side at a very fast pace.

It was the body of a woman, another of the mercenaries who sailed limply through the air and collided with the oncoming attacker. Chris spun to see Zach still fighting the last mercenary that had attacked him and Lei holding the woman who had shrieked down on the ground as she tore at the woman's neck with her teeth.

Chris shook his head as he watched Lei consume the woman she had pinned and mounted and sighed, "Damn if there wasn't a time that would have given me a raging bone..."

The impact that struck Chris' side wasn't overly hard, but it was enough to jar him off his feet as the remaining mercenary tackled him. Chris twisted as he hit the earth and brought up his forearm just in time to stop the rapidly descending tip of the combat knife from penetrating into his chest. The blade was sharp and slipped through his forearm, lodging between the radius and ulna bones, until the hilt hit and stopped it's momentum. The man tried to rip the blade away but the back of the blade was serrated and, as sharp as it may have been, the living flesh and bone of Chris' arm held the knife in place. Chris cried out in pain, but didn't stop fighting as he pulled the man's head down and wrapped his legs around the back of the man's head. The hold was a jujitsu chokehold called a "triangle choke" and once it had sunk in there was no way to escape it. The mercenary realized his mistake and abandoned the knife, trying to pull his head free, but Chris reached up and grabbed his right foot and cinched it solidly into the space of his left knee. Then Chris flexed his thighs and arched his back to increase the pressure until he heard the telltale gurgling sounds that indicated he had the hold properly applied. With the blood cut off to his brain the mercenary passed out in seconds, but Chris held the hold for almost a minute until the screaming muscles in his legs and back demanded he let go.

Chris flopped on his back and tried to unwind his legs from

around the man's neck but found that his legs had cramped into position. Using his hands he pulled one leg out from under the other and forced them straight. Not wanting to waste more time and potentially allow the man to recover again, Chris crawled the ten feet to where the other mercenary lay, still holding onto his gun. Chris looked into the man's still seeing eyes as he pried his unfeeling fingers off the weapon, aimed it at the unconscious man he had just choked out and pulled the trigger twice. The explosive sounds of the double tap to the head were thunderous and made Chris' ears ring, but he still swerved the weapon to the paralyzed man and aimed.

Before he could fire a sound made Chris look up to see Zach holding the last of the mercenaries aloft by the neck. The man was struggling and trying to tear away the giant's hand but was making no progress. Then the muscles in Zach's arms flexed as he closed his grip on the man's throat and crushed the tissue and bones underneath, rendering the mercenaries body limp in his death grasp.

Chris looked back to the paralyzed man on the ground next to him and saw that his eyes had gone wild with fear as Chris lowered the gun.

"No, it's all right," Chris said sympathetically, "I won't leave you like this."

Chris reached over and pulled his knife out. The curved blade sliced straight through the man's carotid artery on it's way out, but the man didn't even flinch as the part of his spinal cord that sent pain messages to his brain had clearly been severed. Chris tried to get his mouth into position to catch the blood geyser erupting from the man's neck, desperately trying to swallow as much as he could, but it was like trying to drink from a fire hose, and most of it splashed over his face and chest before the torrent quickly subsided.

Zach released his grip on the now dead mercenary he held in

the air and let the lifeless body fall to the ground. He looked to Lei and saw her straddling a dead woman, face and chest covered in blood while running her hands erotically over her body. He frowned at the scene but, as he saw she wasn't in need of assistance, turned to Chris and saw him lying motionless over another of the mercenaries. The merc's eyes were staring lifelessly into the distance...dead, but Chris was draped strangely over the man and appeared to be shuddering. It was concern that made Zach turn toward Chris, but he stopped when Chris removed his mouth from the ruin of the mercenary's throat, sat up and began laughing manically.

Lei sauntered over to the door and ran her hands over its smooth surface as she pressed her ear to it.

"Little pigs, little pigs, let us come in," Lei purred creepily as her hands left streaks of red blood on the door where she caressed it.

Chris' laugh abruptly stopped and he stared intensely at Lei, as if she had just recited a passage from the bible in its original Aramaic tongue. He turned to the mercenary he had just fed upon and then started searching the area for another that might be still alive.

"Are any of them alive?"

Lei purred, "Mmm, not mine."

Chris looked to the twisted bodies that lay at Zach's feet and shook his head, "Damn."

Lei cocked her head, "Aw, what's wrong sugar?"

Zach walked over and gently guided Lei away from the door before running his hands over it, apparently studying it.

Chris was pacing now and speaking out loud more to himself than to Lei, "The way they moved, and the way they attacked. It makes sense, but a collective group? Has that ever been documented?" Chris pulled out a cellular phone from his pocket, but cursed a moment later when he saw he had no Internet connection.

Lei was sobering from the blood drunk euphoria as well, "Okay we need to focus here." She took a couple deep breaths, "We need to get past the door, even though it is likely being covered inside by several guards armed with automatic assault rifles."

One of Zach's hands paused near the doorknob and he gently touched the heavy wood door with his fingertips. He stepped back from the door a couple paces and studied it a moment longer before he nodded and turned to walk away.

"Wait!" Lei called to him, but Zach never turned around.

Chris was still lost in whatever thought had come to him, "Christ, if that was what we were dealing with it would be unprecedented in medical history, I'm almost sure of it."

"Chris!" Lei called to him, "How are we going to get in there?"

Chris seemed to wake from his daydream and turned to the door, "I don't know but," he looked at the ground and noticed something, "The ones we just killed all had two of those special combat knives on them. Try to keep one of them alive, if there are any more inside."

Lei put her hands on her hips angrily, "That isn't really our focus here!"

"I know," Chris responded, "I'm just saying if it's possible."

There was a sound of bushes rustling as the villagers emerged from the forest. Zach was standing at the exact point where the first small man emerged carrying his hunting rifle. The two exchanged words as more villagers poured in from the surrounding foliage until nearly thirty people stood around holding various versions of their ancient rifles. They followed, as Zach led them back to where he had fought the trio, many of them highly disconcerted by the sight of the dead and mangled bodies lying on the ground. Disconcerted, but not shocked or revolted, as they had all seen their share of the cruelties that people could inflict on each other. It just wasn't all that uncommon in this part of the world.

Zach turned and called to one of the boys in the back of the pack. The youngster, maybe thirteen, ran forward enthusiastically and saluted Zach. Zach said something in Thai and the boy nodded before removing a fanny pack that he had cinched around his waist. Zach thanked him and unzipped the pack, then removed two M67 Delay Fragmentation grenades.

Chris' eyebrows shot up, "Well, well. Where the hell did he get those?"

Lei was nodding, but still looked concerned, "Those will probably get us through the door, but we still have to worry about the guns beyond the..."

Zach held the grenades in one hand and pulled the pins with his other, his large long fingers prevented the activating levers from disengaging, leaving the grenades active, but un-triggered, as he knelt over and lifted the largest of the mercenaries off the ground. The villagers all seemed to know what was about to happen as they worked the bolts on their rifles or pressed a lead shot into newly powder packed rifle barrels. Lei and Chris were just staring wide-eyed and unsure if they should run for cover.

Zach effortlessly dragged the body over to a spot about fifteen feet from the door and looked at Chris and Lei as if waiting for something. The pair just stood there gawking until Zach inclined his head at the villagers who had moved as a group to one side of the building. Recognition hit them simultaneously and they jogged over to where the villagers readied themselves while Zach set the body down on the ground in front of him. He altered his grip until he had a solid grasp of the thick fabric of the mercenaries vest and checked the grip by flexing his bicep and doing a bizarre kind of curl exercise with the body.

"What the hell's he going to do?" Chris whispered to Lei.

Lei shook her head and shrugged her shoulders in return, "I

don't know, but he seems to have a plan."

Zach glanced over to the group and one of the villagers gave him a "thumbs-up" signal. Zach nodded, and with one hand he lifted the body completely off of the ground. He released the arming levers on the grenades and shoved the two round cast iron balls of death into the dead mercenary's pants.

"Holy Shit!" Chris screamed, "Get away from..."

Zach spun around in a three hundred and sixty degree turn, the body of the mercenary gaining the momentum of centrifugal force until Zach completed the turn and threw the mercenary's body at the heavy wooden door. Over two hundred pounds of flesh and bone was launched as if weighing no more than a football and it crashed into the heavy door with a sickening sound that was part wood cracking and part human body caving in under the force of the impact.

Chris watched and was surprised that the mercenary's body didn't simply fly straight through the door, noticing it was actually the door molding that framed the door that had given way. The wood that the hinges and doorknob had been screwed into were regular plywood and shattered as the body hit. Still the objective had been attained as the door, though still upright, had given way on one side as the body fell through the new opening and came to rest about a foot inside the doorway.

Zach had continued his spin after he had thrown the body and raced for the spot where the villagers were waiting, most of which were covering their ears in anticipation of the explosion. Chris whispered to Lei, "And how is it, exactly, that we aren't going to get blown up as well from this distance?"

Lei had been covering her ears, but Chris' words had somehow penetrated and she turned wide-eyed to him as she realized the truth of what he was saying. Lei opened her mouth to say something, but Chris never heard it, as the grenades exploded.

Chapter 54

"Just shoot him."

The bastard had said, "Just shoot him." "Him" meaning me! At those words my whole body tensed and, as the adrenaline burst through my system restoring what little strength was left in me and I pulled against my restraints with everything I had.

The light from the outside hallway flooded into the room as the doctor opened the door and ran through. I watched as Pollard followed, but turned to face me in the doorway before he looked away and gestured at someone to come over.

I stopped trying to flex my whole body against the restraints and concentrated on my right arm. I willed everything I had into my stronger arm and pulled against the restraint for all I was worth. Pain shot through my wrist and a ripping or tearing sound came from the area. I had the random thought that the sound might have been the tissues of my arm tearing when my hand and arm burst free of the leather that had held it fast.

I reached up to my throat and tore away the restraint around my neck and head, which came away easily compared to my arm restraint, before reaching over to my other wrist, in order to help my other arm pull free. Pollard had seen me break the restraint and all the color drained from his face as he backed out of the room and let the door shut just as one of the guards arrived. I pulled my second arm free, and was working on the restraint around my waist when I heard the doorknob click as it turned.

Then there was a boom and a rumble that managed to shake the ground on a barely perceptible level. I frowned, but saw that the door knob quickly turn back to it's original position as the sound of people running and shouting came from just outside the door.

Realizing that I had just received a reprieve from my own execution I desperately tore at the remaining restraints, completely freeing myself, yet when I tried to stand, I promptly flopped to the floor. I had nothing left, my legs felt like Jell-O and the burning pain in my arms made me just want to crawl into a ball and sleep. Instead I crawled on my elbows and knees for the door. Sooner or later they would come for me and deliver that bullet to the brain that had been promised. So I crawled and with every shift of my weight the agony in my limbs and core increased. I don't know what I thought I was going to do when I got near the door, but a part of me was screaming at me to just keep moving and be ready when the guard returns. I suppose I was just hoping for an opportunity, but I doubted that I would be able to capitalize on anything that presented itself.

I still had another five or six feet to crawl when the doorknob turned again. I tried to roll onto my belly, but I only managed a half turn before the pain stopped me. The door began to open slowly and the room suddenly came alive with sound as men screamed both in pain as well as what sounded like battle cries. The number of different voices raised were far more than I would have expected, and an image filled my head of a civil war battle just as the two opposing armies met in the center.

The door continued it's cautious opening swing and it was all I could do to raise my hand to block the bright light from the hall.

"Steve!" a woman's voice called out. No, not just any woman. MY woman! It was Lei and the next thing I knew she was on top of me, arms around my neck and her mouth over mine.

When she finally parted her mouth from mine I was panting for the lack of air and no strength to resist Lei's amour to get a breath.

"Oh God, what did they do to you?" Lei's voice broke, and it seemed to take all her will not to actually break into tears.

"I'm fine," I somehow managed through gritted teeth, "Just real weak."

Lei set my head down on the floor and I found myself staring at the ceiling as she ran to the door, "Chris! Get in here now!"

Then she was back again, "Steve, Chris is here and he's coming."

"It's...okay," I managed, "I'm okay." I looked out in the hall and saw a small group of men armed with what appeared to be Pangas, which was kind of an all-purpose knife/machete used for cutting meat or chopping wood.

They hacked mercilessly at the guard, who screamed as his blood splattered over the men and the white walls of the hallway.

I must have reacted to the sight because Lei tightened her grip on me and whispered urgently, "They're from the village and they brought us here."

It took a moment to have that set in, but when it did I felt my body ease and I let my weight drop into Lei's arms.

"So, what did you blow up getting in here?"

Lei smiled, "Just the front door, and a big chunk of what looked to be a reception area. After that we just gang rushed our way in."

Chris appeared in the doorway, "Steve!" then he took a closer look at me and bolted to my side, "What happened?"

"They were using electricity, why?"

Chris looked at Lei who was staring at me intensely. Chris turned back to me, "Steve you look like death. I mean your pallor is almost as pale as Alpha's."

I just stared at Chris as he felt my wrist and then throat for a pulse.

Chris lowered his hand, "It's just a guess but I think he's severely hypovolemic. Lei he needs..."

Lei was already on her feet and out the door. About five seconds later she came back in carrying one of the guards and dropped his limp form on the floor next to me.

I looked at the body it was a mess of deep hacks and gashes indicating that the man had probably died from blood loss, "what do you expect me to do with that?"

Lei looked at me with frustration written all over her face, but her voice sounded patient as she said, "Steve, honey, you need to...eat."

When I hesitated Chris chimed in, "Go on man. It's not like he needs the blood anymore and the longer you wait the greater the chance it will decay and become useless.

I cocked my head at them, "You think there's anything left in there? Looks to me as though it's probably all over the floor out in the hall."

"Oh just do it you pussy!" Chris cried out with mock exasperation like a child would to pressure a friend into doing something disgusting.

I shook my head, "Take me into the hall."

Lei got it before Chris did and she hauled me up and started walking me to the door.

"Um," Chris muttered, "What are you...?"

Lei didn't turn as she said, "get those clothes off of that guard. They look like they'll fit."

Lei pulled me another couple feet and set me on the ground next to the guard I watched get hacked apart by the villagers. The man was lying in a pool of his own blood. I rolled to my side and started lapping at the floor and with each sip the pain in my body diminished. I knew that it was the euphoria that was taking away my symptoms and that the damage that had been done, had not been undone, but slowly I took in more and more blood, as my body assimilated what it needed from every drop I swallowed. Within a minute or two, I felt functional again and shakily rose to my feet.

Chris walked over and handed me a pair of pants. They were tight around my thighs but fit well enough to work and I tried to push a t-shirt over my head while Lei led me by the arm.

"Where are we going?" I asked once I had slipped both my

arms through the shirt.

"Out," Chris said sharply as he stopped to peer around a corner.

"What? Wait," I stopped walking and nearly fell over as my weak legs had trouble coming to the abrupt stop.

"Huh?" Chris had already stepped around the corner and had to come back to see what the problem was.

"We can't leave without Whelan. That bastard can't..."

Lei gripped my arm tighter, "It's okay, he won't get away."

I shot Lei a frown, "What do you mean?" It was at that point that I realized the villagers' presence meant that Lei and Chris had found Zach. So where was he?

The obvious question slipped from my lips, "Where's Zach?"

"We saw the doctor as we were fighting our way in. Zach ran after him and we came for you."

Panic shot through me, "We have to get to him now!"

"What?" Lei asked in surprise, "Why?"

I shook my head, "The doctor is responsible for his adopted daughter's death, he's going to be sloppy when he gets to him and we can't risk Whelan getting away again."

Chapter 55

Doctor Whelan had retreated to the large laboratory and examination area where he sat at a random computer terminal and hastily downloaded his data onto various zip drives. He was in the process of downloading the last one when the sound of air escaping from one of the heavy doors indicated the seals on the doors had released it's pressure. There was a loud clang and then the sound of heavy footfalls on the metal grating echoed throughout the otherwise silent chamber, gaining in volume as their creator grew closer and closer.

"C'mon, c'mon!" the doctor urged the download bar as if trying to use his will to move it faster.

A shadow appeared overhead, covering the area where he sat, and although Doctor Phineas Whelan rarely felt fear, he did feel a souring of the contents inside his stomach as adrenaline shot through him. Slowly he tilted his head upward to where the metal grating of the stairs transformed into a walkway before leading down to the ground level, where he was working. The doctor peered up through the grating and pieced together the face of his magnificent creation, peering down at him through the grating. He was standing and staring at the doctor with his blood red eyes. The creature's face was such an expression of rage it would have frightened a marble statue into running away.

The doctor heard a slight chime and broke his vision away long enough to see the download had finished. He ripped the zip drive out of the USB port without properly ejecting the disk and pushed it into his pocket before bolting for the exit door.

The giant on the walkway leapt over the rail and landed heavily on the ground just behind the doctor, grabbing him by the collar of his lab coat. The doctor felt his feet leave the ground and his body go airborne, as Zach threw him to the far side of the laboratory as easily as if he weighed no more than a stuffed animal.

The doctor landed on his right shoulder, felt a crunch and pop within the joint and then his body skidded to a stop against the far wall. The pain of his shoulder dislocation made the room spin and brought on a wave of nausea he thought would overwhelm him.

Dr. Whelan turned his eyes to the computer terminals and saw his creation slowly walking over to where he was lying. Understanding the danger he was in caused a momentary cessation of his pain and he desperately fumbled in his right pant pocket with his left hand, fingers awkwardly pushing their way into the fabric sheath as they tried to lock around the object he always kept there.

His long middle finger and his index finger just grazed the smooth metallic side of the object he was fishing for, but couldn't wrap his fingers around it with enough strength to pull it free. He looked up to see that the giant had covered half the distance between them, and he screamed in frustration and pain as he pushed harder into his pocket and managed to pinch the small box between his fingers.

He had to be careful to not jerk the object out of his pocket, for fear of losing his grip on it, so he proudly used a considerable amount of restraint, as he slowly eased his "Flash Box" out of his pocket. A hand the size of a baseball glove snatched him around the throat and squeezed. The doctor gurgled out a yelp as he felt his body rise off the floor. He could breathe, but just barely as Zach lifted him to a standing position and pulled him close. They were nearly eye-to-eye as Zach growled and his hand began to tighten around the doctor's throat, but the doctor raised his flash box and managed a garbled, gurgling word.

"Sm-Smile," could barely be understood as it passed through the doctor's lips, but he pressed the button on the flash box directly in front of Zach's eyes and, instantly, the pressure around the doctor's throat eased.

His whole body dropped to the floor, landing in a painful

crash, as Zach froze in place, letting him drop. The doctor screamed again in frustration, as the pain of his dislocated shoulder began to overwhelm him, and he could barely find his feet to stand. Realizing he would need to reset the joint, he looked around the lab and his eyes locked on the solid stairway railing. He tried to stand but any movement, even the slightest twitch made his shoulder scream in agony.

"Fuck!" the doctor shouted to the open space of the lab, and then his eyes fell to the flash box in his hand. He sat back down on the floor and pinched the box between his knees so he could twist the dial on the device. Having been made to resemble a pocket sized digital camera meant putting all of the adjustments on the top of the device and the doctor began turning and setting the dials with his left hand. He finished altering the settings on his flash box and plucked it out from between his knees before turning it to face his own eyes. He had never used the device on himself, and given what he had designed the box to do, he was hesitant to use it on himself now.

Then he heard another of the heavy doors open from another side of the room. More people were coming in through the adjacent rooms. The doctor knew it was now or never and he pushed the button.

The white lights flashed in a preprogrammed sequence and completely blinded him for a couple seconds, but as his vision returned, his pain vanished. He gasped in a huge breath of air in relief and rose to his feet. He quickly moved to the computer terminals and peered through the glass of the observation room to see three people, two men and a woman cautiously moving between the seats as they worked their way to the front of the room. The doctor thought he recognized one of the men, but gave him little thought as the sight of the woman brought all his fears to life.

"You!" he hissed and, although there was no way they could

hear him through the heavy glass and airtight seals of the room, all three of the people in the observation room looked to the glass, and directly at the doctor.

The small group stared at each other for a moment before the doctor pivoted and started typing on a keyboard at the nearest computer terminal. One of the men raised a rifle and fired, but the bullet ricocheted off the heavy, and apparently bulletproof glass, forcing them all to drop to the floor to keep from being struck by the ricochet.

The doctor's fingers flew over the keyboard and as he hit the "enter" button the laboratory seemed to hum to life. The air seals on all the doors made their tell tale inflation sounds as they locked into place and the air vents hummed as they mechanically swung from open to shut.

The people inside the observation room ran for the door that led to the inside of the lab only to find it was sealed shut as well. One of the men moved to the computer terminal inside the room and slid the mouse across the table and began rapidly clicking on the things that appeared on the screen. Then his face dropped as his two partners moved to stand next to him with questioning looks on their faces.

Chapter 56

"What'd he do?" I asked Chris as he stared at the computer screen.

Chris looked frustrated at the screen and began scrolling through the information that was loading, "Looks like he locked himself inside the lab. I can't say for sure but it appears to be an air tight and pressurized system in place. Worse, he's overridden the commands and I can't bypass his access."

"What's that mean?" Lei asked.

"It means," Chris sat back in his chair with a sigh, "that we aren't going to be able to get him out of there."

"Can't we just break the glass?" Lei asked.

"It's pressurized. Even if we could get something to penetrate it, the sudden drop in pressure would cause a kind of implosion. All he'd have to do is move to the far side of the room and he'd be okay, but in this small space the glass would shatter and probably kill us...and that's assuming we could break it in the first place. Bullets didn't do the job."

"So we wait him out," I volunteered, "he can't stay in there forever."

Chris shook his head, "Look at the..." Chris noticed something in the room, "How'd Zach get in there?"

We all turned to where Chris was looking and saw Zach standing motionless like a statue on the far side of the room. We were staring at the surreal image and didn't notice the doctor fumbling with something in one of his hands. It was the slightest glint of light on stainless steel that warned me as I turned to look at Whelan and saw his hand come up with the Flash Box. Instinctively, I dove for Chris and Lei and tackled, more landed on them than actually tackled them, and forced them to the ground, as the series of strobe flashes illuminated through the clear glass.

A second or so later I was checking each of them, "Both of

you, say something now!"

Lei was breathless, but answered, "I'm okay."

"You can get off me anytime, thank you," Chris said in a muffled tone before I realized I was sitting on him, "And what the hell was that all about?"

"Stay down!" I commanded, "he's got that damn Flash Box thing."

"Oh, not that thing again," Chris said remembering all the trouble we had as a result of the damn thing a couple years ago.

"So what do we do?" Lei asked.

A deep voice called out over loudspeakers, "Hello? Anyone still functioning in there?"

It was the doctor speaking in a mocking tone via some kind of intercom system.

"How's he doing that?" Lei asked.

"The whole place must be wired," Chris responded as I rolled off of him.

There was a slight tapping sound above our heads, but none of us dared to look.

The doctor's strange deep voice called out in a tone of familiarity, "Hey, if you guys are still conscious, I call truce. Honest, I want to talk with you."

I looked at Lei, who shook her head "no" to me, before I shrugged my shoulders and slowly lifted my head up.

"Look I'm putting the box down over here," the doctor's voice spoke in a singsong tone as if he were talking to children.

I raised my head quickly and then dropped down again in case he was lying. The image I saw in that split second was indeed the doctor standing away from the glass and putting the flashing device down next to a keyboard. I repeated the process and saw that the doctor now had his empty hands held up and the device resting on table as he walked back over to the glass.

I stood up and glared at him, "You're going to have to come

out of there eventually you piece of shit."

"Oooh!" the bastard said as he saw my expression and made a puppet hand that was intended to mock the words I was saying, "Such a fierce look! Very scary, now if you'd like to talk you need to push the button next to the microphone so I can hear you."

I glared a moment longer and then looked down to the table and found the button he was talking about, "I said that..."

The doctor cut me off angrily, "I can give a shit what you were saying!" the bass and anger in his voice was disconcerting even given his frail body and I found myself jolting back in surprise.

Then his voice calmed and he flowed right into a scientific tone, "Now let's talk about how we are going to get through this little impasse."

I laughed, "What impasse is that exactly? You are going to have to come out of there eventually. We have the compound, which means we have food, water and time on our side. What have you got?"

The doctor didn't look flustered at all by my words, "There's never as much time as you think. Trust me on this. I didn't get into this alone. I have partners and they are very powerful people who will come looking after their investment when communications end."

I tried not to let it show on my face, but I had thought the same thing. Truth was we didn't really have command of the compound either. The mercenaries were on the defensive, but we had to get the villagers out of here before the trained professionals they were fighting figured out a way to turn the tide.

Lei got to her feet while Chris sat back into the chair and began clicking away again at the computer and said, "Keep him talking, maybe I can figure out a way to override his control."

I didn't nod my agreement and hoped Chris would get the hint when I asked politely, "So what do you suggest?"

"A trade," the doctor said with a smile, "You let me go and I don't kill your big friend over there."

I looked away from the doctor and took in the image of Zach standing motionless on the far side of the chamber.

"What did you do to him?" I asked as I heard Chris' fingers rapidly typing on the keyboard.

"Same thing I did to the rest of your people two years ago," the doctor said as he turned to look at the big man in the distance. "Strange reaction, that. I had expected him to fall limply to the ground the way most people do when I hit them with the strobe. Still, it was effective enough as I only needed to immobilize him."

"And how exactly do you intend to kill him? With your bare hands?" I mocked.

"Oh no, of course not. The doctor started to reach into the pocket of his lab coat with one hand, but the arm did not seem to respond properly. It was then that I noticed the severe disfigurement of his right shoulder that even the oversized lab coat couldn't hide.

The doctor looked down at his shoulder, "Oh right, one second."

The doctor walked over to the stairway and, with his opposite hand, I saw him lift his right arm by the wrist until his right hand was able to grasp the railing. He then took in a nervous breath and fell quickly away from the railing. I could see the "pop" of the shoulder joint as it went back into place, as over the speakers a sound like a muffled gunshot burst through. I winced at the sight knowing the pain that such a maneuver would invoke, but the doctor merely tested his arm and nodded with satisfaction before walking back over to the glass.

"Now where were we?" the doctor said as if nothing had just happened, "Oh yes, how do I plan on killing your friend?"

The doctor plucked what appeared to be a small eyeglass case out of his pocket, "I always keep this little case on my person as it has come in handy on several occasions." He slowly unzipped the case and looked at Lei, "I bet you remember the contents well, don't you bitch?"

My eyes shot from the case up to the doctor as he insulted the woman I love. I turned to Lei and found her crossing her arms over her abdomen and the neat three-inch scar that extended from one side of her navel. Two years ago Lei had been at the doctor's mercy and the sadistic sonovabitch had started torturing her, not for information as much as some perverse pleasure. He had just started dissecting her when he had been interrupted as Chris, Alpha and I broke our way into the Pharmanetics building and interrupted his fun.

"I see you do remember," the doctor laughed as he waved the same scalpel that had cut into Lei's flesh in front of the glass. "You remember how sharp my little knife is and how easy it would be to slip it across your large friend's neck and bleed him out."

I looked down at Chris, but the look on his face told me he was no closer to finding an answer.

"Do you remember how it felt to be under the influence of my little flash box?" The doctor asked Lei, "How you could still see and feel everything, but were powerless to do anything about it?"

I turned and saw Lei shiver at the words. I moved to her and put my arms around her, pulling her in tight to my body.

"Aw, so sweet. Clearly I am not easily forgotten. I could take my time with your friend, you know, run the blade over his abdomen and let his guts drop out on the floor as you watch him die slowly." The doctor laughed, "Hell, given enough time I could even skin him alive. It would take him days to die, and all the while you will be sitting there waiting for me to come out."

The doctor extended his arms and gestured around the room, "This is a laboratory. There's a water source in here, as well as I.V. bags of glucose for my experiments, so I bet I can outlast you, but even if I can't, I guarantee that your friend won't make it."

I held Lei tighter and she rested her forehead against my chest as I asked, "Chris? Anything?"

I couldn't see Chris shake his head, but the tone of his voice was enough despite his words, "Still trying."

"And you can tell your friend to give up on the computer. The system is mine."

I looked back to the doctor, but movement on the far side of the room caught my eye. There was a blur of movement and then the doctor's body was wrenched to one side as something massive hit him. I have no idea how Zach beat the flash box's effects, but he was operating again at full steam and was slamming the doctor repeatedly against the heavy glass. Amazingly the doctor seemed to be ignoring the damage each blow was sustaining on his person, and he swung his scalpel at Zach's chest, carving a horrible gash diagonally from the top of his left pec to the base of his right. Zach reacted to the trauma and punched the doctor hard in the chest. We could hear ribs shattering as the doctor flew back into the glass and his body fell to the floor. Again the frail man got up and charged crazily at Zach, but Zach caught the wrist that held the scalpel and squeezed. The doctor turned his eyes to his wrist watching as his bones were pressed against each other until they were crushed to splinters, but he didn't scream in pain. Instead launched a kick up into Zach's groin that staggered the big man making him let go of the doctor's ruined extremity.

The doctor was wheezing and red foam was starting to bubble up and out of his mouth as he tried to distance himself from the monster he had created, but Zach recovered from the blow and quickly drove the doctor to the floor. Zach sat on top of the doctor smashing a fist into his head once, twice and then a third time, until the doctor lay motionless on the floor of the chamber.

Frowning and out of breath, Zach stood over the doctor and gazed down at the unconscious man as his chest rose and fell with each labored breath. Zach looked around the room and began walking toward the observation room. We three were smiling, but

Zach was still wearing that emotionless look on his face. The blood from the gash in his chest had completely saturated the clothes he was wearing and his face was getting pale. He mouthed some words but they were in a language none of us could understand.

I pushed the button on the microphone and asked, "Zach, do you know how we can unlock the doors and get you out of there?"

Zach tilted his head in that confused puppy manner again, but then seemed to comprehend what I was saying as he pointed to the console next to the computer. There were a series of dials and gauges that appeared to be monitoring the pressure, air quality and proper seal of the laboratory chamber. There were several switches as well but there was no way to indicate which one might be the key to an "Unlocking" mechanism for the lab.

Zach was pointing to the switches and Chris slid the chair over and looked through the glass.

"Do you know which switch?" Chris asked.

Zach nodded and pointed.

Chris placed his fingers on the first switch and looked at Zach, who shook his head "No."

Chris moved to the next and repeated the process as Zach continued to indicate that he was touching the incorrect switch. Finally Chris seemed to find the right one as Zach nodded in the affirmative.

Chris looked at me and I shrugged my shoulders back at him. I knew what Chris was thinking. Something didn't feel right, but I couldn't think of what the problem might be. I turned to Lei, who I found staring at Zach with a concerned look on her face.

"Lei?"

She shook her head, "I don't know."

Then a surprising force rocked the entire building. The electronics blinked on and off before righting themselves and all of us staggered a bit as we looked around in surprise.

"What the hell was that?" I called out.

Chris moved back to the computer and opened the security system. A black and white image flickered to life on its screen, relaying a picture of the outside jungle, which was either on fire, or scorched to blackened ash.

"That looks like a big explosion, but what went off?" Chris asked as he panned the camera around.

A thought occurred to me and I said, "Can you aim the camera up?"

Chris nodded, "Sure but all we'll see are the tops of trees."

We all watched the image as the camera slowly panned up to reveal a large hole in the jungle's canopy and empty sky beyond. Well, almost empty...there was one white vapor trail carving a line into the sky and its source was obviously our location.

"Someone shot a Goddamn missile at us?"

Lei nodded, "Or at the camp."

"Shit, do either of you have my two way radio to Larson?"

Chapter 56

"You there Major?" Steve's voice came from the speaker of the two-way radio that Larson had attached to his belt. He had been wondering if Steve and the others had survived the initial missile strike, and now felt a slight degree of triumph at the sound of Steve's voice.

Rogers had heard it as well and he raised the barrel of his pistol so Larson could see it in his peripheral vision.

"Don't answer that," Rogers said in a calm, but warning tone.

Larson shook his head in disgust, "You aren't even going to let me warn them?"

Rogers frowned, "They're in the hot zone. You know as well as I do that it means they are to be considered contaminated and can't be allowed to leave without being cleared first."

Larson growled, "And, as there will be a 30,000 pound bomb about to land on their heads, they're certainly not going to get the chance to be 'cleared' first."

Rogers smiled, "Looks that way."

Steve's voice called out again, "Major? Are you there? What just hit us?"

Larson ground his teeth as he steered the Jeep around one of the many large holes in the dirt road.

"Pat, this is so wrong. You haven't been out that long, man. My God, we would never have abandoned anyone like this when we were in the same unit."

Rogers smirk faded and his eyes dropped just a bit at those words, but then he said, "People change, Major."

Larson turned his head away from the road for a split second to ask, "Is it really that simple for you?"

"Of course not!" Rogers exploded, and Larson worried that in the sudden anger he might pull the trigger by accident. "This goes against everything I believe in, but those three...whatever they are, aren't really our people or our concern."

"And what about Zach?"

Rogers paused, "We never really knew Zach did we? I always wondered how that big bastard was so damn good without any formal military training. Turns out he was one of them all along."

"One of them?"

"Some kind of goddamn monster."

Larson purposely shifted the steering wheel, aiming the Jeep toward the nearest and deepest hole in the road. The front of the Jeep dipped severely and then shot up in a violent bounce that caused both of its un-belted passengers to come out of their seats. Larson was prepared for the jolt and had readied himself, but Rogers careened wildly around in the passenger chair and was forced to move the gun away from Larson in order to brace himself. Larson whipped his right arm out and struck Rogers' wrist, sending the gun flying backward out of the Jeep. Rogers responded by throwing a short punch into Larson's face with his left arm, but when the blow caused the Jeep to veer off the road he stopped trying to fight.

Larson slammed on the brakes and grabbed Rogers with both hands, but to his surprise Rogers merely held his hands up in surrender.

"I don't want to fight!" Rogers screamed wide-eyed and frantic, "We can settle our differences once were out of the area!"

Larson ripped the radio from his belt, "Steve! Come in! Steve!"

Initial static turned into a tinny but clear voice, "We're here Major! What's going on?"

Larson told them everything, including the impending MOP strike.

When Steve's voice returned it was calm, but tight, "How long do we have before the next set of missiles?"

Larson turned to Rogers, who promptly answered, "They're

probably already on the way. The idea will be to break through the trees to get a clear visual of the target so they can be as surgical as possible with that MOP."

"Did you get that?" Steve asked after Rogers stopped speaking.

"Yeah," Steve replied, "What happens after the next missile strike?"

Rogers spoke up without prompting, "Satellites will confirm the blast site as being fully exposed, or not. If not, then more missiles will rain down until they get the exposure they are looking for, and then the MOP will follow."

Steve asked, "How long between missile strikes?"

Rogers shrugged, "Maybe ten minutes?"

"Okay, going to sign off now."

"Steve!" Larson nearly screamed into the radio.

"Yes?"

"I...I don't know how...I'm sorry this happened."

There was silence on the other end for a beat and then, "If we make it out you and I will be having words, Major."

Larson knew there was zero chance of Steve, Lei, Chris or Zach making it out of the blast zone, but he nodded saying, "Understood. Good luck."

The radio went silent..

Chapter 57

"They're going to blow us up," Chris said with a certain degree of humor in his voice.

"Lei and Chris, you get to the villagers and get them out of here! Try to get them as far away from this place as you can!"

I didn't know why I was bothering. We had no transportation, even if we managed to survive the missile attack, there was no way we'd survive such a massive explosion.

Chris looked at me, "Kinda pointless, no?"

I shook my head, "Maybe it will take them longer to level the place than they thought. Maybe it will give us enough time."

Lei looked at me and shook her head defiantly, "If this is the end I'm not leaving you."

"Dammit," I cursed and knew that when she wanted to dig in her heels on something, it was nearly impossible to change her mind.

"All right," I surrendered, "At least gather up the villagers and get them running. Who knows? Maybe there will be a miracle and somehow they make it." When neither of them moved I sighed, "Can you two at least do that for me?"

Chris was up and moving in an instant, but Lei stepped to me and lightly kissed my lips, "What are you going to do?"

I shrugged, "Try and get Zach out of there. Give him a chance too."

Lei nodded and caressed my face with one hand before turning and running after Chris.

I turned to the observation glass and saw that Zach had been watching us the entire time. He made the same motion again at the electronics console and I walked to the switches that Chris had been in front of before the missile strike had hit us.

I looked at Zach, "Okay big fella, which one do you want me to hit?"

Zach pointed again and I placed my hand on the switch. Again the feeling of wrongness shot through me and I paused before flicking the switch. I have never been particularly intuitive. I trust my instincts, of course, but this was different. My instincts told me when there might be danger lurking in a dark alley, or whether or not an enemy was packing a gun. This was more of a feeling like I had forgotten to do something but, for the life of me, I wasn't going to remember what it was.

I looked at Zach even though I knew he couldn't hear me without my pressing the transmit button on the microphone, "Is this the switch you want?"

I hoped my body language would convey what I had said well enough. Zach just looked at me for a second and then nodded.

I nodded as well, and flicked the switch. Instantly the main lights shut down to be replaced by red lights, and a siren came through all the speakers. Shocked by the sudden noise and light I stood abruptly and tried to find the source of it all. My head cleared a second later and I realized that the switch I had thrown was the culprit and tried to push it back into its original position. The switch clicked back into place, but the process that had started didn't shut itself down.

I looked to Zach, and through the blood red color that was in his eyes I could tell he was staring right at me. I ran over to the microphone and pressed the transmit button, "What did I just do?!"

Zach was the picture of calm as the sound of a generator hummed into life. I looked around, but saw that nothing had changed inside the observation room. Zach walked over to where the doctor was lying on the floor of the lab. The big man grabbed him by his shirt and dragged him over to the computer terminals. Zach lifted the doctor with one hand and set his gangly body in a chair and spun the chair to face the display screen.

I could hear the doctor wheezing with every breath as the laboratory side of the sound system was open and the doctor's deep voice sounded raspy when he spoke, "You're pumping the virus into the chamber?"

Zach just looked at the doctor without responding.

The doctor coughed and spat out a mouthful of bloody foam, "Heh, going to kill me with my own creation hmm? Think that you'll survive because I've given you the vaccine already?" The doctor began cackling, which was probably about as close to an actual laugh he could muster with those broken ribs.

A dark green mist started flowing from the air vents and the doctor turned to look at it and smiled.

"Well then, the joke's on you." the doctor's teeth were pink from the blood he had coughed up, "I gave myself the vaccine as well." Then he inhaled deeply, or tried to, and then exhaled with a theatrical sigh, "Ah, fresh as a mountain breeze."

Zach just watched the doctor for another couple of moments as I frantically began flipping switches, hoping that one of them would either stop the process or open the door.

When Zach finally moved, he dipped one of his large hands gently into his pocket. When he removed it, pinned between the two fingers, was a small square of paper that I could tell immediately was the passport photo of Pha, his adopted daughter.

The doctor looked confused when Zach held it out for the doctor, but he took it and frowned at the picture. Realization came across the doctor's face and he made a show of dropping the picture on the ground and then gently stepped on it with one foot.

Zach looked down to where the photo had landed before rearing back and launching a kick into the doctor's leg that shattered the knee joint beyond any hope of repair. The doctor yelped in surprise, but then smiled at the giant that loomed over him, "Yeah? Fuck you!" he then pointed to his head, "Can't feel a thing."

Zach cocked his head again as the green mist stopped flowing from the air vents and hung ominously in the room like a cloud of green smoke. Then he brought his foot back and stomped down on the doctor's other knee. This time the joint was so ruined that the lower leg bent in an abnormal direction, but the doctor didn't even cry out this time.

The doctor shook his head, this time apparently unfazed by the trauma that had just been done to his body, "Nope, still nothing."

Zach looked around the lab and his eyes fell on the flash box on the table where the doctor had set it down. The doctor seemed to follow his gaze and a sudden realization seemed to come to him as his face lost all of its color, his eyes went wide with fear and his mouth quivered as if speaking, but no words emerged.

Zach resumed his looking around the room as if waiting for something, and then the viral cloud in the room began to swirl. Air was being forced into the chamber and a new mechanical humming started.

The doctor looked around the room and panicked. He tried to get up from the chair, but had forgotten that his legs were ruined and completely incapable of supporting his weight, regardless of whether he could feel the pain or not.

"NO!" he screamed over and over as he tried to drag himself across the floor.

Zach retrieved the flash box and calmly walked over to the observation glass. He stood right in front of me and gently rapped on the glass to get my attention.

I looked up from the computer console and the buttons that I was haphazardly pressing over and over to no effect. I pressed the transmit button on the microphone, "Zach what's happening? How do I get you out?"

Zach shook his head at me and pressed one huge hand against the glass.

I looked at the hand, and then at Zach's face and saw pink tears falling from his eyes. They weren't blood tears, really, they were more like regular tears tinted slightly by blood, and when I saw his eyes they had lost almost all of their redness. Zach eyes were now an amber yellow, just like mine, and the sight of them sent emotions running through me I had never felt before.

I pressed my hand against the glass on top of Zach's, imagining I could feel the warmth of his hand through the heavy glass. Zach's head moved in a barely perceptible nod, and he pushed off of the glass walking to a spot in the room where the doctor still appeared to be attempting to drag himself.

Surprisingly the doctor had covered a decent amount of the distance and Zach knelt in the space, waiting as the doctor continued his attempts to crawl despite the ruined knees and recently dislocated shoulder.

He was only a few feet away when an audible ticking sound came from the speakers as another gas filtered into the room.

A mechanical voice called out:

"Final decontamination procedure initiating in 5..."

I felt my own tears falling from my eyes, as the mechanical woman continued her countdown.

4...

The doctor screamed in desperation, holding out a hand to Zach in what seemed to be a wordless plea for his life.

3...

Zach looked at the hand and then extended his own. In his hand was the flash box and he aimed it at the doctor.

2...

The doctor's eyes went wide with fear for the second time, as Zach pressed the button and a burst of strobe lights, kind of like a red-eye reduction feature on a camera flash, illuminated the doctor's face.

1...

The sound coming over the loud speakers now was practically inhuman in its level of agony, conveying what must have been intolerable pain. Whatever the flash had done to him otherwise, the doctor could once again feel his pain.

...ignition sequence activated"

Fire erupted from what appeared to an uncountable number of gas spigots imbedded in the walls, floors and ceiling all over the walls of the lab. The entire room was filled so completely with fire that the heat immediately could be felt as it came through the glass, making me flinch and turn away for fear of being burned from the heat.

Behind the roar of the flames was the sound of the doctor screaming even louder, and when I could finally look back into the room I saw the silhouettes of two figures in the center of the room. One, unusually large and unmoving, had apparently fallen over on his side while the other flailed and contorted wildly as pieces of its extremities seemed to melt and drip off its bones as it's cries of agony grew even louder.

Then, as the oxygen in the room was depleted, the fire died out and left one unmoving and scorched body lying near the center of the room and, next to it, only the ashen remnants of another. A mechanical voice sounded after a chime, "Trace contaminant level: 0%. Air quality restored. Disengaging auto locking sequences."

The door leading to the laboratory clicked to the unlocked position as a pain in my chest threatened to overwhelm me...and then I remembered to breathe again.

Chapter 58

Rounding up the villagers was less difficult than Lei had thought it would be. The explosion of the initial missile strike prompted the remaining mercenaries to begin looking for ways to evacuate the area. Perhaps they had been ordered to drop everything and run, if something like that should happen, but more likely it was pure instinctual self-preservation that told them the day was lost.

Lei thought it ironic that no matter how far they ran, they had no chance of getting far enough away. The depressing thought made her sluggish, and if not for Chris she might have simply abandoned the villagers, gone back to Steve, climbed into his arms and waited for oblivion to take them. She thought there was almost something poetic about it, dying in your lover's arms while looking into each other's eyes until a brilliant and blinding flash transports you to whatever lies beyond. She had lived a long time, by human standards, and technically she was an octogenarian. She didn't look it, and despite the way her life had begun she had few regrets. Maybe the time she had lost with Steve, as they both refused to talk to each other from simple pride, but that time seemed irrelevant now.

No, her life's only regret, was that she had never officially been able to call Steve her husband. Silly, perhaps, but sometimes a young girl's dreams of marrying her knight in shining armor didn't die completely as the years passed her by.

That thought dominated her mind, as she and Chris guided the villagers to the surface and watched as they disappeared into the forest to rejoin their loved ones, in celebration of their victory over the evil foreigners who had tried to wipe them out. They didn't tell them that those moments would be the last they would spend on earth. Lei thought it was both a cruelty and kindness, to have kept the information from them. Kind because they would return to their people and be welcomed with hugs and cheers. Cruel because how much tighter would they have hugged their children or other family members, if they knew it was all going to end in a matter of minutes?

The thought of being with Steve overwhelmed her and Lei turned to go back into the building when something struck the side of her neck. She slapped at it, thinking it was a wasp or bee, but her palm struck something solid and she plucked it out of her flesh. She stared at it and staggered as the world began to spin. She saw Chris still looking at the jungle where the villagers had disappeared and only started to turn toward her as her vision clouded and she started to fall.

Lei heard Chris call out for her, but his voice seemed so far away and she didn't feel her body hit the ground or understand why everything was turning black before she drifted away.

Chapter 59

Chris had turned just in time to see Lei begin to topple over like a drunkard who was finally passing out. Concern had caused him to take an initial step toward her, but movement from the jungle behind Lei made him retreat a step. He heard the tranquilizer dart zip past his ear, and then saw a man run out of the foliage wearing all black commando gear, like the other mercenaries they had faced earlier. Chris shot one more quick glance at Lei who was now lying on the ground and appeared to gazing aimlessly off into the sky and then retreated a few steps before drawing his Karambit from his belt.

The man came in low, and one of his hands shot up toward Chris' face. No light glinted of the blackened blade he held and Chris just barely managed to juke his head back fast enough to avoid the tip striking his eyes. Pain erupted from his thigh as a second blade swept past and bit deeply into the muscle, but not so much as to reach the large artery that lay beneath the muscle. Chris spun with the second strike and brought the Karambit around catching the third strike blade to blade, which unbalanced his attacker and Chris reversed his movement to slash the blade across the man's abdomen. The wicked curve of the Karambit was designed to slice open a throat or disembowel an enemy with ridiculous ease, but the attacker seemed to sense the danger and twisted out of the way quickly enough that only his clothing suffered any damage.

Chris spun with his strike and the two men parted. They faced off and began to circle one another as the sound of an automobile engine came to life from some place unseen. Chris couldn't risk a turn of his head to look, but he could hear it as the vehicle's wheels crunched the ground beneath its tires, coming to an abrupt stop behind him. Chris continued to circle his opponent until the vehicle came into view. Chris' eyes veered from his opponent only for a split second to see a man in a dark business suit dragging Lei's body to an expensive SUV that was unusually outfitted with off road tires and suspension.

"NO!" Chris screamed and he inadvertently took a step toward the vehicle, but a quick fencing style thrust of the combat knife from his opponent prevented him from running to Lei's aid. Chris blocked the thrust and parried the next as the sound of the vehicle's door slammed shut, then the engine fired as the vehicle reversed its way out of the area, and back into the jungle.

Apparently, the man attacking him hadn't expected to be abandoned and he broke off the attack to see where the truck was going. Chris tried to take advantage of his assailant's momentary disorientation, but the man recovered and parried the Karambit away from the strike to his spine. Chris blocked and thrust as the attacker held his ground and did the same. A feint to his left gave Chris' free hand a chance to strike and dislodge one of the two knives the man held, but he recovered and exploited the moment to disarm Chris as well.

Now, with only his hands as weapons, Chris reached out and caught the wrist that held the last remaining knife. He was going to twist his body and flip the man to the ground, but the man used his free hand to reinforce his knife hand, and the leverage drove Chris to the ground instead.

Pinned Chris pushed against the wrist and the bodyweight of the man lying on top of him. The guy was strong and he had all the leverage, so Chris knew that although the tip of the knife wasn't falling toward his heart yet, his muscles were going to give out first and he realized he couldn't fight this fight fairly and win. He desperately tried to think of something that might help him survive, but his mind was a blank.

All the training, time and promise of a new life was for nothing because he was going to die today. And at that exact moment, one thought entered Chris' head. He wasn't still a wimpy, nerdy, medical examiner. He wasn't the lanky little boy who had been shoved into lockers in high school, or had his head stuck in a flushing toilet in grade school and again in junior high in order to give him a "swirly" for the amusement of other students. He wasn't that simpering clown who hid in the basement of the police precinct gathering information, while other people took action out in the real world.

No! Now he was a real live, blood drinking, woman stealing, and night stalking, badass, masculine vampire! Sure, he was going to be killed either by a missile strike while he was out here in the open, or a MOP if he tried to hide inside the building, but he was not! Repeat NOT! Going to be killed by some bully with a blade!

Chris screamed as loud as he could right in the man's face, while he bucked his body and shifted to the right, letting his arms go slack. The blade dropped down and sank deeply into his left shoulder, and the pain of the injury made the entire left side of his body feel as though it were on fire, but the blade was in his shoulder and not in his heart. Chris used his still working right hand to pull the mercenary's knife hand to the side, as the man reacted to having missed his target and tried to reverse his force in order to pull his blade free. Chris raised his head, opened his mouth and caught the wrist and knife hand in his teeth. He felt the flesh part under his front incisors and canines while his molars crushed through flesh and lodged into bone.

The mercenary screamed in pain, desperately trying to free his hand, but Chris bit down even harder and kept the extremity locked in place like a vise. Fingers lost their sensation, dropping the blade harmlessly to the side of Chris' head. Chris thought about reaching for it, but instinct told him to reach with his free hand, placing it behind the man's head, grabbing a handful of his hair. With every ounce of strength he had left, and while still holding the man's hand and wrist in his mouth, Chris pulled the man's head down onto his own crown.

The top of the forehead, where it begins its curve to the top of the head, is a near perfect parabola and one of nature's most indestructible geometric designs. It is also reinforced with a thicker bone plate than the top of the skull or the facial bones and when Chris slammed the man's face into that part of his head, it hurt. The impact would probably leave a welt or bruise on his head, but the mercenary's nose shattered on impact. The fracture made a popping sound, followed by a burst of blood that flew from the man's nose, while his eyes rolled in disorientation from the concussion.

Chris pushed the man's head away to an arm's length, and then pulled him down again striking his already shattered nose a second time. Chris bucked his body again, this time dislodging the man who was on top of him. He rolled his body, taking the mercenary along for the ride until he ended up in the top position.

Chris spat out the man's hand while the mercenary coughed out a mouthful of blood that had flowed into his throat from his ruined nose. Chris raised a fist and was going to finish the fight, but the mercenary's eyes suddenly cleared and he let out a snarl that was as feral and inhuman as anything Chris had ever heard.

It made Chris hesitate, but in the end did the mercenary little good, because as frightening as that final sight had been, Chris had already moved beyond being scared. He dropped his fist down hard, in the perfect spot on the man's jaw for a knockout, and sent him into an immediate state of unconsciousness.

Chris fell from the limp form beneath him and took in a few deep breaths. Almost as soon as he caught his breath the adrenaline of battle wore off, and the pain in his shoulder began to grow to a nearly intolerable level.

He managed to stand turning to walk back to the laboratory building when he had a thought and turned back to the unconscious mercenary lying on the ground. He thought for another second and then lifted his head to look at the part of the jungle where the SUV had gone with Lei, and shook his head in frustration.

"This is really going to hurt," he mumbled as he moved back to the mercenary and grabbed hold of the man's wrist.

Chapter 60

I didn't go inside the lab. I just looked at the unmoving bodies as they sat motionless on the floor of the lab, amazed at the sacrifice I had just seen. Zach had sacrificed himself to make sure the doctor not only died, but that he suffered for all the things he had done. He had literally allowed himself to be burned to death in order to metaphorically spit into the doctor's eye as he gave the sadistic bastard the death he deserved.

I had wanted to be the one to kill the man so deeply that all I felt now was a surreal numbness. I didn't necessarily feel cheated, as I rationalized that I couldn't have equaled such a horrible end to the man, but I did have a certain degree of vertigo, once I realized I had reached the end of two years worth of pursuit. The concept, of the end of my hunt for the last man responsible for the deaths of so many of my people, had always left me puzzled when I thought about it, because I really didn't know what I would do afterward.

I slumped into one of the comfy leather chairs and let my eyes focus on nothing as they drifted to the ceiling. I wondered if the next set of vapor trails were visible in the sky yet? And if they were, did they mean that a regular explosive missile was on its way, or perhaps a two and a half megaton bomb that was the MOP?

I closed my eyes and thought about a time when Lei and I spent several weeks at a beach house a couple of years ago. It had been our reunion and was as sweet as love can be. It made me long for her and listen as footsteps approached the door to the observation room.

I had been expecting Lei to return after she corralled all the villagers out of the area and was surprised when Chris returned alone instead. Actually, he wasn't alone as he was dragging a body behind him. My initial reaction was to panic, but I relaxed as soon as I saw it wasn't a woman.

"Why are...?" I had started to ask, but when I saw the look on Chris face and the blood seeping from a shoulder wound, I lost all interest in why he was dragging an enemy around.

"Where's Lei?!" I blurted out, completely insensitive to the fact that Chris was obviously wounded.

"Gone," Chris huffed out as he unceremoniously dropped the man's wrist and fell to his knees. "They took her. Drove off in some modified Lexus or whatever."

I shook my head as if to clear it of aberrant thoughts, "Wait, what! Who took her?"

Chris shook his head, "No idea. She just fell over when this guy jumped me. I was too busy fighting him to stop the other man, who drove up in his SUV and just picked up Lei and drove off. Left his buddy behind as well." Chris snorted, "You should have seen the look on that guy's face when he realized he was being left behind."

My head couldn't focus and I took a couple steps toward the door before I realized that we didn't have a vehicle of our own to give chase. Assuming we could even locate them at this point.

The man on the ground let out a moan, but Chris and I ignored him.

"Chris we...we have to..."

Chris held up his hands as he calmly said, "I know, bro. I know, but we don't have a vehicle of our own to make a break for it. I didn't even know there was one in the area to take Lei away in."

My shoulders dropped and Chris' face dropped with it, "I'm sorry," then his face cheered a bit, "Hey, maybe whoever took her will be able to get far enough away when the MOP explodes!"

I screwed up my face at Chris.

"Well...I mean, at least she'd be alive to fight another day."

A strange garbled and nasally voice behind Chris asked, "What explodes?"

Chris and I turned to look at the man Chris had brought back into the lab with him. The man was holding his nose with one hand and cradling his other near his abdomen.

When neither of us responded he asked again, "What explodes?"

I glared at the man and my voice rose in my throat, "Who took the girl?!"

The man frowned and considered me for a moment. Then he nodded, "Sure, I'll cooperate with you, but first tell me...what is going to explode?"

It took all my self-control not to give in to the urge to run over and rip out the man's throat. The thought of savoring real blood for one last time was overwhelming, but somehow I managed to answer him instead.

"You saw the first missile strike?" I asked.

The man nodded.

"Well, that was the Navy clearing the jungle so the satellites over our heads could get a clear view of your compound. They're going to carpet bomb the place in order to make sure they have a perfect target to drop the MOP bomb on top of...meaning right where we are now."

The man's eyes widened as much as their swollen sockets would allow.

"They wouldn't! The Thai government..."

I cut of his obvious thought, "Doesn't want a death plague epidemic on their hands."

The man seemed to think about that and the truth of it rang in his ears.

He cursed, "Goddamn Pollard!"

Chris and I looked at each other as I repeated, "Pollard?"

"The guy who left me behind was military intelligence, but he had to have known that he couldn't out run a MOP."

"He's CIA?" my thoughts immediately turned to Rogers, but I

shrugged and suggested, "Maybe he didn't know that was the plan."

The mercenary shook his head, "No, he had to know."

Chris shook his head, "If the military is anything like the LAPD, then there are times when one division isn't aware of what the other is doing or planning."

The mercenary still looked defiant, but then he seemed to soften and nodded, "That is probably true." Then his demeanor perked up, "Are any of these supercomputers able to send a simple e-mail?"

Chris and I looked at each other before I asked, "Why?"

The man scowled at me with as much venom as he crooked nose would allow, "Is now really time for lengthy explanations?"

"No," I answered, "So give us the really short version."

Quickly the mercenary said, "It's like you said, maybe Pollard, and therefore, the C.I.A. isn't aware of what the Navy is planning. If he were to find out, maybe he could stop it."

Chris and I looked shocked, "He's got enough clout to call of the air strike?"

"That's just it," the mercenary explained, "It isn't an air strike."

"It isn't?" Chris asked.

"No. It's containment, through the use of a massive combustible, and therefore, not an act of war or aggression against an enemy."

I probably had a confused look on my face when I said, "And that matters, how?"

"It just does, trust me."

Chris and I looked at each other but the mercenary spoke again before we could, "Got any better ideas?"

Chris was already on the move to the computer as he said, "Nope!"

The mercenary started to follow, but I put a hand on his shoulder, "No tricks."

He tried out that scowl on me again, "Or what? You do something worse than drop a bomb on my head?"

I let go and he moved to the computer as Chris hit a final key.

"Okay, you are clear to send an e-mail," Chris seemed to consider something as he spoke, "How is this going to help us?"

"Pollard carries a smart phone. He doesn't always answer it, so calling him might not work, but he does always look at the screen. It's like an obsession."

Chris got it immediately and nodded, "Better put something eye catching in the subject line."

The mercenary had finished typing his message to Pollard and then moved the cursor up to the subject line and typed:

"MOP Containment Imminent!"

"That catchy enough for you?" the mercenary asked.

Chris smiled, "Works for me. Steve?"

"Just send it already and let's hope he realizes that if he doesn't call it off, then his bacon is going to fry as well!"

The mercenary nodded and pushed the "Enter" key.

I turned to look at the images on the security screen and saw the white plume of multiple vapor trails in the sky.

Chris moaned, "Mmmmm...bacon," and less than a second later the ground shook again. This time, the sound of the explosions were loud enough to deafen us all, as dirt and other debris flew in through the doors. All three of us were lifted into the air by the concussion, sent crashing through the protective observation glass and into the laboratory. As I landed I could see a brilliant light growing in intensity before my eyes...and then everything went black.

Chapter 61

Larson was leaning against the side of the Jeep when he heard the explosions. Over and over again the sound of explosive ordinance boomed as it rained down again and again. He didn't turn to look as the missiles flew through the sky and then dove sharply toward their target. Nor did he bother to watch the explosive aftermath when they struck. He had seen it all before, but this was the first time he had ever left anyone behind at ground zero. That fact wasn't sitting well with him, but what could he do? He and Rogers had managed to extend their distance to nearly six miles to the coordinates that someone had sent to Rogers, which was apparently far enough away from the expected collateral damage area of the MOP that was going to be used. When they arrived they found a hastily set up command post that was supposed to monitor the blast as well as take them into custody in order to proceed with their debriefing.

Rogers walked over from what served as a refreshment area and carried two cups of coffee. He held one out to Larson who simply glared at him.

"For what it's worth, I'm sorry." Rogers said as he lowered the cup.

"Are you now?" Larson nearly spat the words, but his heart wasn't really in it so they came out in more of a tired tone than in one of righteous indignation.

"Actually, I am." Rogers confessed, "Okay, so I didn't like them and I admit that they completely freaked me out, but Zach was one of us."

Larson stood and his eyes burned right into Rogers', "You don't have the right to include yourself in our company. Zach would have walked through fire to get you out, as would have anyone else in the old unit."

Rogers' didn't back down, "And what good could we have

done?! You saw the devastation the biologic caused! We aren't immune to it like those freaks..."

'We could have given them a chance!" Larson was pointing a finger at Rogers' as he spoke, "We could have given them more time!"

"And let them walk out of a hot zone as potential carriers of the next black plague?!"

Larson shook his head dismissively, "You don't know they would have been carriers."

"And you don't know that they wouldn't," Rogers countered, "They might not suffer the disease, but that doesn't mean they can't carry it back to civilization."

Larson tried to argue some more, but all he could do was ball up his fists and scream, "DAMN IT!" in frustration. He knew Rogers was right, and protocol had been properly followed, but he still didn't like it.

Rogers remained quiet as Larson's anger ran its course. Once he realized Larson had sufficiently cooled, he extended the coffee to him again, "C'mon, take it."

Larson shook his head, but stood from the folding chair and took the cup. The coffee was black and very bitter, but the warmth alone made it worth drinking. He had nearly finished it when a young man in a business suit ran over to Rogers.

"Sir, we have a satellite feed and there's a phone call for you inside." he gestured at the guard shack.

Rogers nodded, but held up a hand to cut the man off, "Okay, how long until the..."

The young man cut him off, "I really think you should take this call sir."

Rogers frowned and looked at Larson who also appeared confused. They both knew something was up and together they walked in silence to the guard shack.

Rogers walked over to the satellite phone and lifted the

receiver, "This is Rogers?"

Larson watched as Rogers' eyes opened wide in surprise, "But, sir are you sure..."

Larson could see that whatever information Rogers was getting wasn't sitting well with him.

"Sir," Rogers tried to continue, "You can't think that simple ordinance can contain..." Rogers paused and his eyes narrowed and he raised his voice, "That's insane!" There was a pause before Rogers said, "No sir I am not trying to question the..."

Larson could practically hear the person of authority on the other end of the phone as he reeled in Rogers. He had received similar "Talking to's" in his own day and knew the level of frustration that they caused. Finally, Rogers expelled a long breath and closed his eyes, "Yes sir."

Rogers set the phone back on its charger and looked wildly at the smoke that was rising from the area of the jungle that had been bombed.

Larson asked calmly, "What's up Pat?"

Rogers looked to Larson and then moved to a spot where his laptop was sitting. On the screen were images as photographed from the satellite orbiting above their heads at that precise moment.

"Pat?" Larson called out.

Rogers collected a breath and then said, "Looks like you got your wish Major."

Larson frowned, "What?"

Rogers kept staring at the screen, his eyes searching for something, "They've called off the MOP."

Larson jumped to his feet and ran over to look at the laptop screen, "What! Why?!"

Rogers shook his head, "The mission is back in CIA control. Apparently the agent in charge said the area was contained and that retrieval crews can be sent in for clean up."

Larson was so ecstatic about the news that he almost missed what Rogers had said.

"Did you say retrieval crews?" Larson asked warily.

Rogers sighed and nodded, "Looks like the plan wasn't to stop the spread of biologic weaponry as much as it was to collect it for ourselves."

As elated as Larson felt, a sense of dread began to fill him.

"Can the CIA do that?"

Rogers chuffed, "Apparently."

Larson shook his head, "That can't possibly sit well with you."

Rogers never looked up from the computer screen and said, in a matter of fact manner, "No, it does not."

Larson looked at his friend's face, and there was a glimmer of the man he had formerly known.

Larson smiled, "You know, for a minute there, I thought I recognized you."

Rogers turned to face his old friend, but he merely shrugged his shoulders before returning his attention to the screen.

Larson was still smiling when he said, "So what are we looking for exactly?"

Rogers shook his head and tapped a key on the keyboard. Instantly the black and white image turned to a thermal scan.

Larson frowned, "Half the area is charred or on fire. What do you hope to see with the thermal?"

"Fire doesn't get up and walk away." Rogers said and pointed to a spot on the screen. Larson looked at the image but could only see the large flickers of what had to be flames. Rogers tapped a few keys, and then clicked his mouse on the area he had indicated. The screen jumped and the spot on the screen zoomed in to take up the full screen.

Within the image was one very large figure that seemed to be carrying and dragging three more as it moved away from the blast site.

Chapter 62

It was nighttime when I awoke in the hospital. There were doctors and nurses moving all around but none of them seemed to speak English. Either that or they were just choosing to ignore me. I did a quick inventory of my physical condition, but as there were no splints or casts over my extremities and my breathing was slow and easy, I figured that I was probably okay. I tried to sit up and there was a great deal of soreness, but nothing much worse than what an overzealous workout might bring. However, the moment I sat up a siren went off and nurses came running in along with a couple of doctors, all of whom were trying to make me lie down.

They all were also wearing what appeared to be some kind of gas mask.

I was so freaked out by the scene that I didn't notice as one of the doctor's stuck me in the arm with a syringe until I felt the effects of the drugs he had pumped into me. I didn't pass out, but it was powerful enough to make me flop into the nurse's arms that shifted my body around and set me back onto the bed. It was all I could do to watch as they began to fasten restraints onto my arms and legs, securing them...me... to the hospital bed.

Evidently, the drugs weren't supposed to improve my mood as I desperately tried to get my body back under my control. In the end I just watched helplessly as they stuck an IV in my arm and then walked out past some clear vinyl curtains. Whatever was in the I.V. must have started to take effect because I suddenly felt dizzy and sleepy.

The next time I opened my eyes, not knowing how long I had been out but realized it could have been hours, or even days later I saw Larson staring down at me. He was dressed in his regular Navy fatigues and seemed none the worse for wear.

"Welcome back," he said pleasantly to me.

I nodded and then started to scan the room. I was in a regular hospital room now without vinyl curtain or restraints tying me down.

I tried to talk but my throat was so dry that it came out more as a croak. Larson shifted in his chair and handed me a bottle of water.

"Just small sips, okay?" he said patiently.

The water felt cool on my lips, but once it got to my throat it felt as though it was burning the whole way down. After a few painful sips though, my throat and body, felt a great deal better.

I looked up at Larson and asked, "Lei?"

His face dropped a bit and his eyes left mine to look a the floor as he said, "I don't know."

I nodded solemnly. It was the answer I had expected. Then my mind seemed to clear even more, "Chris?!"

Larson held his hands up in a gesture to calm me, "We found him. He's fine and recovering same as you, although he did have a nasty shoulder wound that needed tending. The doctors are amazed that it didn't get infected." Larson shot me a knowing glance as he said that last part.

I breathed out a sigh of relief as I tried to remember everything that had happened up to now. I remembered being caught, breaking free, Zach's and Dr. Whelan's horrible deaths, hearing about the MOP...

"The bomb!" I shouted.

Larson shook his head, "Never happened."

"What?" I stammered, "Why?"

"Some CIA agent in the field called in an 'All clear', and the drop was aborted."

I smiled, "Damn, it worked."

Larson's face screwed up in confusion, "What worked?"

I told Larson all about what had happened after we had parted ways in the jungle. I stopped when I got to the part about how Zach and Dr. Whelan had died in the lab's decontamination fire.

"I'm very sorry about your friend." I said, but Larson looked more confused and uncomfortable as opposed to grief stricken regarding the news. Then he shook his head and said, "Go on."

I told him about how Chris had brought the last mercenary back to the lab and how we had tried to contact someone named Pollard, who was apparently the field agent working for the CIA the entire time.

Larson took it all in and then leaned in close, "Do yourself a favor, and never repeat that part about Whelan and the CIA ever again under any circumstances."

When I frowned, Larson quietly elaborated, "the United States of America would never allow information to surface about any corroboration between itself and any terrorist organization, nor any practices that would be in defiance to guidelines set forth within the agreed upon war tactics as laid out by the Geneva convention."

I shook my head, "I couldn't care less about any of that right now." I looked at Larson, "I have to find her and if Pollard has her, then I am about to become the CIA's primary concern."

Larson nodded, "Of course. I'm already working on it."

I narrowed my eyes, "How?"

"We still, unofficially, have that mercenary Chris captured in custody."

I growled, "Fat lot of good that does us, if the government won't let us question him."

Larson smiled, "I never said the government had him."

My eyes widened as Larson continued, "I said that 'we' still have him."

I sat up and looked Larson in the eyes, "And just who exactly is 'we'?"

Larson shrugged, "Me, Chris, you...and some big scary guy named Alpha who somehow managed to arrange the whole thing. Says he knows you?"

I felt a smile spreading across my face, "You could say that."

Larson shrugged again, "Well, whoever he is he certainly knows how to get things done. Frankly, I have no idea how he managed to pull that mercenary out of the government stronghold and have him placed in our custody, but I ain't arguing."

I felt my smile widen even more, "Yeah, he has that way about him. So when can I get out of here?"

"You tested negative for biologic contamination," Larson rolled his eyes as he said that, "Not that this is news to you, but the 'powers that be' took some convincing."

Suddenly the whole vinyl curtain thing made a lot more sense.

"I was in quarantine, wasn't I?"

"Yep, seventy two hours worth, but you can leave as soon as you feel you have the strength."

My heart dropped a bit at the realization that I was more than seventy-two hours off of Lei's trail. Larson seemed to read my mind and said, "We'll find her."

I looked up at Larson and he nodded at me, "Believe it. I do."

I nodded and held out my hand to him. Larson looked at it briefly before he clasped his own hand around mine and we shook on the unspoken promise to one another. We would find Lei and when we did, whoever dared to take her was going to die, regardless of what flag they served under.

"Mind if I ask one question?" Larson asked as he let go of my hand.

"Not anymore," I said with a smile.

Larson smiled back, "Okay, so Rogers and I were watching as you and the others climbed out of the rubble, but when the Haz Mat team found you it was obvious that the three of you hadn't been in any condition to remove yourselves."

I looked at Larson and waited for the question that was now screaming inside my own head.

"So, do you still think Zach is dead?"

Chapter 63

The view from the pinnacle of the mountains overlooking Patong Bay is about as breathtaking as any view in the world. The natural jungle parted near the top, giving anyone who would risk the hike up the mountain a perfect sense of isolation, where they could peer out and feel as though they were literally standing on top of the world. There were higher peaks in the world to be sure, but none were anywhere near Thailand.

Zach didn't know exactly what drove him to make the climb to the top of the mountain, he was too single minded on completing the task he had already decided upon, but something drove him anyway. Now that he had reached the top he couldn't help but stare out and take in the sight. Without question the view filled him with awe, but didn't give him any peace. At best the scene distracted him for a moment and then his mind drifted back to Pha and the way the whole world seemed to melt away when she smiled. He closed his eyes and pictured her smiling at him as they read a bedtime story together and felt the tears start to form in his eyes.

Zach opened and closed his eyes rapidly to clear them before looking out once again to the view. The world in front of him hadn't changed, but it had lost a great deal of its beauty when compared to the smile he had just pictured in his head. Zach swiveled his right hand around and felt the heavy weight of the Desert Eagle handgun that he held in it. He had removed it from the ground as he crawled out of the crater that the lab had become, tucking it into his belt, as he had dragged the three others to safety. The fire had scorched and singed him when it had gone off in the lab the same way it had so many times before, but each time his skin didn't seem to be as susceptible to burning, unlike everyone and everything else that came in contact with the fire. He didn't know why this was the case, but there were so many things about himself he didn't fully understand...and now he never would.

He lifted the gun up and checked the magazine for what must have been the tenth time. He eyed the large, hollow point, .50 caliber Desert Eagle rounds, and was well aware that a full magazine wasn't necessary. Just one would do the trick, or it had better, because it was likely that he wasn't going to be in any condition for a follow up shot.

Zach replaced the magazine into the grip listening for it to slid completely home with a mechanical click. He took one last long look around, felt the simple pleasure of a deep lungful of air and then in one simple fluid motion raised the weapon, pulled back and released the slide, chambering the round so the gun was ready to fire as he set the muzzle against his temple.

He willed his finger to squeeze the trigger, but they wouldn't respond. He pinched his lips together, gritting his teeth and tried again, but still his fingers wouldn't obey him. He was about to squeeze the gun's trigger with all his might when a voice spoke to him from behind.

"I always thought my timing was inherently poor."

Zach froze as the sound of the words broke the serenity of the moment for him. He lowered the gun from his temple, slowly turning to see the source of the voice. The sight that met him had Zach initially thinking he was seeing a ghost. The man that stood calmly watching him was very tall, although not as tall as he, and big bodied, but once again, not as big as he. The man was dressed all in black, which accentuated how purely white his long hair and skin were against the dark cloth. Despite the gothic appearance of the stranger's skin and clothes, it was his eyes that commanded attention...or rather the two obsidian black orbs that sat in the sockets where his eyes should be. The appearance should have been frightening, but they instead appeared well rounded, having a life to them, expressing something other than horror. It was more along the lines of looking into the eyes of a stag, or a stallion, when the whites couldn't be seen.

The man spoke again, "But this time I am glad to see that I haven't arrived too late."

Zach cocked his head to one side, "Too late for what?"

The stranger's eyes widened, "Interesting, I was told you weren't talking. I see you've found your voice."

Zach nodded. A lot of things have come back to him since the fire in the lab, just like grandmother said they would. Zach looked away from the man and at his gun, "Are you here to stop me?"

The man smiled, "Absolutely."

Zach raised the gun up again and pointed it at the stranger, "Who are you?"

The smile immediately left the stranger's face, "They call me Alpha now, but you once knew me as Alphonso Diemo, and later as the Comte de Navarre."

The words were familiar to Zach, but with his thoughts, prior to the recent events being so jumbled, he couldn't place where he might have heard them before.

Zach shook his head, but lowered the gun back down to his side, "You know me?"

"Oh yes," the man called Alpha said warmly, "In fact, I believe I can say with complete confidence, that I know you far better than you know yourself."

Zach smiled, "That...is not saying much."

Alpha shrugged, "I suppose not, but would you like to know more?"

Zach looked down to the gun in his hand, "Do you think it matters now?"

Alpha looked into Zach's eyes, "I can see your eyes."

"What?"

"Oh nothing," Alpha said causally as he waved a dismissive hand in front of his face, "I was told that your eyes were nothing more than red spots in your head." Alpha confessed, "I'm going to have to tell my sources to double check the details of their information."

"What sources?"

"Two of the men you pulled from the crater belong to me."

Zach winced, "Belong?"

Alpha held up his hands, "As a part of my family, so to speak. They filled in the details and I was quite surprised by what they told me."

"Why?"

Alpha stood up from the boulder he had been sitting on and began to pace back and forth as he spoke, "Because it sounded so familiar. In fact, it sounded too damn familiar to be a coincidence. Memories, along with a guilt I have been holding onto for longer than any sane person should, told me that I had to find you."

Zach raised an eyebrow, "How did you find me?"

Alpha smiled, "I'm afraid that I have been very sneaky as of late. I really don't know much about computers, but that young man, Chris, is an absolute...what's the term?" Alpha looked at the sky as if the answer was written there and then snapped his fingers, "Hacker! That's it, a hacker. Anyway, he tapped into a few military satellite systems for me and we used their surveillance cameras to look for your heat signature. Took some time, but there weren't that many people who walked from the wreckage that had been the camp. In the end, you weren't that hard to track down."

Zach eyed the man called Alpha nervously, "So, why track me down at all?"

"As I said I needed to see you face to face."

"And as I asked before, why?"

"Because I had to know if it was really you. That you were alive."

Zach chuckled and gestured with the Desert Eagle a couple of times, "Not for long."

Alpha's face dropped and he looked very sad, "Yes, I noticed that." Alpha was silent for a few seconds and then asked, "Is this about the girl?"

Zach turned away from Alpha and his voice cracked, "Of course it is...and what would you know about it anyway?"

The emotion drained out of Alpha's expression and he answered in such a monotone that one might think he was otherwise completely apathetic.

"I know that you always wanted a son...and a daughter."

Zach chuckled, "Oh really? And how could you possibly know that about me?"

The man named Alpha smiled, "Let me guess. You were going to make her English name 'Abigail'?"

Zach froze. He had never written that down. Never discussed that with anyone, not even Pha. There was no way this man, strange though he might be, could possibly know that.

Zach straightened, "How could you know that?"

"Because Abigail was the love of your life. Your OLD life."

The words played in Zach's head and a wave of vertigo threatened to overcome him. He dropped the gun, staggering to one side he dropped down to his knees. Just to keep him from falling over. Alpha knelt down next to him, saying, "Right now my own daughter is missing, and in the hand's of men who have only the worst of intentions for her." Zach shook his head in an attempt to clear it as he looked at Alpha who continued, "I know I need your help to get her back alive."

Zach frowned, "The girl..." he searched his garbled thoughts for the name of the girl who had helped him and fought alongside him in the past few days, "Her name is Lei, right?"

"Yes."

"How exactly do you think I can help?"

Alpha smiled at him and sardonically said, "You have your talents."

Zach looked at the man, looked deep into those limitless black eyes and said, "No."

Alpha's white eyebrows shot upward in surprise, "No?"

Zach shook his head, "No. It won't bring my daughter back, and frankly, I just am too tired to care about anyone or anything anymore."

He raised the gun back up to his temple, "Now if you do not wish to watch this I'd suggest you..."

"Are you curious why your skin doesn't burn like all the others who were reduced to ashes?"

Zach froze, his mouth still open with the half spoken word on his lips.

"Or perhaps where you are from?"

Again Zach's mouth moved, but no words came out as he tried to answer.

Alpha spoke again, but now his voice changed and an accent that hadn't been present before colored all his words "Or, most of all, where the rest of your family is?"

Zach's eyes shot to Alpha as a small moan found its way out of his mouth from somewhere deep inside him.

Alpha saw the reaction, "Yes, your family Zach...or should I call you by your real name?"

Zach felt as if the world had begun to spin as a sense of vertigo threatened to overwhelm him, "M-my real...?"

Alpha nodded slowly, "Yes, your real name...William."

Something inside his head, like a dam that had been blocking his thoughts, broke wide open as memories suddenly came flooding in all at once and Zach...no, not Zach...his name wasn't Zach...it was William. He said it over and over in his head, "William." It was his name...

"William Bartholomew McCullen..." he said it out loud, as if he had always known it was his true identity. More memories came flooding in as he spoke and now there was nothing to hold them back and they swept over him. The last of the damage that Dr. Whelan's torture and the mind control treatments that held him in bondage was stripped away and William's arms dropped while his body began to sway as he teetered toward the edge of the cliff. Alpha sprang forward, grabbed him by the clothes he wore before he could fall, and together they dropped back to their knees, as William began sputtering, his own rough English accent returning, "Good Lord...I remember." he looked to Alpha, "I remember it all.

Alpha nodded, "I'm so sorry William. I had no idea you were still alive or I would have sought you out sooner."

William was staring off into the distance remembering the past, "They...they burned me alive, didn't they?"

"So they tried. So I had thought," Alpha confirmed, "When I had recovered from my injury I returned to our home and found you and Abigail dead in the front walkway. You were little more than a charred corpse...and Abigail..."

William nodded, and tears filled his eyes again, "Oh Abi. My beautiful Abi. What they did to you."

Alpha looked at William, "I am so sorry."

William held up a hand, "Not your fault sir."

"No. No 'sir' to me. Not anymore." Alpha insisted.

William laughed, "You are an honored Count, while I..."

Alpha stiffened, "Are my brother, as certainly and stronger than if we had shared parents."

William smiled, but then his face turned horror stricken, "Alphonso! I had a son! I-"

Alpha immediately grabbed onto William and quickly said, "He survived that night! You had done it. Everyone that had been in our charge survived because of you and Abigail."

A glimmer of hope seemed to flicker into William's demeanor, "My son...is...is he like us?"

Alpha knew what William was asking and his face dropped. It was a very rare thing for any of their people to live without aging. True the aging process happened slowly for all, but only a select few would live on and on. Alpha didn't want to deliver even more grave news, but he knew William could always spot a lie, even a white one, "No, I'm sorry my friend but he died over four hundred years ago."

William's head dropped, but Alpha continued, "William, look at me. Your son was nearly one hundred and fifty years old when he died and the father of three, grandfather of six, great grandfather of fifteen and great-great grandfather of thirty beautiful children. He was a strong, intelligent man who led our people to the new world, the Americas, and helped establish our presence there. I couldn't have been more proud of him, and I know you and Abigail would have been so very proud of the great man he had become as well."

William had begun openly crying as he took all of that in and said quietly, "Are...are any of my..."

"Your grandchildren still alive?" Alpha finished what William was having trouble saying, "After all this time families have become so diluted and integrated that I'm sure there are hundreds, but any direct decedents I simply can't say...with one exception."

William looked up at Alpha and quickly wiped the tears from his eyes, "One? Truly? But if everyone is so... How can you...?"

"Because in all the centuries we have lived the only ones from our community capable of resisting age are our descendents." Alpha smiled, "You have family my brother. You are not as alone as you think."

William dropped the gun and looked out over the cliff at the view that was spread out before them.

Alpha's face grew serious again, "There's more William, and I will tell you everything, but my daughter needs me and I need you."

William didn't answer, but his head nodded and he fought to stand. Alpha helped him to his feet, "There's something else."

William listened as he retrieved the massive sidearm from where he had dropped it and slid it into his belt, turning to look at

Alpha. The expression on Alpha's face was a mask of anger as whatever he now thought about was burning a rage inside of him.

"What is it?" William asked.

"The man that escaped with my daughter, I had thought he was a CIA operative, but it turns out he was a mole for someone else."

"A mole?"

"A spy."

"Ah, I see. So who has your child?"

Rage overwhelmed Alpha and his voice came out in a hiss, "An enemy who has declared war on our people. His name is Dimitri Lagos and he, like us, is an ancient."

William looked surprised, "There are others like us?"

Alpha nodded, "The world is a much smaller place now. We know of our kind all over the world. Dimitri is the ancient of the Russian collective."

William nodded more in understanding Alpha's words than in any sort of agreement, "But why would one of our kind want to war with another?"

"He doesn't want us to interfere with what he is planning, and thought that by taking Lei he could guarantee our cooperation."

William shook his head, "Stupid. So we kill them all, yes?"

Alpha nodded, "Yes, but you should know something else."

"What?"

"When you were being experimented on by the late Dr. Whelan, he was manipulating your brain. It was, of course, his specialty and through all the torture and the drugs he used, you have to understand your mind was not your own."

"So?"

Alpha stepped back from William as if suddenly afraid of what the giant might do, "Your daughter...Pha. She's not dead."

"WHAT?!" William roared and rushed forward, grabbing Alpha by the shoulders and lifting him effortlessly off the ground.

"She's alive William. They tricked you into thinking they had killed her to break your mind and spirit, but they kept her as a prisoner in case they ever lost control of your mind. A security measure they could use against you."

William was shaking all over, but he set Alpha down and growled, "Who?"

"Initially I believe it was Whelan's plan, but now Dimitri has both our daughters, and by God, we are going to get them back!"

William stood up straight with his body still quaking from the news that his daughter was still alive.

"And then…" Alpha's voice became a snarl, "Then we are going to kill them all!"

Something around William's eyes twitched as he spoke, and Alpha watched in awe as the whites and pupils of William's eyes began to darken until they turned completely blood red.

www.ingramcontent.com/pod-product-compliance
Lightning Source LLC
LaVergne TN
LVHW050915080826
845145LV00001B/100

* 9 7 8 0 9 8 3 7 6 8 3 2 6 *